The Earthborn Series: Book 2
Stygian

By Spencer Helsel

Stygian

For Adam and Sammy

Acknowledgements
First and foremost, I want to thank my wife Jessica, again, since I would not have gotten this book done without her constant support and help. After losing the first draft in Germany, the second one was difficult to restart. You were there for me, babe. You're my favorite.

I also want to thank two former students in particular who pushed me to write this: Skylar and CeCe. You did so much to encourage me to publish and keep working. Sincerely, I can't thank you enough.

Thank you to my parents, Kim and Greg, who have financially and emotionally supported my passion. You raised me to believe in myself and that has made a world of difference. I hope to raise my sons the same way.

I also wish to thank a new friend and editor, Katherine Weber, who offered her services to help make this a wonderful book and my sister-in-law Amanda who helped by giving me a much-needed extra set of eyes.

And, of course, I want to thank any who bought my second novel. I hope you enjoy it. Keep an eye out for the third installment, *Pyrophoric*.

Customer Reviews for The Earthborn Series, Book 1: Empyreal

"...very cleverly combines Biblical stories and mythology to tell a gripping and fast paced story..."

"An interesting twist about the battle between Good and Evil. Enjoyable, light read; perfect for curling up with."

"What a great read, I couldn't put it down. I was impressed with the flow of the story, the descriptive writing and each one of the characters."

"If you like adventure books, you'll love this! It's like Buffy the Vampire Slayer meets Harry Potter... and then some! Funny and exciting; I can't wait for more! It's such a good read!"

"If you're looking for a series to dive into, this is the one!"

Part I
Archdemon

Chapter One

Yvette del Lucio shouldered her purse as she left the St. Catherine of Sienna Free Clinic and walked to her bus stop. The mid-October California heat was unusually intense; shimmering off the asphalt and dancing in the air as she walked. She fished a cigarette from her purse and struggled to find a lighter. She hadn't smoked in hours. Her hands shook for one.

As she walked, she passed Lightpoint Academy; her daughter's old school. It was the only part of her walk she slowed for; the only part that made her stop her hurrying to get home to Ricky. She paused a second, staring silently at the two-story building with its stadium bleachers and football field along the sidewalk. Like every time she stopped here, everything flashed through her mind again:

Ricky's fight with her daughter, then Daniella beating him up, and finally Ricky kicking her out. And shamefully, Yvette sticking by Ricky instead of her daughter, screaming at her to get out of her life.

Yvette hadn't seen her since that day. Only a day later, Yvette woke up from her alcohol-induced stupor and realized what she did. And to her horror, she hadn't seen or heard from Dani in over a year.

Yvette stared up at the school and tears threatened to spill from the corner of her eyes. She wiped them and quickly started her walk again through the blazing heat. All around her, the usual sights of the city lulled her back into her life away from her regret. The familiar heat waving off the asphalt, the haze of the Los Angeles skyline in the distance; they were the things she saw every day.

The only thing she didn't see was her daughter standing at the top of the bleachers, watching her pass.

Daniella, or Dani as she liked to be called, kept behind the veil; the supernatural barrier between the ordinary world and the supernatural one in which she now lived. The veil could be controlled to make one practically invisible, which Dani preferred. She had followed her mother for the last several hours and didn't want to be seen.

Normally, she never needed to be completely invisible. The brown Novice raiments forged of nearly-impenetrable Arachne weave, with the trousers, laced boots, and belt synching her top over her shirt kept hidden by the magicks woven into them without any concentration. Very few, if any, mundani ever saw them and if they did, it took only seconds for the veil to convince them she wore normal clothes. Similarly, she didn't have to worry about someone spotting her empyreal-steel saber-sword and dagger. Pointyend and Pigsticker naturally blended, too.

But Dani couldn't let her mother see her. It'd been months since she visited; over a year since her mom saw her in person. It would cause too many questions if Yvette spotted her, even though she would be grateful to see Dani. She knew her mom regretted kicking her out. Yvette tried to call her on her old, lost cellphone. She put up flyers with Dani's face on them, posted about her disappearance online, and even opened an investigation with police.

But she wouldn't be found. Numen were never found. Rarely did her kind have family and most fell off the map where no one would look for them. But Dani was different. She was a runaway, as far as anyone knew. People looked for runaways. Dani needed to hide from her mother; for her protection and for Yvette's.

Because Dani wasn't the same person anymore.

The same night Dani ran away, she became an Earthborn; a Numen, using the old Greek word. Technically, she was always a Numen, but like all Earthborn before they were "called," Dani lived unaware of her powers until the solar eclipse, which brought out her magical side. And just like one hundred and forty-four other Numen who were "called" that night, hers appeared as the moon covered the sun.

Yvette made it to the bus stop while her daughter watched from two stories above. She noticed the tremor in her mom's hands as she lit the cigarette and inhaled the acrid smoke, calming her. She reveled in the simple pleasure and relaxed. Dani knew her mom; smoking was the only thing that settled her. It was easy to see.

It was also easy to see the bruises, even from far away.

Ricky was abusive. Dani leaving didn't change that. Recently, Dani broke Ricky's nose. He didn't see her do it. Being a Numen had privileges like hiding behind the veil and punishing abusive drunks, but it didn't stop Ricky from hurting her mother. She still lived with him. There was no stopping it. And she couldn't do more. Any contact, even this, was forbidden. Numen could not interfere in the lives of mundani, especially those that knew them before. Getting too close was dangerous.

She felt a presence at her back and sighed heavily. She didn't have to look to see who it was. She already knew.

"What are you doing here?" she asked.

"I'd ask you the same thing." Ethan said evenly, betraying nothing in his voice. "You're not on assignment."

"How would you know?"

"I asked Mastema."

Dani cussed. Of course he talked to her Guardian. They were friends. "He's pissed, isn't he?"

"That's an understatement. He wanted to come, but I asked him not to."

She was minorly grateful for that.

Dani turned to look at him and wished she didn't. Ethan was handsome. It made being angry at him _really_ difficult. He was a few inches taller than her, with even dark-brown hair that curled and matched with his honey-brown eyes. He had some Italian in him with his dark complexion.

He also stood out amongst the others. Ethan was very normal for a Numen, which was saying a lot. Because Earthborn lived so long—nearly immortal and aging so slowly centuries passed like years—they carried over a lot of things from the past: curse words, prejudices, superstitions, and unhealthy habits of thinking women were objects. He didn't have any of those. In fact, he was kind of sweet and considerate.

At least when he wanted to be.

"What do you want? Are you following me?" she demanded. His expression said nothing, but Dani had gotten pretty good at reading it. "Well that's a yes. I guess I should ask how long you've been following me instead."

"A few minutes. It wasn't hard to figure out where you went." He glanced sideways down at her mom. "Dani, you know the rules. I should report you for being down here."

She only glowered at him, but it was enough to make him angry.

"Hellfires, Dani! I'm trying to be the good guy here. It's dangerous for you."

"Oh, how sweet." Her voice took on a tone like vinegar. "My big, manly protector."

Ethan ignored that. "You know what I mean. This puts you in a lot of danger."

"From the Elders?" She heard that excuse before. She didn't care.

"Because of the demons and you know it."

She didn't have a comeback for that, mainly because he was right. Dani was a Numen, but that didn't just mean she had powers. Earthborn, as they were commonly called, stood for Earthborn angels. They were angels born human who inherited their powers to protect the world from the demonic; the beings of Hell that sought to kill and destroy everything in existence. It was their destiny. Because of their powers, demons could easily identify them, which made them targets. And that meant the people around them were targets as well.

There was more than one reason Dani kept her distance from her mom. Ethan reminded her that being close to her mother meant the demonic might try to use Yvette to get to her. And she hated him for it.

Consarned logic, she cursed silently. She crossed her arms in a huff. "I can protect myself."

"That's not the point. How did you get down here, anyway?"

"That's my little secret."

"Which Mastema is trying to figure out up there." He pointed skyward where their celestial fortress-city, Empyrean, hung hidden in the skies above Los Angeles. "Do you have any idea what will happen if the Council finds out?"

"Jeez, why can't you two just give me a break?"

"Dani." He made her name a warning, something he did a lot. "How?"

And she hated that. "Okay, okay, fine. Look, it wasn't like I had a master plan or anything. I just...fibbed to the Gatekeepers on watch that my Guardian gave me a mission down here to complete."

He expected something more sophisticated. "And they believed you?"

"Yeah. They didn't even ask me anything about it. They just summoned me a ride. Can anyone say gullible?"

"No, not gullible. Dani, normally we don't lie to the Gatekeepers."

"Well, maybe you don't."

"Dani! You're a Novice for crying out loud! Lying to Gatekeepers? Seeing your mother? Do you have any idea what kind of trouble you're in?"

She had a vague one. Dani was a Novice; a Numen-in-training. That meant she learned under the tutelage of her overbearing Guardian, Mastema. She didn't exactly have any favors or get-out-of-jail-free cards she could use with the Elder Council, the ruling body of Empyrean.

Ethan shook his head, partly out of amazement and partly out of annoyance. "Dani, Mastema is on thin ice with the Council. So are you. If you step out of line too far, you could be in a world of trouble and take him along with you."

Dani hadn't thought of that and felt a little guilty. Mastema had done a lot for her.

But she put on a brave face, trying not to show she was worried. "Don't worry. It'll be fine."

Ethan didn't believe her.

Yvette's bus arrived. Stamping out of her cig, she climbed aboard. Dani watched her go. She took a seat three rows back against the window, looking so fragile and broken. Her face seemed sunken in, like the world took something out of her. Maybe it had. As stupid as it was, Dani wanted to get on the bus with her. She wanted to help her; get her away from Ricky and everything she abandoned her mother to.

But she stayed where she was. The bus hissed and with a grumble of the engine, it pulled away.

Dani softly whispered under her breath. "Bye *mamita*."

She turned and jumped off the top of the announcer's box she stood on, summoning Aer underneath her to float down to the bleachers.

Ethan followed. "Are you okay?"

She felt the sting of tears but pushed it aside. "That's none of your business."

She took a seat at the top, looking out over her former school; the painted football field, the two-story building, the parking lot where she and Nathaniel hung out. She missed it. She missed normalcy. She wanted to drink it in before going back to Empyrean. She may have had friends and a purpose there, but sometimes, she just didn't feel protected by its walls and its soldiers; she felt trapped by them.

Ethan sat beside her, his long adamantine Montante sword, Stormthrower, lying across his lap. They sat in silence; for how long, she didn't care. She didn't want to talk; to him, to anyone. And for good reason. Her life was complicated. Hell, complicated didn't even begin to describe it.

Dani was the only female Numen in existence. The. Only. One. Every Earthborn, for thousands upon thousands of years, were men; always between the ages of thirteen and eighteen, always found within the shadow of a solar eclipse. Dani was the sole girl. It made her the leper in her new world and it made it difficult with Ethan, too.

It made it difficult with her and Ethan, anyway.

"Do you want to talk?" he asked.

"About what?"

"About us."

Her chest tightened. "What about us?"

She could see the hurt on his face. "Dani, come on, you know what I mean."

"No, I don't." she growled a little. "Do you mean how I had to save you from Alecto because she knew I cared about you? You mean that?" she leveled her gaze at him sternly. "Or do you mean the part about not believing me when I said that someone in Empyrean is working for demons?"

Ethan frowned. "That wasn't what I meant."

"No? I guess you wanted to talk about the good things: how we feel about each other, how I like you, how we can't be together. Stuff like that? Sorry to disappoint you, but I'm not the kind of girl who dwells on her mushy feelings for a boy. I've never been that way." Which was true, though it sounded cold coming out of her mouth now. "No, Ethan, if we're going to talk, it's going to be about how you don't believe me. Nothing else matters now."

Alecto, a Fury who was supposed to be on their side, led a group of demons into their city half a year ago and killed dozens of Earthborn and Gifted in the process; however, the only way she could do that was if someone allowed her in. She used a special entry called a "ladder," a portal, to by-pass the defenses, which could only open from inside Empyrean. That meant someone they knew and lived with betrayed the Numen. Ethan was unwilling to believe Dani's suspicion.

"We talked about this."

"No, *you* talked!" She shot back. "The problem is that *you* didn't listen to me. This isn't some difference of opinion we're having. We're talking about someone who handed over the city to demons."

"Alecto was inside the city. It could have been her."

"She attacked Nathaniel and I in the parking lot of the Hellfire Club, remember? The portal closed behind us with her outside. Someone else opened it." She glared at him. "You think I want this? You think I want to suspect every person around me of working for demons?" Of course, she suspected them of worse things like attempting to kill her, but that was beside the point. "Ethan, someone had to let Alecto and those demons in. The Council isn't going to investigate and based on how you're acting, neither are you." She shook her head. "I just don't get it. You saw how they hurt me during the Trials. I just don't get why you won't believe me."

"Because," he told her, "it's one thing to be a disgusting human being, but to work with demons is lower than low."

"Well, some Numen we live with redefine low, so I have no trouble believing it."

She went to leave in a huff, but he caught her arm. The expression on his face made her stop. She hated him for it.

"I'm sorry." He said sincerely. "I know you're only doing what you think is right."

"Don't you dare try to be reasonable."

He held up his hands. "It's not about me believing or not believing you, Dani. You saw what the Council did when they suspected Mastema of working for the demons. They almost imprisoned him. And they would have done worse to you. I don't want that to happen to anyone else. Besides, no one could do what you're suggesting. It's impossible for one of us to do that."

"Anyone can be bought, Ethan." She shot back.

Unfortunately, he had some quick-witted armor. "Even me?" he asked. "Even me? You're willing to buy that someone sold us out and you say it could be anyone. Does that include me?"

She hated that. Ethan was genuine. It's what made arguing with him so difficult.

He shook his head. "Demons are evil, Dani. Every Numen knows it. Every Numen believes it. They've killed friends, family; anyone we're close to. We would never make a pact with them for anything; even for our own life." He stared her down. "No one would give those things access to our city. Nothing we want would be worth that price."

"Nothing?" she asked. "There's absolutely nothing you would go for?"

"Wealth doesn't mean anything. And women, well—." he cut himself off. "It's not like they could offer me any woman I would want." He burnt with embarrassment.

Dani did too. How much Ethan cared for her made her turn multiple of shades of red. She didn't know how it started, but she fell hard for him. And he fell just as fast and hard for her. She loathed those feelings, and yet treasured them at the same time. *Stupid boys.*

A lot things stood between them: Ethan's stubborn defense of the Numen, for one. And since Numen—being always men—couldn't romantically get involved, it would never happen.

The other reasons were just as complicated, if not more. Their feelings for each other almost got him killed. Alecto wanted to hurt Dani, so she targeted him. She rubbed her hands together, feeling the itch of power she couldn't speak of. Even months later, that memory made her angry.

A long silence passed between them. To say it was awkward would put it easily at the top the list of All-Time Most Understated Observations of Human Existence; top five at least. But it was enough to make them put their daggers away, metaphorically speaking.

"We should get back." He told her.

"In a little bit." She said. "I like it here. I want to stay for a bit."

"What is this place?" He asked. He read the large sign behind the bleachers. "Lightpoint Academy. This is yours and Nathaniel's old school?"

She nodded, tucking up her legs to her chin. "Yeah. It was before we moved into Ricky's house, at least. My mom didn't want me going to public school. She worried I'd flunk out. A lot of kids do. She didn't want me to end up like," she paused, laughing, "like her boyfriend. Funny. She wanted me to do something with my life but ends up staying with a guy who won't."

"Sometimes parents want to protect their kids from what they already know."

She turned her head. "Did you go to school? You know, before?"

He smirked. "You mean before becoming a Numen? Dani, I lived in the Eighties, not in the Dark Ages."

"Same difference; weird hair, weird clothes, and definitely a period we don't need to relive."

He laughed. "I take your point. I hope synthesizers and leg warmers don't become a fad again."

"I'd take that over mullet rock any day."

He chuckled louder. So did she. It was a good sound.

The end of school bell rang. Students poured out of the building; loosening ties, unbuttoning uniforms, while they climbed onto buses and into cars, headed off campus. Others started walking while the football team headed onto the field for practice. Dani watched them enviously.

They descended the bleachers and headed inside. She wasn't sure why she wanted to go in. It wasn't like she had the fondest memories of Lightpoint. She never fit in. She never had a large social group. Mostly, she hung out with Nathaniel, which only furthered her social outcast status by hanging around with a foster kid.

But the building was familiar. The tile floor, the beige walls and blue lockers; Lightpoint was a part of her old life. Other than her mother, she didn't have much of that left.

"I had Math class in that room right there with Ms. Periquet." She pointed to the right. "And across the hall was History with Ms. Thompson, and down the hall was English with Mr. Berry."

"Good times?"

"It's school. What do you think?"

They kept going, Dani strolling the recognizable nooks and crannies of her former years. Not much had changed. The library still stunk of old musty books. The principal office, where she had to sit for four hours after punching a boy in the nose, was still as depressing as ever. The gym sat at the back of the building. Dani hated the gym. The floor was uneven and unpolished. It smelled like sweaty socks and hormones. Lightpoint's basketball team was the worst in the county. They lost every game. Yet the boys thought they were God's gift to women. One of them even thought he could get what he wanted, when he wanted, from Dani just because he had a jersey. His hand found its way onto her rear end.

Her fist found its way to his nose. Hence spending the day in the Principal's office.

On the stage across the basketball court, which the Principal used during assemblies, a group of girls hung a banner for the upcoming Halloween Dance. A blonde with a Valley girl accent and a tennis skirt/pink sweater combo barked orders to the three other Stepford look-alikes to hang it. A fourth stood by her like an assistant, checklist in hand.

"I hated dances." Dani grumbled, watching them from mid-court. "It was awful."

"Why? Dancing is fun."

"Not when you're a pariah freshman who punched the team captain in the face."

His eyebrows shot up. "What?"

"He had it coming."

On stage, the blonde screamed loudly, "It needs to be higher!" she stamped her foot. "It has to be perfect! Everything must be perfect!"

"I'm sorry, Amy." Said one of the girls on the ladder. "I don't want to fall. I could break my arm."

"Well at least you'd break it for a good cause. And it's President Amy, Agnares. Don't make me remind you again."

Dani shook her head. "The Student Council Association. I hated the SCA, too. Elections were crap. Prissy girls like that Queen Bee-ed their way to the top."

The one with the clipboard reminded the SCA prez, "President Amy, the dance is more than three weeks away. We have time to make it perfect. There's no rush."

"No rush?" The fierce glare in the blonde's eye cowed the other one. "Do you not understand what is at stake here? Do you know who's coming?"

"Yes, President Amy. Of course, President Amy."

"Seems like a real taskmaster." Ethan muttered.

"An overseer in a brazier." Dani grumbled. "I've known a ton like her."

"I said higher!" the SCA President stomped her foot like an impudent child. "Higher!"

"See what I mean?" Dani folded her arms. "Total bully."

"Hey!"

They both jumped. The blonde turned and glared right at them, which was impossible since they were behind the veil. But her eyes fixed on Dani and Ethan.

She put her hands on her hips with a total it's-my-party-and-I-cry-if-I-want-to glower. "If you got something to say to me, say it to my face."

Dani blinked. "Are you talking to us?"

"Well who else?" she gestured to the empty stage. "You want to complain about how I do things? Let's see you do better."

"You can see us?"

President Amy made a *pfft* sound dismissively. "Numen. You all think you're so big and bad. Well let me tell you something, sweetie. I'm the biggest and baddest of them all. When I say jump, my demons ask how high."

'Demon' struck a chord. Almost in unison, Dani and Ethan drew their swords. Dani's single-handed saber glimmered a soft, mellow gold as she held it point-towards the girl—who in fact couldn't be a girl. Normal girls couldn't see through the veil.

Demons could.

President Amy laughed. It was a high-pitched giggle that sent a chill down Dani's spine.

"Please." She held up her hand. Hellish orange flames sprouted from her palm and flowed over her fingertips. "You are so outmatched here."

Chapter Two

She looked like any other bully Dani despised in high school. Maybe that was why President Amy disturbed her. From her platinum-blonde ponytail, to her pristine white sneakers, to her just-so outfit; she was the image of the All-American girl. Except she was Dani's worst nightmare: a prissy, stuck up demon.

Ethan kept one hand on the grip of his sword, the other at the base of the blade. He spoke out of the corner of his mouth. "Move towards the exit."

Amy, apparently, had excellent hearing. "Ugh! If there's anything I hate worse than Numen, it's cowardly Numen!"

With a wave of her hand, flames engulfed the exit behind them, cutting them off. More ignited in every window above them. They were trapped.

"Now that's better!" President Amy giggled. "Just stay right there until I finish my to-do list." She turned back to her subordinate with the clipboard. "What else is on the checklist?"

Flustered, her assistant quickly flipped the page, "Almost ninety percent of the school bought tickets for the dance. Principal Berndt and the other administrators will be there. There's already about thirty or so chaperones. All-in-all, most the school will turn out; an almost-complete slaughter of the entire student body."

"Almost?" Amy demanded angrily, flames brightening around her clenched fist. "Almost? I don't want 'almost' Astarte! I want them all! Don't you get it?" she slapped the girl hard enough to burn a handprint into the other girl's cheek. "Everyone has to be there! Everyone! This must be perfect! The whole school must be sacrificed! Understand? How many haven't bought tickets yet?"

The other girl hurriedly flipped through the pages. "I—I don't know the exact figures! I think—I think maybe fifty or so, but I'm not sure."

"Not sure?" Amy demanded, her flames glowing hotly. "How many?"

"Like, fifty or something, but they're all the freaks and losers. Who cares?"

"I do!" The fire shot up both of Amy's arms. "I am going for perfection here! Perfection! When we're done killing these Numen, I want those fifty freaks signed up. I don't care how you do it. I am not putting together a partial sacrifice to our lord! If I don't have one hundred percent participation, Astarte, I'm giving him you in their place!"

Astarte's face paled, groveling in her Ralph Lauren cardigan and pumps. "Yes, President Amy. Of course, President Amy."

"Good."

Dani and Ethan backed up, but before either of them could get far, the demoness wheeled on them.

16

"Oh no you don't!" she screeched. The two helpers on ladders jumped down to stand at her back. "Where do you think you're going?"

"Far away from you, you putrid piece of hell-scum." Dani shot back.

"Please. Like you could get out of here before I barbeque you." The demon sneered. "You know, I was going to go to Chipotle later, but I guess I got Mexican delivered. This is way better."

"Seriously, who the hell are you?" Dani demanded. "You know, other than a racist priss?"

Amy giggled, placing her ember hand to her mouth cutely. "I told you. I'm President Amy. I'm Student Council President, captain of the cheer squad and the debate team, and I am the leader of thirty-six legions of demons." Her smile turned to a snarl. "And you two were not supposed to be here, which doesn't matter much now. I'm glad you're here. I get to kill you. Ever since Alecto bought the farm and released us with the Horn of Gabriel, there's been a price on your head; the only female Earthborn. Anyone who guts you gets a gold star. I haven't been out of the Furnace long myself, but this happy coincidence will put me at the top of everyone's favorites list. High school has been such a bore and this is such a happy coincidence!"

"Yeah. Happy. That's the word I'd use for it." Dani said sarcastically, trying to use bravado to cover the bone-shaking fear in her voice. "So, what, you and the Bimbo B-Squad want to fight us? Good luck. I killed a Fury. She was badder than you on her worst day."

An evil look passed across Amy's face. "Is that so?"

Her airhead crew fanned out behind her. As Dani watched, their faces deformed. Bony lumps grew from their eyebrows, breaking the skin and sprouting stout horns. Their hair fell out in clumps, leaving disgusting trails across their molted skulls. Bat-like wings exploded from their shoulders, each tipped with a hooked fang. Tails grew from under their skirts and their shoes tore apart as clawed feet ripped out of them.

Dani swallowed her words.

"Succubae." President Amy said, fire spreading across her body. Her voice took on a darker, deeper tone beneath her giggly schoolgirl one. "A present from my great lord, for whom I will throw a welcome home party on Halloween. And this school is the main course."

The succubae were terrifying. They were demons of lust, but the only lust Dani saw in their eyes was bloodlust. They could take human form, pleasant to the human eye, but they were not pleasant to look at now. The one called Astarte leapt down from the stage, flapping her wings. Agnares and the third followed suit.

"A great second coming is on the rise!" Amy proclaimed. "The demon lords have returned to Earth! Judgment's trumpet has sounded!"

"Got a plan?" Dani asked Ethan, gripping her sword tighter.

"Stay together. Don't let them corner you."

"And?"

"I suggest killing them."

She shook her head wryly. "Good plan."

President Amy was now a walking human-shaped inferno. She swiped with one hand and hurled a ball of demonic hellfire. Dani and Ethan jumped apart as it blew a hole in the gym floor, spouting flames and the smell of hellish sulfur. Dani rolled, coming to her feet as the first succubus charged.

"Kill them!" The demonic SCA President cried. "Bring me their heads!"

So much for the plan to stay together, Dani didn't say aloud.

She took her stance, heavenly empyreal sword ready. Astarte flapped her wings, launching to attack with her clawed feet. Dani rolled under the beast, the demon's tail lashing out like a whip as she passed. Dani spun and sliced with her blade, separating a few inches of the tip from the rest of the appendage and spilling black, tar-like blood. The demon screeched.

A second succubus landed on Dani's shoulders, throwing her to her chest and knocking the wind out of her. But even as she fell, her instincts kicked in. Mastema trained her relentlessly. *Do not become foolish in battle*, he told her about a billion times. *Always be aware, even in the midst of pain*.

Dani landed hard, but even as she lost the ability to breathe, she reached back and grabbed the grip of Pigsticker, her dagger. She drew it and flipped over, hacking out with the now-ignited blade. The edge slashed open the demon's right thigh. It screamed, spilling blood onto what remained of its Armani Jean sling-backs.

Dani sat up and stabbed into the demon's midsection as she sucked in an agonizing breath. The vile creature, a mixture of demon and debutante, disintegrated into ash as the blade sliced through the heart. She yanked her dagger free and rolled back as it broke to pieces.

Across the gym, Ethan spun his sword Stormthrower around him with expert grace, switching grips naturally as the demon Agnares tried to attack with her claws and wings. His blade caught her with a downward stroke, separating the wing almost completely from her body. It screamed. Grabbing the sword by the bottom of the blade, he swiped back and forth, opening its stomach before stabbing home through the heart. Agnares would never have to follow her bossy president's orders again.

"You little wench!" Screamed Astarte, who Dani forgot about. Missing part of her tail, leaving an oozy trail of blood behind her, she stalked towards Dani. Her fingernails extended into claws. "You're going to die!"

Dani hefted her sword and stood. Her lungs burned, croaking. "Then come and get it, you pageant reject!"

Furious, the succubus launched into the air towards her.

Dani was ready. She practiced this move a hundred times. She feinted left and then went right. Astarte's aim was off. Dani sliced with her sword, taking off one of the demon's wings. It dissolved into musky dust and the demon fell past her. Dani whirled off her feet, using her momentum to bring her dagger around and shove it straight between her shoulder blades.

Astarte exploded into a cloud of chalky ash. Gone.

Succubae destroyed, Ethan and Dani turned towards the stage. She could see Amy's face through the flames. She was not at all worried by the deaths of her underlings.

"Impressive." The demonic SCA president cackled.

Dani raised her sword. "You're next."

"Really? You think so?"

Amy held her hands aloft. Fire swirled between them. In a bloom of flames, it curled outward and shot towards her in a flowing funnel of death. Dani leapt back, lifting off with a blast of Aer and launching away from the ground as the floorboards reduced to smoldering charcoal. Gouts of fire followed as she landed high on the opposite wall, half-running and half-flying across it. Championship banners wafted as Aer flowed from Dani's hand as she passed, then incinerated as Amy chased her with molten air, cackling madly.

Ethan lifted off the ground, bringing Stormthrower back to strike as he launched at the demonic inferno. Amy cut off the flames and blasted him with a bolt of fire, striking him in the upper chest and pin-wheeling him out of the air.

"Ethan!" Dani screamed.

She kicked off the wall and sprang towards him. Amy summoned another ball of fire, much larger than the first blast. Ethan skidded across the ground, his tunic and flesh underneath seared. His sword dropped from his hand.

Amy unleashed another torrent of flames his way. They curled through the air towards him. But before they could reach him, Dani landed and extended her hand.

White-light exploded from her palm and struck the flames, smashing them apart. Searing pain radiated from her palm, but she poured her anger, defiance and desperation into it. The beam of light broke through the hellfire, swirling it back. Amy screamed, pouring on more fire, but she couldn't stop Dani.

"No you don't!" Dani yelled, light and flame surging into one another.

"What are you doing? You can't do this!" Amy shouted. She pressed both hands together, unleashing more flaming floods.

Dani gritted her teeth and pushed, too. "Yes, I can!"

Her light powered through the inferno funnel, forcing it aside as it split up the middle. Amy's eyes widened as the luminescence surged down the column of flame towards her.

"No!" she cried. "No! No! No! You won't ruin my perfect party!"

The light pushed Amy's flames back until it reached her. She screamed as the white glow curled over her hands, consumed her power and poured down her arms. The light extinguished her flames and consumed her demonic, blonde pixie frame as she fell to her knees. Skin and bone and then everything else crumbled under Dani's power. The Student Council President collapsed as her remains obliterated in a flash of light.

"Go eat Chipotle in Hell, *perra fea*." Dani cursed, lowering her hand and spitting in her direction.

The light dispelled, and she sheathed her sword. Her lightbringing usually hurt, but she ignored the sting in her palm as she knelt next to Ethan.

"Are you hurt?" It was a stupid question to ask him. The demon's hellfire scorched a large hole in his raiment top and burnt to the flesh underneath. His chest looked like charred meat.

He grunted. "I'm not _not_ hurt." The joke did little to cover up his pain.

She hovered her hand over the wound. "Let me help."

He slapped it away. "Dani, no!"

"Ethan, I need to heal you."

"Not like that!"

It was the last and one of the biggest contention points between them; the thing that stopped them from ever acting on their feelings. Dani was a lightbringer. She was the only one, at least as far as she knew. It was rare gift that allowed her to destroy demons like Amy by channeling her negative emotions into bursts of light, as well as heal poisons and wounds by channeling her positives ones. She learned to use it secretly because she feared what would happen if anyone found out.

Lightbringing was named for the original Light-Bringer: Lucifer. The Devil. The father, creator and basically god of all demons. So naturally, if any of the other Numen found out what she could do, her status as outcast would change to enemy right quick. Only Ethan and her Guardian Mastema knew.

"Please," she begged, "you're hurt. I need to help."

"Then," he spasmed, choking for air, "then help me...get back to the Empyrean...where I can...heal..." He spoke through clenched teeth, barely able to move.

20

"I can't get you there in time. Ethan, please!"

"No."

"Ethan!"

"Please…Dani…don't…" His eyes rolled into the back of his head. His voice was thready. When she took his hand, it was clammy and cold.

"Ethan?" she pressed her palms against his cheeks. "Ethan? Ethan!"

But he didn't respond.

"No! No, you are not doing this to me!" she slapped him, trying to wake him. "Ethan! Wake up! Wake up, damnation!"

She cursed to herself. Closing her eyes, concentrating, heat rushed down her arms to her hands. Her hands coursed with white light under her skin.

"I'm sorry. I don't have a choice."

Like sunlamps blooming to life under her palms, light exploded out from them into Ethan's cheeks. It hurt, but she pushed it aside. Unlike with President Amy, unlike with others she destroyed, Dani didn't use anger.

Ethan's face came to mind. She envisioned what he looked like when he smiled. She visualized clearly how he helped her when she first came to Empyrean; how kind he was to her. She remembered, just before the attack on the city, she kissed him. She focused on that. She focused on the taste of his lips, the scent of his skin, the feel on his arm around her. She used the feelings she never spoke of or showed and poured them down her arms into her hands. And instead of a violent burst of light that destroyed, she brought forth something pure and healing. She curled the power around her fingers and pushed it down into him. And then she prayed for it to work.

Ethan sucked in a lungful of air. His body seized. His eyes flew open. Through the blinding rays of light, Dani watched as the fresh burn scar on his chest healed over in a matter of seconds. Skin and muscle knit back together. Layers of flesh reclaimed what the demon destroyed and weeks of healing passed in seconds. Ethan spasmed uncontrollably as his body painfully healed to whole. Dani held him, keeping his head still until he settled back down to the floor.

Dani pulled back her power and withdrew her hands. He gasped again, hand slapping to his once wounded peck. All that remained now was a burnt-out shirt and tunic. He sat up.

"You—!" he began.

"Saved your life." Dani shot back, rising. "You were going into shock. Despite being pretty durable, nobody—not even Numen—are going to survive part of their chest being seared off like flank steak."

He checked himself over, looking for any trace of a wound.

"A thank you should be in order." She held up a warning finger. "And if you dare try to tell me I shouldn't have done that, I'll kick your ass. I am not going to watch you die."

21

Ethan winced. He may not have liked what she did, but he wouldn't argue with her. "Thank you."

She extended a hand and he took it, both of them getting to their feet.

"How do you do that?" he asked. "The lightbringing thing, I mean. I get destroying demons. It's like your empyreal swords: you channel your hate and anger. But healing? What do you use?"

Dani blushed. There was no way she could tell him about that. "We can talk about it later. Come on, we'd better go." The gym still burned around them. It filled with smoke. They could hear sirens in the distance. "We need to get out of here before someone sees us."

He nodded. "Judah's place is probably best. It'll be safe ground."

"Right."

She picked up his fallen sword and handed it to him. When he took it, their fingers brushed. Dani reflectively snatched back her hand. So did he. They both nearly dropped Stormthrower.

They locked eyes. Then both of them ignored what they knew each other thought.

Chapter Three

Black smoke curled from Lightpoint Academy's gym and filled the school. The fire alarms blared as first responders arrived. Firefighters ran in while others poured on water from hoses. No way would Amy's dance happen now.

Dani and Ethan flew over Sun Valley into south Los Angeles towards Judah's club.

The Hellfire Club wasn't a normal nightclub. For one thing, it was hidden by the veil. Dani was unclear how Judah, the club's owner, could do such a thing. He was human; a centuries-old human, but human. To most people, Hellfire appeared as a perpetually empty construction zone but somehow, it boasted a full club with two stories and a vibrant night life. Of course, most of its patrons and staff weren't strictly homo-sapiens; not one-hundred percent, anyway.

As they approached, the veil lifted. The building with its neon lights formed out of the earth. Dani and Ethan aimed for the empty parking lot behind it. She didn't know who on earth would both own a car and go to the Hellfire Club. It was hard to imagine a dog-headed cynocephalus or a walking pyre-like jinn taking their family sedan out for a night on the town. And because the staff was comprised of magically animated, six-foot-tall clay creatures called golems, she didn't think they commuted to work. The mental image alone was too strange to believe.

Ethan and Dani touched down. Two large golems, both with the same clay-grey complexion and both wearing Hellfire shirts, stood at the back entrance.

"Password?" One asked. He was tall, muscular (could you be muscular without actual muscles?) and broad. He had what looked like a flat-top haircut, with no actual hair.

"We don't know the password." Ethan told it.

"Password?" it repeated.

"I just told you we don't know. Is Judah here?"

"Password?"

"I just—ugh! Is Judah here or not?"

"Password?"

Golems were frustratingly stupid creatures. They owed their entire existence to a magical scroll in their head. It didn't come with advance computing skills. When they first formed, they were simple things. Bouncers at Hellfire were usually the worst, since Judah used the smarter ones for more complicated tasks like bartending or waiting tables. Dani only met one who was halfway intelligent, but Rudolf was dead.

Ethan looked at the other one, a big bald guy with a square jaw. "Are you any smarter?"

The golem blinked. "Password?"

"Of course not." He shook his head and yelled, "Judah! Will you get out here?"

"I'm coming good sir! Just hold your horses!"

A large, burly man with a thick black beard about the size of his own golems appeared behind them. Judah was human, but Dani sometimes thought he wasn't completely that. He was well over six feet tall and though he was imposing, he was the gentlest man Dani ever met. Brushing his clay creations aside, Judah stepped out wearing a fine-tailored, custom-made suit for his rotund form. He smiled broadly, extending his arms.

"Ethan! How fare you this fine morning?"

They hugged. "Good, if you'd tell your goons to let us in."

"Don't be crass." Judah *tisked*, hugging Dani and turning to the pair of guards. "Adam, Steve, let them in. Dani and Ethan are always welcome. No password is required."

"Password?" Steve asked dumbly.

Even Judah looked irked. "I apologize, my friends. Adam and Steve are some of my newest creations. That is why they are on the day shift. Come, come." He waved them through. "Please, rest yourselves inside. You're just the people I wish to see. I have a new bartender. Perhaps you can tell me if she is any good."

They scooted past and followed Judah's large back into the club.

Hellfire was a mixture of a lot of styles. There were the usual strobes, modern deco furniture, and glossy finishes of a modern club on the main floor, but around the edges draped thick, heavy curtains for booths that reminded Dani of Victorian England. *Baroque*, Ethan called it. Overhead hung a gold and obsidian chandelier, which in the dark went unnoticed but in the day shone with brilliance. It was like the entire establishment didn't know if it were antique or modern, much like its owner.

"You know, my boy, if you would just learn the passwords, you and your fellow Numen could use them for vespertide. It would be much easier." Judah gave them stools at the bar. "Now where is my new serving wench?"

"Serving wench?" Dani asked. "Isn't that a little sexist, Judah?"

"Nonsense." He waved it off. "Her people invented the term. Idunn! Idunn, we have customers!"

No answer.

"The girl is a goddess," he said almost apologetically, "but I wish she were better about being on time. If I am to get things up and running again, I need someone dependable."

"It sounds like you already like her for the job. What's the problem?"

24

"I don't like her."

"You said she's a goddess."

"That's not a figure of speech, my darling. She is an actual goddess; a Norse one to be exact. I only interviewed her because her husband performs poetry here on open mic night. He brings in a crowd. Idunn! Customers!"

"I'm coming!" barked a voice from the back. "Keep your beard on!"

The woman who owned the voice came striding across the floor with the air of a don't-mess-with-me attitude, which Dani admired; however, she was nothing like what Dani expected. She looked like she weighed a hundred pounds on a good day. Her hair was soft, like golden straw, and woven into two braids from her brow to the back of her head, then down in an interlaced weave to the small of her back. Her skin had the complexion of marble and her eyes, filled with enough anger to frighten a demon, were like twin green emeralds. And she shimmered like a small sun in the gloom of the club.

On one shoulder, she balanced five full cases of elixir-filled bottles that easily weighed over a hundred pounds. Stockboys used gurneys to cart around what she carried with one arm.

"Your stock room is a mess, Judah." She said, walking behind the bar and depositing the bottles. "Who arranged it? Mindless idiots?"

"Golems."

"Same difference. Who's this?"

Judah's jaw tensed. "Paying customers. Idunn, I hired you because of your husband. Please don't make me regret it. The last thing I want to do is find a new bartender."

Idunn snorted. "That's why you hired me and yet, the job you hired me to do—you know, tend bar—is one of five things you have me doing because some Fury destroyed most of your last employees. Now, Judah, I get that I'm a goddess and let's face it," she flipped her braid, "all kinds of fabulous, but I'm just one goddess. Yes, I once oversaw an orchard of the rarest, most temperamental fruit in Creation—do you know how difficult it is to grow golden apples?—but I'm only a single, white immortal female."

"I know your last job was taxing. I've read the sagas. But you're missing the point." Judah warned. "I said the last thing I want to do is find a new bartender, but if you're not going to wait on my customers, then I will have to."

Idunn put her hands on her hips, gave him the stink eye and turned to Dani and Ethan. Her smile was as plastic as a Barbie doll.

"Hi. Welcome to the Hellfire Club. What can I make for you, since my boss is a tyrannical despot?"

"They'll have two of your golden appletinis." Judah ordered for them. "Trust me, friends. I hired her for more than her looks. It's her signature drink."

"We'll take two then." Dani quickly removed several adamant shekels, the money of Empyrean, and handed them to her.

To say Idunn could move fast was an understatement. In a blur of golden hair, goddess glow and fury, two martini glasses filled with a gold liquid appeared in front of them.

Idunn folded her arms and looked at Judah. "Should I go now boss? I have a billion things to do before the main rush tonight and your club is still a disaster."

Judah glanced at Dani and Ethan. "Is she worth the headache?"

Dani picked up her glass and sipped the liquid. Since Numen couldn't get drunk, they used elixirs in their place. Most created sensations or warped the mind. This elixir was like drinking dreams and colors. Almost immediately, it warmed her down to her soul and took her to a happy place she never even knew she had.

"She's a keeper, Judah." Dani told him.

Ethan agreed with nothing but a dopey smile.

"Fine, you can keep your job." Judah sighed.

"Oh my Odin, thank you so much boss!" she sneered and then disappeared.

With her gone, Judah leaned against the bar and rubbed his eyes. "If I thought running a mystical nightclub would be this hard, I wouldn't have created it less than a century ago."

"Then why did you?" Ethan asked.

"It was Prohibition. I thought it was a good idea." He noticed the burn on Ethan's tunic. "My, my, what trouble have we been into today?"

"We ran into some demons." Ethan said evasively.

"Really? My stars, I do hope you are both alright. You do not look worse for wear."

"It's a scratch."

"A scratch?" Judah raised an eyebrow. "Is that what they call battling the spawn of Hell these days? Last I recall, demonkind was quite deadly. Ethan, my boy, you do not need to act so tough on my account. Unless, of course, it was much more severe than you let on and something else," he glanced sideways at Dani, "aided you in your healing."

Judah wasn't very gullible, it seemed. Dani said nothing and nervously sipped her drink.

Ignoring him, Ethan glanced over his shoulder, noticing an occupant in one of the booths; an older, bearded man in a suit. "Isn't it a little early for bar rats?"

Judah chuckled. "Aye, but he's not a bar rat. He is a human alchemist from Virginia here to sell me some homunculi."

"Homoncu-what?" Dani cocked an eyebrow.

"Miniature, human-like creatures. They are very difficult to make."

"Any more difficult than golems?"

"Ah, no, but after Alecto destroyed most of my creations, I was forced to make more. And as the two outside show, they aren't the best I've ever done. So, I'm trying something new for my waiting staff in addition to my immortal pain-in-the-backside barkeep. Homunculi could be exactly what I need."

"Why are they so difficult to make?" Dani raised her glass and sipped once more on the delicious liquid.

Judah lamented. "Well, it's difficult to get the necessary magician semen and horse wombs suitable to make them."

She nearly spit the contents of her drink back into the glass.

"At any rate," he waved nonchalantly, clearly disliking his newest business partner, "the alchemist is pushing for a high price. You'd think people with the ability to make gold out of lead wouldn't be so miserly, but such is life! I will make a call to get you a ride back to Empyrean and I promise to be discreet. I am to assume this trip was not sanctioned by the Elders?"

Dani and Ethan both shook their heads.

"Very well. Excuse me. Enjoy your drinks. I must go haggle the price. I pray it does not cost me an arm and a leg. I do hate regrowing those."

Judah left, which meant Dani and Ethan were alone again. They quietly sipped their drinks.

"So," Dani ran her finger around the rim of her glass, "I assume vespertide is still not happening?"

Ethan shook his head. "There's a few backdoors into Empyrean still left. Some of the Gifted talk about coming down, but after what happened with Alecto, I'm pretty sure no one is using them until they know it's safe."

"So, you're not still seeing Airlea?"

Ethan frowned a bit more and shook his head, sipping his drink. "Would it matter if I were?"

That was a good question; one Dani didn't fully know the answer to.

"I guess it's good no one comes down right now." Dani said. "I mean, after all, if someone who goes to vespertide is responsible for Alecto−."

Ethan's fist came down hard on the bar, his jaw clenched. It was enough to cut off anything else Dani meant to say.

"You just won't let that go, will you?" he asked.

Dani shook her head, not trusting herself to be calm if he wasn't going to be.

"I'm not thirsty anymore." He shoved his drink away and stood up. "I'm going to find out what's taking Hermes so long." He stalked off.

She felt the familiar sting in her eyes and rubbed them. *No. No crying.* Dani had never been one for dating before and now, in her new life, it seemed there wasn't much point to it, either. Boys were stupid.

She stared into her glass. She could have been nice. She could have been the bigger person. But she was tired of that. She'd been the bigger person since she discovered she was a Numen. She just couldn't do that anymore.

Idunn appeared again, carrying more boxes. She noticed Dani sulking on the stool and came over.

"This is the part where I take a rag, wipe down the bar and ask you what's on your mind." The goddess said, leaning over. "I'm out of rags and don't give a crap what the bar looks like. But are you okay? You look like you have man-problems."

"How so?"

"Well, in my experience men are problems."

Dani failed to suppress her smile. "You sound like you know first hand."

"You ever live in Valhalla? The place is swarming with the medieval equivalent of jocks with big egos and tiny...uh...swords." She smirked. "Do you know how many bad puns I had to endure over the centuries? There are only so many euphuisms for a girl's body using apples and none of them are clever."

Dani smiled appreciatively. She knew very few women. Even one like Idunn, all business and sass, was kind of nice. "Thanks. I appreciate it, but talking about boys isn't something I really want to do. I've got bigger issues."

Idunn put some bottles away. "What could be so bad?"

Dani shrugged. "I failed to stop the release of the most ancient demons in existence and possibly put the world at risk."

Idunn paused her restocking of the bar. "Oh...yeah, well, that does sound like it sucks."

"I still appreciate someone to talk to."

"Anytime. That's my job: look pretty, serve drinks, and solve problems. And, if I'm lucky, I get to beat up a drunk. That's always cathartic."

"I can imagine."

"Anyway, you need anything, you just holler at me."

"Holler? Are you from the deep south?"

"Cold north actually."

Idunn disappeared in a rush, leaving a trail of golden light and Dani to wallow, though now, a little less depressed.

She sat there, staring into her glass as the golden liquid swirled with hues of light, trying to lull her back to a happier time in her life. All it did was piss her off and she downed half of it out of spite.

"Hey sweetness," said a familiar voice behind her, "you got the look of a camera-ready woman in need of a Hollywood talent agent like myself." Dani turned around. "My name, honeypot, is..." The voice trailed off when she locked eyes with him.

Dani came face to face with a man she knew as Dogmund. Or rather, a cynocephali dog-person named Dogmund. As with all cynocephali, they were human-like from the shoulders down except for the dog fur. From the neck up, however, they were some breed of wolf or canine. Dogmund was dressed in jeans, T-shirt and blazer, his black Labrador face going from confident to sickeningly-afraid. Dani glared at him.

"Oh, you," he quivered, "I, um, I didn't know that was you." He looked about to pee himself. And for good reason. The last time Dani saw him, she threatened to cut off his Kibbles and Bits. "I'm sorry. I—I shouldn't have...I know you don't like the name sweetness..."

Her hand reflexively went to her sword hilt. "Swindling girls in bars, Dogmund? I seem to recall, you said you were a lawyer." She stood up. "So, which are you? Hollywood talent scout or lawyer? Or are both of those just lines to tug on a girl's leash?"

Dogmund whined, "No, no, not lines! Of course not! I'm totally a lawyer. I just, uh, do a little talent scouting on the side. You know: diversify the portfolio. I deal in all kinds of talent: legal services, models, procuring weapons for knights. It's all about cash flow. I got seven mouths to feed."

"Seven? Really?"

"You know how litters go."

"Uh-huh. And I assume there's a wife involved?"

"Yes! Yes! A wife and kids! You wouldn't," he swallowed hard, "hurt a guy just trying to provide for his family, would you?"

"Even if he were, say, scamming girls in a bar behind his wife's back?" she drew Pointyend a little bit from her scabbard. "Maybe I would. I would enjoy it, too."

"Hey! Hey! No scamming! No scamming of any kind!" He was going to wet himself for sure and pass out for good measure.

She snapped her sword back into the scabbard, making him flinch. Then she stuck a finger in his face. "Bad dog." She sat back down, her threats over.

Dogmund swooned with relief. "So," he licked his chops, "you're a full-fledged member of the Numen, huh? A big bad warrior with swords?"

She picked up her glass. "That's the idea."

"How's it going?"

She frowned over her rim. "How do you think it's going? I'm a girl in a city full of guys."

"That bad, huh?" he took a seat next to her. "Sorry to hear that."

She sipped some more of her elixir cocktail. "Yeah, well, whatever. We all don't choose our lots in life."

"That is very true." He signaled to a golem bartender. "But just because you get put into a situation out of your control doesn't mean you can't control things in it."

"Tell that to everyone around me. I got some friends, people are nicer, but it's not like things have changed. It's a boys' club."

"Well, sometimes all a boys' club needs is an alpha bitch."

She set down her glass threateningly.

"No! No! No!" he held up his hands. "I didn't mean to call you a female dog! I meant that all they need is a strong female! An alpha!"

Dani resisted the urge to cut him.

"They need someone who challenges them." Dogmund explained. "Every alpha in the pack forces change, or otherwise they all just go on believing the same thing. That's never good no matter how well intentioned. And no matter how," he searched for a good word, "amazing the girl, they'll regret the intrusion."

Dani grimaced. That was true of Ethan, not to mention a bunch of others. They were good people, but blindly believed they could do no wrong. That made it difficult to be one of them.

"You're making sense." She told Dogmund. "I don't like it when you make sense, or be nice to me."

He shrugged, Labrador jowls hanging open in a smile. "I can be a good dog sometimes."

"Uh-huh. You still don't get a treat."

A new drink came for Dogmund, who lapped it out of the glass on the bar. "Anyway," he said between slurps and gulps, "I'm sure things will get better."

"Don't count on it." She told him. "Unless you know the future, I'm going to keep on being pessimistic."

"You want to know the future?" he brightened. "I can help with that!"

"Excuse me? What do you mean you can help? Are you saying you have a crystal ball?"

"Oh no, no, no, crystal balls don't work. Obsidian ones do, but those are expensive. No, what I'm talking about is a client of mine!" he yipped. "I mean, not a _client_ client since she's not a client yet. I'm trying to sign her to my label, but you know these Hollywood types."

She gave him a flat scowl. "No, I don't."

Flustered, he continued. "Anyway, she's the best! You'd love her!"

"The best what?"

"Witch, of course!"

Now that Dani had to question. "Witch? As in flying brooms and big pointy hats and warts on the nose?"

"Well, I don't know about warts but I can say she's the real deal. I promise you. I've seen her a couple of times. Everyone who does says she is spot on every time."

"Spot on about what?"

"The future!"

"She's a psychic?"

"No, no, no! Psychics are crackpots and L.A. hippies trying to sell herbal remedies. No, she's an honest-to-God witch! Powers and everything! But I think she prefers 'medium' to the W-word."

Dani's head spun. "What the hell is a medium?"

"She can talk to the dead." Dogmund explained, as if it were the most natural thing in the world. "She can commune with spirits beyond the grave, even summon them, and ask them questions to know the future. Trust me," he told her, as if that was something she would actually do, "I know it sounds wacky, but communing with spirits has been around a lot longer than any crystal ball and card-reading hocus pocus. If you want to meet her, I can arrange it for you."

"How?"

"She's visiting Hellfire." He pointed up the balcony above their heads, towards a back booth. "She comes around every few decades. Judah lets her use a booth since its good for business. She charges a small fee and, of course, I'll need a surcharge for setting you up, but—." He stopped and swallowed hard when Dani leveled her gaze at him. "I mean it would be my pleasure to set up a meeting for free. You interested?"

Talk to a witch? Dani's life hadn't exactly been normal for the past year, but asking a witch or medium? Was she seriously considering it?

She glanced up at the balcony again. "Are you sure it's not just an act?"

"If it is, it's the best I've ever seen. She told me my wife's litter of pups was going to be four and it was four, dead on."

"I thought you said it was seven?"

Dogmund's ears went back sheepishly. "Well, I'm hoping to have three more."

"Keep lying to me and I'll make sure that won't happen."

Dogmund ducked his head. "No reason for death threats."

"I wasn't threatening to kill you."

He shook himself. "You're mean. So, you want to talk to her?"

"I don't have a lot of money."

"Lucky for you, she doesn't ask for money."

"What does she ask for?"

"That's between you and her." He said cryptically. "So? How 'bout it?"

Chapter Four

They took the stairs to the top-floor balcony. Behind the lights, in the gloom and shadows, it was a hushed-quiet. Dogmund led Dani back to the most secluded part of the club; a VIP area with a set of steps ascending to a curtained-compartment in the corner. Instead of red drapes, they were black, merging with the shadows around them.

"Wait here." Dogmund told her. "I'll see if she's available."

But no sooner had his foot (paw?) touched the bottom step, the black curtain pulled aside and from within a voice said clearly, "Mr. Dogmund, that is not necessary."

The voice was female. It was one of those voices too exotic to place; full-bodied, but soft; commanding, and yet relaxed. It was as if the person who owned the voice spoke with an implicit authority. You knew they deserved respect.

Dogmund bowed and glanced at Dani. "She'll see you, I guess. Should I take your, uh, swords?"

"No need." The female voice said. "She is in no danger from me, nor I from her."

"Yeah?" Dani asked arrogantly. "How do you know?"

"I simply know, lightbringer."

The word froze Dani's blood. How could she know?

A hand, thin and elegant like that of a piano player, waved to her from inside. Swallowing her panic, Dani forced herself up the steps and followed the voice in.

Within wasn't a booth. It had the same round table like the ones downstairs, with a silvery serving tray resting atop it, but instead of the cramped corners like the other booths, this space was three times the size; a small, dimly lit room. It was difficult to see, even coming from so much darkness outside. A single lantern hung above the table. And other than Dani, there was only one other occupant.

She stood behind the table when Dani ducked in. From head to toe, she clothed her whole body beneath a black dress, shawl and hood. Only her hands were visible, folded in front of her. They were weathered and wrinkled with age, with nails of midnight black.

"Please," she gestured to the nearest chair, "sit."

"I don't like being in a room with someone I can't see."

"And you would not be here if you did not want to hear what I have to say." Dani couldn't see them, but she could feel this woman's eyes on her. "You chose to come. It does not take a gifted sight to see you want answers. I can give them."

"You called me lightbringer." Dani said. The hidden form did not react. "How did you know? Only two other people know my secret."

"Three, if you count the dead Erinys Alecto."

If Dani ever doubted this woman was a psychic—or a medium, witch, whatever—she didn't anymore. Instead, she took a seat at the table, though her hand strayed close to her sword.

"Can you read my mind?" Dani asked.

"There are creatures, even humans, that can do such things, but the mind's passings—the emotions and the thoughts that make us human—are fleeting. I cannot follow them anymore than I can follow the invisible wind, so I do not try."

When she moved, the witch was not graceful. She moved slowly with age; painfully, her spine bowed as she walked with a cane. She eased herself into the seat with a creak of bones but even this close, Dani could not see her face. The shadows clung to the inside of her hood as if by magic.

"My gift, as so many call it, is not of this world. It is of the next." She told Dani. "The spirits speak and I listen. I call and they come."

"Who are you?"

"My name has long since been forgotten," the witch told her, "but you may call me En Dor. It is the name that most address me as now."

"Endor? Isn't that a planet in Star Wars? What does that have to do with witches?"

The moment she said it, she wished she hadn't. She couldn't see the woman under the hood, but she could feel the indignation and anger like a hot breeze. If Dani didn't know any better, she would have though the lantern's light dimmed.

"It is my ancestral home." En Dor told her. "It is a village in the ancient lands from which a great king once summoned me on the eve of his death. It is a settlement near a very important spring, lightbringer, not a planet in a Hollywood movie."

"Please don't call me lightbringer."

"I ask, then, that you not call me witch."

She guiltily bowed her head. "I'm sorry."

"It is of no consequence. You are here for another reason."

"I don't know why I'm here."

"Sometimes our truest heart can be found when our mind is at a loss."

She didn't know what that meant. Dani shifted uncomfortably in her chair.

"You come for answers. All who seek my counsel do. Even those who would revile me wish to know what I know. It is the hypocrisy of your kind. But I am at your service."

"I told Mr. Dogmund that I have some money but you don't take it. How do I pay you?"

"Payment for physical needs is paid for in physical things. Payment for spiritual matters lies not in the here and now, but in the elsewhere."

Dani shook her head. "That sounds like a bunch of mumbo-jumbo."

En Dor extended her hands across the table, waving for Dani to take them. Hesitantly, she slid her palms over the old woman's. En Dor's hands felt soft to the touch across the tops of her fingers, but calloused and worn across her palms.

"Payment in matters of importance are never made as we want them to be and it is never determined when or how. Our debt is often paid by our own actions, or at times by someone else. All that is known is that your debt will come due one day, Daniella del Lucio. The question is: no matter what the price, are you willing to pay it to know what you desire?"

She licked her lips. The woman was unnaturally enigmatic, but what she said didn't sound like sunshine and rainbows with talk of paying debts. It made Dani scared to know what the woman meant, or even the answers she could give.

"Will you be able to tell me everything I want to know?" Dani asked.

"In time and in a way."

"That is not an answer."

"It is the answer I provide."

It's like talking to a fortune cookie, she thought, but Dani didn't doubt her power. "I need to know about the demons Alecto released. I need to know about what my lightbringing means. I need to know...I need to know what dangers lie ahead and if anyone in Empyrean is responsible for the attack. I'm willing to pay to know, so long as I'm the one to pay the price. Can you promise me that?"

"Sacrifice for the sake of others?" The medium nodded. "It is admirable, but foolish. Life gives us choices and consequences not within our control. I ask if you are willing to pay any price, not one in your own terms. Decide: are you willing?"

Dani bit her lower lip. After a second, she nodded.

"That is acceptable." En Dor released her hands. "You have asked the spirits, and they shall answer."

Dani felt no stir of magic, but somehow, something had changed. En Dor reached to the silver serving dish, picking up the simple flat plate with silver stemmed goblet and pitcher. En Dor placed them between her and Dani.

"Casting is the way of divination and summoning." En Dor said. "Invoking spirits to change the course of events and reveal the hidden truths has been used by magicians for centuries; throwing bones, throwing arrows, considering the entrails of animals. But in the holiest of oils, consecrated and infused with the power of the soul, the cup reveals what nature cannot."

She began whispering; softly at first, repetitive, and in a language more ancient than English. With goblet in one hand, pitcher poised over it, she spoke not to Dani but to someone else; *something* else. She recognized some of the words. They were an ancient language of the angels. She never heard them spoken outside Empyrean. En Dor, however, spoke them with understanding. She chanted, growing louder with each recitation.

Dani felt the air stir, like a breeze through the booth. Magic had a feel to it unlike anything else in nature. Each spell had its own touch. The more harmful ones felt prickly and threatening. This one felt cool and tingling, like a buzzer dipped in ice against her skin. She tried to keep still.

A strange sensation crept up Dani's neck. It was like they weren't alone in the booth anymore; as if someone were just out of the light in the shadows. Her hand gripped around her sword and dagger hilt. Her ears began to ring, as if someone were playing music just out of earshot. And the music was growing.

En Dor tipped the pitcher and the oil slowly dripped from the lip into the goblet. It splashed in flecks. She continued to recite. The energy picked up. The song became louder. Dani felt her heartbeat thump faster. More chanting, more oil; a splash this time.

A hand fell on her shoulder. She nearly drew her sword. Dani turned but no one was there. The thick curtain fluttered. Drops of oil landed within the basin of the cup. Another brush, now along her arm.

Dani stood and drew her sword, the blade coming to life in a flare of gold.

"They are here." En Dor warned. The wind now swished through the room. She couldn't see anyone, but it was as if people darted in and out of the booth, running along the shadowed walls. En Dor continued. "Spirits we invoke thee. Spirits do we ask of thee. Answer our question. Reply thine answer."

More wind. More movement. Dani searched frantically around. Something brushed her leg and she jumped. "What the hell is going on?"

"Spirits we invoke thee." En Dor repeated. "Spirits do we ask of thee. Answer our question. Reply thine answer."

Dani's hair fell from her braids as if undone by a magical hand, whipping about her face. Her blades glowed brighter as her fear spiked.

"Spirits we invoke thee!" En Dor chanted louder. "Spirits do we ask of thee! Answer our question! Reply thine answer!"

"What's going on?" The wind roared; deafening.

"Spirits we invoke thee! Spirits do we ask of thee! Answer our question! Reply thine answer! Answer us now so we may know! Answer us now so that we may go!"

And then, with the air lashing around her at tornado-like speed, everything went silent. The gale stopped. The invisible figures suddenly departed. The hood of the witch raised and she looked to Dani.

"Speak." En Dor told her.

"What—?"

It hit her. Dani's vision blanked. From the shadows, visions flashed out of the dark and color exploded in a rush of chaotic images. Dani reeled against the table, dropping her sword. She felt something like this before in a cave with an archangel. His memories flooded her brain. This was like that, but instead of experiences, it was like the world lost sense.

A shadow crawling across a crescent island.

A star inscribed upon double-doors of a shrine.

An inky black shape rising from a dead body.

A large building with a neon tree decorated with mouths.

A golden medallion, engraved with a symbol, laid in fiery coals.

A rickety sign above a gravel-and-dirt path.

A fish in a murky river.

A man sitting on a bench by a lake.

A set of double-doors, a small sanctuary beyond on the shore of a lake.

A massive storm of black clouds and shapes darting between them.

A dark beast standing on a sandy beach, the same terrible storm behind it.

Ethan. Kleos. Roxelana.

Her mother.

Someone screamed and it may have been her.

Dani collapsed, hitting the table and falling to the floor. Nausea swept up through her stomach. Turning, she wretched but nothing came out.

Someone called her name.

Dani looked up. The medium of En Dor still sat at the table, goblet in front of her. A pair of dark eyes shone in the light under her hood, the barest outline of a thin, elderly face stretched into a smile.

"Dani!" Someone screamed again.

The eyes bore into her.

"Dani!"

The Witch of En Dor whispered softly. "He is coming."

Chapter Five

With the sound of metal on wood—a sword drawing from a scabbard—Ethan threw open the curtain with Stormthrower in hand. He pointed his adamantine blade at the woman across the table. Judah came behind him, along with two others Dani barely recognized in her state. Cowering behind them was Dogmund, who made no move to stop any of them.

"Hold, fiend!" Ethan warned, glaring at En Dor. "Return your forked tongue behind your fangs before I cut it out!"

En Dor didn't move. The two others with him, both covered with adamantine Earthborn armor and white tunics, drew their swords as well. They were Elders.

Judah stepped between them. "Put up your blades!"

The one on the right Dani didn't recognize. He was tall, muscular with tanned Middle Eastern skin. His beard showed wisps of grey, which meant he was centuries, if not millennia, old. Across his brow, he wore the golden circlet crown of an Elder, the angelic markings unique to his responsibilities on the Council. Dani couldn't read it, but she did see the long, two-handed saber he carried; an axe-like scimitar with a flared end. It was an executioner's blade.

The other Elder, however, Dani knew. As her vision swam back into focus, she recognized Elder Heman by his short hair, his clean-shaven face and his deep scowl. It was hard to forget a man who wanted her dead.

"I said put them down!" Judah warned them.

"You do not command us." The newcomer said, his stare unwavering from En Dor. "You bring this witch into your establishment? You defile yourself?"

"You do not give commands here, Elder Maalik." Judah told him. "I would remind you that you are not in your city."

"And I would remind you, sorcerer, that you are outnumbered."

Dani had never seen Judah angry. Frightened? Yes. Apologetic? Yes. But now his massive fists clenched as he put himself between the Earthborn and the medium.

"You will not give me orders in my home." The club owner said. He opened his palm. Something like lightning crackled between his fingers. "This is my domain. I allow what happens here. If you challenge my authority, so be it, but the consequences are your own."

He glanced at Ethan. They had been friends longer than Dani knew them. Now they stood facing one another, ready to come to blows.

Ethan glanced at Dani, then at Judah, and then at En Dor. He lowered his sword and stepped back.

Dani got to her feet. "Please," she said, "don't. I'm fine."

Heman regarded her with contained fury, but returned his sword to its sheath. Elder Maalik did the same. Judah's lightning-magic slowly dissipated.

"We heard screaming." Elder Heman said, sounding slightly happy about it.

"I just had a dizzy spell." She lied. "I'm okay."

"I would ask you all to leave." Judah said, his eyes falling on Dani. "All of you. You have upset my guest and are not welcome here."

Ethan sheathed his sword, offering his hand to Dani. She didn't take it, glancing at both Heman and Maalik. Holding hands in front of them may not be such a good idea. Besides, after their spat she had no intention of touching him. Instead, she walked around Judah, joining them at the door. She frowned apologetically to the club owner.

"I will see you again, Daniella." En Dor called out.

Dani paused at the threshold, glancing over her shoulder. "I doubt it."

"I do not."

With a shiver, Dani followed them out.

She knew better than to make any of her usual half-dozen sarcastic comments as she followed the Elders outside. She learned to hold her tongue a little.

'A little' being the operative phrase.

"I'm guessing there's a reason two Elders came to get little ol' me?"

They scowled together like some sort of evil twins, but instead of addressing her, Elder Heman commanded Ethan, "Please inform this Novice how her actions not only nearly got you killed today, but are in violation of our laws."

"This Novice can hear you just fine." She shot back.

"Dani." Ethan's tone was nothing but cautious.

"Listen to him, Novice." Heman scowled. "You left Empyrean under false pretenses. You allowed yourself to be attacked by demons—."

"Allowed myself to?"

"—and whilst waiting for retrieval from your ill-begotten journey, you consulted with a witch, violating our most sacred laws of purity."

She didn't bother hiding her contempt. "They prefer 'medium' to 'witch.'"

Both Elders turned matching shades of irritated crimson. Maalik growled, "I do not care for what she and her kind wish to be called. I have the freedom to speak as I wish and I would remind you and the _witch_ to hold your tongue."

"And you don't see the double-standard in that statement?"

"No."

She rolled her eyes. "Of course you don't."

The two Elders looked about ready to throttle her, but a peel of thunder sounded above them and something like a miniature star exploded as it crossed into Earth's realm, dropping from the sky. A fiery golden carriage, with a team of equally fiery horses, hurtled towards earth like Santa Claus on a suicide run. Then, at the last second, it turned up level and touched down hard on the asphalt and powered down the street until the team of sun-stallions skidded to a stop in front of them with sparkling embers.

Sitting at the front, the psychopomp Hermes leapt from the carriage seat, landing gracefully with a flutter of wings that were attached to his head under a wide-brimmed floppy hat.

"We did not call for thee yet." Heman told him.

"I was bid by another to come." Hermes answered formally.

"Another?"

The door to the carriage swung open and out stepped Elder Jeduthun. Dani wasn't exactly thrilled to see him. He was older than the others, with grey and white hair, a long beard and a constantly-wrinkled brow. He was a Co-Consul, one of two leaders of the Elder Council, which meant that Heman and Maalik reported to him. And they were not happy to see him.

"Elder Maalik, Elder Heman," he stepped down and bowed in greeting. There was little fanfare or respect in the gesture. In fact, he seemed almost bored by their presence.

"Elder Jeduthun, there is no need for thee to come." Heman told him. "We are handling this affair. It is not wise for three Elders to be exposed on Earth. It is dangerous."

"I believe if we encountered any, together we could handle them."

Dani knew that was true. She saw Jeduthun's power up close and personal. His ability to control sound could incapacitate almost a dozen opponents without lifting a finger.

"Why have you come?" Maalik demanded. "It is rare that any of the Council leaves the city."

"This is true, which is why I find it odd two Elders saw it necessary to personally retrieve one Novice."

"There is the Guardian as well." Maalik said defensively.

"Yes." Jeduthun smiled tightly. "I'm sure that makes it necessary now."

The three Elders began to argue, though in a strange and polite way, like how politicians did on live television; civil, but with thinly-veiled hatred.

Hermes stood to one side with her and Ethan, waiting. He caught eyes with Dani. As he normally did, he wore no tunic top; only a shawl over his thin adolescent shoulders and a set of pants with a wide-brimmed hat. Hermes wasn't a Numen. Technically, he was a god; one of many that

40

worked for Empyrean. They called them psychopomps, or guides, and they ferried Numen to Empyrean or around the world like angelic chauffeurs.

"Hey Dani," he said softly. He twirled his long, double-snaked staff around, "long time no see. You're looking good."

"You too Hermes. How are the kids?"

He chuckled. "To the Devil with it all Dani, you just don't know when to quit with the sarcasm, do you?"

"It's one of my endearing qualities."

"It's going to get you killed one day. Of all the people to piss off, you piss off Elder Maalik. Even I know better."

"Who is he?"

"You don't know? I'm a guide and even I know."

"So enlighten me."

"He's the new Arbiter of Punishment." Hermes said, the tone of his voice subtly betraying his fear. "The last one died in Alecto's attack. Maalik is the new dean of discipline, you might say. You know," he nudged her, "the one who gets to decide exactly how to torture you if you act out of line; what goes where, how hot the thing is, what that thing is used to cut off. Word in the bird's nest is that he enjoys his job."

Cold trickled down her spine. She glanced at his executioner's sword again.

The heated argument amongst the Elders ended abruptly. Jeduthun held up a hand. "That is enough!" his voice was firm, unyielding. "I have already spoken with the rest of the Elder Council. Though Novice Daniella's actions were not in line with our creed, it has been decided that her punishment should not warrant Elder Maalik's," he glanced sideways at her, "intervention. As such, this discussion is tabled until the appropriate punishment can be discussed by the full Council."

Both Heman and Maalik were livid. Dani hadn't seen that kind of unbridled fury since, well, since she killed a Fury.

"Novice Daniella and Guardian Ethan are to be returned to Empyrean immediately." Jeduthun gestured to them. "Come. Your chariot awaits."

Glancing sidelong at the two pissed-off Elders, she boarded Hermes' carriage with Ethan and Jeduthun. When the door closed, their guide took his position with the horse team.

With a quick flick of the reigns, the carriage took off like fireworks from a cannon, nearly sending Dani's front teeth back into her molars.

Crossing into the realm of Empyrean was something nearly impossible to do. Technically, Empyrean floated on a mystical mountain above Los

Angeles, but no aircraft could reach it no matter how high it flew. It existed in another dimension; something Ethan once described as "beside Earth."

Hermes' chariot became less turbulent and the air smoothed out. Then, with a burst of sunlight, they broke from the clouds.

Empyrean sat in the crater of a mountaintop. The beginnings of a forest began halfway down in the crags, becoming more and more lush as they neared the top. A river gate poured crystal-like cascades from a valley in the side, the water washing off into the clouds below. Set into the mountain a little higher up were the white-stone-and-pearl triple gates: the Gates of Pearl, one of four entrances to Empyrean. Each of the Cardinal directions had a set.

The Numen Citadel was barely visible over the rim of the crater; spires, towers, and buildings mixed into the massive trees, creating a hybrid of nature and home. Some dwellings hung from the massive branches high above the crater floor, while others were built into the trunks or on the ground.

Across a massive bridge lay Sanctuary Hills; home of the Gifted refugees who took shelter from the demonic in Empyrean's safety. Novice Village, home to every trainee except Dani, also sat along its lush hillside.

The chariot veered towards the Gates. From their pedestals jutting over the cloudy abyss below, the Gatekeepers signaled for them to open. Dani could see dozens upon dozens of red-clad uniforms amongst the battlements around the gates. The Head Gatekeeper, Asaph, had doubled patrols and guards since Alecto's attack. She could feel hundreds of bows and arrows trained on them as they neared. In the corners, circular platforms held ballistae, catapults and other defenses ready for the signal to unleash hell on anything attempting to attack the mountaintop.

Swooping in through the open gate, the chariot touched down and skidded to a halt. Dani felt her stomach flip. She'd never get used to Hermes' driving.

"You can't make that landing any less rough?" she asked as he hopped down and helped them out.

"Why?"

"Because one of these days, I'm going to barf in here."

He bowed with a low, sweeping gesture of sarcasm. "M'lady, it would be an honor for you to wretch in my cabin."

"Get knotted."

"Yes ma'am, but another time, perhaps."

Dani liked Hermes. He was one of the most normal people she knew up here, which said a lot considering he had wings growing from his head and rode horses made of sunfire.

"He also was one of the few to be honest with her. Tending to his horses, he murmured, "Looks like the welcome wagon is here.""

Dani glanced over her shoulders. A contingent of Gatekeepers marched down the steps towards them. At the lead, one of her least favorite people scowled from under his helm. Elder Asaph did not look pleased.

"How bad do you think it'll be?" she asked him.

"It won't be a picnic."

"Guardian Ethan, Novice Daniella," Asaph scowled, "you are to be summoned before the Elder Council."

"Can I say no?" Dani asked him.

"No."

"Well alrighty, then."

Dani enjoyed talking to the Elder Council about as much as running blind-folded and naked through a cactus field.

The Elder Council was comprised of twenty-four of the oldest Numen in existence, each appearing middle-aged or older. They collectively held thousands of years of experience, more than any Numen in Empyrean, and they were the biggest bunch of codpieces to boot.

"This is a violation!" Heman roared from his seat, having arrived only moments ago to spew the usual amount of hate in the form of frothing spittle. "This Novice defied our laws and endangered this city by her actions!"

"I would remind you," Elder Castus told him, "that we have a different matter at hand." He turned back to Ethan and Dani. "It was a demon, you say? What kind?"

Dani and Ethan stood before the blazing braziers that lit the Throne Room, which could fit thousands of Numen and Gifted into the two levels of seats on either side. Dominated by a large mirror-like pool, the glassy surface reflected seven large fires. Behind the lamps sat the Council, each seated on a throne lined into two rows, with a final throne above them. This final throne was always empty, reserved for a Numen Dani knew little about; some guy named Metatron that every Numen venerated as a prophet. It was special. A rainbow shimmered in the air around it, separating it from the rest of the thrones. No Council member could, or would, ever try to sit in it.

Ethan reported. "It was demon unlike any I've ever encountered. It called itself President Amy and could change its form at will and control hellfire. It also commanded a group of succubae to do its bidding."

"Succubae? Is that so?" Jeduthun's expression gave away nothing, but Dani knew that was when he was deepest in thought. "And it referred to itself as 'president?'"

Dani rolled her eyes. "It's important that demons run for student council?"

She regretted mouthing off. She was well-known around Empyrean for it, but now wasn't the time. She had learned when and where to push the envelope lately. This wasn't one of those times.

"'President' is a title in the demonic hierarchy." Jeduthun told her. "It is the ancient system of rulers amongst the spawn of Hell, though most demons care very little for titles now. The beings of Hell have not invoked the hierarchies since the War in Heaven, as I recall. Elder Atid," he turned to the Head Chronicler of Empyrean, "you are the most knowledgeable of the Old Ones. Do you recognize the name President Amy?"

Elder Atid was a balding, olive-skinned man with glasses, which Dani learned were magical spectacles called seerglass. As she watched, symbols so small only he could read them scrolled across the surface, as if summoned by his thoughts. Then, they stopped and he nodded. "Yes. If what I see is true, I believe they are referring to a demon named Auns, or President Amy, attested to in goetia."

"Go-what?"

"The texts of sorcery to summon angels and demons. She commands fire and—"

"—thirty-six legions of demons. Yeah, I remember." She shuddered to think the depths of Hell had blonde bullies.

"She is an archdemon."

The statement made every Elder silent. Even Dani shut her mouth. Alecto, before her death, claimed to release dozens of older demons from imprisonment using Gabriel's Horn. And when Dani look at the Elders, she could see the same expression on all their faces: worry.

"Archdemon," the word sounded sinister on her lips. "As in, the ones I warned you about months ago?"

"Do not be snide." Heman snarled.

Dani almost answered his tone with her own, but Jeduthun cut her off. "Archdemons are the eldest of the demons. Some are the very first creations of the Devil himself. Others appeared much later. They begot the demons we fight today."

"But archdemon is still pretty bad." Dani noted.

"President is not the highest title," Jeduthun conceded, "so the demon you faced may not be as powerful as others, but yes: bad."

"She was plenty powerful." Ethan said, reflexively touching his chest.

"There are many in existence." Elder Atid continued. "And if one has been slain, there is hope the others released by the Horn of Gabriel can be as well."

"Not all archdemons were released." Castus noted. "Many who fought in the War were destroyed during the rebellion or bound to Hell with the Devil, but others were rumored to remain on Earth; sapped of all power and strength and unable to take corporeal form. Now that those who were bound are released, they may organize."

"They already have." Ethan reminded them gravely. "President Amy had succubae at her control. They are rare and very difficult to control."

Dani shook her head. "Great. So, Alecto released the most hardcore inmates of Hell's dungeons. Awesome."

"Do you find this funny?" Heman demanded angrily.

"No. I find it very _un_-funny. Remember, I'm the one who killed Alecto. I understand how serious this is."

He snorted, but said nothing. Dani was still surprised that after exposing Alecto's conspiracy and killing the Fury, she still got those kinds of responses.

"Amy wasn't just out to kill a few humans." She pressed. "She was planning a sacrifice. She talked about a 'great lord' or something coming to Los Angeles. She planned to kill everyone in the school for it. There's something bigger out there and its coming."

"We must convene." Castus agreed. "We will decide what to do about this impending threat."

Dani couldn't believe it. Did she just hear him right? "Discuss? We tell you there's an archdemon trying to organize a mass slaughter and you want to discuss it over coffee? Or do you all prefer tea and crumpets?"

Ethan scolded her. "Dani! Elders, I apologize. She has a valid point, but the Novice should have spoken with more respect."

"Oh, you little—!"

She pushed it too far. Castus, who rarely got ruffled, snapped, "That is enough! You have made your point, Novice. Do not test this Council's patience."

Her eyes flicked to Jeduthun, who gave the slightest sign to her to back off. Ethan seemed in agreement. She nodded and shut her mouth for now.

"As for the Novice's transgressions, we will table the discussion for later. You broke a law. There will be consequences. Do you understand?"

Suddenly, she was five years old and her mom was yelling at her. "Yes, Elder."

"Good. Return to your Guardian and training, Novice. Dismissed."

Dani and Ethan left. As soon as they were outside the Citadel, Dani wheeled on him, punching him hard in the arm. "What was that all about?

45

'But the Novice should have spoken with more respect.' Zounds Ethan! I thought you'd stick up for me after I saved your life!"

"I'm trying to make sure you don't end up in Elder Maalik's hands, which will happen if you aren't careful."

"Well, I'm trying not to kick you so hard in the testicles they end up behind your eyeballs, which I will make happen if you ever say something like that again!"

He sighed heavily. "Dani, no one—not even you—can help if they constantly fight everyone on their side. Cooperation must happen. It doesn't make anything you say less valid."

"No, it just makes playing nice harder to stomach." She still wanted to nut-knock him, but calmed herself. "But I get what you're saying, even if what you're saying is completely stupid." But she stuck a finger in his face. "But fair warning: I'm really, _really_ mad at you, so if you want to keep your jimmies where they are, don't ever do that again...unless you are keeping me out of a literal dungeon. Once, I'll forgive. Twice, your boys get pulverized."

Instead of responding, he simply said, "You have a very vivid way of describing how you hurt people."

"It's why you love me." She quipped.

Almost immediately, she wished she hadn't said that and looked away. *Love*. It wasn't a word she should have used with him. Instead, she shoved her shame right down into a secret box, locked it away and tossed the key off a metaphorical cliff. Then she left Ethan as quickly as possible.

Today with him hadn't gone very well. Hopefully her reunion with her Guardian would be better.

Chapter Six

It wasn't.

"What in that baseborn, idle-headed mind of yours thought that lying and sneaking out of the city was a wise idea?"

To say Mastema was harsh was like saying Ebola was a mild case of the flu. Her Guardian—a tall, muscular shaved-headed man with midnight black skin and a demanding mean-streak—didn't show affection often. Usually it took nearly dying or nearly killing him to get him to show any concern.

"Put aside what happened already," he told her, "and the numerous demons who wish you dead. What were you thinking by angering the Council? Do you realize the consequences of your actions?"

"How does the answer 'no' grab ya?" she asked slyly.

Frustrated, he turned his back on her and walked out onto the fallen tree log that bridged the Crystalline River, the main source of fresh water in Empyrean. It was only a day after Dani's little stunt, but Mastema knew every detail, all the way down to her use of lightbringing. He wasn't happy.

Like most Novices, Dani trained with her Guardian either in her village or in the lush, green valley called the Vale, which separated the Novice villages from the rest of the city. They stood, bowstaves in hand, while the river gushed beneath them in quick rapids towards the river gate. It wasn't very high, but the roar of the water was a little unnerving.

"This is not humorous, Dani." It took Dani slaughtering a group of demons to get him to call her that. "You could have been killed. You could have been seen by your mother. Anyone associated with this scheme would be subject to the Arbiter of Punishment. I experienced the custody of the one before Maalik. He was half the man Elder Maalik is now."

Dani felt terrible. Mastema supported her numerous times, to the point of being thrown in shackles. It's why she put up with his aggravating B.S.

"Think before you act." He told her.

"Yes dad." She griped.

"Do not call me that. If I were your father, I'd throw myself from the cliffs."

He continued to walk out over the river. Dani followed. She still had to look forward to the Council's eventual punishment, but for now, she needed to train. She was still a Novice. There were still demons to fight.

"What exactly are we doing?" she asked, nearly falling off a dozen times before righting herself with Aer.

"Learning." He said.

The log was thin, about as wide as a TV tray; sloped and bumpy. It was difficult to walk on. Useless as a bump on a log. She got it now.

"To what? Balance?"

"Amongst other things."

"Why? I can fly."

Mastema walked, moving from the shore of the riverbank into the open. He turned, walking backwards with ease and without the use of his powers. He flicked the bowstaff behind his shoulder.

"Too many Numen rely upon the *arche*." He said, using the ancient Greek word for the Numen abilities. "They are useful tools, but they are not infallible. To rely solely upon them is to give your opponents a weakness to exploit. Learn to focus and fight with more than just your abilities. Now, focus your mind. Use your core muscles to keep yourself upright. Find your center."

"'Focus your mind' 'Find your center'; you're just saying meaningless gibberish now." She nearly slipped and fell. "*Carajo!*"

With his front foot, he smacked the tree trunk and it wobbled. Dani tumbled sideways but as she fell, she summoned the Aer and stopped herself horizontal above the water rapids. She then summoned Water to her palm to push upright again.

"It is not gibberish to those who truly wish to be masters of themselves." Mastema told her coolly.

She glared him. "Jerk."

"Lout."

"Culus."

"Latrine slurry."

Dani attempted to balance. It was harder than it looked, even after a year of training. Numen had greater physical strength than the average human. She was in the best shape of her life because of her Taskmaster From Hell's Armpit.

"Balance." He repeated.

"Oh, thanks, I didn't think of that." She used the bowstaff to steady herself. "You know, I don't see anyone else doing stuff like this."

"That is because their Guardians are fools." Mastema continued backwards without having to look. "Mastery of Fyre, Aer, Water, Erthe and the Aether is important, but too often we overlook our greatest natural gift: our mind. It is our greatest weapon. Our decisions, our wits, our ability to out-think our foes; these can mean the difference between life and death. When we panic, our powers fail us. I am attempting to teach you that."

"By dangling me over a river?"

"Yes. I am trying to help you."

"Then help me Obi Wan Kenobi. You are my only hope." She sneered.

He hit the log again and she tumbled, this time summoning her power and whipping herself around back up to standing. "Stop that!"

"Then learn control, which includes your mouth."

She balanced again, using more muscle than power. The searing pain of her muscles working to keep herself together was excruciating. She barely kept herself centered on the piece of wood, following him across the makeshift bridge into the open. Mastema moved as if he were simply taking a stroll.

Cocky culus, she thought. "You've got to be joking. No one can do this."

Mastema, slowly, lowered himself down a seated position on the log, crossing his legs. He placed his wrists on his knees, staff between his hands. "Have you ever known me to joke?"

"To say a joke? Not really. To be a joke? Meh."

"Do you plan on defeating demons with wit? No? Then I suggest you take this seriously." Her Guardian had a way of sucking the humor out of almost everything. "Now come to me."

She shook her head, legs trembling in exertion and fear. "I'm going to fall."

"And?"

"If I fall, I'm going to die."

"Are you scared?"

"Are you an idiot? Of course, I'm scared. Everyone fears death."

"And that is the power of fear." Mastema told her. "Fear is more powerful than almost any force on this planet. When creatures fear, they have three responses."

She knew that, but thinking and balancing at the same time was difficult. "Well, there's fight and flight and..." she tried to think of the third.

"And fail." He finished. "To become immobilized, to become powerless in the face of fear; that is failure. We can run, we can fight, but all too often we are paralyzed by fear. Indecision, hesitation, losing hope; fear takes from us that which would save us."

"And walking on a tree trunk takes what away, exactly? Because it is so not taking away the fear."

"Mastery of one's self takes it away." He told her. "I am training you to conquer fear, for fear is what you will face one day."

"I have powers, Mastema." She reminded him, almost falling again. "I can literally destroy things with light. How is almost drowning going to help me where lightbringing can't?"

Slowly, with such control Dani was actually envious, he rose to his feet again. "One day you will not have your powers. Now, come to me."

Slowly, Dani walked forward. She didn't have his confidence. Her whole body sung with panic, pain and sweat. She stumbled.

"I can't!" she gasped, trying not to look down. "I—I can't do this!"

"You can." He told her. The tree wobbled a little beneath them. "You can do this. Look at me and only me, Dani. Try to focus."

She wasn't really looking at him before, but when he said her name her eyes snapped up to him. His face was a solemn, serious mask, but underneath it she could see that same look he gave her when she destroyed the demon nest in L.A.; the same one he had when she bested him in sword-to-sword combat.

It was one of pride.

"You can do this." He told her. "Fear is an illusion."

She took another step. And then another. And then another.

"You are doing very well."

Any moment, she'd fall, but she kept going.

"You can do this." He repeated, reaching out towards her. "You can."

His hand brushed across the back of hers as she came to stand next to him. She did it. She made it to the midpoint of the river. No powers and yet, there she stood.

Mastema nodded. "You are learning."

"Thank you."

"There is only one other lesson that remains."

"What's that?"

With a gentle shove, he pushed his Novice off into the water below.

She was halfway through her first cuss word when she hit the rapids and plunged under. The push was too quick and unexpected to summon Aer or Water to stop. Submerging deafened her. The river swirled and soaked her through. She clung to her staff as she swept downstream, breaking the surface a second later for air as she churned downriver.

"You jerk!" she screamed.

She hit a rock and her head smacked back. She saw stars. Then she was face first in the rapids. They pulled her down, tumbling her over the bottom and down the slope towards the river gate. When she surfaced again, it came right at her.

"Oh God!" she strained to swim sideways for the shore, but she was going too fast. The river narrowed. She sped up. Beyond the gate, the blue sky, clouds and empty space beckoned.

A one-way ticket to death.

Dani panicked. It was difficult not to. She tried controlling the water around her, but her abilities failed against the natural tide of the river. It moved too quickly. She couldn't bring herself to pull herself out using Aer.

She tried to dig the bow staff into the riverbed next, but it caught and snapped in half. The broken bow flung her back into the water, doing nothing to slow her. She kicked back to the surface, trying to swim, but the waterfall was only a few feet away.

"*Dani? Dani!*" a voice cried from overhead.

Something white shot out of the sky towards her with powerful beats of her wings.

"Caesar!"

Caesar screeched, her impressive wingspan catching air pockets and sailing downward. Caesar was a caladrius, one of the most powerful supernatural birds. Her crown-like head-plume folded back as she pivoted left, aiming for Dani.

"*I'm coming!*"

The river gate loomed. Dani vainly swam backwards but the falls rushed her forward and over the edge. Overhead, Caesar swooped in, claws extended.

Dani dropped over the edge into the sky. But even as she fell, talons snatched by her by the shoulders of her tunic. Claws dug in and yanked her sideways with a hard jerk.

"*Gotcha girlie! Can't let my bestie down!*"

"Caesar!" Dani screamed, grabbing hold. They swooped upwards, her friend's wings flapping hard to gain altitude. Caesar was powerful, but even she couldn't carry Dani for long. They turned, gaining as much altitude as she could muster and headed back into the city. Dani didn't dare look down.

"*Almost...there...!*" she grunted. "*You gotta...fly...!*"

They shot over the river gate and Caesar aimed for the far bank.

"*You gotta fly, toots! I'll give you all the altitude I can!*"

A burst of air knocked them skyward. Even as they shot up, Caesar let go. Dani swallowed her fear and summoned Aer, launching outward under her own power. Unfortunately, she hadn't thought it through.

More under the power of velocity than her own ability, Dani soared forward the rest of the way. Too close to the treetops and with not enough time to gain altitude, she collided headlong into the first tree and bounced off it.

Then she tumbled from the sky.

THWACK! THWACK! THWACK! One branch after another broke under her and pin-wheeled Dani like a rag doll. She had enough sense to put her feet down as she passed the branches and fell towards the forest floor. She summoned a burst of Aer to slow her descent so when she landed, she didn't break something. Or rather, any more somethings.

Dani landed hard in a clearing below. Her ankle twisted and something popped inside it. She cried out in pain and collapsed to the ground.

"*Dani!*" Caesar burst from the treetops, swooping down to land next to her. "*Oh my God! Honey! Are you okay?*"

Dani groaned something.

"*What's that?*"

"I said I am going to KILL HIM!" Dani screamed.

———————————————

It was bad—not as bad as it could have been, like if she fell off the side of the mountain into oblivion—but she sprained her ankle and probably ripped a tendon. Panacea would heal it.

In the meantime, she plotted a dozen or so ways to murder her Guardian in his sleep.

"I can't believe he did that!" She wrapped her bare ankle in a bandage; something she took to carrying with her during training. She broke and sprained things a lot these days. Her ankle was bigger than a grapefruit and different shades of black, purple and yellow. It barely fit into her boot. "What the hell was he thinking?"

"*Well, he did ask me to help.*" Caesar said from her perch. "*I was on standby in case you couldn't get out of the river. He tried to make sure you didn't die.*"

"A lot of good that did," Dani grumbled, "but thanks for being there for me."

Caesar bowed in her head in a quick nod. "*Anytime, chica.*"

"That still doesn't excuse that *idiota* from pushing me off the log, though!"

"*Maybe it's his way of Wax On/Wax Off. Are you going to make it back up to your house okay?*"

"Trust me: I'd rather fly than walk on this thing." She painfully got to her feet, unable to put any pressure on it. "But I need to find an opening in the canopy to take off. Walk with me?"

"*Sure.*"

"I'm lucky I didn't die." She grumbled, limping with one barely-usable foot.

"*You've always been lucky like that.*"

That was much was true. There were several times recently that Dani wasn't supposed to have made it, but she did. "I swear, one of these days I'm going to cover him in catnip and feed him to the Tigris."

Caesar fluttered ahead. "*Yeah, well, there's a lot that I would like to cover that delicious man in.*"

"Oh my God Caesar! Eww!"

"*What? I'm a lonely bird and he is divine chocolate.*"

She shook her head. Her friend, though very much a bird, always had a wandering eye. "So, I take it you haven't heard from Nessus?"

Nessus was Caesar's beau. He was also a centaur.

Caesar sighed. *"Yes, well, being deployed into Hell sort of puts the damper on the relationship."* She fluttered down to the nearest rock. Though she was a bird, it wasn't difficult to see she was sad.

"When was the last time you heard from him?" Dani was anxious to hear about her friend. Nessus saved her from several very horrible fates before he left. She was in his debt.

"Well, he can't exactly text me from the frontlines in Asphodel, but we communicate through messengers. Snail mail sucks, by the way. That doesn't change if you're mundani or supernatural. But he gets leave sometime soon."

Dani had to take a break after a few more feet, leaning on the rock on which Caesar rested.

"I miss him Dani. I'm worried about him."

"I'm sure he's fine. Nessus is strong. He'll make it through." She leaned against the rock, trying to lighten the mood. "Besides, him fighting in Hell isn't exactly the biggest obstacle for you two."

Caesar turned a hawk-eye on her. *"What do you mean?"*

"You're a bird, Caesar. He's a centaur. Isn't that kind of...I don't know...weird? How would that work, anyway?"

Caesar laughed with a soft, chirping sound. *"Anima forma."*

"Excuse me?"

Caesar turned to face her. *"Some of our kind—supernatural creatures, like me— can change our physical form. We can become something else."*

"You _what_?" How did she not know this?

"Oh, come on, everyone knows this. Why do you think stories like The Little Mermaid exist? Supernatural creatures from gods to birds change if they fall in love with someone not of their species. In my case, I take an anima forma; my 'soul-form.' It means that I take the form of the person I love."

Dani stared. "Caesar, I had no idea."

"Mostly, we turn into humans. At least, that's what happens in the stories, since most of us fall in love with humans instead of each other, but I'm hoping if Nessus would return..." she trailed off, looking away. *"Dani, I know I joke a lot, but with Nessus...it's different. He's my alos misos."*

"Your what?"

"My other half. My soulmate. If I could, I would take my soul-form for him."

Dani smiled. It was sweet. And part of her, a part she would never admit, was jealous of Caesar. She had something with Nessus that Dani didn't have: hope for a relationship.

"Dani, why are all the good guys gay, married or in Hell?"

Dani laughed, standing up painfully again. "Caesar, I am _so_ the wrong person to ask for dating advice."

Chapter Seven

Dani trudged uphill as best as she could. She ignored the searing pain. Still, a year of Numen combat training toughened her against things that would have sent her screaming to the hospital before.

Dani's and Caesar's conversation turned from boys to something vastly more important.

"So, Ethan still doesn't believe Alecto had an inside man?"

"Nope."

"And I take it he doesn't know you have me spying on people to figure out who it is?"

"Nope."

"Why?"

"Because he's an idiot."

Since Dani could speak the language of birds, a rare gift in Numen, she asked her friend to keep an eye on things around the city. Some would call it spying, but Dani called it being smart. Caesar followed Numen and Gifted secretively, hoping to discover who might be involved in the attack. So far, they found nothing.

"Are you ever going to tell anyone?" Caesar asked as they left the tree line, with clear sky now overhead.

Dani rested against another boulder. "Why would I do that?"

"Because the first people you had me follow were your friends."

Dani ears burned with embarrassment. It was true. She knew that whoever allowed the demons in could be anyone, including her closest friends. The first people she had Caesar spy were Ethan, Nathaniel, Bouden, Kleos, and even Mastema. She needed to know who to trust.

"They won't understand." She said guardedly. "I'm doing this to keep people safe."

Caesar got quiet. She understood. She was the only one who could.

Dani stood, still in pain. "I have to go Caesar. Thank you for saving me."

"I got your back, Jack...er, Jackie." Caesar couldn't smile but Dani could almost feel it from the way she spoke. *"I'll see you at the wedding?"*

Dani cussed. She forgot.

"Don't be too long!" her friend chided and took off.

"I'll be right behind you!" She called, preparing to take off. "Just as soon as I kill my Guardian."

Dani flew back towards her house, which was nestled along the cliff-edge of Sanctuary Hills, overlooking the Vale. It used to be called the Arn, an ancient word for 'eagle' and named for a group of people who could speak to birds. It seemed like an apt place for her to live, so much so that when those who died in Alecto's attack left a space for her to live at Novice Village, she declined.

The house she lived in was small; only a sleeping area, a small table for a kitchen, and a bath-tub. But it was more than just a place to sleep. It was built by the centaurs as a way to say thank you. It had a roofed-pavilion on the Vale-side of the shack for training. The walls were covered in vines, which grew almost every kind of fruit or vegetable that Dani could want. A fountain got it's water from a natural spring in the yard, giving her an endless supply. And erected next to her home was one for Mastema.

Mastema sat, cross-legged, mediating in the open. It took all of Dani not to drop out of the sky and kick him in the face, if for the simple fact it would probably break her ankle.

She landed tenderly instead. "You could have killed me."

He opened his eyes. "But did you die?"

She rolled her eyes and tried to limp past him. "You know, sometimes I think you're less Obi Wan Kenobi and more Jar-Jar Binks."

Mastema stood swiftly, blocking her path. "Today's training was vital, Dani. You will face darkness; worse than you have before. You already know it is out there. You and Ethan nearly died fighting it."

"And yet, President Amy is dead."

"Do you think it's a coincidence that you came across a demon such as her? You think I only speak of one such creature?" His questions shut her mouth before her next snide remark. "They are out there, Dani. Alecto told you: the archdemons, first-born, have returned."

"There have always been demons." She said flippantly, though she realized she sounded just like the Council; playing down the threat.

"True. Demons have always existed, but they are only the children. The fathers and mothers of demonkind have come back. If Alecto is to be believed, the strongest archdemon of them all—Belial—is among them. There is no telling when or where, but one day he will show himself. I must prepare you."

"By knocking me off a tree?"

"By forcing you to face your own darkness: fear. You put on a show, but I know you. I see through your veneer of bravery. You are scared, but you can't let that fear control you. You saw what simple panic did today. You nearly drowned."

"Thanks for that, by the way. And honestly, though, can you blame me for being scared? If I let my guard down, even a little, I get hurt. Sometimes, it's the people I care about doing the hurting."

"Fear is the enemy of strength." He sighed heavily. "A human philosopher once said that the only thing to drive out darkness is light. Fear is one type of darkness. It can only be conquered by two powers, the most important of which is yourself."

"And the other power? The other light that stops darkness?"

"It comes only from others in the form of love."

Dani shook her head. She was used to Mastema's strange teachings; deep, thoughtful, but totally cheesy. She knew he meant well, but sometimes he sounded like a fortune cookie on crack.

"How about we make a deal?" she asked. "How about you teach me all about mastering myself and conquering fear, but without something that makes me almost fall to my death?"

"I'm not sure that is possible."

She patted him on the shoulder. "Try. Now, if you'll excuse me, I have to heal a nearly-shattered ankle in time for a wedding."

Sanctuary Hills was alight as the sun dipped low in the horizon. Amongst the Gifted that fled Earth from the demons, festivities were limited, but who could resist a wedding?

Above the Sanctuary Hills market, Adare's house crawled with people. Dressed in all sorts of strange, exotic clothes, the many attendees for Roxelana's nuptials took their seats. In addition to multi-colored lanterns, each of the attendees received small bouquets of strange flowers which gave off their own radiance in the dark. Elementals—the fairy-like sentient nature that existed all throughout Empyrean—added their own flare. Sylphs, the air elementals, danced across the sky and their soft wisps ruffled the banners. A few fiery salamanders burned in the lanterns, intensifying the light with tiny pulses. Dani even spotted little, earthy gnomes spying from behind rocks and bushes. It was as if everyone wanted to see Roxelana wed her husband; Numen included. Alecto's attack unified the mountaintop. Amongst the attendees were Guardians, Powers, Gatekeepers, and even Elders.

And Dani was part of the wedding party.

She stood with Shea and Airlea, two of Roxelana's closest Gifted friends. She wasn't allowed to wear Gifted clothes, but she wore her best raiments and a blue sash for the occasion; the color of the wedding. Shea wore some sort of formal, medieval-looking attire which accented his emerald-green eyes. Airlea's dress was a mixture of modern-chic and Renaissance flare. As always, she looked pristine with her golden locks and sapphire eyes.

On the other side stood Roxelana's soon-to-be husband. Dressed in an island tribal-robe, he was a type of Gifted called a Naacal. Dani knew almost nothing about him or his people, since he was from another city. All she knew was his name: Akela. And though he had a strong jaw, shaven head and stern appearance, he smiled warmly as wedding music played and Roxelana appeared.

Arm-in-arm with Adare, she looked radiant. Her sparkling purple eyes were accented by beautiful makeup, which shimmered in a way mundani cosmetics never could. Her dress had the same medieval flare common with Gifted outfits, but embroidered with jewels into the gold lace. As she appeared, the glow of the flowers in the guest' hands intensified, sprinkling luminescent seeds into the air. It lit up Roxelana's face, which glowed with its own light for her beau.

Dani smiled warmly as the elderly Adare guided her through the crowd up to the front. As she did, vines sprouted from the garden and formed a gazebo around them.

Finally together, the two turned towards Adare, who would marry them, and Akela removed a long, white rope that he laced around his and Roxelana's wrists. Dani grew up calling it a *lazo*; a wedding knot. They tied their wrists together to symbolize their joining.

And Adare spoke the words that made that symbol a reality.

The celebration spilled down to the market square once the ceremony finished. Still joined by the hand, the happy coupled greeted all their guests as musicians played and people danced. Elixir-drinks flowed happily into people's cups while Numen entertained, throwing Fyreworks in the sky or making Aershapes for the younger children. Sylphs danced about to the songs, mirrored by the revelers below.

"Dani!" Roxelana and her husband peeled away from the crowd of well-wishers and she wrapped her in a fierce, one-armed hug. "Thank you so much for being here!"

"I wouldn't have missed it."

"I finally get to meet the famous Dani." Akela spoke with a strange accent that Dani couldn't place. "I do not know how to thank you for saving Roxelana from the demon attack."

"It was nothing." Dani assured him.

"From what I have been told, it does not sound like it. The whole of Empyrean talks of you. You saved many lives that night."

"Yes, well," she smiled tightly, still not fully comfortable with her new-found fame, "I didn't save everyone. We lost too many people."

Just as quickly as the good mood came, Dani killed it. Neither of them had to mention Korë to understand. She smiled tightly, as did Akela and Roxelana.

"So," she said, switching subjects, "how are the living arrangements going to work? I'm assuming Adare doesn't want two newlyweds living under her roof. Are you building a home in Sanctuary Hills?"

The pair made a face; one Dani knew as the we've-got-bad-news face. Her mom used it all the time.

"Well," Roxelana said slowly, "here's the thing: Akela is from Beri'ah. It's the celestial city of the Pacific. His whole tribe is there."

"There is a large Gifted community on the island; twice the size of the one here." He added. "We call it the Crescent. I have a beautiful home above the beach. Roxelana will be very happy there."

Very happy there. The realization caught up for Dani. "You're leaving?"

"We won't be far." Roxelana promised. "I mean, the cities trade all the time. Shea's work brings him to Beri'ah at least twice a month. We'll see one another."

But the promise was a weak one. The two girls already had a strained relationship in Empyrean. Gifted and Numen weren't supposed to fraternize; a rule they broke quite often. It made things difficult for Roxelana and Dani. How much more difficult would it be if they lived in different cities?

Roxelana saw Dani's expression and unlooped her hand from the lazo. "Honey," she said to Akela warmly, cupping his face "could you see if your tribesmen are ready for the bridal song? I'll stay here with Dani."

"Of course." He kissed the side of her head and walked away.

Roxelana then looped her arm through Dani's. "Talk to me."

"It's nothing. It's fine, it's fine." That was her mother's favorite lie. She avoided Roxelana's knowing look. "It's just a shock."

"I know." She conceded. "I meant to tell you earlier, but all of this was so sudden—."

Roxelana only knew Akela since the attack; only a few short months. Maybe that was what bothered Dani so much. She was getting married very quickly. And in that time, she forgot to tell her friend she was leaving.

She stopped herself mid-excuse. "I'm sorry. I should have told you."

"It really is fine." Dani assured her. "I'm not a Gifted. We don't live in the same world. I wouldn't expect you to drop everything for me. You have another life; an important life. Akela loves you and if moving to Ber-whatever—."

"Beri'ah." Roxelana reminded her.

"Right, Beri'ah, is important to you, you should go." She tried to joke, flipping her hair like some airheaded cheerleader. "I mean, I would NEVER move to another city for a boy, or whatever, but if you want…"

Roxelana giggled and nudged her. "Stop it."

"No you stop it!"

"No you stop it!"

The two burst into laughter. It felt good. It lightened her soul; something she needed.

"He really is great." Roxelana told her. "I love him."

"I know you do."

She took Dani's hands and turned, looking her in the eye. "You'll be okay without me, right?"

Dani tried joking again. "Oh, come on, you're not THAT important to me."

"Dani," Roxelana, just like Ethan, could make her name a warning, "I worry about you. After everything last year, after Alecto and this whole business with demons; I worry."

"It's my job to fight demons. It's a Numen's destiny."

"You and I both know you're not a normal Numen."

Wasn't that the truth...

Chapter Eight

Combat exercises for Novices changed after the Trials. The following morning, after training with Mastema at her house, Dani climbed the hills into the heights of Empyrean's crater to the Training Grounds.

She didn't carry her sword or wear her greaves and bracers. Most Numen didn't go armed around the city. It was too much to lug around and you looked stupid carrying your weapon everywhere you went. But ever since the attack, Dani took to carrying Pigsticker across the small of her back within easy reach of her left hand.

The Training Grounds were now the sole place for Novices to practice their combat skills. Other than Studies and for announcements from the Elder Council, they didn't go to the Citadel much anymore.

When Dani arrived, most had already broken into groups. Some had wooden practice swords, honing their weapon-strikes. Elder Caspar instructed a group in aerial combat maneuvers. Elders Azariah and Atar had another group and she spotted some friends waving her over.

"Watch out!"

Dani had only a split-second to duck as a silvery flash slashed by her ear. With a loud *thunk!* an adamantine weapon smacked into a wooden target next to her. She could feel some strands of hair flicker away, cut off by the edge of a blade.

"Are you okay?" A familiar voice asked. "Dani, what the hell? Weren't you looking?"

Kleos stood over her. The black-clad Guardian's hair matched his raiments. His bearded face frowned as he offered her a hand up.

"Sorry." She mumbled, burning with embarrassment.

"My charge could have taken your head off."

Dani blinked. "Charge?" Kleos' charge, Dink, died months ago in the attack. It took her a second to realize a Novice stood beside him.

He was a few hairs taller than Dani, with a similar complexion. The boy's black hair was longer, nearly to his shoulders. Dani liked that; a throwback kind of style that he kept back in a loose ponytail like Kleos. Too often, guys cut their hair like a Bruno Mars knockoff. Bunch a' *babosos*.

Dani recognized the Novice, since there weren't any new faces in Empyrean, but she had trouble placing his name. Seeming to understand, he extended his hand.

"Ignacio." He introduced himself. "Ignacio Pérez. Most people call me Izzy."

"Why Izzy?"

"Because no one seems to call me Ignacio and I don't want anyone calling me Nacho. I'm not a food."

She giggled. "I'm Dani."

"I know. We've met."

"Really? Where?"

"The Vale during the first Trial. I saw you, right before a gigantic boulder swallowed me whole."

Now Dani remembered. "Right. I remember."

"Sorry about almost killing you." He stepped by her and pulled the weapon from the target. "Kleos is all about distance fighting."

"Why go in close when you can cut them down from afar?" his Guardian asked. "Izzy is my new charge. The Council saw fit to have me take another after Dink." He said his former pupil's name bitterly. "I was severely wounded guarding the Vale Bridge, so I wasn't there when he died. The Council absolved me of responsibility for his death."

Dani remembered. "You still helped me escape to help Ethan."

"And to get revenge on Alecto. I wish I was there to kill her myself."

"Trust me, she's dead."

He took solace in that. "Izzy's Guardian died in the attack on Novice Village, so they transferred him to me."

He hefted his weapon. "I'm still trying to get the hang of this."

Dani stared at his axe, which didn't look much like an axe. It had a crescent arch in the front for the axe-blade, but a point jutting from the top and one towards the back as well. Below, just above the handle, was another point thrusting forward.

"What the hell is that?"

"It's a hunga-munga."

"That cannot be a real word."

He shrugged, grinning impishly. "Technically, it's also called a mambele, but I like hunga-munga. It's a weapon from South Africa. Good for fighting and for throwing."

"It looks like something out of *Buffy the Vampire Slayer*."

He shrugged again. "Like I said, I like it."

"And you need to train with it." Kleos said sternly. "Back to training. Good-bye Dani."

"Bye Kleos. *Adios* Izzy."

"*Hasta luego, chica fuerte!*"

She paused for a second. "*Chica fuerte?* Tough girl?"

He shrugged for a third and final time. "If the name fits..."

Chica fuerte. She liked that.

She went to join the training session with Azariah and Atar. They stood before what looked like an archery course, but instead of bows and arrows, large fire-pits were erected in front of them.

"Now, you all know the basics of using the elements," Azariah told the large group, "but to use them against your enemy requires much more than simple focus. It is visualizing what you wish the elements to do and having the will to bend them to you."

The Elder had grey touching at his temples and a trimmed beard, matching his stern expression. He unfolded his arms from over his broad chest and extended his hand. Flame curled off the pit through the air and into his hand. The blaze hovered over his palm like something alive.

"Fyre is the standard attacking element of our kind. The Fyreball is the most effective method. Demons fear fire, despite originating in a realm of it. Some can even use fire, but for it to be used against them is their greatest fear." He turned uphill to a target arranged a few meters away. "To use the Fyreball, you must direct it. Visualize how far you wish it to go. Keep that image in your mind. Then, allow your body to direct it."

Azariah cast forth his hand like throwing a frisbee and the Fyreball leapt from his palm and shot the distance to the first target, which exploded into flaming bits.

The Novices clapped.

"Now, keep a few things in mind." Azariah began, but stopped when he spotted Dani. "Novice Daniella, thank you for your punctuality. You are only a few minutes late today. I'm glad we are getting more prompt."

Dani was notorious for being late. "I'm sorry, Elder. My Guardian wanted to ensure I was good and tired today."

He chuckled. "I'm sure." He began giving pointers on keeping the fire alive in his palm.

"Do you think they are ever going to let that go?" she murmured under her breath. "I haven't been late in weeks."

"I think there's a better chance of Mastema doing a Broadway number in a pink jumpsuit." Nathaniel whispered from next to her.

Dani grinned at that image. Nathaniel did too.

Nathaniel was Dani's oldest friend. They knew each other long before they became Earthborn; collected on the same night of the solar eclipse. Nathaniel was Ethan's charge.

Nathaniel was tall, lanky, and even though his time in Empyrean shaped his build, he was still the same awkward kid she went to school with at Lightpoint. He had brown hair, neatly trimmed and new glasses; seerglass, like Elder Atid. He still hadn't learned their full potential yet.

"Um, excuse me, but I'm learning here." Bouden joked.

Bouden was short, skinny with auburn hair and his own set of specs. He was one hell of a quick study when it came to history, spells, and elixirs; the quintessential Numen book nerd. He was the only one to rival Nathaniel on book-smarts. Bouden easily surpassed every other Novice when it came to academics and made no bones about it. He knew he was the smartest person in the city, but was also about the gentlest soul Dani had ever met.

Nathaniel punched him in the arm. "Ow! Hey! What was that for?" Bouden demanded.

"For being smart."

"I can't help it if you're a dunce."

"And I can't help it if I have an involuntary urge to smack you every time you run your mouth." Nathaniel shot back. "Don't get lippy."

"Well, at least I add some sparkle to the conversation—"

Nathaniel smacked him again. "Hey!"

"Like I said: I can't control it. It's a disease, really."

Bouden hit him back. Nathaniel hit him again. The two traded blows until Azariah roared. "NOVICES!" They quickly stopped. The Elder glared at them. "I am trying to instruct you on something that may one day save your life. I assume your life is still important to you?"

"Sorry, Elder Azariah." Bouden said innocently. "It won't happen again."

"See that is does not." He turned back to instruct.

Bouden drop-fisted Nathaniel right between the legs, sending him to the ground. The words Nathaniel mouthed angrily back up at him would have made his mamma blush.

The great angelic warriors, ladies and gentlemen. Dani smacked them both upside the head. "Will you two stop it?"

They broke off into teams of three, with each team taking a fire-pit to practice. Bouden easily summoned a ball of Fyre, but couldn't accurately launched it at the target. Dani did moderately well, having learned to summon Fyre before, but Nathaniel sucked at it.

"So how was Earth?" Nathaniel asked, failing to summon even a little flame to his hand.

"What do you mean?"

"Oh, come on, Dani," Bouden said, "you know the rumor mill here. Everyone knows you lied and snuck out of Empyrean. And we know you and Ethan took down a couple of demons. Spill. What happened?"

"How come I'm always the topic of gossip?"

He summoned a ball of Fyre and tried again. He almost hit it. "Because everyone is bored and you're more entertaining."

"Right." She rolled her eyes, trading places with him. "What do you want to know? I went down, saw my mom, and got attacked. Ethan got hurt. End of story."

"Is that the end of the whole story?" Bouden asked.

"What's that supposed to mean?"

"You and Ethan were out there by yourselves for a whole day."

"Meaning?"

"Meaning..." he wagged his eyebrows.

Dani rolled her eyes. "Seriously? I kill a bunch of demons and all you want to know is about my love life?"

"At least you have a love life." Nathaniel grumbled. Nathaniel once had a thing for Dani, but that time had long since passed.

"Yeah, well, mine is not up for discussion."

"So there was at least something to discuss?" Bouden asked.

This time, Dani hit _him_ between the legs.

They took turns, one after the other, practicing the move, but she heard some snickering behind her. A group of Novices stood to one side, watching and whispering amongst themselves. At the forefront was the bear-like form of Andreas; the usual ringleader of the group. He was a big guy; muscular, short-cut black hair, tanned complexion. There were a few faces she didn't recognize, but among them was lanky Lester, a Texan with a mean-streak and blonde hair and Michael, a dark-skinned Novice built like a barrel. She had a special kind of ire for him.

She held up two fingers, knuckles towards them in the Numen form of giving the bird. Then, for good measure, gave them the bird anyway.

"You'd think after I saved Andreas' life he'd be nicer." She said.

Bouden laughed as if she should know better. "You're such an optimist. The day he warms up to you is the day Hell freezes over. And after discovering that there is such a place, I can definitely tell you: that won't happen."

To an extent, Dani didn't care. She dealt with boys all her life. On the other hand, though, continually dealing with the likes of them was tiring, frightening and frustrating all at the same time. Watching her own back made her neck hurt.

"Novice Andreas!"

All Novices jumped as Azariah stalked towards them.

"Yes Elder?" Andreas asked.

"I was under the impression this was training."

"It is, Elder."

"Then I suggest you get back to it."

Andreas' shameful cowing was enough to give Dani a bit of a smile. He glanced at Dani and she blew him a kiss. He steamed.

They practiced for a few more minutes before the end of lessons were announced by a trumpet blast. Studies would be next, but Dani had no intention of going. Both Bouden and Nathaniel silently jutted their chins towards Elder Azariah. Dani had to ask him now.

"Yes, Novice Daniella?" Azariah asked.

"I was wondering if it were possible to send word to Elder Atid that I, Novice Bouden and Novice Nathaniel would not be coming to Studies today?"

The Elder's eyes narrowed. "You wish to miss Studies?"

"Yes, Elder."

"Why?"

"We wanted to spend some time in the Hypogeum to pay respects to Novice Ailbe. sir."

The Elder's expression softened. "You mean the Novice killed in the Fane?"

"Yes, sir. He was a friend. We wish to light a candle of remembrance."

The Elder nodded solemnly. "Many of us — Gifted and Numen — have done the same. I will send word to Elder Atid. Let your heart and your mind guide you and keep you."

She nodded, reciting the Numen Creed back. "Let the light shine upon you, Elder. Thank you."

He touched two fingers to his forehead. She returned it and left. When she came back, Bouden asked softly, "Did he buy it?"

"He did." She shook her head. "I hate using Dink as an excuse."

"We better hurry." Nathaniel said nervously, picking up a pack of books he brought, as planned. "We won't be able to use that excuse again."

The three of them flew off towards the Hypogeum in the Citadel. The tomb of the Earthborn lay through the Fane and below the city in the caves of Empyrean's mountain. They landed, passing past the guard shrine to the Archangel Gabriel, with its Horn resting on its new pedestal. Dani ignored the thrumming energy from the angelic artifact and took the long sets of stairs down into the cold, dank darkness.

The Hypogeum was a massive network of catacombs built into the depths of the mountain. Lining the cave walls, rows of tombs—each one the final resting place of a fallen Earthborn—filled the cavern. Dani never appreciated what it meant to be a warrior until she saw each tomb, with some stories high from the interlocking pathways through the catacombs. Thousands upon thousands of Numen died in the untold centuries of war with the demonic; faceless generations lost to Hell. Now, not only Numen but Gifted, dwelled here.

Two of the tombs called out to them.

Dink saved Dani's life from Alecto at the cost of his own. Bouden, one of Dink's closest friends, carried his bow now. They found his tomb and laid their hands on it. As the two stayed there, Dani floated down further until she found another, smaller tomb. Korë's name was etched into the plaque. Dani touched it lovingly, remembering the young girl she couldn't save.

After paying their respects, the three floated away to another part of the Hypogeum; the part they really came for.

The Song of Sacrifice, the massive and monolithic memorial to the War in Heaven, covered the tomb wall near the entrance. Like in every city, the Song was the last thing the angels made before leaving Earth. As Dani discovered, the angels could not handle the aftermath of their bloody fight with Lucifer, the rebel angel. They almost obliterated the universe. So, they left. But as angels sang into existence everything in the universe, they also sadly sang this engraving into it. It was a record of their war, of who had died and—as she recently found out—of a prophecy of what was to come.

She didn't know how, but the nearly-all-powerful children of God knew the future and left a prophecy as a warning.

A prophecy about a lightbringer.

Over the past few weeks, Dani tried in vain to discover what the lightbringer prophecy meant. Unfortunately, translating ancient angelic script was not something she did well. When Caesar certified that both Nathaniel and Bouden were not the ones who brought the demons into the city, she enlisted their help—albeit without telling them why.

Nathaniel and Bouden quickly removed scrolls and tomes on the angelic language they "borrowed" from the Athenaeum and went to work translating.

"Okay, so," Bouden held up one tome covered in celestial symbols, looking up to the prophecy section of the Song, "we know this much: you're right. The text speaks of a lightbringer, whatever the hell that means."

"Lucifer, obviously." Dani lied "What else?"

"The text is pretty difficult." Bouden murmured, looking over the book. As he did, tiny glowing symbols appeared on his seerglass specs, which he then used to compare to the wall. "I mean, angelic writing is kind of weird."

"Weird how?"

"Well, the best way I can describe it is like," he searched for a metaphor, "is like it's a river. At one end, you see the lake, and then farther up you see the inlet and before that you see the rapids. In order to figure out where the lake comes from, you need to see the inlet, and in order to see where the inlet comes from you need to see the rapids. The angelic language is fluid. It builds on itself, like a song towards a crescendo. Without the first part, you don't have the second, or third, or fourth. It's frustrating."

Dani took a seat on a nearby rock crevice, scroll open in her lap. "If anyone can do it, it'd be you Bouden."

"Ah-hem!" Nathaniel coughed.

"And you too, Nate."

He shook his head when she used his annoying pet name.

They translated as best they could, but it was difficult. Some words only made sense if other words—or word parts, prefixes, suffixes, or God knew what else—were used. Otherwise, the meaning changed completely. How the hell did anyone communicate like this?

As they worked, Nathaniel sat next to her. "So, about your time on Earth...?"

"Drop it, Nate."

"I'm just saying: things are uncomfortably tense between you and Ethan. He sulks around Novice Village like a kicked puppy. I thought you two had a thing?"

"We can't have a thing. The Council wouldn't allow it."

"Is that the only reason? Because it doesn't seem like it to me."

She hated that. Nathaniel could read her like a book. Unfortunately, she hadn't told him anything about traitors or the fight between her and Ethan. And she didn't want to. Nathaniel fit in somewhere for the first time in his life. The last thing she wanted was to ruin his new life by telling him someone sold them out to demons.

"Like I said: drop it."

"Okay, well, I'm your friend. If you want to talk, you know where I live."

"Yes, I do. Thanks."

"Hey guys!" Bouden called out from the base of the Song. "I think I might have something!" He stood, book in hand, glancing from it to the wall and back.

"What is it?" Dani asked.

"So, the prophecy part here," he indicated a section of the wall, "is all the stuff about Gabriel's Horn, right? I think I might have cracked the next portion of it." He pointed high to a grouping of symbols in angelic script. "This is after the Trumpet of Judgment blows. The next section is a bit unclear, because the translation is a bit weird, but I think I might understand most of it. You see this word?" He indicated the book. "That is the same word up there."

Nathaniel checked. "What's the word mean?"

"Well, loosely translated it means 'consuming darkness,' but usually that means 'demon.' And you see this symbol here?" He pointed again. "It's usually reserved for angels; really important angels, like Gabriel."

"Archangels?"

He nodded.

"So putting that together would mean...archdemons?"

He nodded again. "I think so. If I have the translation right, it supposedly says, 'and one archdemon will rise when his seal is broken by truth. Covetous possessiveness will take hold the one he seeks.' After that it gets unclear again."

Nathaniel shook his head. "So, not a light-hearted children's rhyme, then?"

"Nope. But it seems to allude to something powerful. You said Amy was strong, but this sounds like the Grand Pooh-Bah of demonkind."

"Do you think it's Belial?"

"Who knows?"

Dani didn't like the sound of that. "'Covetous possessiveness?' What's that?"

"It's just a loose translation, but I guess angels got really specific when they talked about demons. It's like a personal moniker for the demon; a translation of its name. The word here means something like trying to take ownership, but in this case of someone instead of something."

"Someone? You mean take ownership of a person? Like a slave?"

"I kind of thought it might be related to this word here," he suggested, comparing his notes and the shimmering symbol on his glasses, "because it appears together in this section."

"Can you translate that word?"

He nodded. "The translation is pretty clear, but it doesn't make sense." He showed her. "It means lust."

Chapter Nine

She took it back: she didn't enjoy talking to the Elder Council as much as running blind-folded and naked through a cactus field.

She would enjoy that more.

Dani returned the following week, this time with Mastema, to receive her punishment.

"Novice Daniella," Castus stood, "you are charged with a violation of our laws. You trespassed our borders without permission. As such, you are sentenced to servitude."

"Servitude?"

"You are to act as servitor to a Council member to remind you of your duty to serve this city faithfully. You will be in their employ until they deem you no longer a threat to our security."

"And who am I supposed to serve?"

To her disgust, Heman stood. "I have volunteered to take on this burdensome responsibility."

"Your mom is a burdensome responsibility." She muttered under her breath, but low enough that no one could hear.

Jeduthun stood as well. "Elder Heman, if I may: as Arbiter of the Powers, are you not engaged in numerous duties already? To take on a servitor may, in fact, be distracting."

Dani didn't like being called 'distracting' but she knew Jeduthun enough to know when he played political word-games. He was trying to butter Heman up to get her out of working for him.

Nonchalantly, Heman shook his head. "I do not believe so. It may be helpful to me to have an assistant in my duties; and to her fellow Novices to doll out a lesson the importance of following the law."

Dani didn't like the sound of that. Being his servitor did not sound promising. Or safe, for that matter.

They left the Keep. Mastema uncharacteristically offered to cook dinner that night and departed for the marketplace. It should have made Dani feel better. Instead, she worried. Mastema was never that nice. Was it because he knew what punishment lay ahead for her?

As she was about to take flight, she spotted a familiar couple coming across the Vale Bridge.

"Today's the day, huh?" she asked.

Roxelana and Akela were prepared for their journey to Beri'ah; their new home. Her friend wore a traveling cloak and they had wedding gifts and other personal belongings packed into a cart pulled by a weird-looking animal called a qilin; a bearded and scaly creature with horns. A harness around its shoulders helped pull the cart along.

Roxelana separated from Akela and hugged her fiercely. "Yeah. It's time."

"Good luck." She squeezed.

"You'll hear from me soon. I'll send a whisper or a messenger."

Dani tried to believe that. She smiled at Akela. "Take care of her. Treat my little queen like the *reinita* she is."

Roxelana giggled. "I'll be fine. Good luck yourself. Try not to get into any more trouble."

"No more than necessary." Dani joked.

They kissed each other's cheek, hugged once more and then Roxelana joined her husband as they headed through the Citadel to the West Gate. Dani watched them go.

"Bye best friend." Dani whispered softly.

"Try not to get into any more trouble," she said. *Oh, I wish I had that luxury.*

As the sun began to head towards the horizon, Dani flew north towards The Dalles. She had to talk to someone and knew only one place to find him.

The Dalles was not a place Numen frequented. The rapids that streamed through a tight valley sprayed mist into the air. The mist, it seemed, hampered Numen abilities and navigating it by air was nearly impossible. People easily got lost. The only way up was on foot, which in and of itself was treacherous. But Dani had done it before, and for good reason. She had another good reason now.

As she came out of the mist wall, she was greeted by the most amazing sight: from the orange-and-purple-hued sky overhead, a waterfall descended as if from the air itself. It simply appeared and flowed down onto the rocks. Kleos, a friend of hers, surmised the river came from Heaven. Dani wasn't sold on that idea, but it was a nice thought.

It flowed into a lake-like reservoir which then churned through the gorge and down into the valley. Dani went around to the far cliff, and then clambered down a little walkway until she slid behind the falls into a cave.

"Hello?" She called out to the darkness. "Gabriel? Are you there?"

Only silence greeted her. She knew it was a long shot. After all, didn't ultra-powerful archangels have better things to do then hang out in a cave?

It was the dirty secret of the universe. The majority of Numen believed, as she once did, that they were inheritors of the great, noble struggle of the angels against demonkind. As the War in Heaven had been the forces of Heaven verses the forces of Hell, they were just the newest soldiers in the struggle.

That story ended up being total bull.

The real story was that the War in Heaven nearly obliterated most of the universe, save for Earth. Angels were not the benevolent caretakers of humanity, but in fact nothing more than children. They slaughtered each other, not to mention the rest of existence, because they didn't know any better. They couldn't grasp what it meant to wipe out ninety-nine percent of life in the cosmos.

After the War, as punishment by God, angels were forced to grow up. Dani still wasn't sure what that meant, but whatever God did, He forced them to fully understand what it meant to murder. Angels were so horrified by their actions that most of them disappeared. Very few, if any, were seen again.

But Dani discovered that not all were gone. She met the creator of Empyrean, the Archangel Gabriel, last spring. He lived like a cave man up here in The Dalles; unable to leave his blessed city.

"Gabriel! Archangel of Truth, Trumpeter of Judgment and Lord of Hide-and-Go-Seek! Get the hell out here!" She was pretty sure pissing off an archangel wasn't the best policy, but since he once threw her shoulder out of place, she figured she could give him a little attitude. "Please! I need your help!"

"You ask in a very strange manner."

Dani jumped. His voice filled the cave. She looked around, but there wasn't a body to it. "What's with the disembodied voice routine?"

"Do I need one form to speak with you?"

"No, but you're giving me the willies."

"Turn, Daniella. I am behind thee."

Dani turned around and wished she hadn't. The falls that covered the cave entrance transformed; moving against gravity to create the beautiful face of Empyrean's founder. Gabriel usually appeared a gorgeous, tall man—or woman. She wasn't really sure. Dani only used 'he' by default. His smooth, soft features formed in water with eyes made of deeper sapphire than the rest of the falls.

"It is good to see you, Daniella."

"Scratch the disembodied voice routine." She whistled. "You went full Wizard of Oz-slash-Zordon."

"You are a strange mortal. Do many find you entertaining?"

"You know what? You'd be surprised, but they don't. But that's not why I'm here. I need your help."

"As I have before, I will assist thee in any way I can."

"Alecto is dead, which I guess you know."

He nodded. "I sensed it, yes."

"But the person who helped her—the enemy in our midst you warned me about—is still out there. And it's gotten worse. Alecto freed a bunch of demons she called 'demon lords,' which the Song of Sacrifices translates to 'archdemons.' I don't know what that means but I'm going out on a limb here thinking that you do."

"You have not asked for aid. How am I to assist you with this?"

"I need information. I know you're not about to jump into this fight, but I need to know what's coming. The demons were trying to throw a welcome home party for something really dangerous. I'm guessing it's one of these 'archdemons.'" She pulled out a piece of parchment she wrote Bouden's Hypogeum translation on. "'And one archdemon will rise when his seal is broken by truth. Covetous possessiveness will take hold the one he seeks.' It's from the Song of Sacrifice, which you and the rest of the angels wrote. I need to know what it means."

Gabriel's churning face grimaced. "I am unsure."

"How can you be unsure? You wrote it. You know the future."

"Angels are not omnipotent, Daniella. We can glimpse possible futures, but not the one that is guaranteed to come to pass. The future is not fully determined."

"Please," she said earnestly, "anything you can tell me will help. The 'seal broken by truth' makes me think it has something to do with your Horn of Truth. I got a feeling that whatever this 'covetous possessiveness' thing is, it's bad. I need to know what I'm facing. Does it mean Belial?"

"No." Gabriel told her. "This 'covetous possessiveness' refers to a demon of darker intent. He is the origin of many evil things in the world."

"A friend of mine says it's a reference to lust."

"The word you use as 'lust' does not explain this creature." The face in the falls splashed as he spoke. "This monster lived long after the War. It was a creature bred of lust, as you surmised, but not of the modern concept of the word. It is," he searched for the word, "domination; the need and will to own the very soul of the one it seeks to control. It remained on Earth after its master Belial and god Lucifer were struck down; seeking to corrupt humanity. This creature is from the bowels of Creation's existence and is a darkness none wish to recognize in the human heart. I'm sorry, but I cannot tell you more. I do not even know its name."

"Can anyone tell me?" she asked. "There has to be other angels out there, right? You're not the only one."

"I have been in seclusion for a very long time, Daniella. This cave is my home. There may be records of the demon, but I do not know for sure. I know this demon you seek has not walked the Earth in over a millennium, since it was bound within the lands of Egypt."

"Bound by who?"

"My brother."

Dani blinked. "You have a brother?"

"I have many kin." Gabriel told her. "I was youngest of the first angels, what are now called Archangels. My older sibling is the one who intervened in binding this darkness."

"I thought angels couldn't or wouldn't interact in our world."

"We can only do so much. We do not make war as we once did. We give assistance to humanity when we can, just as I once gave to you. Our ability is limited."

The ache in Dani's shoulder still reminded her of his 'assistance.' "This archangel: who is it?"

"You call him Raphael."

She knew the name, but from where? "Raphael. Ok, so, where is he?"

Gabriel shook his head, which nearly soaked her in river water. "I know not. I have not heard from him in ages."

"Do you know how I can find him?"

"I do not. Even when he was active in the world, he could only be found through his bannerman."

"His bannerman? What the hell is a bannerman?"

"He is one that carries a warrior's standard into battle." He said that as if it made any kind of sense.

Dani shook her head. "*Okaaaaay*, where can I find his bannerman?"

"I know not, either."

She rolled her eyes. "Of course you don't."

"The Angel of Joy and Laughter has not been seen since the destruction of the universe, though his legacy lives on amongst humanity."

"Wait, wait, wait, the Archangel Raphael's banner-dude is the angel of laughter? How does that have anything to do with war?"

"Remember, Daniella, we were not meant for war. We were meant to be creators; not destroyers. Our war was never supposed to happen. It was by our own hand we took up the sword of conflict."

Dani sighed. *Great.* She learned almost nothing and now had more questions than when she arrived. "Please, Gabriel, if there is anything you can tell me that might help, please tell me now. Can you try to find your brother? Or this demon? Can't you sense them like you sensed Alecto's attack?"

Gabriel was silent. The very beautiful face in the water grimaced in thought. When he spoke, his tone was as solemn.

"I cannot find my brother or the demon. They can hide themselves from me. I can only give to you two warnings. The first is to trust your heart and your mind, even in the darkest of times. They are the vehicle by which the divine works." His eyes intently bore into her as he spoke. "The second is this: do not allow the darkness that is rising to know of you. Do not seek to find it. Do not let it feel your strength of will, for it will want to stamp it out. I have seen this demon first hand. It is an all-consuming shadow that will twist even the purest of hearts. It will never rest. It will never tire. And if it finds you, its focus will be upon you and it will seek to take you."

"Why?"

"Because it will want to consume you."

Night had fallen by the time Dani flew back home. Once below the Dalles' fog, she could fly. She took her time, mulling over what Gabriel told her. His warning was cryptic, but ominous.

She skimmed the trees, her fingers brushing the top branches. Overhead, the moon was full; blotting out the stars in the night sky. The glow illuminated everything around her.

It was why, as she raced across the treetops, she spotted something flying up into the air ahead. She narrowed her eyes. It was right in her path and arched towards her.

An arrow.

"Whoa!"

Dani dove left and the arrow shot by her; way off the mark, but waking her from her reverie. But as the arrow sung past harmlessly, she wasn't prepared for a second one that zipped from the branches right for her.

Someone used the first arrow to steer her into the path of the second.

Dani summoned a pocket of Aer around her hand and batted the weapon away, but as her *arche* connected with the bolt, it exploded with a concussive blast that knocked her out of the sky.

She tumbled, smacking into a branch that cushioned her fall like a bed of scrap metal. As she tumbled through the next few branches—a sickening repeat of her fall with Caesar—she had more mind to land on the forest floor without a painful snap of her ankle.

She landed, but no sooner were her feet on the ground than an arrow lanced past her; close, but she escaped by chance. Dani threw herself against a tree as a fourth shot went wide.

Who the hell is shooting at me?

"I don't know who you are," she screamed, "but you messed with the wrong Numen!"

No answer. Dani drew Pigsticker and knelt to make herself a smaller target. She listened for her attacker.

Nothing.

Dani glanced around the far side of the trunk and nearly lost her head to another arrow.

Damnation, that was close, she thought. She could try to fly, but whoever shot at her proved they were a good shot. She had her lightbringing, but even as she thought to summon it, she realized she didn't know where they were. She couldn't hit them.

Finally, she heard movement. Underbrush rustled.

"I hear you." She called out. No sense in staying quiet if they knew where she was. Maybe if she got them to talk, she could get a bead on where they were. "Do you know who you're firing at?"

Finally, a response. "A trespasser." The voice was soft; not feminine, but young. It was a boy's voice. "You encroached upon our lands."

"'Our lands?' Whose lands?"

A hard *thunk!* and an arrow lodged into the tree behind her.

"You missed." She called out.

"No, I did not."

Dani realized what he meant and threw herself forward as the arrow, just like the one above, detonated and blew a chunk out of the tree. Wooden shrapnel rained around her as she landed on her stomach.

She heard galloping. Dani rolled to her feet, Pigsticker still in hand, and saw a moonlit figure coming through the trees. He appeared to be riding a horse, but she knew better. She'd seen plenty of centaurs before.

The figure drew back his bow and fired. Dani dodged, now able to predict his shot. She rolled across the ground as the arrow flew past. She got to her feet and ran, using the trees between them for cover. The centaur rode in at an angle. Dani moved to cut him off.

She dodged behind a tree, which absorbed another arrow, and she kicked off the ground. Leaping up into his path, she slashed with her dagger and struck the bow and arrow out of his hand. Then, as she sailed past, she put both feet onto the next tree and pushed off back at her attacker. She meant for a graceful spin to strike with her heel like Elder Caspar taught her, but instead she flipped backwards and collided with him as he slowed to draw his sword. She plowed into him and tumbled them both over, with him onto his side while she ended up on her back.

Dani flipped to her feet just as he started to rise. She kicked him hard across the jaw. Her blade ignited in the moonlight as she leapt on top of him and pressed it to his throat.

"You move, you die!" She warned.

In the large moon, it was easy to see his face. He was young. If he were human, he would have been twelve at most. Clean-shaven, baby-faced with olive skin, he wore a tunic and no armor with a quiver over his shoulder. His lower horse-half was spotted.

He brayed angrily, still moving to draw his weapon.

"I will kill you." She warned again, pressing the tip of her blade in.

He relented, easing his hand away.

When he glared up with his deep, dark eyes, Dani couldn't help but be reminded of Nessus. He looked just like a younger version of him.

"Who are you?" she demanded.

"A warrior never gives his name." He said.

"Warrior?" she asked. "You're, what, a foal?" That was what child centaurs were called, right?

"I am not a foal!" he growled. "I have taken my first ride in the wilderness! I am a colt!"

"Bully for you." She stripped his sword—a single-edged, double-handed cavalry blade centaurs used—and tossed it away. Then she stood, putting away her own weapon. She offered him a hand.

"I do not take assistance from an enemy."

"Kid—." She started saying, annoyed with this little punk already.

"I am not a kid! I am a colt!"

"Whatever! You barely look legal to drive."

He stood, towering over her. "What does that mean?"

Whoops, wrong species. "Nothing." Dani told him. "Now, come on, who are you? I'm Dani."

"I know who you are."

"Then you know I'm a friend; not a trespasser or an enemy. One of my friends is a centaur. His name is Nessus. Do you know him?"

The boy sniffed, wiping dirt from his nose where Dani threw his face into the ground. "Nessus is my uncle."

"Your uncle?"

"My name is Orion; named for the great archer of legend."

"I see that." She picked up one of his fallen arrows. It looked like any other, but was warm to the touch. Magic? She only knew centaur trick-arrows that fired binding chains, but could they do magic as well? "You made these?"

"My uncle says I am gifted with them." He snatched it back. "He taught me to use a bow."

"Nessus taught you? What about your dad?"

The boy frowned, teetering uncomfortably. Instantly, Dani hated for asking about the obvious.

"I'm sorry."

"It is no business of yours."

"Yeah? And what's your business firing arrows at me?"

"I told you: you were trespassing. My duty is to protect the border of my village."

"The centaur village up the way?" she nodded in the direction of Nessus's home.

77

"I am the eldest male." Orion puffed out his chest proudly. "As such, it is my duty to protect the Forest Foothill Clan until the return of our warriors from their mission. A mission," he scowled, "that you put them on."

Dani frowned. *Great. Looks like the Council's rumors precede me yet again.*

Orion the centaur gathered up his fallen arrows. Dani's blade had cut his bow in half and he discarded the pieces.

"I'm sorry about your family." Dani said. "I didn't mean for that to happen. Nessus is my friend. I wouldn't put him in harm's way."

"But you did."

"Well, there's debate on that. You're not going to attack me again, are you?"

Orion retrieved his sword. "I will let you live."

"Oh, thanks." She grumbled.

"Leave our borders, Numen. You've caused enough trouble."

"Yeah, sure, whatever." She turned to leave, now on yet another centaur's short-list, it seemed.

But she didn't get far before she heard him say, "Why did they have to leave?"

The question stopped her. She turned around. Orion's face frowned with deep sadness that Dani understood all-too-well; the one that comes from separation from a parent.

"Why did he and the others have to leave us?" he asked aloud.

As angry as she was at this kid...er, colt, Dani didn't want to leave. Instead, she crossed back over. "Because they're braver than half the warriors in the Citadel. Because your uncle is the greatest person I know, human or otherwise."

"I want to make him proud."

My god, he really is just a kid. It was weird for her to think that, considering she was only seventeen. But after everything that happened, her old soul was a few decades older.

"You do." She said. "You will." What else could she say?

"You don't know that. You don't know me."

"You're right." She sighed. "But I'd like to, if you want. I told you the truth: Nessus is my friend. You're his nephew, so that makes you my friend." *Friends who try to kill each other, apparently.* She didn't say that out loud. "Do you know Caesar, the caladrius?"

"My uncle's *alos misos.*"

Dani recognized the term. *Soul-mate.* "He called her that?"

He nodded.

She grinned. Apparently, their relationship wasn't just one-sided. To Orion, she said, "If you need me, call out to Caesar. She'll hear you. And then I'll come meet you."

"Why?"

She shrugged. "If you need someone to talk to, or if you need help protecting the borders of your village; anything you want."

"Why would you do that for me? I tried to kill you."

"To be fair, some of my own people tried to kill me and I still have to work with them. But at least with you, you thought you had a good reason. They're just jerks."

Orion's mouth twitched. Was that a smile? He slid his arrow back into his quiver. "Thank you, Daniella the Numen."

"Call me Dani."

Chapter Ten

Well, this is going to suck, she thought as she got up and dressed the next day. Instead of training with Mastema and then uphill with the other Novices for training, Dani flew across the Vale to meet Elder Heman for her punishment. Awesome.

And Heman didn't disappoint. As an Elder, he had many duties to perform and found a way for Dani to help with each one.

It began at the Powers barracks, which served as a training ground and gathering point for the forces of Empyrean before going out on missions. She had to muck-out sun-stallion stables that some of the psychopomps used. Dani learned first-hand what happened to food the stallions ate. She was also forced to gather used and broken armor to be taken to the Forge.

Then she had to survive the Forge.

Dani dropped off the broken equipment with the metalsmiths, but Heman then had to ensure that she got the smiths fresh water for their forges and to drink. Novice-turned-serving-wench was not fun, especially since she suspected the smiths were ruder than needed on purpose. And then she had to schlep a bunch of newly fixed armor back to the cart for Heman, who watched on condescendingly.

By mid-day, Dani was gathering, counting and then re-counting—to ensure accuracy, of course—a shipment of armor to another celestial city.

"Count them again." Heman growled when Dani told him they were short several helmets. "They are here."

"I counted them twice."

"Then count them for a third time." He shook his head. "It is beyond me how you, of all Numen, defeated the Fury Alecto. How could someone with such an addled brain possibly defeat the greatest warrior of the Hellions?"

Dani's fist burned with the answer, but she tamped down the urge to lightbring him into oblivion.

"Did Guardian Ethan really kill her and you just took the credit?"

His insult was cut short by the arrival of a Powers commander, Plutarch, with a small collection of helmets. "Elder Heman," he had his Powers place them with the others, "you said to bring these?"

Dani glared. *He meant to keep them out?*

"Very well," Heman said dismissively, "let us move on. We have another matter to attend to at the Training Grounds."

They crossed the Vale Bridge on foot, since Heman wouldn't allow her to take the easy route of flying. When they arrived, only a few Novices remained on the grounds while everyone else departed for Studies.

Kleos was there with Izzy, and frowned when he saw her with Heman.

"Elder," he called, approaching, "may we be of assistance?"

"Not necessary, Guardian Kleos. Novice Daniella missed her training exercises this morning. I will aid her." He sneered at her. "In fact, I have just the exercise to suit her special talents."

She didn't like the sound of that. She liked it less when the three Novices he apparently had in mind to 'aid' her arrived.

Michael, Lester and Andreas were like the Three Stooges, but less funny and less talented.

"I'm sure you know your fellow Novices."

She jutted her chin towards Lester. "You mean the one who had to sit out the entire battle for the city because he got hurt," she turned on Michael, "or the guy who needed five people to back him to fight only me or," her eyes fell to Andreas, "the one who ran away to hide while demons killed his friends?"

With that one sentence, Dani earned the ire of every one of them all over again. Her and her mouth.

Heman was unfazed. "Be wary, Novice. Divisiveness breeds only ill-contentment. Of course, we expect such things from you."

Bite me, she thought. She knew better than to keep poking the bull so she didn't give any other snide comments.

Kleos and Izzy watched silently from where they stood. She could tell by Kleos' face that what was happening was not good. If anything, he was there in case something bad happened.

"Now, to correct your discordant behavior," Heman went to a weapon rack, "I thought some simple training would be in order. You will not need your knife." He extended his hand for it.

Dani handed over Pigsticker; not that she wanted to.

Heman tossed it away as if it were nothing. "Excellent. Pick a weapon."

Since the other three were already armed, she took the wooden armament provided to her. There were mostly longswords, broadswords, axes, and bowstaves. Nothing small. Dani's empyreal-steel swords were light and quick. She was used to fighting with them. These weapons were designed for bigger combatants.

She chose a broadsword and stepped back. "Which one of them am I fighting?"

"All of them." Heman told her.

"I mean who am I fighting first?"

"I know. That is why I meant: all of them."

Kleos spoke up. "Elder Heman, what is the purpose of this?"

"The purpose, Guardian," he used Kleos' title to remind him of his place, "is to judge what the Novice has said to be true. She claims to have defeated a Fury and an archdemon in battle. Surely, with such talent, defeating three fellow Novices should be quite easy." He turned back to her. "And, should she fail, she will at least learn to respect the Elder Council and not defy its laws."

Kleos turned his eyes on her. She could tell he wanted to help, but there wasn't much he could do. Even Izzy looked concerned, standing aside with his weapon uselessly.

She knew Heman was about the most horrible human being she ever met, but she assumed he tried to hide it. Unfortunately, whenever she thought the people here hit rock bottom, they brought in a backhoe to prove her wrong.

Dani stepped into the open, facing her three opponents. Michael had a sword. Lester had a bowstaff. Andreas had a two-handed club. All of them were bigger, stronger and meaner. This wasn't going to end well.

"Begin!"

Michael attacked first. He swung right for her head. She brought her sword up to block, but unlike her empyreal weapon, it could not absorb her emotions to make it stronger. She blocked, but pain radiated down her arm and through her hand from the blow. She blocked once, twice, three times. If it had just been him and her, she could have put up a fight.

But it wasn't.

Lester struck to the back of her thigh, sending her down to one knee. She screamed, having enough sense to roll under Michael's next attack. Mastema taught her to fight solo. She was used to being on the run from multiple opponents.

She rolled to her feet and struck, catching Michael low on the front-most knee and taking him down. Lester swung, bowstaff arching high. Dani caught it with her sword above her head, using her free hand to balance the blade, but the dull edge was sharp enough to bite hard into her palm.

She didn't see Andreas until he struck her in the back.

She remembered the pain, both in her shoulder blade and as she fell forward onto her hands, weapon tumbling away. She remembered Andreas striking to the small of her back. She remembered Lester's boot in the side of her face.

What she didn't remember was Heman telling them to stop.

She was in agony. One kick or club-strike after another landed. She curled up into a ball to protect herself as all three laid into her until Heman finally called for them to cease.

They stepped back. Dani was bleeding from her lip, from a cut above her eye and she knew she had several severe bruises. When she peeked through her arms, Heman looked bored.

"Elder Heman, I must protest." Kleos stepped forward. "There is nothing to be learned from this."

"Quiet, Guardian." He snarled and turned back to the boys. "That was sloppy. You fight as one, remember? You cannot prevail against any opponent no matter the strength if you do not fight together. Novice Michael, she should not have landed that blow."

"I apologize, Elder. It will not happen again."

"See that it does not. Novice Daniella, why do you remain on the ground? Stand."

She got up slowly. Heman kicked her weapon over to her. She retrieved it begrudgingly. "Got any notes for me?" she asked bitterly.

"Only for you to understand there is an order to things in this city and that you must learn your place in it."

Dani spit blood on the ground in front of him. "Uh-huh."

"Again." He ordered. "Take position."

Dani limped over to stand in front of the three, she was fairly certain a blackout was in her future. The idea she could take them on toe-to-toe was ridiculous. Three opponents, all with considerable reach over her, all wanting to beat the ever-living hell out of her; how was she supposed to fight with a weapon too heavy for her, or that she never trained with for that matter?

Mastema's nagging voice came to mind as it always did. *Will you just lie down? It asked. Will you give in? Will you accept death and shame? I do not believe you will.*

Yeah, thanks, she sighed silently. *Got any other helpful advice?*

And, in fact, it did. *Do not focus on where your enemy is, but where he is not. Every terrain offers a better chance in battle. The difference between the weak and the strong, the slain and the victorious, is who takes note of it.*

She looked around. The hill sloped, which meant taking the high ground was her best bet. And, when she looked uphill, she saw a long board which functioned as a barrier for arrows and throwing knives. Usually, it was where targets were mounted. She got an idea.

Your opponent is but a mortal, Mastema once said. *They fall to desires like everyone else. Find their weakness. Exploit it.*

Heman raised his hand to begin.

"Hey, Michael," Dani sneered through red-stained lips, "remember that one time when I shamed you in the Vale like the little weasel you are? Want to go another round?"

"You're dead." He snarled. "I'm coming for you."

"Good luck with that. Anyone as cowardly, spineless and," she glanced down slightly at his waist, "small as you wouldn't know what to do with a girl even if he got her."

That was all it took. Heman didn't even get to announce the beginning of the bout.

Michael screamed, swinging the sword. He was a big guy so he had a lot of power. Dani used that. When he swung, she flipped her sword to her non-dominant right hand and caught his sword arm with her left. He grabbed her right arm with his free one and together, they charged uphill towards the barrier.

But she wanted that.

As he drove her back, she braced up. She turned, tossing him hard against the thick, wooden wall and his head snapped sideways on impact, dazing him. Dani spun, putting him between her and the other two. Then she head-butted him in the face, breaking his nose.

His head snapped back and Dani spun him, her sword up across his throat. She couldn't—and wouldn't, even given the chance—cut his throat. She wasn't evil. She didn't kill Numen. But her practice sword choked him out, keeping him in place.

Andreas and Lester attacked together and Dani moved Michael to one side and then the other, absorbing the blows to the stomach, chest and face like a human shield.

Andreas rushed. Dani kicked Michael into him, snatching his sword from his loose hand. She blocked Lester's next attack with the staff, using the second sword to strike his hand. Screaming, he dropped it.

Dani struck again, this time between his legs. His knees buckled. Normally, she would take pity on an opponent, but after these three chuckle-nuts nearly beating her senseless, she wasn't in a forgiving mood.

She kicked the side of his leg and broke his knee sideways, dropping him like the garbage he was.

Dani blocked the next blow from Andreas, which knocked one of her swords out of her hand. She rolled, coming up under and catching him off guard. Her first strike was to the knee, the second to the ribs and the third to collarbone. Andreas' club fell from his hand.

Dani struck. Hard. Multiple times. She didn't know how many, but he was on the ground in seconds with her over him. She used her bare knuckles and beat him.

Again.

And again.

And again.

And again.

"NOVICE DANIELLA! CEASE! CEASE!"

She kept going.

"NOVICE! STOP!"

Heman cast out his hand and with a blast of Aer, hurtled her into the wall. She landed hard and slid down. She glared at the Elder, but also in horror at the three she disabled and took down. Mastema would be proud. She was just sick.

Heman stared in both shock and fury at the three lying on the ground, then at her. "How dare you—!"

"Elder Heman!"

No sooner had Heman begun to advance on Dani then Jeduthun and Castus arrived. Kleos and Izzy stood at their side. Apparently, they couldn't do anything except for retrieve another Elder to put an end to it. Though, Dani saw, she didn't need them.

"What is the meaning of this?" Castus demanded. Both Elders looked utterly horrified; two wounded Novices unconscious and one screaming in agony from a broken leg.

Jeduthun knelt and whispered into Lester's ear. Lester stopped screaming, eyes rolling into the back of his head and passing out. One of Jeduthun's powers over sound could make people pass out if he used the right frequency. It was a mercy now.

"What is the meaning of this?" Castus demanded.

Heman pointed angrily at Dani. "This impudent Novice nearly killed three of our men!"

Jeduthun caught Dani's eye and said, "What I see is one who stood remarkably against three. What lesson was to be taught here?"

"I attempted to show Novice Daniella how to combat three opponents at once, since she will perpetually be alone," his voice turning sour, "as no true man would ever stand beside her in battle."

"I would think any man would, considering the skill by which she dispatched these three." Castus surmised. Healers arrived, taking the unconscious Novices away. "It appears she does not need this lesson."

Jeduthun took Dani's sword from Heman.

"I would think it best if Novice Daniella were to be in my care for the remainder of her punishment. Would you not agree?"

Heman scowled.

"That will be all, Elder."

Disgruntled, Heman cast one ugly look her way and stalked off.

Jeduthun gestured for Dani. "My dear, we should attend to your wounds, though I imagine your recovery will take less time than your peers."

Dani followed a healer towards the Citadel. Her hands were still warm; her lightbringing coming to the surface. As she passed Jeduthun, she saw him look down at her sword.

The grip was singed black.

85

Dani broke a rib. She was lucky it was just one.

She had contusions all over her body. She had a fracture in her cheekbone. The panacea and other elixir concoctions would take about an hour or so to work before she was fully healed.

The other three would be there two days.

Jeduthun stayed quiet at her bedside until the bandage from her face was removed. "You look no worse for wear."

The Ward was empty save for the three she put there. Situated behind the Citadel, it was protected by its own courtyard when wounded needed shelter during an attack. Until Alecto, no one thought that would be needed. They were wrong.

"You should see the other guy. Oh, wait, you already have." She didn't usually gloat, but there was nothing to say she couldn't sound a little proud. "How much trouble am I in?"

"None." Jeduthun assured her. "Heman should have been wiser in his choice of punishments. Unfortunately, three Novices paid the price."

"We're all accountable for our actions. They could have said no."

"And they would have been wiser for it, too." Jeduthun's smile was reserved. "You are an interesting person, Novice Dani. Or rather, I should call you Daniella, shouldn't I?"

Dani and Jeduthun weren't on the best of terms. In fact, she wasn't exactly sure where she stood with him. Jeduthun often supported her, but he only did so because he didn't trust her. It was strange.

And a little bit scary.

"Dani is only for my friends."

"Ah yes, I remember." He nodded. "Well, as it stands you are now my servitor for the remainder of your sentence. I hope that I can be of better assistance in correcting your behavior."

"Doubtful."

"I suspect as much. Though I am glad we once again have a chance to talk. Ever since I helped you to escape, your life has become quite interesting, even for a Numen." His smile twitched. "I also notice the absence of a particular Guardian."

She blushed. Jeduthun was unfortunately aware of her love life. "Ethan and I are having a disagreement."

"Care to explain it to me?"

"Do pigs fly?"

He chuckled. "In our world? Sometimes."

That didn't surprise her, but she wasn't telling him anything about possible traitors, prophecies hidden in the walls or angels in the river. "Thanks, but I'd rather keep my secrets to myself."

"Of course. I have come to expect secrets from you."

"And I've come to expect you to try to find them out, anyway."

"I am glad we have an understanding, then."

Sometimes, Dani was painfully aware that Elder Jeduthun was one step down from a supervillain.

But he also had a lot of information. And right now, Dani wanted help with a question. "Can I ask you something?"

"Depending upon the nature of it, yes."

"It's about the angels. You know," she said sarcastically, "the ones you Council guys have been lying about?"

Jeduthun let the jab roll off him. "What would you like to know?"

"I want to know about an archangel. His name is Raphael."

Jeduthun's brow perked up. "The Archangel Raphael? They called him Raphael the Healer. What about him?"

"I want to know more about him."

"Why?"

"Because I'm totally fangirling on him." She said flippantly. "Let's skip the why. What do you know about him?"

Jeduthun frowned and sighed. "Well, as I said, he is the Archangel of Healing, as Gabriel is the Archangel of Truth. He has many duties, as does our patron. He is the patron angel of the city of Beri'ah."

Dani perked up. "The city Roxelana moved to?"

Jeduthun frowned. "Do I know that name?"

"It's just a Gifted girl I know. Go on."

"Well, he is the patron of healers, but also of travelers, the blind, apothecaries—."

"Did he ever kill a demon?"

The question caught him off guard. "Kill a demon?"

"Well, did he?"

"He killed many demons."

Of course, she thought. *He's an archangel! He probably killed thousands!* How could she ask Jeduthun questions if she couldn't be specific? She tried another question.

"Who's the angel of laughter?"

"The angel of laughter? You mean Raphael's bannerman?"

"Yeah."

"Well, there are many names for him. A great deal of angels went by different monikers; some known, some not. In antiquity, he was called Sechoquel. It means Laughter of God."

Well, that didn't help her. She knew his name, but how was she supposed to find an angel by name alone? Jeduthun wouldn't know his whereabouts any more than Gabriel.

"This is all very specific to the Archangel Raphael." Jeduthun commented. "Why do you ask of this?"

She was about to answer with her best lie when a trumpet blast interrupted her. Trumpets were used to announce all kinds of things: the time of day, meetings in the Throne Room, the changing of the guard. There were various types too: long drones, short bursts, high-pitched chimes. But this one was familiar and made her blood run cold. It was a deep, resounding blast that shook her teeth, followed by three very quick warning blasts. She only heard it once before and never wanted to hear it again.

Jeduthun rose to his feet. "We are under attack."

Chapter Eleven

Empyrean was in an uproar.

The Gifted working in the Citadel fled towards Sanctuary Hills. Gatekeepers flew to the gates while Powers and other hosts got to their assigned positions. Dani followed Jeduthun through the crowd to the West Gate, where they met Castus.

"Elder Asaph has sealed off the city," Castus reported to his fellow Co-Consul, "and has requested two-dozen reinforcements. I will see to them in case of an assault."

"Very well." Jeduthun marched towards the West Gate. Dani followed on his heels.

"Novice Daniella, I believe you should return to Novice Village with the others."

"Like hell." She muttered, though she felt naked without her weapons and armor, and following the Elder into almost-certain danger.

Jeduthun chuckled. "I thought as much. Very well. Here." From within his cloak, Jeduthun handed over her dagger, Pigsticker. It wasn't much to fight with on its own, but she strapped it to her side.

They entered a side entrance to the West Gate's inner archway; a reinforced porthole that led into the battlements surrounding its inner cloister. Once inside, she could see out into the sky beyond. The clouds around Empyrean, normally white and lush, were now dark and crackling with lightning.

"What's coming?" She asked. "A demon?"

"I do not know." He said, not even looking back as he strode briskly down the fortified line of Gatekeepers. "An omen such as that means something has broken through the firmament without permission."

"Firmament?"

"The true name of the veil that keeps our city separate from the rest of the world." He explained. "Only a guide or something powerful could break through, and only something tainted with the scent of Hell would disturb the clouds."

Dani remembered Alecto when she came to Empyrean. Despite being invited, her Chariot of the Underworld wreaked all kinds of havoc.

They made their way down a long corridor, which opened into the forward ramparts that ringed the terrace. From here, archers could rain down death on anyone trying to enter the city. Already, two rows of Gatekeepers assembled, with one row at the windows and a second standing in reserve.

There were other defenses, too. As Dani and Jeduthun came to the front, ballistae with long, adamantine tipped-spears turned to aim at the cloud wall. Gatekeepers stoked Fyre inside of large basins to create flaming projectiles or Fyreballs to hurl down on anyone foolish enough to attack. Dani also noticed that the whitestone gargoyles, which normally sat like grotesque observers, now moved on their own; hellish-looking monsters with spears, or clubs, or stone swords. She always thought they were just for decoration. Apparently not.

"Gargoyles?" Dani asked. "Seriously?"

"Every gargoyle on earth and in the celestial cities is imbued with a spell to serve the Numen." Jeduthun explained. "They act as our eyes and ears and, when the situation calls for it, soldiers."

"Are they alive?"

"No more than golems."

Which didn't answer Dani's question.

"You know," she murmured as they passed another defensive row of archers, "I never understood something."

"And that is?"

"Why do we not have, like, assault rifles and grenade launchers? Couldn't we just make adamantine bullets? Then we could go all Rambo on the demons."

He chuckled. "That truly would be a grand invention, though I must confess, I know not this Rambo."

"It doesn't matter. But, still, why not?"

"You assume that modern firearms can launch an angelic metal." He glanced over his shoulder. "They cannot."

She hadn't thought of that. "But bows and arrows can?"

"Bows and arrows made of mystical lotus or mistletoe wood can."

They reached the front. Elder Asaph stood, helmet tucked under one arm, shouting orders to his men. His armor shone silver in the light and sun rays glistened off the hilt of scimitar.

"Elder Asaph," Jeduthun bowed, "what can you tell me?"

"Nothing, at the moment, Elder Jeduthun." His eyes fell on Dani. "Novice Daniella."

"Elder Asaph." That was about the extent of their pleasantries.

"You are not armed for combat."

Dani flexed her hand and touched her dagger hilt. "I have what I have."

"You will be a hindrance, should it come to a fight."

"I'll take care of myself."

Asaph didn't want to argue. "Very well. Have the Powers assembled?"

"They are as we speak." Jeduthun informed him. "Our forces have come to bear."

"Then now we wait." He slid on his helm, the visor lowering over his eyes, and drew his scimitar.

Dani had never been in a siege. The fight for the city last spring was an ambush. There was no time to prepare. But this was different.

A siege was boring as hell.

Ten minutes. Fifteen minutes. Twenty minutes. Time crawled by. The lightning crackled, but nothing came out. Asaph periodically sent messages to the troops, moving people to different stations, but for the most part, all they did was stand there.

Dani took a seat against the rear parapet. She drew her knife, digging out some dirt under her nails with it. She didn't know how long she sat there.

Then, as if echoing down the line, someone shouted a warning. Others took it up. She shot to her feet.

Breaking from the clouds was a single object. She had to squint to see it. It soared upwards, flapping its gigantic wings to gain altitude. Whatever it was, it came in low and then tried to get higher. As it approached, it looked more and more like an eagle; or rather, an eagle the size of an eighteen-wheeler. The bird shrieked as it powered towards them. She could see something across its back, but it was too far away. And as it neared, Dani could see it was covered in stains of red blood.

"Make ready!" Asaph called.

Bowmen nocked arrows.

The eagle got closer and Dani could see that on its back wasn't just something, but a person. He had a shaved head, beige skin, and an outfit that looked familiar.

"On my mark!" Asaph called. Officers relayed orders down the line. "Bring me a mirror!"

Two men marched through the crowd, carrying what looked like a large, glossy black disc. Asaph pulled it from their hands using Aer, running his fingers across a spell on its backside.

"Show me." He commanded.

The mirror surface—what kind of mirror she wasn't sure—shimmered and like he commanded, it showed a close-up view of the eagle and its rider.

"Prepare to fire!" Asaph called. Gatekeepers followed, drawing back their bows.

Dani, however, recognized the rider.

"WAIT!"

It didn't even occur to her that screaming was out of line. But she didn't care.

Asaph glared at her from under his helm. "Novice! Quiet!"

"No, don't fire!"

"Why? We have no idea who—!"

"It's Akela!"

91

Roxelana's husband soared upwards across the back of the blood-stained eagle. In the mirror, she could see he looked hurt.

"Who?" Jeduthun asked.

"Akela my friend's husband. He's a Gifted." She explained quickly.

"We do not know him." Asaph pointed out.

"Look at him: he's hurt!"

Jeduthun frowned at the image. "He is riding a psychopomp, who is also clearly injured."

"It could be a trap." Asaph argued. "We do not have any guides out at the moment."

"He's from another city." Dani insisted. "Beri'ah."

She spotted Jeduthun's questioning stare. They just talked about Beri'ah, along with a lot of other things about Raphael.

"Open the gates." The Elder told Asaph.

"Elder Jeduthun, we do not know for certain if there is no danger!"

"The beast is wounded. See for yourself." Jeduthun was already moving, with Dani at his heels again. "If it should be a threat, our forces can deal with it. Open the gates."

Asaph said something like a long, drawn out curse under his breath, but gave the order. Then he gathered a troop of soldiers and descended with Jeduthun and Dani.

They went down to the terrace as the gates swung open. The massive bird soared in and Asaph shouted orders. "Archers on guard! First platoon on me!"

Dani almost choked. As the eagle came to land, the wave of stench hit her like a wall.

Sulfur. Thick, rotting egg-like sulfur.

The creature stunk like demonic brimstone.

The bird landed and with a death-throe-screech, it fell. Akela toppled from it. Both slid to a stop at the foot of the steps.

"Akela!" Dani made to run to him, but Asaph held her back.

The bird collapsed on its stomach, head resting on the first step. Slowly, groaning, Akela shakily rose to his feet. His Naacali robes were torn and marked with blood. He bled from the corner of his mouth as he stumbled over to the dying creature.

He drew a dagger.

"Hold!" Asaph screamed, though she wasn't sure to whom he was yelling. The Gatekeepers lifted their spears and the archers readied to fire.

Akela collapsed next to the eagle. He murmured something, but Dani couldn't hear from across the terrace. Her eyes shifted to the eagle. It gasped visibly for air. Its feathers were frayed, torn or ripped out. Caked in blood, head lying sideways, it stared back at her. When she met its gaze, locked onto her.

And then it spoke. "*Please...*"

Dani jumped. She could speak to Caesar, but she never spoke to another bird before. The eagle rasped. "*Please...*"

"Novice!" Asaph screamed. "What are you doing?"

She hadn't realized it, but Dani stepped from the protective ranks of the Gatekeepers towards it.

"Daniella!" Jeduthun cried. "Return here at once!"

Dani walked slowly forward.

"*Please...help me...*" the creature begged.

Akela chanted something like a prayer. Dani could almost feel the creature's pain. It was in agony. Tears stuck at the corner of her eyes.

"*Protect...me...*"

Dani was halfway across the nearly-silent terrace. Akela didn't seem to hear or see her. He sadly chanted on.

"*They came back...*" the eagle crooned cryptically. "*They killed...the whole city...*" it swallowed painfully, "*everyone is dead...*"

The bird's eye bore into Dani as he spoke.

"*He is coming for you.*"

"Me?" Dani finally asked.

Akela raised the dagger. The eagle's eyes turned up toward it.

"*Protect me—.*"

The guide's final words were cut off as the dagger plunged into its neck, right behind the head; a nearly-instant killing blow.

Akela moaned. "I'm so sorry...thank you..."

His eyes shifted up to Dani, but he didn't appear to be looking at her. Then they rolled into the back of his head and he collapsed.

"Akela!" Dani ran to him.

She slid down next to him. Akela moaned, unable to speak louder than a whisper. The Gatekeepers arrived, but Dani wouldn't leave him.

"Akela?" She shook him softly. "Akela, where is Roxelana?"

He moaned again.

"Akela, answer me!"

"She is gone." He cried as the Gatekeepers seized him and pulled him up. Healers arrived with a stretcher between them. "They are all gone."

They stripped him of his dagger, put him on the stretcher and took him. Dani stared at the blood on the blade, and then down at the eagle that lay dead on the ground.

He is coming for you.

She heard those words before. En Dor spoke them.

Beri'ah, Raphael's city; it wasn't a coincidence.

"Novice Daniella?"

They came back. They killed the whole city, the eagle said.

"Novice, answer me!"

She broke out of her trance and looked up. Jeduthun stood in front of her. "What?" she asked.

"Are you alright?"

She looked down one more time at the eagle, and then shook her head. "Something's wrong."

"What do you mean?"

"Something happened to Beri'ah." She met his gaze. "I think they were attacked. I think they might," she bit back the fear in her voice, "I think they might be dead."

"Who might be dead?"

"Everyone."

Akela was taken to the Ward instead of Gifted healers of Sanctuary Hills. He was covered in wounds. They fed him calming elixirs to put him under; to stop his rambling. He kept repeating the same thing.

"Shadows...shadows...shadows..."

They meant to prevent rumors from spreading by keeping him in the Citadel, but as soon as Dani returned to Sanctuary Hills, many of the Gifted already knew.

Airlea confronted her at the Bridge. "Is it true?"

"Is what true?"

"Did Akela come back? Did something happen to Beri'ah?"

"I don't know."

"Dani, I know you know something. Don't lie to me!"

"I'm not, Airlea. I don't know anything."

"Did Akela come back or not?" she demanded angrily.

Before she could answer, a dark presence landed at her back and every stepped away. Mastema's voice was darkly calm, "That is enough."

"Arugh! Earthborn!" Airlea cursed. "You act like you're protecting us, but the moment we want to know something—!"

"You will know when we do." He answered coolly. "Until then, leave my Novice alone."

Airlea steamed, but her sapphire eyes were cold. She stormed off past Shea, who looked on confused and worried.

Mastema turned back to Dani. "Are you well?"

"You never ask me if I'm alright."

Her Guardian nodded. "True, but I ask nevertheless."

"I'm fine." She lied. "Any news? Has Akela said anything?"

"No."

Dani chewed the inside of her lip, walking back towards her home. Mastema walked beside her.

"You are thinking of something." He noted. "What is it?"

She shook her head. "Beri'ah."

"And?"

"It's the city of the Archangel Raphael."

"Does that have some significance?"

She filled him in on what he didn't already know: her excursion to study the Song, her suspicion about the archdemon and its involvement with Raphael—

—and, for the first time, where she got her information.

"The Archangel Gabriel? He appeared to you?"

"You don't seem so shocked." She noticed.

"I have come to expect very odd things from you, Dani. Normalcy is not your strongest attribute."

"Uh...thanks?"

"If what you say is true, the creature he warned you about has attacked Beri'ah."

"He warned it would come after me; not another city."

"It is not a coincidence that it attacked Raphael's city, if Raphael was the one to defeat it first." Mastema frowned. "And if what you say is true, it may still come for you yet."

"I'm worried."

"About yourself?"

"About Roxelana." She shuddered as if from the cold. "Akela said she's dead."

He bowed his head. "My condolences."

She shook her head. "I won't believe that—I can't believe that—until I know for sure."

"And in the meantime?"

"In the meantime, I need to talk to the others."

"Others?"

"Bouden, Nathaniel, Kleos; even Ethan. I'm going to need their help. If this thing really is out there, I need their help."

"What will you tell them?"

"Everything."

Chapter Twelve

"Wait, wait, wait," Bouden said, "you were *spying* on us?"

Nathaniel stared at him like he was crazy. "That's the part that sticks out to you? Not that she was visited by an angel?"

Night fell. Dani called her friends down to her house; all of them. Bouden, Nathaniel, even Izzy—who only came because of Kleos—sat on the floor. Kleos leaned against one post of her pavilion; Ethan another. Mastema stood by her side. Everyone looked equally pissed about her spying and equally surprised about her other revelation.

"Okay," Bouden frowned, "I can see her visiting an angel. I mean, look where we are." He gestured around to Empyrean. "But spying on us?"

"I had to be sure." Dani said defensively.

"Had to be sure? Of what?" Bouden gave an uncharacteristically hostile look. "You mean that one of us didn't betray this city and get one of their best friends killed?"

"Don't bring up Dink. He was my friend, too."

"Then you should understand how utterly insane it is to even *think* we would have something to do with that!"

Dani couldn't meet his eyes. Instead, she looked up where Caesar perched in the rafters. "*I told you they wouldn't be happy, honey.*"

"And you can talk to her?" Nathaniel asked, glancing up at the caladrius. "That's one of your powers? Like Jeduthun's sound-thing or Ethan's stormthrowing?"

She nodded. "She's my friend. She helped me, but only because I asked her to."

"Some friend." She heard Ethan mutter.

Dani glared. "Look, I didn't know who to trust. You, of all people, can't complain. You didn't believe me when I told you about Alecto."

He folded his arms, still pissed. But his jaw clenched with an anger he couldn't let out, since it was directed at himself.

Bouden sighed, angry but in typical Bouden fashion, thoughtful. "You should have told us, but," he glanced sidelong at Ethan and took a different route, "I get it."

"Me too." Nathaniel said.

Dani was thankful for that.

Izzy shrugged. "Hey, I'm new to this, but if *chica fuerte* thought keeping it close to the chest was right, I got no complaint."

Nathaniel asked, "*Chica fuerte?*"

"*Jolín!* You've known this chick your whole life and you don't even know that much Spanish?"

"*Darle un descanso*, Izzy." Dani told him. "Besides, it's not important right now." She looked from Ethan to her own Guardian, to Kleos. "Kleos? You've been quiet."

He stood with arms folded, but looked less angry. He shrugged. "You went with your gut. Isn't that what we train our people to do? Make a decision and see it through?"

"She lied." Ethan reminded him.

"Uh-huh. I'm still failing to see how that's a bad thing."

It felt nice to have his support. It still sucked not to have Ethan's.

"But you still messed up when you lied to us." Kleos finished. "We could help a lot more if we knew."

"I know and I am sorry I lied." She conceded. "And that's why I am telling you now. This is big; bigger than me, bigger than you, bigger than all of us. Beri'ah was attacked. We still don't know what happened there or what attacked it, but if the Song is right, then it's something terrible. I need your help to stop it." Her eyes fell on Ethan. "All of your help."

Ethan nodded, putting aside his anger. "If this 'covetous possessiveness' archdemon is here, we need to know more about it and quickly. The Council will want to investigate."

"Will they send scouts?" Izzy asked.

Kleos shook his head. "They won't risk it. They'll send a full force of Powers. If anything is there, they'll wipe it out."

"Unless that's what it wants." Dani offered. "It destroyed an entire city of Numen and Gifted."

That idea was met with silent horror.

"So, we figure out exactly who or what this archdemon is and we do it fast." Ethan said again. "Bouden?"

Bouden looked a little insulted, "Why me?"

"Because you're a nerd." Nathaniel sneered.

"Tough talk, four-eyes," but he knew why everyone looked to him on the book-smarts. "Fine. You said this demon was once captured by Raphael? That'll give me a start. I can look through the lore about the first demons. There may be something in there."

"It's a start. When can you go?" Dani asked.

"As soon as we leave here, so long as Elder Atid lets me, which he will. Let's face it: I'm his favorite."

"Brown nose." Nathaniel jeered.

"I will punch you, you know."

The boys laughed, and Dani had to admit, it felt good to get a little levity on this.

But their laughing cut short when Caesar screeched from above them. "*Someone's coming.*"

"Who?"

She listened. "*No idea, but there's two and they're armed. I can hear the wind on their spears.*"

"What is it?" Ethan asked, coming off the post.

"We have company."

They didn't arm themselves, but their hands strayed near the weapons they carried. Dani stepped to the edge of the pavilion, ready.

Two Gatekeepers descended from the air into the square. Both were armed, but unlike last time strange Numen came to get her, these two didn't want to attack her.

"Novice Daniella?"

As if she had to tell them. "That's me."

"Elders Jeduthun and Asaph request your presence in the Ward."

"Why?"

"To question the Gifted."

Akela. He must be awake. "Okay. I'll be right there."

"I'm going with you." Mastema said, grabbing his khopesh.

She didn't have to guess why. On top of everything else, they both had a similar suspicion about this visit. They spoke quickly, both understanding what might happen in the Ward, and then took off.

Dani and Mastema followed the guards across the Vale towards the Citadel, which had defenses visibly on high alert. Alecto's attack taught them to be vigilant and this was a high-alert moment.

They couldn't land directly in the Ward, since the Elders added angelic spells as an extra precaution to prevent anyone from accessing it from the sky. They went through the Citadel, where Asaph and Jeduthun met them.

"For the record," Asaph said without a greeting, "I am against this."

"Against what?"

"We wish you to interview the Gifted." Jeduthun said. "He has asked for you multiple times. You are close, supposedly."

"Which is a violation." Asaph pointed out.

Jeduthun waved it off. "If we punished every Numen for breaking that law, both of us would have been thrown in the dungeon once upon a time."

The revelation shocked Dani, but she didn't ask. And Asaph didn't have any comeback. "Fine. Let her through then."

Mastema waited outside while they took Dani in. Akela was the sole patient awake, as the other three she beat up earlier were still sedated. He sat up in bed expectantly and smiled when Dani appeared.

"Dani," he smiled in the soft glow of the lanterns, "thank you for coming."

"Akela." She glanced sideways at Jeduthun and Asaph. "You wanted to talk?"

He also looked to the Elders, who excused themselves to the other side of the room while she took a stool next to Akela's bedside.

"I am glad you came." He said. He took her hand, which kind of freaked her out. "I needed to see you."

"Is it about Roxelana?"

There was a strange look that passed over his face, but it disappeared and he nodded. "Yes. You were her friend, which is why I wanted to see you."

She took her hand back. "So, what is it?"

"Roxelana," he started hesitantly, "she told me you could speak to birds. Is that true?"

She nodded. "It is."

"Did you speak to my guide? The one that brought me here?"

She nodded again. "That's what you wanted to ask about?"

"Yes. Why?"

"I thought," she paused nervously, "I thought you wanted to tell me about Roxelana."

"I do." He insisted quickly. "It is only...only I do not think you wished to hear what I have to say."

"But I do. She's my friend."

"Of course." He bowed his head sadly. "I am sorry, but my wife is dead."

The news hit her heart like a brick. Dani pulled back the tears. "How?"

"I do not remember. Everything was chaotic. I lost her in the flight from Beri'ah. All I remember is what happened briefly before I arrived here." He took her hand, again. "I wish not to cause you pain, but I must know: did my guide say anything to you before he died? Did he know what happened?"

They came back.

They killed the whole city.

Everyone is dead.

He is coming for you.

Protect me.

"No," she lied, "he couldn't. You killed him before he could."

Akela nodded sadly. "We knew one another well. He guided me many times. I was honored to end his suffering."

"Of course. Is that all?"

"I wish only to ensure you are well." Akela squeezed her hand. "For Roxelana."

"I'll be fine." She withdrew her hand again. "You should rest."

"I will. Will Empyrean go back to Beri'ah? Search for survivors?"

"I don't know. Maybe. I have to go."

"Of course. Until I see you again."

She left. She had nothing to tell Jeduthun and Asaph, but when she stepped outside, Mastema waited for her.

"Is he well?"

"Yep."

"Did he ask you questions?"

"Yep."

"Is he is hiding something?"

"Yep."

They both knew before Dani came here that something was wrong. Akela, a Gifted, survived the attack but Numen did not? He killed his guide instead of healing it? The biggest warning signal was how he acted.

"He didn't care about Roxelana." Dani told him. "All he asked about was if the eagle told me anything and if we were going to Beri'ah."

"Beri'ah was a city full of Numen. You think Akela had something to do with what happened?"

"Maybe. I don't know."

"If we do not know, we need to be cautious. He should be allowed to think the ruse worked." He frowned. "So, going to Beri'ah is a trap?"

"Oh, it's totally a trap."

Chapter Thirteen

They didn't tell the Council; not yet, anyway. It may have been a mistake, but if Akela was involved in some plot with whatever demonic force attacked his city, capturing and torturing him would not get them what they wanted. That would be the Council's first move. They needed to figure out what he was up to.

His change of behavior was disturbing, though, especially watching him with the other Gifted. He appeared to be completely normal. And yet, Dani couldn't shake her suspicions. Once released from the Ward, he went to Sanctuary Hills. The whole mountain knew about the attack on Beri'ah now, so there was no sense in secluding him in the Citadel.

Shortly after his release, the Council decided what Dani already knew they would: they had to go to Beri'ah. The Powers would marshal for a full-scale assault, in case whatever attacked was still there.

Dani acted as Jeduthun's servitor during the meeting. She wasn't sure, but she suspected he asked her to accompany him on purpose; to allow her to listen in on their discussion.

"As Arbiter of the Powers, I will lead the assault." Heman volunteered. "It is my duty."

"Very well," Castus said.

"As I am duty bound, I will never shirk my responsibility." He continued. "This Council needs strong leadership in the face of this threat."

Dani saw several approving nods from other Elders. She also saw the worry on Jeduthun's and Castus's faces.

"I should accompany you." Jeduthun pointed out. "After all, strong leadership should require a Consul."

"That is unnecessary."

"I insist." He looked to the others. "We should take several Guardians and their Novices, as well."

"Why?" Asked another member.

"As the Powers will be engaged in searching the whole of Beri'ah for survivors, other less-critical duties may be performed by a small team. Namely, searching for Gifted or protecting the Nacaali Akela as he accompanies us. I assume we wish to bring him, as he is the only witness?"

The Elders agreed, though Heman looked slightly miffed by Jeduthun's intervention.

The Council broke and Jeduthun came to speak to Dani.

"What are you doing?" She asked. "Why are you going with them?"

"I told you once: I do not fully trust this Council. And as you have seen before, it is for good reason."

Dani didn't know what he was talking about, until she thought it through. Heman and Maalik came to get her from Hellfire without the rest of the Council. Heman once tried to stage a coup, until Asaph put him in his place.

"You think Heman is doing a power-play." She realized. "You think he'll look like the hero and take over the Council."

"We may be Earthborn, but we are human. Law and order balance against power and ambition."

"And taking Guardians and Novices?"

"True, anyone could go, but it is a convenient lie to take you."

"Why me?"

"What does Beri'ah have in common with Empyrean?"

"It's a celestial city."

"And?"

"It has..." she trailed off, thinking. Then it snapped to mind. "It has a Fane."

"And inside?"

"Ours held the Horn of Truth. You think Beri'ah's Fane has something of the Archangel Raphael's?"

"I suspect as much. And I would rather you retrieve it than Elder Heman. I will choose some of your companions to accompany us, as well."

Dani had to give Jeduthun credit: he wasn't stupid. All she was worried about was that he might get them killed.

Once the assault on Beri'ah was announced, things moved quickly. In two days, the Powers prepared to depart. So did Dani and her friends.

Mastema, Ethan and Kleos were chosen to go, along with their Novices. Dani was surprised when Jeduthun also selected a Guardian named Nazir and his Novice, Michael.

Just what I need, she grumbled to herself.

The Gifted pleaded with the Elder Council for word from the Crescent, the Gifted community. Many had friends or even family that lived in the other celestial city. They wanted to know what happened to their loved ones. Dani got a few requests, even one she didn't expect.

"Please find out what happened to Roxelana." Airlea pleaded. "I just need to know what happened to my friend."

Despite her ire for the Gifted girl, Dani promised, "I will."

"And if she is dead," she looked on the verge of tears, "could you...could you bring her back to us?"

Dani understood. "I will." She repeated.

Shea saw them off as well. He wished Kleos and Izzy good-luck, and then wished Dani luck as well. "Come back to us."

"I'll try my hardest."

Bouden, whose Guardian wasn't chosen, looked downcast when he met her at the marketplace before crossing the Vale. "I hate they didn't choose me."

"They did that on purpose."

"Why?"

"Because I asked them not to take you." Dani told him. He looked angry. "I need you here, Bouden."

"Why?"

"Because if we get there and things go south, you're the only one left who knows the truth. Keep looking for the demon. If we don't make it back—."

"Don't say that!"

"—if we don't make it back, warn the Elder Council about it. Tell them everything, including," she hesitated, "including about the prophecy."

"Why?"

She hadn't told Bouden or anyone else about her powers from the Devil. She still didn't. "Because it may come true."

He didn't fully understand, but he nodded. "If I can't go, at least take these." He withdrew what looked like small, black discs and handed them to her.

"What are these?"

"Obsidian mirrors." He explained.

They looked like smaller versions of what Asaph used to see Akela at a distance. "What are they for?"

"Think of them like magic walkie-talkies. You touch the angelic sigil," he pointed a symbol drawn into a circle on the back, "and speak the name of the person you want to speak with. That'll allow you to talk to the others."

Dani smiled and accepted the gifts, putting the four disc-mirrors into a pack she carried. "Thanks."

"Be careful."

"I will."

Dani flew to the West Gate, where Empyrean's Powers gathered. Dani had never seen so many of them in one place. The whole of Empyrean's army formed into neat columns, ready to march through the open double doors onto the West Gate terrace. Their helmets were made to look like two wings swept back to a tip behind their heads. The visors locked down into place. Their round shields, large enough to cover their torso, were emblazoned with Empyrean's fiery-wheeled crest.

Unlike Guardians, a Power's job was to stand and fight, not run. For them, retreat was not an option. Hence, the armor.

Dani wove her way through the crowd towards the front. She spotted Mastema and the others.

Heman wore his silvery adamantine armor with pride; a large round shield emblazoned with Empyrean's sigil on one arm and broadsword in his belt for the other. Jeduthun was also there, but unlike the war-like visage of the other Elder, Jeduthun remained in his robes.

Dani and the other Novices dressed like their Guardians; light armor and simple raiments. Mastema was armed with his hooked khopesh saber, but she spotted the hilt of several knives and daggers assorted around his person. Nathaniel had his one-handed axe and shield. Ethan's two-handed sword, Stormthrower, hung from his belt on loose-binding rings.

Kleos and Izzy were both armed as always.

Unfortunately, the others with them weren't as familiar or as friendly a sight: Michael and his Guardian Nazir. Michael still sported a shiner under one eye, which felt something close to opening a present on Christmas Day. He carried his two-handed longsword, a beast of a weapon like Ethan's, across his broad back. Nazir, who made Michael seem like a choirboy in comparison, was armed with a short knife called a Cassock dagger, and a thin, hooked saber known as a shamshir.

"What are you looking at?" Michael asked.

"God's biggest mistake."

He actually growled a little under his breath.

"Enough." Mastema told her. "This is no time for games."

"Listen to your Guardian." Michael sneered.

"You would do well to do the same." Mastema told him. "We go into the unknown. Childishness will be the death of you."

That shut Michael up.

The last addition to their party arrived. Two Gatekeepers escorted Akela to the front. He looked nervous, but Dani swore it was more nervous-excited; like he was eager.

He smiled in her direction, which creeped her out.

"Let us begin." Jeduthun said.

Heman gave the signal to the Gatekeepers above. With a loud grind, the West Gate's doors swung outward. Jeduthun led the Guardians and Novices to one side while Heman, with sword drawn, stood before the Powers and shouted, "Forward!"

As one, Empyrean's army advanced. Each step was a clang of armor and heavy footfalls. Heman led them towards the edge.

"How do we get there?" Dani asked. "Guides?"

Ethan shook his head. "It's too far for that."

"Then how?"

"Watch."

Jeduthun, who stood closest to the edge, extended his hand over the void under Empyrean. He murmured something under his breath; an incantation Dani recognized as the angelic language.

Ethan touched her elbow softly, "Look, about before—."

"Please don't." Dani cut him off.

The Powers neared the edge. Jeduthun continued to chant.

"Don't what?" Ethan asked.

"The last time we went into a fight, we kissed." She told him, swallowing an equal amount of anger and fear. Why was it so hard to talk to him about this? "I really don't want to start a trend with doing," she didn't even know what to call it, "*this* every time we go into some life-threatening situation. I don't want that to be the only time we're honest with one another."

She finally looked at him. His mouth shut, realizing what she said was true.

"You don't like some things I do or say, fine. I can accept that, but I'm not changing. End of story."

"I never want you to."

"Yes, you do. You wish I weren't a distrustful outsider to your precious society. You wish I didn't have... certain abilities...."

"But what's about to happen. If we don't at least say—."

She held up a hand, stopping him again. "No, Ethan, I'm not Twilight-ing this with you. Whatever you want to tell me, you tell me when we're safely back home. Deal?"

He nodded. "Deal. Can I at least tell you to be careful?"

"You can try."

"Be careful."

The Powers were almost to the edge. The wind around them stirred with magic. The air smelled like it did right after a rainstorm; the sharp, clean smell of ozone. The clouds darkened into shades of grey, and then new colors emerged. A florescent green burst to life amongst the sudden storm. Green rays swirled outward in a circle, forming into the unmistakable bands of lights she knew only from pictures of the Artic.

"Is that...?"

"An aurora borealis. Northern lights." Ethan nodded. "It's a gateway. The solar winds act like a portal between two places."

Heman, at the lead, jumped from the terrace and dove towards the aurora below. The Powers soldiers marched past in a wave of armor and violet, following in one, massive column.

She was in awe.

The remainder of the force departed as Heman and his first ranks hit the luminescent barrier. They disappeared in a flash of light. Each Power was a tiny emerald burst of energy before vanishing.

"I shall take you." Jeduthun told Akela. With a wave of his hand, a pocket of Aer lifted him from the ground. Together, the two dropped out of sight. The Guardians went next, choosing to go first in case danger waiting on the other side.

Dani looked at Nathaniel. "Ready, Nate?"

"Sure, *chica fuerte.*" They smirked at each other, attempting to lighten the seriousness of what they were about to walk into.

They dropped off the ledge together. The gates fell away.

The sound of the world disappeared behind the rush of wind. Her clothes flailed about her, deafening everything else; including her cry of joy. The four Novices dropped together towards the aurora. In seconds, it was right in front of her. Her eyes widened.

And then they hit the magical barrier.

They broke from the clouds with a jolt. They weren't under Empyrean anymore. Instead, they flew towards an island unlike anything Dani had ever seen.

It was a crescent in the middle of a vast, sapphire ocean; lush and green, with valleys so wide a 747 could fly through them without its wings touching. The whole island was covered in jungle. And as they approached, falling into formation behind their Guardians, Dani spotted buildings below, nestled in the arc of the island itself.

The Gifted community. The Crescent.

Attached to one tip of the island was the largest part of the civilization; a whitestone Numen Citadel. Unlike their Citadel, the one here seemed to be built on a large flotilla. Its massive walls jutted up from the ocean's waves, with towers arranged along a defensive wall. From the side not attached to the island, a long whitestone bridge stretched across the gap to the opposite tip of the island's arc, with even more towers arranged along it to protect the Gifted community.

But what amazed Dani most wasn't this island, but tiny ones that floated around it. Like balls of jungle, mountain and rivers, twelve smaller islands hovered in the air above Beri'ah's waters. Each one was connected by rope bridges or pulley systems to the main island, or had what looked like landing pads for some vehicle or creature that could bring goods to them. As Dani and the others passed, Powers soldiers peeled off, landing amongst the different landmasses to search the buildings.

Nazir and Michael arched down towards the Citadel, while Dani and the rest of her friends continued across the bridge towards the Crescent.

They landed on the beach. Above them, storm clouds cast a cool shade across the island. As soon as they landed, they drew their weapons.

"We need to hurry." Mastema warned. "Elder Jeduthun was specific: search for survivors and then joined the rest in the Citadel. We do not want to delay long."

Dani removed the mirrors, handing them out. "Take these. If you get lost or get in trouble, contact everyone else."

They split up.

Dani went uphill with Mastema while the others went in either direction along the beach. The Gifted houses here were like Hawaiian beach-front huts; bamboo or something like it made up the walls, while some sat on stilts from the surf or were built into the ground, which made it impossible to see where the roof ended and the ground began.

Dani didn't know what to look for. There were stables here, but for what she wasn't sure. She didn't see horses or animals of any kind. More eagles like the one that brought Akela? Something else? They checked a few along the way. Each one was empty.

Dani noticed there didn't seem to be signs of a struggle. Every so often, they found overturned chairs or ceramic dishes left uncleaned, but no broken doors, burned homes, or blood.

Everyone was just gone.

"It is eerily quiet." Mastema noted.

"Thanks, Captain Obvious." She paused at the entrance to one home and spotted something. "What's that?"

A small wooden perch, like a small cage or bird house on a stand, stood outside of almost every home. Every one they found was empty thus far, until this one. This one had something in it.

It was a bird, about the size of an owl, though it had feathers of blue, green and black. Instead of two feet, this one had three.

It lay dead inside its cage.

"A qingniao bird." Mastema said.

"What are they?"

"They're native to the Pacific and the Asian continent." He examined it. "This one has its neck broken."

"Why would anyone kill a bird?"

"They're used for messengers because of their speed and ability to fly long distances." He gave her a knowing look. "If you were to attack an island, what would be your first move?"

She knew. "Stop anyone from sending a distress call."

She felt warmth in her obsidian mirror and heard Ethan's voice, "We found something."

Dani picked up the mirror and saw his face in it. "Where are you?"

"About a mile up the coast from you; near the top of the first hill."

Dani flew to him. He and Nathaniel stood in a circle of huts, waiting with the others.

"What did you find?" Dani asked hurriedly, landing at a jog.

He glanced over his shoulder at a hut.

Dani didn't see what was so important at first. The place was similarly deserted as the rest of the Crescent, but when she looked closely, she saw something hanging to one side of the door.

A lazo. Roxelana's and Akela's wedding knot.

"Dani, I'm sorry." Ethan told her.

She touched the *lazo*. Inside, the hut held no sign of her friend.

"Where is everyone?" Nathaniel asked aloud. "This place gives me the creeps."

Dani left the knot and turned back to the others. "I want to see Akela."

"Why?"

"Because if my friend isn't here, I want to know where the hell she is."

Ethan chewed his bottom lip. "Dani, he said she's dead."

"Yeah, well, I don't believe him." She looked around. "This place is vacant. There is no trace of anyone who lived here, so where are they? If they were dead, there'd be bodies." She shook her head. "I don't like this."

"We thought this would be a trap."

"Yeah," Dani agreed, but shook her head, "except where's the danger? There isn't anything here."

Or anyone.

Chapter Fourteen

They returned to the Citadel. The only live occupants of the once-Numen fortress were Empyrean's Powers, which moved through the streets in teams searching for survivors. The Keep wasn't like Empyrean's. It was forged from the same whitestone, but looked more Asian in design. Before it was a large like dais the size of a helicopter pad. Inlaid into the stone were intersecting lines that formed what looked like a star, surrounded by a circle.

Dani landed, staring at it. "Is that a pentagram?"

Ethan landed besides her. "Pentalpha."

"A what?"

"It's the symbol of Beri'ah."

Dani stared at the symbol. Why did it look familiar?

Ethan led the way down the steps towards the Keep where Jeduthun and Heman waited.

"What did you find?" Akela asked, looking worried.

Dani wanted to say something, but chose not to; not yet, anyway. Instead, she turned to Jeduthun. "We found no one in the Gifted community. We could keep searching if you want."

Jeduthun shook his head. "Do not bother. We have found no one in the Citadel or on the aerial islands. It is as if the entire Numen and Gifted population vanished." He turned to Heman. "Have we searched the peaks of those mountains on the horizon?"

"Not yet," Heman told him, "but I will put a search party together." He departed.

Jeduthun turned back to Dani. "You should search the Fane. Eventually, Heman will himself. I would rather you do it."

Dani nodded. "May I take Akela? He can show us the way." *And I need a minute alone with him.*

"I would be happy to." Akela started walking.

Everyone else besides Jeduthun followed. The Elder gave her a knowing look as she departed.

The streets swarmed with Powers as Akela led them across canals that crisscrossed the Citadel. They appeared to be some sort of transportation routes, but Dani didn't know what for, since Numen could fly.

"It is for the ocean creatures." Akela told her. "The Numen here welcomed many outside creatures."

"What? Like mermaids?"

"Amongst others."

There were gardens, too; not the ones like in Empyrean meant to grow food and medicinal herbs, but what looked like places to rest; like human public parks, but with tranquil pools of water and flowering trees. Meditation gardens.

After the third canal, they arrived at the Fane. Unlike the Fane of Empyrean, this was built at the very heart of the Citadel. Still, it reminded Dani of a vault. It sat in the middle of a wide-open space, like a circular shrine surrounded by whitestone and adamantine supports. Walls that could slide back were closed, giving anyone inside a safe place to hide.

But what stopped her wasn't the doors, but what was inscribed on them: a star inscribed upon the double-doors of the shrine.

It looked exactly like it did in Dani's visions from En Dor.

"Dani?" Ethan noticed. "Are you okay?"

She shook herself. "I'm fine."

Akela led up the steps to the door, but stopped. "Gifted cannot open the Fane." He said apologetically.

Dani stepped past him and touched where the two doors met. With one brush of her fingers, they parted and she pulled them apart.

The inside glowed from faint light filtering through a skylight at the center of the rounded roof above. Just like the Fane of Empyrean, the shrine was circular, arranged with lanterns around a central dais. A pool formed around the feet of a statue; a man in long, flowing robes holding a staff. Raphael, supposedly.

Unlike Empyrean, stairs started behind the statue and led down, most likely into Beri'ah's Hypogeum where they would have tombs and their own Song of Sacrifice.

Dani and her friends entered, followed by Akela. She looked up at the statue and cursed.

"What is it?" Akela asked.

"They took it."

The statue of Raphael held the staff in one hand. It was nothing but stone; not a magical artifact. The other arm stretched outward toward the doors, but ended abruptly at the forearm. The hand and wrist were shattered into pieces. Whatever had been in the hand—whatever angelic object once hidden here—was gone.

"I do not understand." Akela said behind her. "Who took what?"

"We think the Fanes are places to hide artifacts from the original angels." Dani explained, her friends fanning out to search the space for anything that might be important. "The shrines may be a place to conceal them, even from us."

"Truly?" Akela asked behind her. "Astonishing. You figured this out?"

"Yes."

"I knew you were as intelligent as you are beautiful."

Dani stopped, a flicker of cold shivering down her spine. "Well, whatever was here, is gone now. Do you know what was in the statue's other hand?"

Akela spoke from almost right behind her. "Yes."

"Good."

Dani spun, drew her sword, and pressed the tip to Akela's throat. Everyone else drew their weapons, too; surrounding him.

In Akela's hand was a black-steel dagger, drawn from beneath his robes. Dani knew the metal as stygian; a hellish steel forged in the Underworld and deadly to Numen.

"Nice try." Dani snarled. "Next time, try not to do exactly what every bad guy in every B-rated flick does: lead us into a trap." She pressed her sword a little more. "Drop the knife."

Akela did as he was told.

"Kick it away."

He complied.

Dani gripped her glowing sword tighter, bearing her teeth. "Where is Roxelana?"

For his part, Akela didn't move. He was surrounded by six armed Numen. He should have been worried.

Instead, he smiled. "I knew you were special."

"Answer me." She threatened. "Or I'll just kill you and find her myself."

"You cannot find her. She is gone. I told you that."

"I don't believe you."

"You should." He said. His smile wasn't sinister. It was calm; adoring. He looked at her as if he worshiped her. "I would never lie to you. I would never hurt you." Then another look passed across his face. "I would never, unless I had to."

With a wave of his hand, the doors to the Fane slid closed on their own, latching and sealing them inside.

His eyes changed. Red cracks broke across the whites of his eyes; a shade the color of blood.

Then, with another stroke of his hand, a wave of shadow exploded from him and knocked them all back.

Dani tumbled through the air and landed in the shallow pool around the base of the statue, water spraying around her on impact. She slid through it to the feet of Raphael. Mastema smacked off the side and cartwheeled into the water a few feet away. He didn't move. The others swept in opposite directions, all taken by surprise.

Akela didn't move as Dani slowly rose back to her feet, sword thankfully still in her grasp.

She hurt, but she raised her blade threateningly. "Stay where you are!"

He didn't. He took a step towards her.

"Stay back!"

"So strong." He admired. "I love that about you."

When he spoke, her whole body shuddered. It was his voice, but it was as if someone dubbed over it; speaking the same words in a different way. The other voice was softer, gentler, but it slithered up Dani's spine and made her skin crawl.

"So many beautiful women in the world," Akela told her, "but none like you. Your soul is like fire."

"What is that? A bad pick-up line?"

"It's only the truth." The two voices said. Akela's cracked eyes bled like tears of adoration. "Why do you still hold your sword? I told you, I won't hurt you—unless, as I said, I have to. But you don't need to be afraid."

"Uh-huh, you freak."

"Freak? I am your destiny."

He still walked towards her; not threateningly, but with his arms out like he wanted a hug. Red tears streamed down his face.

"I think we need to talk about boundaries, buddy." She warned. "Stop walking. Stop!"

"Am I not all you desire? Am I not magnificent?"

"Is that a serious question?"

"Dani..."

"Don't call me that." She snarled. "What do you want?"

"You. Only you." He told her, now only a few feet from her. Her friends began to stir, slowly coming to. "Your love, your body, your soul; they belong to me. They were born for me. You," he reached for her, "were born for me to do with as I please."

Dani didn't move to attack. If the others could help, maybe they could take him by surprise.

"I've admired you since I first saw you; at my wedding, do you remember?"

Dani grunted in disgust, saying what she suspected. "You aren't Akela."

"I am."

"If you were, you'd know you loved Roxelana—that you still do."

"She could never compare to you." He said. "Why can't you see that? Why can't you see me for what I truly am? I brought you here so we could be alone. I made myself ready for you. I killed my wife for you."

"You liar!" Her anger flared.

"She stood in our way. Can't you see how amazing I am? I do all of this for you. All I ask is that you worship the ground I walk on. That is what love is."

112

Her friends were almost up. She shook her head. "You're not Akela. You're some freak; some monster in his skin. Who are you really?"

He finally stopped, not daring to come any nearer. "I was he in the beginning that understood a woman's true place. I was given all I desired by right, just as I was given you. I am he who built the Temple to the God of Israel and given Raguel's daughter."

This creep needed a good killing. "Are you Belial?"

"No. I am your master."

Izzy was the first on his feet. He drew back and chucked the hunga-munga like the first day she met him. It sliced across the open space towards Akela's head. But instead of it landing a blow, Akela caught it by the handle before it found its mark.

He turned his eyes on Izzy and his mask of adoration turned to anger. "How dare you interrupt?"

He flung it back. Izzy dodged, but the weapon sliced open his shoulder as he passed.

One moment, Akela was only a few feet from her. The next, he was directly in front of her. She ducked back, slashing with her sword, but his hand caught her wrist. The strength in his grip was unnatural. He twisted.

Dani cried out in pain and dropped to her knees. Her sword dropped from her palm and clattered into the pool.

She went for her dagger next, flipping it up and stabbing him right through the collarbone. The glowing blade sunk deep, but he didn't flinch. Instead, he reached up and squeezed her hand on the hilt. Dani screamed as something popped below the wrist. She lost her grip and he ripped the weapon out harmlessly.

The creature grabbed her around the throat, shoving her against one leg of the statue. His eyes radiated red, pulsing sickly underneath the lids. The enflamed eyeballs streamed red rivers down his cheeks.

"Why are you fighting me?" he asked in the same soft voice, like some little boy who didn't understand. "I put a lot of effort into getting you here. I chose a vessel you knew." He indicated Akela's body. "Look how marvelous I am."

He shoved her into the statue again, smacking her head against the stone.

"Why are you hurting me? Why do women ignore me? All of you belong to me. Every woman should worship me!"

She felt the air escape her lungs. She tried to think. She tried to fight. But when she kicked or struck his jaw, he wouldn't let go. He pressed against her, waist to waist. His sulfuric breath beat hotly against her cheek.

"Your sex has a place they belong, but have forgotten. You tell yourself it is not true, but you know this is your true state." One hand left her throat,

113

keeping her against the stone. "You belong on your back, in service of the ones who are truly in control. I will remind you of it."

Then his hand was between her legs. Dani wanted to scream but nothing came out. Her anger disappeared. Now her heart beat with something worse: fear.

He's not...he's not...

Tears stung at the corner of her eyes. She squeezed them shut.

Stop...please...

"Silence is acceptance."

He released her throat, but Dani still couldn't move; not because of magic, but because of fear.

"You give of yourself to other men, but not to me. You give your heart and your body. But it is my right to take it."

Dani held up her hand, digging deep within herself to find that light to destroy him. Her hand glowed as she pressed it against his chest to force him off.

But nothing happened. The light dissipated.

Dani wept.

"That's right." The monster snarled, stroking her cheek. "Accept my blessing."

But before he could do anything else, he violently jarred off her and flew sideways.

Nathaniel tackled him, hurtling them both across the Fane into the rows of lanterns. Dani collapsed, folding up on herself as they skidded through the debris.

Nathaniel landed atop Akela, axe raised.

"DON'T YOU DARE TOUCH HER!"

Akela hit him with something like black shadow from palm, blasting Nathaniel up into the roof and pinning him there. Akela rose to his feet again, teeth bared, while torrents of darkness cascaded over her friend. Nathaniel screamed, unable to move.

Kleos was up now. Adamantine knives landed—one, two, three—in quick succession in Akela's back. He staggered, but didn't go down. Instead he turned, balling shadow in his palm and firing it at him. Kleos dodged.

He dropped Nathaniel, who landed hard on the ground with a groan of pain. Seemingly bored, he turned back towards Dani, but found Ethan standing there between them instead.

"Move." Akela warned.

"No."

Ethan shoved Stormthrower through Akela's gut. The blow should have killed him, but he only lurched and bared his bloody teeth.

Ethan's eyes widened. "What are you?"

"Her owner."

"I'll never let you near her again."

"Try to stop me."

Ethan yanked his sword free and kicked Akela back, but Akela got his footing and prepared to attack again.

Before he could, the skylight overhead exploded. Lightning crackled down under Ethan's power. It struck his blade and he thrust it forward into the other man as they collided.

The tip burst out of Akela's back. The current of energy exploded through his body. Akela's head threw back and he screamed, but not in pain.

Laughter. He laughed as the energy disintegrated his brain and, blessedly, killed him.

Ethan spun, throwing Akela sideways onto the floor. When he landed, his body sizzled and twitched. Black blood oozed from the wound in his torso. His eyes stared blankly at Dani—

—with a smile still plastered on his face.

Chapter Fifteen

"Dani...?"

Tears blurred her vision. She couldn't see. She only vaguely heard someone speak her name.

"Dani...?"

A hand touched her shoulder.

"Dani!"

"DON'T TOUCH ME!" She screamed.

She nearly cut off the hand on her shoulder. She scrambled back, sword held up threateningly.

Nathaniel backed away, hands raised.

"GET AWAY FROM ME!"

"Dani!" Ethan ran to her. "Dani! Stop! Stop it! It's alright! It's just Nathaniel!" He pushed Nathaniel away, trying to get close to her, but Dani slashed back and forth with her sword. Her skin was crawling every time one of them got near her.

"Stay back!" Mastema appeared, bloodied but alive. She swung at him, but he caught her blow on his sword. "Dani, it is I. Calm yourself."

But she couldn't. Her whole body wouldn't stop shaking. She huddled up again, keeping her legs in front of her. She didn't understand. What was happening to her?

What's happening?

What's happening?

What's happening?

The world dissolved into crystal cascades of tears.

What's happening?

Minutes. Hours. Days. It felt like all of them at once. Her whole life came and went in a silence inside her own mind.

Her friends and Guardian stood around her, unsure what to do. She sobbed uncontrollably. It would come in spurts, wracking her body so hard she gasped for air, and then it would leave, only to come back again and again. She lost control and came back to herself over and over.

Somewhere in there, she found the strength to stand.

"What happened?" Nathaniel asked. "Dani, are you okay?"

She gasped, wiping her eyes. "I'm fine. I'm fine." Her mom's favorite lie.

Her cheeks were stained red. She was at least able to talk. Her hand throbbed excruciatingly; maybe broken. Despite that, it wasn't the worst pain she felt right now.

"We," she swallowed, "we need to go."

Ethan reached out for her, but stopped and dropped his arm. "We do. Something," he looked down at the dead man on the floor, "is not right here."

She shook her head miserably. "We shouldn't have come."

"Then we go. Mastema, Kleos: take the lead. Everyone else behind them. I'll stay with Dani."

"No." Her Guardian stepped in front of her. "You lead with Kleos. I will protect my Novice."

"Mastema—!"

The big man placed a hand firmly on Ethan's chest, pushing him away. "My charge, my responsibility. Now is not the time for romantic gestures. Leave her be."

Dani couldn't bear the thought of Ethan touching her. Her skin crawled. She wanted to scrub it off.

"Go. Now." He warned. "I will not tell you again."

Ethan and Kleos in the lead, Nathaniel and Izzy behind them, they pried open the doors with Mastema gently leading Dani behind them; not touching her, but staying within arm's length.

They opened out into the gardens around the Fane. The wind had picked up. The air was ungoldly cold. As Dani descended the steps with them, she looked back towards the island.

A shadow crawled across it. She felt her heart freeze as she remembered En Dor's visions.

A shadow crawling across a crescent island.

"What in hellfires...?" She heard Kleos mutter.

A body lay a few feet away; a Powers soldier. But standing over it was a dark, shadowy figure. As if made from actual darkness, it looked vaguely human as it turned towards them. The two lead Guardians raised their weapons.

An inky black shape rising from a dead body. This thing looked just like it.

The creature's hand morphed. A long, thin blade of shadow slid into view.

Kleos drew a dagger and threw it. The adamantine blade sliced through the air and through the shadow-person. The creature screamed and dissolved as the knife passed through the heart. It smacked deep into a tree while the monster evaporated into nothing.

"What in the name of God's wounds?" Mastema demanded.

But they couldn't answer. In the distance, dozens of voices began screaming. And then the sounds of battle filled the air.

"Run!" Dani warned.

No one questioned her. They all started at a sprint. Kleos yanked the blade free as he passed and they dashed into the main street, heading back towards the Keep.

Dani turned towards the island again. The storm overhead bathed the entire utopic-paradise in gloom. And from between the buildings, more shadow figures began pouring into the open.

An army.

"Run!" she screamed again.

They flew across the first bridge they crossed on the way here. Powers soldiers appeared, but more shadowmen attacked. Adamantine swords, spears and shields clashed with shadow weapons. Even though the creatures appeared to be made of nothing but smoke, their weapons were solid. The Powers slew dozens as the group fled past, but more and more of the shadowmen arrived and quickly overwhelmed them.

One contingent held their ground at the canal, but the creatures appeared from the water and pulled them in. Their screams drowned with a gargle as they sunk beneath the surface.

Ahead, one Power made to fly, retreating with Dani and her group, but shadows scaled the walls and dropped onto him before he could take off. They sent him sprawling across the ground, shadow-weapons stabbing down into him.

Dani and her friends could do nothing, and none of them dared try to make a break for the sky, either.

The shadows were everywhere. The once empty Citadel now crawled with them. The group didn't slow, only stopping to help those they could. Nathaniel hacked one shadow out of the way with his axe, bashed another with his shield. Izzy curled some Fyre off a blaze that engulfed a nearby building, hurling it in a ball into a group ahead and dissipating them.

They were mortal, but that in no way made them easy to kill.

They reached the next canal. Kleos paused, screaming at them, "Go!" He turned back, waving his hand and summoning a barricade of Aer. The creatures hit the barrier like a brick wall. Momentarily delayed, they screeched unholy cries and bashed their fists and shadow weapons against it. Kleos strained, holding them back.

All around them, Powers fell as they stood to fight or flee. It didn't matter. No one could escape.

Mastema, armed with khopesh, slashed apart several creatures as they tried to climb over onto the bridge.

"Kleos!" He called.

"Go!"

Kleos extended his hands and the wall of Aer cascaded outward, hurling the monsters back into their companions behind them.

They moved ahead of the throng of black monsters. Kleos bought them time.

Mastema grabbed Dani's arm and they made for the last canal; the last barrier before the Keep. More shadow creatures moved into their path. She and her Guardian fought their way through. Dani, still half-dazed, fought alongside him, but her blades wouldn't ignite.

They made it to the next bridge. As he ran to catch up, one creature landed on Kleos, knocking him to the ground.

Izzy stopped on the bridge. "Kleos!"

Mastema pointed his blade to the nearest whitestone on the path, using Erthe to yank it free. He hurled the rock backwards and struck the spectral monster on Kleos' back, knocking it off.

Nathaniel grabbed Izzy's arm. "Come on!"

Not looking, a shadow scaled the side of the bridge and leapt onto his back, knocking him and Izzy down. Mastema, still busy fending off the creatures, couldn't help.

"Dani!" Nathaniel screamed. "Dani! Help!"

She ran towards him, but even as the creature prepared to stab him, she came to a sudden halt. She trembled, shaking on her feet. She raised her sword to strike it down, but hesitated. It was like her whole body went numb and she couldn't move, except for her hand flying to her mouth, as if she would vomit.

Ethan flew past her. He sliced through the creature, banishing it from existence. He kept moving, swinging his sword around and destroying more of the specters before they could jump onto the bridge.

Nathaniel got to his feet. He and Dani locked eyes. Both knew she nearly got him killed.

She backed away.

"Dani!" He warned.

Too late. Something swept her off her feet and threw her clear of the bridge to the other side. She landed hard, air exploding from her lungs as she rolled to a stop. A shadow landed in front of her.

Dani raised her blade and caught the dark, ethereal weapon of the shadow weakly. It swung and cut the weapon from her hand. She was at its mercy.

The shadow stood over her, but it wasn't just a shadow. It was roiling mist of darkness made from shades of black. But it was human. It had a face and eyes like twin black holes. Lips curled back from ash-colored teeth into a look of disgust as I raised its shadow sword above its head.

A long, silvery shaft of adamantine shoved through the creature's chest from behind. It screamed. Dani thought Ethan had come to save her, but when the thing dissolved into mist, Michael appeared behind it.

He lowered his longsword, looking around for any others before offering her a hand.

"What are you doing here?" She demanded.

"I got separated from Nazir. We have to go."

He saved her? She couldn't believe it, but she took his offered hand and pulled herself up.

"This changes nothing." He warned her.

"Thank you anyway."

He nodded curtly. Ethan and the others ran to join them, having bought themselves a few more seconds.

"Are you okay?" Ethan asked, afraid to touch her, but grateful she was alive.

"I'm fine."

"We have to go." Michael told them. "The Elders called for a retreat We're pulling out of the city." He stared back. "This place is lost."

More shadow monsters were coming.

Ethan and Nathaniel went ahead, Izzy and Kleos right behind them, Mastema and Dani bringing up the rear with Michael.

"Don't run so fast." Michael called out. "This sword is a lot heavier than it looks."

A shadow erupted from the cobblestones between him and Dani. He stopped, swinging his blade. The shadow caught it on its own sword. A second silhouette exploded from the street behind him—

—and stabbed Michael through the back.

Michael's eyes widened. The black blade punctured out the front of his chest and twisted. He shuddered. As Dani watched in horror, the second dark creature stabbed him through the front. No blood appeared. It was as if the shadows were only shadows, but the light of life in Michael's eyes vanished just the same.

They seized him around the neck and pulled him to the ground.

Mastema grabbed Dani and pulled her away as he disappeared beneath an onslaught of shadow creatures.

She ran for her life, unable to help him.

They didn't stop running until they reached the Keep. The Elders arranged the Powers into a defensive line around the large dais; the one adorned with the symbol of Beri'ah.

The last retreating Powers arrived with Dani and her friends. The phalanx of Numen battled against a rising tide of shadows, who continued to stream from the Citadel. They kept them at bay, but as Dani arrived,

Numen fell to the attackers while fewer and fewer could come to take their place on the line.

They were losing.

Ethan and Nathaniel reached the line first, helping Izzy through. Kleos drew on two burning braziers on the terrace above, hurling Fyreballs backwards to cover the retreat of Dani, Mastema and the remaining Numen.

A familiar face appeared in the crowd, cutting down a shadow that leapt to attack them.

"Get to the terrace!" Nazir warned, slicing wide arcs with his saber. "Where is Michael? Is he with you?"

Dani didn't answer as Mastema took her to safety behind the lines. She looked up and wished she hadn't. The sky was a monstrous storm. The islands floating above them roiled with black; more shadow creatures overwhelming the Numen there. The bodies of fallen Earthborn rained down as those left desperately attempted to fight off the creatures.

In the middle of the platform, Heman stood, shield up and his sword covered in Fyre, slashing apart the creatures that got through their defenses. Jeduthun summoned shields of Aer to throw the monsters back and protect the Powers.

"Elders!" Ethan yelled over the howl of the storm. "Everyone is out of the Citadel!"

Dani spotted Nazir's expression when he heard. He staggered as if hit, realizing Michael wasn't coming.

Jeduthun looked around. "So few..."

"We must go!"

Healers and injured soldiers lifted off from the terrace, evacuating towards the glowing aurora above. As they passed amongst the floating islands, shadows leapt into their path to pick them off. Some escaped, as the Powers up there attempted to hold the line, but the way was collapsing quickly.

"The Guardian is right!" Heman yelled, casting of a fiery wave from his sword that vanquished a line of shadows. "The Citadel is lost!"

"Very well!" Jeduthun said, tossing a Fyreball into an incoming monster. "Novice Daniella, retreat now while there is still time!"

She shook her head. "My place is here!"

"You are injured!" Jeduthun said with a flick of the wrist, shooting a translucent ball of energy that struck a shadow mid-flight and destroyed it. "Go! Return to Empyrean! Your battle here is done! We will hold them off!"

She looked around. "How do we get everyone else out?"

The look he gave her said it all: they wouldn't.

"The Powers will do their duty and hold this ground to save as many we can. You will go now."

"I can't do that!" She felt so useless.

"Down!" Someone warned.

Dani and Jeduthun ducked and a shadow swooped overhead, able to leap over the line of defenders. Nazir jumped into its path and slashed it apart.

"Go!" Jeduthun told her. "That is an order! We will stay to give you time!"

"No, Elder, you will not!" Nazir stepped between them. "You must leave as well. All of you. Our line is collapsing. Your place is with the Novice and the others who can flee." He pointed to the sky. "The Powers and I are staying. It is you who must retreat."

Everyone stared at him. Kleos spoke up, "Nazir—!"

But he gave him a look even Dani understood. Michael was dead. As his Guardian, Nazir failed to protect him. If his charge would not make it, he was duty-bound to suffer the same fate. He had only one job now: avenge his lost Novice.

When he looked at Dani, she could tell he wished it had been her who died and not Michael.

"I'm sorry." She told him. "He saved me."

Nazir didn't respond. Instead, he told them, "I will stay and assume command. I will send as many after you as possible. By order of the Elder Council, in the name of the one for whom the first throne is left empty, all of you go! Now!"

Dani stared around her. More and more shadows came; more and more Powers fell. Some were killed and pulled into the writhing mass of darkness. Others fell against their comrades, unable to stand and fight any longer.

"Go!"

Jeduthun called, "Elder Heman, forge us a path!"

Heman launched into the sky. With flashes of his sword, he conjured a corona of flames, cutting swaths through the shadows and blasting them apart as he rose. He drove them back in a halo of flames, giving others behind him a chance to follow.

Kleos didn't want to go, but a column of shadow broke through the Powers' ranks on the ground. Numen screamed as they were pulled under by the flowing, black figures.

"The line has broken!" Someone screamed.

"Fly now!" Nazir screamed.

Kleos took Izzy and leapt into the sky. Jeduthun followed, cutting another swath with a blast of sound as Ethan and Nathaniel followed.

Mastema grabbed Dani around the waist without asking and shot into the sky, along with any last injured or retreating soldiers.

Nazir covered them, summoning the Erthe and pelting an advancing wave of shadows with stones from the ground. He slashed and hacked as more approached, destroying them and wading into their ranks instead of waiting for them to overwhelm him.

The ground fell away. Dani watched as purple disappeared under black and the shadows crushed the last of the Powers. Nazir continued to throw stone left and right, slashing wildly with his blades. He was almost too far away to be seen when Dani saw a shadow stab him in the back.

He fell and disappeared into the darkness.

More black ghosts leapt to attack them as they rose. Mastema fended them off as they soared towards the iridescent ring in the sky. Dani threw out her hand, intending to blast away the shadows with her lightbringing.

But nothing came.

Uselessly, she clung onto her Guardian. They hit the radiant portal.

The island of Ber'iah dissolved behind the clouds and gloom.

Part II
Artifacts

Chapter Sixteen

They went to Ber'iah with over four hundred men. Thirty-two came back.

The Ward overran with wounded; so much so, Elder Aleister called for help from the Gifted to help manage them. Triage spilled into the courtyard outside, with screams of pain or moans of the nearly dead filling the surrounding countryside. A few of the injured managed to bring back some of the dead, clinging to the lifeless bodies of their comrades as they escaped. The Elder Council examined them to discern what killed them, as even the monsters that attacked them were unknown.

Some of the injured died shortly after returning. By nightfall, only twenty-seven remained clinging to life.

The day was dark in the city of light.

Dani retreated to her home as soon as she got back; away from anyone and everyone. She ripped off her armor and weapons and threw herself into the corner of her house. Tears streamed down her face.

All your kind belongs to me. Every woman should worship me!
Silence is acceptance.

"Dani?" She heard someone call out. "Dani, are you here?" It was Bouden. He sounded frantic. "Dani, please! Are you here?"

"I'm here." She managed to weakly say. "Don't come in."

He didn't. Instead, he sighed in relief. "Oh, thank God! You're alive! I can't find anyone. The Citadel is chaos over there. I heard—." She could hear the pain in his voice. "I heard so many Earthborn are dead. Is it...is it anyone we know?"

Dani stood shakily. Her hand throbbed. Her head ached. She could feel the bruises. When she finally opened the door out into the courtyard, she could see in Bouden's eyes how messed up she looked.

"Lumme! Dani, you're hurt!"

"I'm fine."

"Your face...your hand...!"

Dani spotted herself in the reflection of the fountain. The side of her face was swollen and bruised. Her hand didn't lie right.

"I'm fine."

"No, you're not."

"I said I'm fine!" she screamed.

Bouden back-stepped, hands raised. "Okay, you're fine. Is...is everyone else?"

"Mostly." She said. "Izzy was hurt. I don't know how bad. Michael is dead."

Bouden bowed his head. He and Michael weren't friends, but they weren't strangers, either. In fact, there may have been some amongst the Powers he knew as well. She felt cold; inhuman. All those deaths didn't matter half as much to her right now. And yet, it was soul-crushing to think how many died.

Nazir once tried to kill her, but watching him die made her want to vomit.

So much so, she did.

Bouden ran to her, helping her to say upright as she wretched into the bushes in disgust and agony.

"Please," he said, "let me help."

"Get away!"

"Novice!"

Mastema arrived, landing at a run and separating the two. Bouden looked so confused. He didn't understand.

"I will attend to her." He told him, even cutting off his next question. "Your friends are alive and in Novice Village. You should go."

"But she—!"

"She is fine. I will ensure she will be well."

Bouden gave Dani one last look and then left. Dani yanked herself out of his arms. "I don't need your help."

"That is not true."

"I don't want you here, Mastema!"

He made a slight bow, as if understanding. "I understand, but I will not leave my charge alone." His dark eyes said he knew Dani's pain was more than physical.

"What are you talking about?"

Caesar soared in overhead, fluttering to the top of the fountain. And then another voice spoke.

"You called for us?"

Airlea and Adare stood at the end of the path to Dani's home.

Airlea drew her a bath; one filled with panacea and other compounds meant to heal her. Adare cooked food, using the fire outside to roast vegetables to go with honey-bread, fruit and fresh chicken. Neither woman spoke, until Airlea checked the bandages on Dani's wrist.

"What was it?"

Dani blinked out of her stupor and looked up. The concern on Airlea's face was out of character for her. Normally so nasty to Dani—and for what reason, Dani didn't know—now she handled her like fragile glass. She changed the dressing, as Dani's hand was almost healed.

"I don't know." Dani answered truthfully.

"Will it come here?"

"I don't know."

Airlea moved to the table, where Adare's supplies of medicines were tucked into a woven basket.

"Why are you doing this?" she asked the Gifted girl. "You hate me."

Airlea returned. "Roxelana would want me to help you."

"You sound like she's dead."

"She is, isn't she?" the old Airlea indignation returned, but more out of anger than spite for Dani. "I've heard the stories. I saw how many of you Numen returned from that cursed city. I know that Akela—." Then she stopped.

"You know what?" Dani asked. "You know what, Airlea? What did Mastema tell you?"

She shook her head, adding something else to the bath Dani healed in. "He didn't have to tell me. I can tell." Their eyes locked. "I might play around with Numen men and you might think I'm some kind of trollop because of it, but that doesn't mean I haven't experienced harsh things in my life. And I know when something bad has happened to a girl." She put aside the empty elixir vial she just poured into Dani's bath. "Something was wrong with Akela. I thought it was losing Roxelana, but it wasn't. He wasn't himself."

"I know."

"He did this to you, didn't he?"

Dani didn't answer except to nod.

"If he could do that to you, then what chance did Roxelana have?"

Airlea was bitter; not towards Dani, but towards what happened to her friend. She could never understand why Roxelana would befriend someone like Airlea; a girl who spent so much time flirting with Numen to get special favors and privileges. But to see her now, Dani could tell she cared about Roxelana.

"She could still be alive." Dani offered.

"If you believe that, you're a fool."

Airlea made to leave. Adare would finish dinner and give Dani her space. But before she departed, Dani stopped her.

"Wait!" Airlea paused at the door. "I don't think that it was Akela."

"What do you mean?"

"I think," it was the one thought Dani couldn't put out of her mind, "I think that whatever attacked me—whatever attacked the city—wasn't really Akela. It was some monster that looked like him."

"So?"

"So, I'm going to find it. And when I do, I'm going to kill it." A part of Dani, one not injured, came surging back. "If it did kill Roxelana, I'll kill it, Airlea. I swear."

She frowned at her and shook her head. "If you believe *that*, you're an even bigger fool."

And then she left.

Dani stood inside Roxelana's hut in Beri'ah. In the cage by the door, the three-footed, multicolored qingniao bird sung beautifully. Outside, the sun was bright and Gifted children played.

She turned towards the sound of laughter. Akela and Roxelana stood in the kitchen area of the hut. Akela kissed along Roxelana's jaw and she swooned in her new husband's arms.

She was a woman in love.

Roxelana turned back to plating food from a sizzling skillet while the smell of wonderful food pervaded the home. Akela pumped water from an indoor pump into a bowl, sipping from it and handing it to Roxelana. Dani watched, happy to see her friend happy.

Akela kissed her again along the neck from behind. She giggled.

Then he bit her hard and drew blood.

"See how much she loves me?" He asked, not turning around. And yet, Dani knew he was talking to her. "See how she adores me? You could have that."

Roxelana bled from the neck as she continued working. Akela turned to her, wiping his ruby-stained mouth.

"Happiness is knowing where you belong."

Dani tensed. Outside, the skies were stormy. The shadow descended over the island again. The qingniao bird was dead in its cage.

"You shouldn't fight me." He told her. Akela's voice was again the soft, eerie one from the Fane.

"Who are you?" Dani demanded. "What are you?"

"I am the thing you fear to want." He told her. "I am the thing all women want: a master. Your master."

"Screw you."

"Is that right?" he asked. "Are you going to, as you told your friend, kill me? Your friend knew better. She knew you could not stop me. And you won't." He extended a hand to her. "You belong to me."

"How did you know what I said to Airlea?"

"Because," he smiled, "I'm in your head. I'm in your heart. You're already mine. You just don't know it."

She turned to flee but ran into Roxelana; dead-eyed, bleeding, blocking her path to the door.

"He owns you." Roxelana told her. Her eyes began to bleed, like Akela's. "He owns all of us."

Dani screamed.

Then she woke. She shot up in bed, shivering.

It was a dream. Only a dream. But she curled up under her covers, unable to sleep.

Two days later, Dani was physically healed, but the nightmare disturbed her. Her lightbringing, which failed her in the city, worked again, but she worried why it didn't when she needed it most.

Izzy was healed as well. The monster posing as Akela sliced open his shoulder nearly to the bone, but thanks to the healers, he would still be able to use it. He even got a battle scar that normally would impress any Earthborn warrior.

But no one felt like celebrating.

Empyrean's Powers lost almost a third of their strength. The defeat had a ripple effect. Any upcoming missions were canceled. Numen withdrew inside the city and until further notice, no coming or going would be allowed—Numen or otherwise.

Ethan came to check on her in two days. Dani practiced under Mastema's watchful eye.

Dani blasted a large boulder target she set up across the square with lightbringing, shattering it to dust. Her hands ached but she fired again, destroying a second. She staggered, her head spinning and Mastema caught her arm.

"Are you okay?" Ethan landed next to them.

"I'm fine." *How many times do I have to tell people that?* "I need to get better at this."

"Your powers take much out of you." Mastema told her.

"Yeah, well, they're my best weapon, so I need to learn to use them more."

He frowned and let her go. "If you rely upon your powers—."

"I've heard the lecture. Let it go."

He did.

Dani was better with recharging after use of her special ability, but it sometimes felt like running a marathon. If that were true, she needed to train to strain herself to use them.

"It's better when I heal someone, but destroying things takes a lot of energy. During Alecto's attack, I couldn't use my powers at all on the Vale Bridge."

She didn't mention she couldn't use them at Beri'ah.

"Mastema, can I have a moment with Dani?"

Her Guardian looked between them, sighed and walked past him. "I will be in my hut." He placed a hand on Ethan's shoulder, whispering so he thought Dani couldn't hear. "She still suffers from her experience in the city. Be cautious."

He left. Dani pretended not to hear as she stripped off her gloves and examined her hands. They looked sunburnt. She rubbed panacea on them.

"You shouldn't strain yourself like this."

"Thanks for the advice." She said wryly.

"How are you, since...you know, everything?"

"Since a monster attacked me?" she asked. "How do you think?"

"I'm really not sure." He shook his head. "I don't understand what's going on with you."

"At least you admit it." She dipped a cup into the fountain and downed the cooling water in one gulp. She spotted his concern. "I'm fine, Ethan. At least, as fine as could be."

"You don't look fine. You don't act fine."

"And how am I supposed to act?"

"Tell me what's going on with you."

"I can't."

"Why?"

"Because even I don't know!"

The anger came way too sudden. The silence deafened the square. She looked down and saw she cracked her cup. "Lumme." She cursed, stalking past him. "Is that all you came here for? To check on me?"

"I was concerned."

"I didn't ask you to be."

He grabbed her arm. "Dani, consarn it, talk to me."

"What if I don't want to!" She raged. She was aware that Mastema now stood in the doorway to his hut, watching. Apparently, this wasn't what he meant when he told Ethan to be 'cautious.' "Has it occurred to you that I don't know what's going on? How I feel? Did it even occur to you that what happened might have been so bad I don't know how to deal with it?"

"He attacked you," he said, referring to Akela, "and I get he nearly broke your wrist, but—."

"You think that's what's causing this?" she demanded. "My God, do you know anything about women?"

He didn't have a comeback.

Dani folded her arms. "I need you to leave."

"Why?"

"Because," she said, "I need space."

"Dani—!"

"If you care about me, you'll go."

Ethan closed his mouth and backed away. He nodded. "I'll go."

"Thank you."

It was all a mess. As soon as he was gone, she hated it. She hated herself a little, too. She didn't know what was going on with her. She could barely make sense of it, let alone tell Mastema.

"Are you alright?" Her Guardian asked.

"Obviously not." She grabbed her gauntlets and strode back to her house. "Can you pick up some things from the market for me? I can lend you some Corinths."

"No need. I will go." He departed. He understood a little more than Ethan, but even Mastema was at a loss as to how to help her.

Dani shined her armor, sharpened her swords, and spent the next few minutes in silence. But as she sheathed her blades, she heard someone in the pavilion.

"Who is it?"

"Bouden and Izzy."

Great, more visitors. She came out to them. Bouden stood with a large book under his arm. He didn't immediately jump right into why they were there. He was more cautious after what happened a few days ago.

"It's fine." She said, reading his facial expression. "I'm better. What's up?"

"I found something."

"Found something? As in, something about the demon?"

He nodded excitedly. Izzy tagged along to hear the news. Bouden opened the tome under his arm. "I went searching through the old legends and found what I think could be the demon."

"How do you know?"

He flipped to the page, blushing. "Ethan. He told me about what Akela-." He cut himself off. "He told me what he said; what the thing posing as Akela said, anyway."

"I don't understand."

"That thing told you it helped build the Temple in Israel. It said something about Raguel's daughter." He found the page. "That led me to the Book of Tobit."

"Book of Tobit? The demon's name is Tobit?"

"No, no, no," Bouden flipped the book and handed it to Dani, "that's the legend. This is the creature."

The tome was on demonology. Though it had no picture of the demon, it did have a picture Dani recognized: a medallion. It was a crude drawing, but engraved into the medallion was a three-faced monster. One face was a goat, the middle was a grotesque man breathing fire, and the third was a bull. Snaking around the edge was a dragon.

A golden medallion, engraved with a symbol, laid in fiery coals. Dani saw that in her vision.

She read the name. "Asmodeus."

"Also called Ashmedai," Bouden told her. "He is one of the seven lords of Hell."

"What makes you think it's this thing?"

"The legend goes that Asmodeus was once a demon captured by King Solomon and forced to help build the Temple of Israel; though that could just be some sick, perverted joke. The story he is most known for is the Book of Tobit."

"The legend states that Asmodeus was a demon of lust; *the* demon of lust, actually. He's the archdemon that created it. He lusted particularly after Sarah, the daughter of a man named Raguel. Sarah was said to be beautiful, but strong. The demon tried to tempt her, but couldn't."

"Tempt her? I don't understand."

"Asmodeus is said to be the father of all incubae and succubae." Bouden explained. "That might explain the demons working for that archdemon you killed."

"President Amy." She shuddered, remembering her blonde backups. "What did he want with this Sarah girl?"

"It says that Asmodeus, as the lord of lust, craved women, but not in a good way. He wanted to possess them."

"As in, take over their bodies?"

"As in mate with them." Bouden sounded sick. "He could not enter their beds unless they allowed him. But like I said, Sarah was strong-willed. She said no. So, Asmodeus resorted to another option. He killed her husbands."

"Husbands?"

"Seven of them; one after the other. Every time Sarah fell in love, he would kill them on their wedding night in front of her."

Dani didn't like the sound of that.

"What makes me think this is him is the part about Raphael." Bouden pointed to the tome. "It's said that Sarah prayed to God for help and he sent Raphael, or at least that's what the legend tell us. Raphael chose Tobias, the son of Tobit, to intervene. Tobias was sent to the city in which Sarah lived, as his father was blind, and was subtly guided towards Sarah. As it so happened, Tobias fell in love with her. They married."

"And Asmodeus tried to kill him?"

Bouden nodded. "Except Tobias stopped him."

"How?"

"That's the sucky part." He closed the book. "It doesn't say."

"It doesn't say?"

"There's talk about a fish or something, but what really happened is vague. He drove out Asmodeus and Raphael was able to bind him."

"Bind him?"

"Supposedly he bound him in the land of Egypt, but it doesn't say what that means."

Dani cursed, walking away. It wasn't helpful, at least to her. She squatted down against the wall, shaking her head.

"You alright, *chica fuerte?*"

"No."

"We'll figure it out." Izzy promised, kneeling down in front of her. "We'll help. I'll help. We'll get through this."

She squeezed his hands affectionately. "Thanks."

He placed a hand on her cheek. She smiled up at him, but still felt uncomfortable with the touch.

Then he kissed her.

The kiss was abrupt and unwelcome. It took only a second for Dani to shove him away. "What the hell are you doing?"

Izzy landed back on his butt. "What?"

She stood, wiping her mouth. "What are you doing? Izzy!"

"Come on!" he said, standing. "*Está todo bien.*"

"No, it is not okay!" She screamed. "Get out!"

"Come on." He grabbed her hand. "Daniella, relax."

"Get off!"

"Hey!" Bouden pushed him out of the way. "Izzy, dude, what the hell are you doing?"

Something silver flashed in Izzy's hand and he turned, striking Bouden in the gut. Her friend's eyes flashed wide as the dagger sliced through the Arachne-weave and into his stomach. The armor took the brunt of the strike, but when Izzy yanked it out, he was bleeding. Bouden collapsed.

"Bouden!"

Izzy turned on her and Dani stepped back in horror. Izzy's eyes weren't normal. They were inflamed, cracked and bleeding.

"We belong together." He snarled.

Chapter Seventeen

Dani ran towards her house. Her swords were there. But Izzy seized her by the back of her raiments and hurled her across the floor of the pavilion.

"Why are you running from me?" He demanded. "I love you!"

Dani flipped onto her back and kept her arms and legs—now her only weapons—between the two them. "Get away from me."

"We belong together!" He snarled. She could hear something else in his voice; something behind it. Something softer.

It was the same voice she heard from Akela.

Before Izzy could get to her, Caesar swooped into the pavilion from above and collided with him. She lifted Izzy up off the ground and hurled him out of the pavilion.

"*You stay back!*" Her friend screeched, soaring around for another pass.

Dani scrambled to her feet. As Caesar came around, Izzy summoned a stone of the ground with Erthe and chucked it, striking her friend mid-flight and toppling her to the ground.

He grabbed his knife again. "You can't let others fight your battles for you."

Dani snatched up the nearest weapon she could find: a practice sword. She held it up threateningly. "Stay back!"

"You can't fight me." The softer voice repeated, though now louder than Izzy's, as if it were slowly taking him over. "I deserve you. No one else does."

Dani screamed and launched herself at him, swinging the stick. He caught it with one hand as if it didn't hurt to block.

She extended her other hand to blast him with light, but again, nothing happened.

"You can't hurt me." He told her. He pushed forward, forcing her back. "You can't fight fate. You can't fight me."

"Fight this!"

Dani head-butted him the face to prove him wrong. Izzy's head snapped back with a snap of his nose. Then, Dani delivered a swift, hard kick between the legs. Izzy dropped to the ground. Apparently, some things still hurt.

"Get," she punched him, "out," a second strike across the jaw, "of my," two more and Izzy was bloody, "friend!"

The last strike sent him to his knees, the dagger dropping from his hand. Izzy dribbled blood from his lip. When he looked up at her, he grinned.

"I'm coming for you." He chuckled.

"So I've been told." She kicked him in the face and knocked him out.

"I could have killed him." Dani told Mastema, watching Izzy and Bouden on the beds of the Ward. "I almost did."

"But you didn't."

Bouden would be well enough, soon. The dagger didn't pierce far enough through his raiments to do too much damage; penetrated his stomach lining and possibly induced sepsis. If he were human or had human doctors, it could have been fatal. As it was, he would be fine. His Guardian, whom Dani hadn't spoken to, was with him.

Izzy was worse off; broken nose, broken hand, broken jaw, and broken cheekbone. Dani did a number on him. Kleos hadn't left his bedside since he arrived at the Ward. Neither had two armed Gatekeepers.

"He is well now." Mastema told her. "He is no longer possessed."

"But he saw it, Mastema. Something got inside him and took over." Izzy said as much before the healers put him under so they could treat him. She shook her head. "Could that have been Akela? Was he alive inside that thing when Ethan killed him?"

"I am unsure. Akela was stronger than Izzy when he attacked you. The beast had more control."

"But that's just it: it controlled him. Akela didn't attack me. Izzy didn't attack me. Asmodeus did."

Kleos finally left Izzy as the healers applied medicinal elixirs to his wounded face. He trembled when he shook hands with Dani. "Thank you for stopping him."

"I didn't have a choice."

"I know." He frowned. "I almost lost another Novice. If he was like Akela, even I would have put him down."

"Well, I'm not in the business of letting a demon make me kill my friends."

Kleos wiped away some tears. "This thing: Asmodeus you called it? What do we know about it?"

"Him," Dani corrected, "at least, that's how it seems. He's an archdemon. The lord of lust, supposedly. And apparently, he has his sights set on me."

"Why?"

She filled them in on what Bouden told her, especially the part about wanting to 'possess' her.

"Unfortunately, it makes sense." Kleos sighed.

"How on earth does that make sense?"

"This thing personifies the very idea it was created to encourage." He told her. "Demons are like that: they embody the worst parts of us, to the point it makes up their very essence. Wraiths embody uncontrolled rage

135

and the depravity of society. Look at them. They're feral monsters. This archdemon is the same."

"So, this thing is, what? Consumed with the need to take me down a peg or something? He's like male ego, weaponized?"

"You know, not all men are a bunch of codpieces," he said defensively, but conceded, "but to an extent, yes. He's the worst part of what it means to be a man. I don't think Izzy let that thing into him. I think it found its way in."

"How?"

"Like you said, he 'weaponized' him by exploiting his weakness."

"Me?"

"No, his feelings towards you. You had nothing to do with it. After you two first met that day at the Training Grounds, Izzy confided in me that he found you attractive."

"So?"

"So, I think that whatever lust he had for you, Asmodeus twisted it. It's like he turned the dial up to a hundred and used it like a backdoor of possession, so that he get to you through Izzy." He glanced back at his charge. "Whatever innocent thing Izzy felt, he turned into something ugly."

Just then, Ethan arrived. Dani asked, "Could he do that to anyone who was exposed to him at Beri'ah?"

"Possibly."

Ethan approached, but Mastema himself between him and Dani.

Ethan looked confused. "What?"

It took a second, but Dani understood her Guardian's thinking and said, "Oh, you've got to be joking."

Mastema insisted that Ethan be kept at arm's length or, if he ever came to see her, Mastema or Kleos would be nearby. Dani understood Mastema's presence, but Kleos? How was he so sure Kleos was safe?

Other boys weren't allowed to come to her home unsupervised, either. Izzy was released but kept at a distance. Even though Bouden didn't go to Beri'ah, he didn't feel safe and agreed to the supervision. Nathaniel was also barred unless the two of them were there.

She was suddenly in middle school again, except this time it wasn't her mother who was overprotective about boys.

Over the course of the week, things got worse. Demonic attacks, emboldened from the lack of Powers, were on the rise. Reports of sightings increased. Dani itched for a chance to get back out there and do something. She knew her attacker's name now; she knew who to hate. Somehow, that gave her the urged to fight back. But she and other Novices were barred from leaving Empyrean.

The following night, while at her house with Mastema and Kleos, she said, "Mastema, I couldn't use my," she glanced sidelong at Kleos, still unsure about sharing her special gift, "gifts against Asmodeus; not in Beri'ah and not with Izzy."

Mastema frowned, eating his vegetables silently.

"Do you know why?" She asked. "Asmodeus could block my ability. How can a demon do that?"

"I don't think it is the demon." Mastema answered.

"Excuse me?"

They were in her house's small eating area. He put his plate down. "Do you remember our lesson in the Vale a month ago?"

Dani hadn't realized it had been almost a month since then. "The one about fear?"

He nodded.

"Yeah. How can I forget? You said fear stops us." Then she caught on. "You think my powers don't work because I'm afraid of him?"

"Possibly."

She glanced at Kleos, who silently held up his hands in 'no comment.' He wasn't about to butt into this conversation.

"That's ridiculous." Dani said. "I want nothing more than to kill him."

"I am not saying you want anything else. What I do say is that your fear stops you from calling upon your gift."

"It's a mental block?"

He nodded again. "Fear is much stronger than we give it credit. Asmodeus may be a demon of lust, but he is still a demon. He understands fear's power. He will use it against you."

"Then, how do I stop him?"

"You conquer that fear."

She shook her head. "How am I supposed to do that?"

"That is not for me to teach. You must learn on your own."

"Yeah, well, thanks for that, Miyagi."

Kleos cleared his throat. "We may also have another problem."

"Tell me about it." Dani murmured, sipping her drink and finishing her food.

"The other things that attacked us; the shadow monsters? Bouden thinks he knows what they are."

Since Izzy stabbed him, Bouden was recovering in Novice Village. Miracle elixirs wouldn't magically heal him overnight. They took time. So, in his down time, he researched.

"You know what kind of demons Asmodeus summoned?"

"They're not demons." He said. "They're shades."

Mastema's expression said it all. Nothing surprised her Guardian; at least, nothing normally did. But he was in shock now. "Are you certain?"

"What are shades?" Dani asked.

"*Rephaim*." He said, still not looking away from Kleos.

"Yeah, like I know what those are. Care to translate?"

"Shades are the returned souls of the dead." Kleos explained. "They're...they're like the leftover, damaged parts of the soul."

"Souls? As in, they're ghosts of dead people?"

He nodded.

Dani didn't like the sound of that. "Kleos, are you trying to tell me that those things that attacked us were the Numen and Gifted from Beri'ah?"

It explained why Kleos looked worried. "I think so."

"That's impossible. First of all, if they were Gifted and Numen, they wouldn't attack us. And second, if they were spirits, how the hell did they fight like that?"

"Shades are spirits, but they're different than an average apparition. They're not natural. Specters, as we know them, remain on Earth upon their death, but shades are summoned."

"Summoned?"

"Usually, by witchcraft, but I guess Asmodeus can do it as well. I didn't realize what they were because I have never seen shades summoned like that; not in such numbers and not in such feral ways. Those things weren't remotely human."

"Asmodeus must have corrupted them," Mastema said, "the way he corrupted Izzy."

"Bouden and I came to the same conclusion."

"Well, at least we can kill them." Dani sighed. "That's something, but that army was massive. We'll need to be prepared."

Kleos thought a moment. "I'm glad you said that. I may have another weapon we can use against them, but I'll need your help to make it."

"Help how?"

"Can I borrow your mother's necklace?"

Dani touched the ring around her neck. It was the only possession Dani had from her mortal life. Thanks to Ethan, she could keep it tucked inside her tunic; a connection not only to her mother, but to who her mother used to be.

She pulled it out. "Why?"

"It could be useful. I promise you, you will have it back."

Dani took it off, curled the chain into her palm and handed it to him. He tucked it into his raiments.

"So, what else?" Dani asked. "I don't like sitting around, waiting for Asmodeus to come after me."

"For now, you are safe in Empyrean." Mastema consoled. "As safe as we can make you, until we figure out what to do."

That was true. Asmodeus was far away right now. He couldn't get into Empyrean without—

"Oh, lumme." She cursed to herself. "That's not true."

"What?"

Somehow, it took her almost a month to put it together. "Asmodeus is coming here. To Los Angeles. To Empyrean."

"How do you know?"

"Because he told me," she said, "and so did his lackeys. Remember President Amy? The archdemon I killed? She was putting together a sacrifice for Asmodeus on Halloween. I thought she was talking about Belial at the time, but if Asmodeus is the baby-daddy of every incubus and succubus in existence, then they were probably doing it for him. Which means...?"

Kleos answered in agreement. "He's coming to Empyrean."

"Ding, ding, tell him what he's won!" Dani said bitterly. "The only question is, since I ruined the Halloween dance at Lightpoint, when is he coming?"

"Still at Hallowe'en, most likely." Mastema told her. "It would be the opportune time, as it is the start of Allhallowtide."

"Wanna run that by me again?"

Mastema explained. "Allhallowtide is a sacred time of year for quite a few cultures. It was celebrated before any of the modern monotheistic religions, but has always been a time of honoring the dead and the spirits."

"So?"

"So, it is a time of year when the veil between the worlds is weakest. Every supernatural barrier, from the veil that hides us to the firmament around Empyrean, is weakened. It is said that during this time, mundani see the most sightings of the supernatural."

"And it starts on Halloween?"

"From All Hallows' Eve—or Hallowe'en—to the second day of the following month."

Dani perked up. "Are you talking about *Día de Muertos?* The Day of the Dead?"

"That is one amongst many days celebrated." He conceded. "If Asmodeus arrives during the weakest point in the veil, he could break through the firmament."

Dani remembered Jeduthun explaining the barrier. "He could get to Empyrean?"

"Yes. He has already shown the ability to enter one celestial city, but if the firmament is weak, he would be able to enter ours, as well."

"Then the walls wouldn't be enough to stop him." Dani said.

"Possibly." That was all he would commit to saying.

Dani remembered another part of her vision from En Dor: *a massive storm of black clouds and shapes darting between them.*

"You said shades are able to be summoned by witchcraft, right? Any particular witch famous for summoning shades?"

Kleos thought. "There's a story about the Witch of En Dor. Why?"

"Because I know where she is." Dani said. "She's in Los Angeles. And I am pretty sure that is not a coincidence."

Chapter Eighteen

There were too many coincidences: Raphael, the demon he defeated, the shades, and the witch who was known to summon them. She had to see the Witch of En Dor again. She knew that was the only course of action and she would not just sit around and wait for Asmodeus to come for her. The following night, she, Mastema and Kleos went to see someone at the Gifted market who might be able to help.

"You want me to sneak you out of the city?" Shea asked. "Why me?"

"You do business with the Gifted in other cities. You travel all over the world. That means you have a way through the Gates, while every Numen is barred from leaving."

"Aren't you already in trouble for leaving without permission?" he asked.

"Oh, come on, that was one time!" But with the threat of Asmodeus looming, she wasn't above begging. "Please. Halloween—or Allhallowtide, or whatever you want to call it—is less than a week and a half away. If I'm right, Asmodeus is coming. He'll attack with his army of ghosts and we may not survive."

Shea understood, but it was Kleos who pushed him to finally agree. "Please, Shea, she's right. She needs to see the Witch."

The market was empty, save for some Gatekeepers down the hill, so he wasn't worried about speaking out loud about something that could probably end his life in Empyrean.

"Okay. Say I agree and say we get her out, what then? How do you know you can stop this demon?"

"Because," she said fiercely, "I can."

It wasn't an argument or an explanation, but the defiance in her eyes seemed motivation enough to agree.

Shea nodded. "Fine. I'll do it."

They made plans to meet up the following day. Gifted were pleading with the Elder Council to be allowed out of the city; to visit other friends and family, to reach other Gifted communities, to look for those who might have escaped Beri'ah. Shea would ask to make a supply trip to another community and Dani could sneak out with him.

"It's a good question." Kleos said as they walked downhill. "What is the plan after seeing the Witch?"

"I have no idea." Dani confessed. "But if the visions somehow guide me and if shades are her specialty, then she's the person to see. I know it." A foursome of Gatekeepers on patrol were marching up the hill. Night had fully fallen. She stared up at the moon, wondering aloud. "It's never really been clear how to do this whole destiny thing. With Gabriel, he didn't give me a mission. I had to work it out myself. These visions I got from the Witch are the same: no guidance. It's like I have to figure them out."

"Kind of a crappy way to communicate destiny."

"In the meantime, I have to worry about this freak turning my best friends against me."

"If it's a consolation, it's only those exposed to his power."

They passed the four Gatekeepers.

"That's not much consolation."

"You will be fine." Mastema assured her.

"How do you know?"

"I just..." He trailed off.

His eyes shifted from Dani to over her shoulder, then widened. He moved, grabbing her by the arm and yanking her forward. Dani jerked into him and they tumbled back.

A spearpoint lanced by Dani's head as she rolled, aimed for Mastema but nearly hitting her, too. When she came to her feet, one of the Gatekeepers they just passed barreled towards her.

Mastema stepped in front of him. Using his adamantine forearm bracers, he parried the edge the tip of the spear and shouldered the man to the ground.

Kleos dodged under a wide arc of an adamantine falx as a second Gatekeeper swung. He twisted through the air and kicked the man in the face.

The next two swept past Mastema and Kleos, headed for Dani. She backpedaled; unarmed. The two were close enough she could see their eyes.

They were bleeding.

"Why do you run away from me?" One demanded.

The other spoke right after him, "All I want to do is love you."

"You've got to be sarding kidding me." She held her hands out in front of her. "Get away from me."

"I love you, Dani." They both said in unison.

"Don't call me that!"

One dropped his spear and lunged at her, hands outstretched. He wasn't here to kill her. He wanted something else.

Dani learned a long time ago how to do this. As he grabbed her, she grabbed his armor and fell backwards. She placed a foot into his chest and used their momentum to topple him over her. Armor was heavy so as they went back, Dani used Erthe and Aer to push him over. She hurled the Gatekeeper over her head and toppled him down the hill.

Unfortunately, the second one lunged on top of her.

"Don't fight me!" he husked from under the helm. "You know you want this!"

"Get off!"

Dani jabbed two fingers through the Gatekeeper's helmet visor and into one eye. He grunted in pain and Dani went for the throat. Unfortunately, whether it was him or the demon that controlled him, he was a lot stronger and resistant to pain than she was. He reared up and backhanded her angrily. It was the first time the creature ever showed anger.

"Why would you hit me?" he demanded. "I work so hard to make myself perfect for you—someone to love and adore; a god for you—and you hit me?"

Before he could rant anymore, someone barreled into him and knocked them both over. Dani sat up, relieved for Mastema, only to find it wasn't her Guardian.

Ethan was over the man. He yanked off his helmet and struck with his bare fist; again and again. He beat the man until his knuckles were bloody. The Gatekeeper's face was likewise.

Kleos expertly took his opponent down. He blocked and grabbed the spear just below the celestial-steel point and drove with his other palm into the nose of his attacker. He struck the inside of the guard's outstretched leg at the thigh and wrenched the weapon from his hands, before thrusting the butt of it up into his neck and dropping him.

Mastema hurled his foe headlong into a market stand and the man didn't move again.

The last one came at Dani. She raised her palm. Her anger coursed down her arm and with a scream, exploded a beam of light right into his chest. Her jerked off the ground and screamed as he fell over the side of the bridge, out of sight.

Dani dropped to her knees and moaned in agony. The man's screams fell away into nothing. He was gone.

She just killed him!

The near-silence was deafening. Mastema and Kleos stood uphill, staring at her. When she turned around, she was crying. She knew what she did. They all knew.

And Kleos now knew something else. "She—She—!"

"You tell no one." Mastema warned. "No one."

"You knew?"

Silently, he nodded. Kleos stared at her again. "She's a lightbringer."

Dani would have said something, but everyone turned to the only sound on the hill. Ethan still hovered over his downed opponent, beating him repeatedly with blows across his bloody face. Again and again, he struck down on the already unconscious man.

"Ethan, it is done." Mastema warned, trudging over. "Stop."

He kept going.

143

"Ethan, cease!"

He grabbed the back of Ethan's raiments, but Ethan slapped his hand away and turned on him.

And to Dani's horror, his eyes were bleeding.

"Get away from me!" He snarled animalistically. His gaze turned on Dani. "What? What do you want Dani? Why are you looking at me like that? Do I scare you?" He stood up, bloody fists clenched. "Is this too much? You want me to stand up for you. You want me to fight for you. Well, I did! Now you look horrified!" He sneered angrily. "What do you want, Dani? Huh? You want me to be a man or your punching bag?"

"Ethan…" she held up her hands, "calm down!"

"I'm tired of you telling me what to do!"

"Ethan!" This time Kleos spoke.

"Shut up! All of you! This is between me and her!"

"Ethan!"

He turned towards him. "*What*?"

Kleos struck him hard with the dull bottom of the spear and knocked him out.

Ethan wouldn't be in the Ward long; a few hours, maybe. But Dani didn't go see him or the three Gatekeepers like she did Izzy and Bouden. She kept her distance. What Asmodeus did to them, to Ethan, was horrifying and the dead Gatekeeper they pulled from the Vale made her sick.

Dani had never killed another Numen before. Based on how she was treated once everyone found out, neither had anyone else. Most of Sanctuary Hills avoided her gaze and her once-leper status amongst the other Novices from before Alecto returned.

She was persona non-grata once more.

Mastema delivered the news about Ethan. Dani was in her house with Caesar, who refused to leave her side now.

"He remembers what happened." Mastema told her. "He remembers everything. He describes it as 'seeing red' though I am unfamiliar with the phrase."

Dani curled her legs up against her chest, resting her head back against the pavilion support.

"Are you well?" He sat next to her. "I am worried."

"I am, too." She confessed. "Mastema, it was Ethan. Ethan! He got to him."

"You knew this could happen."

"Yeah, but I never believed it actually _would!_" she screamed, but got ahold of herself. She hated feeling this way; weak, unable to stop Asmodeus from taking people from her. More and more, she felt alone, even with her Guardian by her side. "I just thought someone could fight him. I thought Ethan could, at least."

"He did." Mastema assured her. "Ethan explained to me that even in the midst of Asmodeus's attempt to possess him, he resisted. I believe he did it for you."

"But Asmodeus still got to him."

He nodded.

"How can you, how can Kleos, be around me, then? Why aren't you two affected?"

Her Guardian frowned. "As for Kleos, his situation is...unique. As for me, you know why. I am a broken man. There is not much left for Asmodeus to twist. Any emotion I could muster would be useless to him."

She twisted her fingers together, admitting. "I'm scared."

"As am I."

The revelation shocked her. Mastema rarely, if ever, showed emotion.

She shook her head. "Not like me. Mastema, Asmodeus keeps coming after me over and over. He won't stop. I have no way of fighting him, especially if he's going to use my friends."

"We will stop him. Tomorrow, when we leave Empyrean and visit the Witch, we will find something that will stop this creature. We will find a way to end this." He took one of her hands in his; a gesture she could barely believe he did.

It was then that Dani was able to admit something, "At Ber'iah, when all of you were knocked down and Asmodeus was in Akela..." she bit her quivering lower lip. "...when he attacked me, he did something to me. Even though it hurt me—even though I wanted him to stop—I couldn't overpower him." She let the one thing she hadn't said aloud to come out. "I'm worried that even if I try, I won't be able to stop him."

Mastema didn't speak at first, as if he already knew what happened to her back in Beri'ah. He protected her then; not just from shades, but from everyone, as if he understood it wasn't just about her physical injuries.

"I told you once fear takes from us the ability to fight back." He told her. "Sometimes, it is not just our physical abilities it steals. It is our mind. It is our confidence. It is our belief within ourselves. Remember my lesson, Dani."

"Don't fear anything? Yeah, sure Mastema, it's just that easy."

"No." He insisted. "That is impossible. My lesson to you was not to fear, but that fear is natural. Fear is human. Instead, you must conquer it. The only way to do that is to embrace it."

"Embrace it?"

"Embrace your fear. Do not push it away. Instead, stand when you are most terrified. Stand when others expect you to fold. Drive out the darkness here," he put two fingers to her chest, "so the light may shine through."

"I told you my powers were useless. I couldn't lightbring. And when I finally did, I killed someone!" The awfulness of that made her stomach roll. "Asmodeus has turned my own powers against me."

"Not your powers." He said. "Not the power of your hands, at least. The power in your heart. Only that light can do that. Only the light within you can do that. And only conquering the fear you feel can free you."

"I can't." she told him, shaking her head. "I can't."

"Yes, you can."

"How do you know?"

"Because I have seen you drive out the darkness before, in ways you will never know."

"Yeah? Like what?"

"Like mine."

She looked back up into the dark, coal-like irises of her Guardian. His face was still devoid of emotion, but when he spoke there was something there; something deep. Intense. Painful. Hidden.

"I would not be standing here without you." He told her. "I would have been swallowed by the darkness long ago had you not arrived in Empyrean. Instead, you," he placed his two fingers over her heart again. "with your foul-mouth, bright soul and insatiable need to anger everyone around pulled me back from that darkness. I came out of the shadows. You were my redemption. You gave me purpose now. So now must you do that for yourself."

She smiled. It wasn't like the other smile she gave since Ber'iah. It wasn't forced, or sarcastic, or full of pain. It was real.

And then the moment ended abruptly. Mastema leapt to his feet, placing himself between her and someone who appeared at the end of her pathway.

Elder Heman marched into the open with a group of Powers at his back. They fanned out behind him; a sick de ja vu of his last time at her house.

"Guardian Mastema," Heman greeted with a smile, "Novice Daniella."

"What is the meaning of this?"

"Stand down, Guardian. I am here by decree of the Council."

"What decree?"

"The Council's latest." Heman said tersely. "I am here to arrest you. Drop your weapon or I give the order to take you by force."

Chapter Nineteen

Arrested. Dani had only come close to being arrested once. It was at a 7-11 and involved a bag of chips. The store owner didn't even call the cops.

But now? Disarmed, placed under guard, she was in the worst prison she could imagine: her own house. The Council gave the order to place Dani under house arrest, which some might think wouldn't be so bad.

Except Heman took some leeway with the order. His soldiers took everything that could be construed as a weapon: their practice equipment, the hooks used for hanging up and drying dishware, and even the dishware. Of course, her gauntlets and swords were confiscated.

These guys took their job WAY too seriously.

"See, now you're just being mean." She said to Heman when they took her pots and pans.

"We must take all precautions." The Elder said slyly.

"Your mom is a precaution."

"That does not make sense."

"Your mom doesn't make sense."

His jaw tightened. Good to know she could still annoy him.

The soldiers were still clearing out Mastema's home even after Dani's was done. Teams of soldiers carried out swords, spears, bundles of knives, bows and arrows, even an extremely oversized axe.

"How many weapons do you have, exactly?" She asked him.

"Some for everyday use, others for holidays, and a few for formal occasions."

She had to look at him to see if he was joking or not. She still couldn't tell.

As they finished, Heman turned on them. "You were involved in the assault of several Earthborn in the last few days, so the Council believes you are a threat to the safety and security of this city."

"Your mom—."

He held up a threatening hand to silence her. "Until this demonic threat can be assessed and we understand if you are colluding with it or not, you and your Guardian are restricted from leaving your residence."

"Colluding? As in, you think I want to _help_ Asmodeus? Are you insane?"

Heman smiled nastily. "It is only a precaution."

"That's total crap! What did Elder Jeduthun or Elder Castus say about this?"

His smile got even wider. "As of right now, the Council isn't confident in Elder Jeduthun's or Elder Castus's ability to lead. Your presence shows they have not exercised the best judgment. They oversee the Council, for now, but it is unclear if they will continue to do so."

Heman left. As he passed out of the clearing around the house, he extended his hand and murmured an incantation. The air around her village shimmered. A translucent dome ringed her home from the pathway to the pedestal over the Vale.

"A ward." Mastema told her. "A magical barrier to keep anyone unauthorized out and us in."

A group of Powers created a picket as a second layer of "protection." Dani was sure that their use, and not Gatekeepers, was intentional. The Powers were loyal to Heman. He learned from his mistakes.

Dani entertained herself through the rest of the day by working out. There wasn't much to stop her from going stir-crazy with cabin fever, so she passed the time challenging herself to severe workouts.

It was times like this that living in a world without electronics and TV sucked.

Eventually, night fell. They had little to cook with, but found a way to warm up some bread and ham. Then Dani and Mastema settled in for the night.

She was in Ricky's living room, surrounded by the stench of cigarettes and stale beer. The place was as filthy as ever. Outside the windows, the world was silent. Only a gentle breeze disturbed the curtains.

How did I get here? *She asked herself.*

The sound of dishes turned her around. Her mom was picking up plates from the coffee table and emptying the ash tray.

"Mama?"

Her mother looked ragged with messy, unkempt hair, and runny makeup. She worked hurriedly to clean.

"Mama, can you hear me?" Am I behind the veil? *Dani willed herself to be seen and called out to her again.* "Mama, it's Dani. I don't know how I got here but—."

Yvette looked up. She saw her. She looked right at Dani, but the moment she did, she retreated to the kitchen.

"Mama, wait!" Dani followed her. "It's me! I came back to you. Mama, me escuchas?"

Yvette dumped the load of dishes into the sink and began to scrub.

"Why can't she hear me?"

"She can." Said a voice. "But like a good woman, she only listens to me."

Ricky stood in the middle of the room. It'd been more than four months since she'd seen him. His greasy hair, his yellow teeth, his thick mustache; everything made him look grimy and soiled.

Dani reached to her belt for her swords, but they were gone. Instead, she held out her hand; ready to summon her lightbringing.

"Back off." She warned.

"You have no power." Ricky told her in a voice that sounded eerily familiar; not his voice, but something she heard before. "You cannot deny me."

She glanced over her shoulder. Her mother scrubbed a plate feverishly. Dani could see that her hands were raw from cleaning. "What did you do to my mom?"

"I reminded her of her place." Ricky's stained smile widened.

She looked at her mom again. How had she gotten here? She was supposed to be in Empyrean.

She turned back to him. "You're not real. This isn't real. It's a dream."

"Yes, it is."

"You're not Ricky."

The thing posing as her mother's boyfriend chuckled softly, sauntering forward. "True."

"Stop." Dani warned, raising her hand higher. "You don't know what I can do."

"You can do nothing, because you are nothing."

His eyes cracked, as if they would bleed. His irises changed color. She could smell the stink of him and nearly gagged.

Dani poured her anger, her hatred, and her disgust down her arm and into her hand. She would not give this thing the chance to hurt her again. But unlike the destructive force she summoned before, no light came this time. She winced in pain. It stung bad enough that she lowered her arm.

Then, Ricky was there, twisting her hand back. She shrieked.

"Women are for one thing." He told her. He stroked a finger down her cheek. "Us. You belong to us."

"You're not real!" she cried, bending under him.

"Does it hurt like it's real?"

Pain rolled down her arm, her elbow nearly tearing away while her wrist was immobilized in his grip. He shoved her down against the fridge across from her mother. She cradled her arm, moaning in agony.

'Ricky' ambled into the kitchen, between her mom and her. He ran his fingers through Yvette's hair, smiling at Dani. Her mother shuddered under his touch. "There is harmony in knowing your place. A place for everything and," he yanked Yvette's head back by the hair, "and everything in its place."

"You're not real." She repeated. "None of this is real, no matter if it hurts or not. I'm dreaming. This is only a dream."

"Dream or not, my power is real."

Dani backed away, realizing there was more truth in his words than he let on. "The dream with Akela and Roxelana. That wasn't a nightmare. That was you."

He glowered. "I came for you. I wanted you. You were mine by right, but instead you throw yourself at other men, like that Ethan, but you ignore me: the perfect man for you. I try to take want belongs to me through other men, but you still deny me what is mine."

"You mean Izzy? Those Gatekeepers?"

The demon's vile grin turned to a snarl. Her mom's hands scrubbed so hard they bled.

"You will love me, Daniella del Lucio, and I will punish you and everyone like you who makes me wait for what I want. I am everything you want and need."

"Don't think too highly of yourself." She said sarcastically.

"Only I know the truth about your sex: that you're slaves to your desires. If men weren't there to remind you what debase, little creatures you are, you would run amok. A firm hand is needed to keep you in place. You've convinced yourselves you do not want it. You think freedom is what you want; that you're worthy of it. You are not. You are only allowed choose to please us, and be free of decision. I will give you that freedom."
He started towards her. "You will know me."

"I already know you, Asmodeus. Trust me, now that I do, I feel like I need a shower to wipe off all the filth."

She meant to piss him off; get under his skin by revealing she knew his name. But he seemed almost pleased by it. He licked his lips. "It is good you know my name. Slaves should know their masters."

Dani nearly gagged in disgust. "Screw you."

Apparently, he had enough. Something changed in Ricky's face; like the mask he wore slipped. Something ugly behind the guise of her mom's boyfriend peeked out. It wasn't Ricky. It wasn't Akela. It was Asmodeus's real face and it was truly horrible.

He grabbed her by the throat and shoved her back against the fridge. The air escaped her lungs and didn't come back.

Asmodeus husked against her cheek. "Every. Single. Spoiled. Self-righteous woman like you I find, I will bring down. I will make each and every one of you," his grip tightened, "every one that rejects me, pay the price for denying me what's mine. You'll be the first, Daniella. I'll make you the example!"

He hurled her to the floor. His burning, bloody eyes bore down on her. Dani scooted away, trying to escape. He followed.

"You are weak! I see you for the feeble, scared little girl you are!"

He dropped on top of her, pinning her to the floor. She clawed at his hand when he grabbed her by the throat again. She couldn't breathe!

"No one is here to protect you. You are nothing! When Allhallowtide comes, I will enter your city as I entered Beri'ah, and I will slaughter anyone who gets in my way. No one can keep you from me. Your friends, your fellow Numen; they will abandon you! You will be alone."

She fought. She kicked and flailed and tried to fight him off, but nothing worked. His weight sank down on her and pinned her in place.

"I am coming, Daniella and I will have my revenge! I was forced to rot in a lonely prison for all this time because of your kind; locked in a cell created by the angels and man. I will not be denied any longer."

She felt herself passing out. Her flailing weakened.

Dani croaked, unable to take another breath. "I...will never...let you...win..."

"You will try, but I will."

The world lost meaning and then oblivion came.

"How long has this been happening?" Mastema asked her the following morning.

They meditated after a morning workout and breakfast, using special gestures Mastema called mudras. Dani wasn't sure how they worked, but he wanted to help her after she told him of her dream. These mudras were meant to calm and compose her.

She didn't think they worked. "A few weeks."

"Why did you not tell me?"

"I didn't know it was him." She shuddered. "He's everywhere, Mastema. I can't escape him. My friends, my dreams; he's gotten into every part of my life." Her chest hurt. She felt violated. "He's made me unsafe in my own home."

"You will stop him."

"How? How do we even start?"

"I think someone's already coming to help us with that."

Four figures appeared at the crest of the hill: Shea, Kleos, Bouden and Izzy. They walked down together with no visible weapons, but Shea carried a covered basket and Kleos carried two knapsacks.

Mastema stood and Dani followed him out into the square.

"Halt." One of the Powers stepped into their path. "On orders of the Council, no one goes further."

"We're here to drop off some food." Shea said good-naturedly. He held up the basket. "Everyone has to eat."

"Gifted," the guard made the word sound like a cuss, "don't tell us what to do."

"Be calm, brother." Kleos advised. "He's only being friendly."

"Is that right?" The Powers soldier asked. "The way I hear, you're a little too friendly with this shopkeeper."

Kleos' smile didn't fade an inch. "Is that right?"

The other guards were closing in. There were four of her friends, including Kleos, but at least half a dozen or more of the Powers. It wouldn't be a fair fight, even if they were armed.

"Walk away." The guard advised.

"Or what?" It was a ballsy challenge for Kleos.

The guard's hand inched towards his sword.

Kleos moved almost too fast to see. While they spoke, he casually closed the distance between him and the guard. It paid off. His palm shot out and blocked the butt of the guard's sword, knocking it back into its sheath when he tried to draw it. His other fist shot out and tagged him in the throat. The man dropped.

Izzy and Bouden tossed something in both directions; glass vials that cracked open with a sound like air from a compressed can. Mist curled around the soldiers. They all stopped in their tracks.

"Stop them!" The lead guard croaked. His hand swirled with Aer. He attempted to form an aerwhisper to send to the Citadel. "What are you waiting for? Stop them!"

But the other guards seemed to have lost interest in their jobs. Some of them stood where they were; transfixed. Others sat, as if bored.

Fellbloom. Lotus blossom elixir. Dani felt its effects once. It turned you into a disinterested slug.

The leader raised his palm to send a message but Kleos kicked and knocked him back into the ward. The guard passed through and his body jerked, twitched and flung forward like he was jolted off an electric fence.

Every guard was disabled.

Kleos extended his hand and murmured a kind of counter-spell in the angelic language. After a few seconds, the ward dropped.

"Get them in." He told Bouden and Izzy. "Hurry."

The boys began herding the elixir-intoxicated guards past the barrier into the ward. Shea jogged down to Dani.

"What are you doing?" She demanded.

"Bringing you these." He ripped the cover off his basket. Inside were Dani's swords, gauntlets and greaves. "We're all here to bust you out."

"What? Why?"

"Because you are leaving." Mastema told her.

Dani took her weapons and armor and began belting them on. "You knew about this?" She asked him.

Her Guardian nodded. "There was a contingency should the Elders try to interfere in stopping the demon. I felt they could not be trusted, so I enlisted your companions to help."

Dani finished with her greaves and slid on her gauntlets. "Where are we going? How are we going to get out of the city?"

"Quickly." He answered.

Once the guards were inside, Dani and the others stepped out and Kleos put the ward back in place. "That will buy us some time." He said, turning to Izzy and Bouden. "You two need to get going."

"Where?" Dani asked.

"The North Gate." Izzy said. "Once they realize you're gone, they'll think you tried to escape through the nearest exit. We're going to make sure they keep thinking that for as long as possible."

"You're a distraction? Why would you do that for me?"

"Because I have to repay you." Izzy said truthfully. "I have to have your back, *chica fuerte*."

She blushed.

"Besides," Bouden added, "if this thing is after you, then I guess you're the only one to stop it. You killed a Fury. The way I figure it, who better to take down a millennia-old all-powerful demon?"

"Thanks." It was partly sarcastic, but also partly true.

"Kick butt, *chica*."

They flew uphill towards the North Gate beyond Sanctuary Hills.

"Where do we go?" She asked her remaining friends. "West Gate?"

Shea shook his head. "It's too heavily guarded."

"Then where?"

"East."

Shea departed for the market, as not to be implicated in freeing Dani. Before they left the guards inside the ward, they poured an elixir into their mouths. Kleos called it lethe. Apparently, when they woke, they wouldn't remember the last several hours. If everyone did their job and wasn't caught, then none of them could be directly connected. It didn't mean it wasn't risky, or that the Council wouldn't suspect them, but it did the most to protect her friends. Dani was grateful.

The East Gate lay across Empyrean almost directly from the West. Unlike the West, South and North Gates, the East was more isolated. Nestled in the rocky crags above the Vale, it lay a little farther south from the Crystalline River's winding path through the Dalles. To reach it, they would have to cross the Vale.

Unfortunately, they had to go by foot.

No more than a few minutes after departing, Dani heard trumpets from the Citadel. They knew. Dropping from the sky, she, Kleos and Mastema crossed the Crystalline to the opposite bank and headed for a long, narrow ledge path that snakes from the Citadel, along the crater, towards the Gate.

"How did you and Shea get my weapons?" Dani asked Kleos. "They were confiscated by the Elder Council."

"A...friend gave them to us."

Jeduthun. Dani would bet on it.

They made their way uphill through the trees. Another trumpet blast. Mastema paused as he listened to it.

"They're coming."

"How do you know?"

"I know Empyrean's signals. The Novices bought us all the time they could, but the Gatekeepers and Powers are being directed to the Vale. We must hurry to enter the mist of the Dalles. We will go unnoticed there."

They were running, using Aer to skip along the ground, but none of them dared to fly. Dani noticed the forest seemed familiar here. Why was that?

An arrow nearly took her nose off. She dropped and rolled across the ground.

"Halt!" Yelled a familiar voice.

Mastema landed in front of her as she came to her feet. Over his shoulder, she spotted a centaur she knew. She couldn't believe it.

"Orion?"

The young centaur had his bow raised and aimed for Mastema's chest. Kleos landed a few feet away, throwing-dagger in hand, but Dani signaled to stop him.

"Wait!" She side-stepped her Guardian. "Orion, it's me. Dani."

His bow wavered. His eyes narrowed. "What are you doing here? What is all the commotion from the Citadel?"

Another trumpet blast.

Mastema cursed. "They are coming. We cannot delay."

"Orion, we have to go."

"I said halt!" He tensed his bow again, re-aiming. "Those trumpets are for you? Why? What have you done?"

"I don't have time to explain."

"Make time!"

Dani sensed something overhead and looked up. Just beyond the far treetops, pinpricks against the sky, she saw a small formation of Powers scouting the forest. If they didn't move soon, there would be no escaping them.

"Orion," she turned back to him, "I made you a promise to help protect your borders. Do you remember?"

He nodded, but didn't lower his bow.

"To do that, I have to leave Empyrean. If I don't, something bad will come and I won't be able to stop it. If you want to keep your village safe, you have to let me go."

He still didn't lower his bow.

"Please. You can trust me, remember?"

His eyes flicked up to the sky and then back down to Dani. An eternity stretched between then and his decision.

A second later, he turned his bow upward and fired. The arrow sung past the treetops into an approaching group of Numen. It exploded in a concussive blast, knocking the Powers apart. They dropped into the trees.

"Go." He told her. "More will come. I can ensure they follow me for a short time. It may give you the distraction you need."

Dani, Mastema and Kleos took off. "Thank you!"

The centaur said nothing. He turned and galloped off in the opposite direction. But he extended his hand out in a wave that told Dani not only did he hear her, but she was welcome.

They made it to the rocks. The mist of the Dalles spread down along the crater and into the forest, so it was cooler here. Light played in rainbows through the fog and wet forest. Dani's braids stuck together.

They couldn't fly here. The fog from the Crystalline dampened their powers, even at this distance. It was why the East Gate was so rarely used by the Numen.

Dani and her friends had to climb.

The three of them clambered up the rocks. As they ascended, Dani heard something that sounded like a boom off in the distance. She heard it once before: Orion's arrows. The brave, young centaur was buying her time. If she made it through this, she would thank him somehow.

She now had two centaurs she could trust.

They made it to the top of the rocks. Climbing wasn't as easy as people made it out to be. Dani had a new appreciation for her powers of flight. As she crawled out onto a pathway at the top, a hand helped her up.

It was Ethan.

"What are you doing here?" She asked. She hadn't seen him since she put him in the Ward.

He ignored her question. "Once they realize what direction you went, they'll come. Come on. The Gate is this way."

"Won't there be guards?"

"We'll have cover."

"How?"

"Some of us have talents of use."

From the fog—as if clothed in it—Airlea stepped into the open. She wore a long, flowing cloak that almost perfectly matched the din of the light and mist around her. She threw back the hood. Dani noticed that when her hands moved, the fog moved.

"You can control this stuff?" Dani asked.

"It is my gift." The Gifted girl turned up her nose. "This wasn't how I expected to use it, though."

"Thank you, anyway." Dani meant it. She may not have liked Airlea, but if she did this, she deserved some thanks.

Airlea turned on her heel and strode up the path. "Coming?"

The way to the East Gate ran from the Citadel along the crater's inward slope. They ran quickly, but fires signaled the escape route in the mist ahead. They slowed. True to her word, Airlea gave them cover. Her hands swirled and the mist thickened. The red-clad Gatekeepers appeared.

The East Gate wasn't as magnificent as the West. Instead of three broad entrances, an inner cloister, and battlements, the East had a single pear-and-adamantine door built into the crater. Adorn by fires, it led into a tunnel through the crater to the other side. Manned by fewer men, it didn't need as much protection. From the outside, it was difficult to spot. From the inside, even if someone got through, they would have a hard time finding their way through the fog. It was perfect for escaping, however.

They stopped. Four Gatekeepers stood guard, all of them armed.

"Airlea?" Ethan asked softly.

She nodded and swirled her hands, adding more fog. Then, when a thick veil gathered around them, she started forward. They followed.

They were only the length of a school bus from them when she couldn't hide them anymore.

Mastema exploded from cover, grabbed the first man and shoved him against the rock-face wall of the crater. Once. Twice. Three times. He fell unconscious. Kleos quickly disabled the one next to him. Ethan dropped a fellbloom elixir down at the feet of the other two.

"My job is done." Airlea told Ethan.

"You should go, then."

Airlea managed a tight, almost-friendly smile towards Dani. "Good luck. I hope you don't die."

"Uh, thanks? Why are you doing this, anyway?"

"Well, for one, Roxelana would want me to. But," she turned towards Mastema and Kleos, "I also find myself without an escort on nights that vespertide occurs. Since Ethan obviously has found," she looked Dani up and down, "someone else, I am in need of new boys to do things for me. What better way than have them in my debt?"

Dani very much disliked this part of Airlea. It was common knowledge that no Numen would ever marry, since the whole celestial-warrior-thing prevented them; however, fraternization with Gifted was very common. Judah allowed it at his club. For Numen, it was a way to relieve certain 'urges.' Dani used to not understand what the Gifted got out of it, but Airlea was the answer. Girls like her grew up in Empyrean. They relied on Numen men to do them favors and give them special treatment. To Dani, it was gross. To her, it was a way of life.

She approached Mastema and Kleos. "You know, both of you are very cute. How come neither of you have come my way?"

Mastema departed with a grunt, disinterested.

Airlea smiled up at Kleos. "Well?"

Kleos said nothing. Airlea took it as an invitation and kissed him.

Dani almost made a gagging noise, watching the super-awkward exchange of spit. But just as soon as she kissed him, Airlea dropped back on her heels and stared him, hand to her mouth.

"Consarn it." She cursed and turned away, shaking her head. "Of course, he is."

With that cryptic expletive, Airlea left. Dani glanced at Kleos, who stood where she left him, stunned. "What was that about?"

"Nothing." He said and walked just as quickly in the opposite direction.

They unlocked the inner East Gate. The path ahead was lit by torchfires. Dani noticed, as Ethan and Kleos ran ahead, that Mastema wasn't moving.

"What are you doing? They're coming. We have to go."

"You have to go." He told her. "I am staying."

"What? Why? You're my Guardian. Where I go, you go."

"And on this journey, I cannot go."

She didn't understand. "Is this about Asmodeus? He hasn't been able to get to you. So why—?"

"Because he might." Mastema told her. He stepped close and put both hands on her shoulders. "Daniella, you saved me once from death. I would never allow myself to hurt you."

"But you haven't—."

"But I could." He insisted. "I am not brainless. Every encounter I had with you over the past few weeks, I did so knowing that the moment I felt any inkling I might hurt you, I would leave. I never strayed far from someone who could stop me if that happened. I never came to you without this."

He pulled a small vial of elixir from his raiments.

"What is that?"

"A very potent poison."

"Poison? Why would you...you would kill yourself?"

"If it came down to you or I, yes. I never trusted any man around you, including myself. Unless I knew you were not in danger, no one could come near you. Including me."

She didn't know what to say.

"I am staying. Take this." He shoved one of the bags Kleos brought with them into her arms. "Novice Bouden packed it for you. Inside you will find items that may help. Now, you must go."

"I can't leave you."

"You can. You are strong. You can stop Asmodeus."

"I don't know if I can do this alone."

"You will not be alone. Kleos will go with you."

"Kleos? Why? I thought you said no man could be around me?"

"He is unique. You are not in danger from him. He will help guide you."

"Mastema, I don't—."

"You go and you go now." And then he did something he never had. It was quick, formal and somewhat awkward, but she guessed he probably had never done it before:

He hugged her.

"Go." He pushed her down the tunnel after Ethan and Kleos. Then, with only a quick look back, he departed into the fog.

Dani ran.

The tunnel through the crater was long, but Dani caught up to Ethan and Kleos outside. The tunnel led to another set of pearl-and-adamantine bars on the other end, which opened onto a small terrace. Gatekeepers lay unconscious on the floor. Kleos was synching on his weapons: throwing blades, armor, and his short sword, the xiphos.

All around them, mist covered the expanse Dani knew was there. She couldn't see it, but the only thing around Empyrean was sky and clouds. It seemed like an endless void. Her chest hurt. She felt vertigo being near it.

She didn't know if she could do this.

Ethan was mumbling some spell with his hand extended over the side of the terrace. When Dani looked down, something shimmered below. It was like a rainbow, but it swirled and moved.

An aurora. He was opening a gate.

"Is that...?"

"The way is open." He told her. "You don't have long." He made the Numen bow of respect towards Kleos. "Good luck."

He returned it and stepped to the rim.

"Go Dani." Ethan urged, backing away.

"Wait!"

Kleos hesitated. Dani stepped away from the rim to Ethan.

"What are you doing?" He asked.

"Ethan…" She wanted to say so much, but for some reason, it wouldn't come out. All she could do was stand there, awkwardly, unable to really put into words what she felt.

He shook his head. "We said we wouldn't *Twilight* this."

He used her own words against her. She looked down, burning red.

"Dani, I can't go. If Asmodeus got into my head again, I wouldn't forgive myself."

"I know." She sighed. "I know, but…"

She did it again. It didn't change anything about what was going on between them, or how upset she was at him; it didn't change the fact they couldn't be together. She saw no way they ever could be.

But she kissed him again. Like before, she decided 'screw it' and went for what she wanted. She kissed Ethan's lips firmly; holding them against hers. It wasn't rational; it was what she wanted. And if some evil entity would try to take away her ability to choose and try to make her a slave, she would choose at least once to make her own decision about someone she cared for.

She broke from the kiss and stepped back. "I'll see you again."

"Promise?" he asked.

Kleos jumped over the side. Dani reached the edge. "I can't."

Then she dropped. Empyrean fell away. Ethan fell away. Everything she thought of as close to safety fell away. Dani plummeted downward into the unknown. She didn't try to control it. There was no way she could. She fell.

The shimmering rainbow portal rushed at her.

Then she was gone.

Chapter Twenty

They exploded from the luminescent clouds, dropping through an intense downpour as they fell. They'd come out somewhere over downtown, with skyscrapers and high-rise buildings looking like toys beneath them.

Lightning crackled so near she felt her skin prickle with electricity. A crack of light nearly blinded her and she screamed, dropping from the Aer.

"Dani!" Kleos screamed from somewhere far off.

Dani swore, her body tumbling instead of flying. The world spun around her; or rather, she spun downward through it. Unable to get her control again, she flailed desperately. She tried to level out like a skydiver, but wasn't able to.

"*Dani!*" A voice called from above.

"Caesar!"

"*I got'cha, girlie!*" Her friend hurled down out of the sky and snatched her by the back of the raiments. Caesar tugged her back, trying to slow her descent. "*C'mon! You gotta fly!*"

Overhead, the multicolored aurora shimmered, but Dani looked back down as the world rushed up at her.

She summoned Aer and began slowing her descent.

Both she and Kleos came in hard. Buildings, cars, and then people all grew to full size until Dani and Kleos came shooting down. They aimed for a large, open, grassy area. Peeling off speed, they slowed, but it was still going to suck.

Kleos hit boots-down first and tore off a chuck of soggy grass on landing.

"Oh hellspawn!" She swore. She dropped her feet to land and broke her fall. Dani tumbled face-first across the wet, damp lawn and rolled to a stop. She disembarked her one-way rollercoaster fall face skyward, staring up as droplets plopped down on her cheeks.

Overhead, the green, radiant aurora borealis faded into nothing. The gate closed.

She lay there for a few minutes. When she was younger, she used to think skydiving would be awesome. She didn't think that now.

Slowly, Dani sat up. They were on a wide, massive lawn facing an off-white stone building with a large obelisk-like tower at the center. At the very top was a golden figure holding a trumpet. An angel.

They just landed in front of a church. She laughed.

"What's so funny?" Kleos asked, slowly getting up to his feet. He had grass stains and mud all down his backside.

"It does hurt."

"What does?"

"When I fall from Heaven."

He didn't see the humor in it, but she was dying laughing. Of course, he probably was never the subject of a bad pick-up line like that.

Caesar wheeled from the sky and came to land on the lawn. "*You okay, chica?*"

"I'm fine. Thank you for being there."

"*Anytime.*"

"Kleos? You good?"

"As good as it gets being on the run." He picked up his knapsack and began rummaging through it. "We should get moving. It won't take Empyrean long to figure out where we went and come looking for us."

"We just nearly got turned into people-sized pancakes. Can't we take a breath?"

"No. Do we know where we are in relation to the Hellfire Club?"

She pointed to the church, "That's the Los Angeles California Temple. It's a Mormon mega-church. If we're there, then we are on the far side of L.A." She checked her gauntlets and swords to make sure they weren't broken in the fall. "We should get flying."

"No." Kleos told her.

"What do you mean, no?"

"I mean that if Elder Heman sends the Powers after us, they could track us through our abilities. We'll need to travel a more mundane way." Kleos shimmered, like asphalt in heat, and suddenly he wasn't a Guardian anymore. He was dressed in jeans and a sweatshirt; no xiphos or throwing knives, no visible trace he was anything but a normal guy. His control over the veil, Aether, was intense.

Dani similarly focused on changing her appearance. Her raiments and swords vanished.

"One more thing." Kleos reached into his "sweatshirt" pocket and removed a long, silvery chain. "This is yours."

"My necklace! My mom's ring!" She took it back, but noticed it was different. Inside the ring on the loop was a purple stone. She held it up, examining it. The stone's color seemed to move as if a liquid energy were inside. "What did you do to it?"

"I used it to create a special amulet." Kleos explained. "It's pretty old magic. We call it a shadelight pendant. Put it on." She did. "Shades are immortal souls; ghosts, almost. If we ever encounter them again, take out the pendant and their presence should set it off."

"Set it off?"

"The magic will repel them."

She grinned. "Cool."

"Yes, well, it only has a limited use before the magic is drained."

"How limited?"

"It'll work maybe three times, so only use it if you're really in trouble."

She tucked it underneath her clothes. It felt good to have it back. And it made her wonder, as she picked up her pack and followed Kleos, "Do you think I could see my mother while we're here?"

He frowned. "No. If Empyrean found out you visited her, it wouldn't matter if we get this mission done. The Council would have your head."

They trudged downhill and jumped the border fence around the Temple onto the sidewalk of Santa Monica Boulevard. There was a bus stop just down the street. They took a seat on one of the covered benches to get out of the rain. Caesar flew overhead, even in the dank weather able to easily stay in flight.

"What else do we have in our bags?" she asked.

"Food. Elixirs. Some helpful charms. These obsidian mirrors." He held one up. "Bouden packed pretty well. He even handed us some combat elixirs." He held one up. The small bottle looked like it was filled with fire. "Don't throw this unless you want to burn down everything around you."

"Good to know." They waited for the bus. "So, want to tell me why you are on this trip instead of my Guardian?"

"Excuse me?"

"Come on, Kleos, I know something is up. You and Mastema are the only two who can resist Asmodeus's influence. Mastema worried that he was finally getting to him, but he's not worried about you. How are you immune?"

"Does it matter?" he asked.

"Yes."

"No, it doesn't."

"You're right, it doesn't. But I'm bored and we're waiting for a bus."

"No, we are not." He pointed.

The public transit bus came rolling up to the stop. Kleos went to hop on, leaving Dani's question unanswered.

They didn't have to pay, due to the veil, and took seats up front. Santa Monica Boulevard was on the wrong side of L.A. from the Hellfire Club. They had to take the bus to the subway station. Unfortunately, automated turn-styles weren't swayed by the veil like bus drivers, which meant they had to get money for a fare. It didn't take long to find someone who wanted to trade cash for a Corinthiacum coin. She was willing to bet that it was worth more than the fifty bucks the guy paid, especially since it was worth more than gold, but they needed the money and didn't care. The pair hopped trains until they arrived at the Montebello/Commerce station near the Outlets and Hellfire.

They had to walk towards the Club. Dani never gave much thought to how convenient flying was, since she didn't have to walk everywhere like before. They lost a few hours taking the mundani way, but at least the rain had mostly slowed to a light drizzle. Pretty soon, they arrived across the street.

She relaxed when the seemingly-empty construction site loomed ahead. Hellfire began to form. A rush of relief washed through her. Safe. They'd be safe soon.

"You think Judah will let us in?" She asked. "I mean, I sort of got him in trouble with the Elders."

"I'm sure he won't..." Kleos trailed off. His arm shot out, stopping her in the middle of the sidewalk.

"What is it?" She asked.

"We have company."

They passed a fenced in parking lot and something melted from grey shadows of the nearest vehicles; several somethings. Inky, translucent shades peeled off and formed a barrier between them and Hellfire. There were at least four of them. Dani glanced over her shoulder. At least six more were behind them.

She reached for her weapon.

"Don't." He warned. "Not yet."

The shadows closed in. Now that Dani knew what they were, she shivered at the appearance of their vaguely human forms. She could see detail she hadn't noticed before; Numen raiments in nearly-transparent shades of black and grey. Hair, faces, and shadowy weapons; they were much more human now, but every one had a feral, angry expression.

"Watch our back." Kleos told her.

Dani turned, putting her back to his.

"What do you want?" Kleos demanded.

"You." Responded one shadowperson. "Well, the girl in fact, but I will gladly take your life as well." The voice sounded familiar.

"Do I know you?" Kleos asked, recognizing the one who spoke, too.

"I would hope. We're old friends, you and I."

One shade stepped forward. He was tall, thin with dark features, even for a shade. His hair and beard were formed out of charcoal colors. Where had she seen him? She knew that face.

Kleos recognized him first. His voice was barely a whisper. "Nazir?"

Dani did a double take over her shoulder. Nazir looked almost as he used to, except of course that he was dead. The last Dani saw him he was fending off an army of shades before being stabbed in the back.

"You look well, Kleos." Nazir sneered. "Alive. Full of color." The shadows around his hand morphed into his long, hooked shamshir saber. "I think I'll take that from you."

"You're a shade?" Kleos didn't seem able to believe it. "You—You died at Ber'iah."

"Yes. It hurt quite a bit."

"What are you doing with these things?"

"They are my people now," Nazir said, "unlike you, who left me to rot."

"You chose to stay."

"Only because it was my duty!" He screamed angrily, his shade-form blurring when he yelled. His voice reverberated across the street. "A duty that was brow-beaten into us. A duty that took our humanity from us and forced me to be," he held up his hands in disgust, "this. It was the same duty that took my Guardian from me, long before you did."

What? Dani had no idea what he was talking about. Kleos did, apparently. He looked ashamed. "Nazir, this isn't you."

"It is. I have a new duty, now. I have a new master. He gave me orders: find the girl and bring her to him. You, however, I am most eager to see. He gave no orders about you, so I can do what I wish."

Dani heard the shades in front of her shuffling closer. Somehow, even as spirits, they disturbed the water puddles. She reached for her sword, but didn't dare draw it.

One of the shades in front of her got closer. She also recognized his face, but didn't know him. He wasn't an Empyrean soldier. He wasn't familiar like that. The one to right, however, was. A cold sweat broke out on her hands.

"Michael." She said, recognizing him.

His big form was easy to identify. His mouth pulled back into a black-and-grey smile. "You. Happy to see you again." His teeth bared in a snarl. "I may not get to kill you, but I'm going to give you to someone who will make you wish you were dead."

Kleos said to Nazir, "This isn't you, Nazir. You aren't him. You're his shade."

"Oh, I am him." Nazir promised. "I am everything I held back once, but I won't anymore. You took Titus from me. You are nothing but a selfish, self-righteous, two faced Janus!"

"Kleos?" Dani asked. "What is he talking about?"

Kleos shook his head, not answering.

Nazir held up his sword, "You can't fight all of us." He yelled commands to the rest of them. "Capture the girl. Kill the Guardian, but leave the final death stroke for me."

"Dani," Kleos whispered, "remember: you've got the shadelight pendant. Only use it if a lot of them are close."

The shades began to advance.

"Oh, I don't think it'll be a problem."

"They're the bad parts of the soul." He reminded her. "That means they're all the flaws of a person. Use it."

And that gave her an idea.

She teased Michael as he came at her. "Lookin' good there, Michael. I like the whole Silent Hill vibe you got going on."

"You're making jokes? You treated me like trash and because of you, I'm dead. Now, you get to be the one treated like trash. Asmodeus'll show you."

"Trash talk. Funny." She teased, trying to goad him just like she had that day in Empyrean. "Only trash I see is the undead, piss-poor excuse for a man in front of me who couldn't handle a woman if he had four sets of hands and a map. Tell me: do you have a problem with all girls, or just me?"

Well, that got him.

Michael's shade exploded forward. Literally. He dissolved as he flew over the ground faster than the big guy ever could in life.

"Kleos!"

She dodged, empyreal-steel sword igniting in her hand as she drew it. She swiped as she rolled. Kleos went the other way. Michael was somehow not fully formed when moving that fast, so he had no weapon and no way to grab her. He blindly charged by, but also so fast she missed him with a slash of her blade.

Dani rolled to a fighting stance in the street, another shade attacking with its black, translucent sword. Dani brought up her weapon of light, blocking and parrying his blow. They may have been shadows and mist, but she could fight them, at least.

More fell in behind the one she was already sparring. She could fight multiple opponents, but she wasn't an expert. There were too many.

"Arrrrrgh!" Michael came flying at her again. She fell back and he swept over her, but another was ready to take his place.

"Grab her!"

Before they could, Caesar gave a piercing cry from overhead so loud it made her ears bleed. They may have been dead, but it worked on them, too. They staggered away and Caesar plummeted from the sky, talons outstretched. She lashed her claws through the head of the shade Dani battled. His body dissolved into nothing.

She rose to her feet, using the distraction. She slashed left and right, dispatching another. Up and ready, she came face to face with the first shade she recognized and this time, she knew who he was.

He was from Ber'iah; the one who nearly killed her. He was the one Michael destroyed. And apparently, he didn't stay dead. The creature stabbed. Dani dodged, drew Pigsticker and attacked back, but this one was faster. She faced two opponents and though she held her ground, they were harder to kill.

Then she made one last move. Slashing with her swords, she forced them back and grabbed for her raiments. From within, she ripped out her mother's necklace; the one Kleos transformed into a charm. The shadelight pendant.

Something like a purple wave of light exploded from the amulet. It hit the two shades. They screamed, falling back, and as they did, they dissipated into nothing. Gone.

The charm worked...well...like a charm.

Michael was the only one left. He formed into a solid body, a long black shadowsword in his hands.

"You're going to die." He warned.

"You would know. You're one step ahead of me."

"I can't die." He teased, bearing cinder-colored teeth. "You cut us apart with those adamantine weapons and we just reform."

"Maybe, but not right away."

"But eventually. And we'll keep coming. We don't sleep. We don't eat. And all I want is to see you on your knees, begging for your life." He stalked forward. "Asmodeus is going to make you beg. He's going to make you his slave. There ain't nothing you can do about it."

Dani swallowed, her hand shaking on the grip of her weapon.

"I might be dead, but at least I don't feel any pain. The master? He'll make you feel a pain so horrible you'll beg to be like me. But you won't." He shook his head. "No, you're going to serve him any way he wants."

"Enough talk. Go to hell." Dani raised her empty hand and poured all her anger towards Michael into it. She fired a blast of pure white light that smashed into him and exploded his shade into mist. "Reform after that, you undead piece of crap."

Her hand hurt, but she went to help Kleos, who by now dispatched the other three shades and was dueling Nazir. Unlike Michael, his Guardian was an expert fighter. Swords clashing, Kleos was at the disadvantage. Nazir's hooked saber was much longer than Kleos' xiphos. He slashed and hacked, keeping Kleos off balance. Her friend couldn't parry and the xiphos was not meant to be a dueling weapon.

"Caesar!" Dani called, running that way. "Help him!"

Her friend banked hard and shot down towards Nazir, but as the shade knocked Kleos to the ground, he raised a hand and fired a ball of shadow at the caladrius. Caesar grunted as it struck and knocked her from the sky.

166

"Caesar!" Dani raised her hand to blast him with lightbringing.

Nazir was faster. Another ball of dark energy struck and cartwheeled Dani into the windshield of a nearby parked car.

Through blurry, painful vision she watched Nazir turned on Kleos, saber raised. "You took Titus." Nazir snarled. "Join him."

The sword came down but before it could, Nazir cried out in pain. He fell to his knees, his shadowy figure blurring around the edges. Dani felt the prick of magic as she pulled herself off the hood of the sedan. Nazir thrashed wildly, screaming in agony.

A new arrival stood a few feet behind him, hand raised. Her black-nail fingers curled and she twisted her hand. Nazir cried out once more and then fell, dissolving into nothing.

Dani staggered over to Kleos. "Are you okay?"

He nodded, wincing as he sat up. Caesar fluttered over to them, landing on Dani's shoulder. *"Girl, you okay?"*

"Thanks for the save." Dani nuzzled her.

"Who's the chick in the burqa?"

Dani, Kleos and Caesar all turned their attention towards the Witch of En Dor, who stood calmly a few feet away, one hand on her cane and the other at her side.

"A friend," Dani told her, helping them all up, "I think."

"It is good to see you again, Daniella." En Dor said. "As foretold, we meet once more. And I believe you've come with more questions."

Chapter Twenty-One

The Hellfire Club was warm and dry; two things Dani wanted to be. En Dor took them to the same booth as before to give them a place to hide.

The Club, since it was towards the evening, was much more crowded. They wove their way past two jinn making out while multi-colored flames danced about them. A pack of cynocephali out on the prowl stalked by; looking for either their next meal or a date or both. And something that looked like a miniature giant was hauled off by two golem bouncers, who were having a hell of a time doing it.

The Hellfire Club. Weird place.

Caesar took a perch near the curtain entrance as a lookout. En Dor gestured for them to sit and pulled a rope next to the door, summoning a waiter. Dani almost relaxed until their waiter arrived.

He looked human; with a California tan and wiry muscles under his Hellfire uniform shirt. He sported short red hair and the most startling violet eyes Dani had ever seen.

But more startling than that, he was about three feet tall.

"Hello, I'm Peter," the tiny human said, putting out napkins for them on the table, "and I'll be your waiter. Can I start you off with food? Something to drink? A complimentary dry spell for your wet clothes?"

Dani stared.

"Nothing to drink or eat," Kleos told him, "but a dry spell would be great."

"Of course." The little man waved his hand and suddenly, Dani's hair and clothes were brand new and unsodden. So were Kleos'. The miniature man bowed. "Anything else I can assist you with today?"

What the hell was this guy?

"Is Judah available?" Kleos cut in. "We'd really like to speak with him."

"I'm sorry, but the master is unavailable."

Dani had enough mind to ask. "Is Idunn? She's one of the bartenders. Could we speak with her?"

"She is on break. Her husband is about to take the stage, but I can ask for you." And then he was gone.

Dani was still staring when he left.

"He's a homunculus." Kleos explained, taking a seat. "They're artificial, miniature humans imbued with special magicks by their creator. I guess Judah got a new wait staff. I wonder how he made them?"

"He didn't. He ordered them." She remembered. "He couldn't get the magician semen or horse wombs he needed, or something like that."

"Yeah. Our alchemists usually can get the latter, but not the former. Magician semen is really hard to come by." He said that like it was the most natural thing in the world.

They turned their attention to their cryptic hostess, who took a seat across from them at the table. She didn't have her silver serving dishes for divination this time. Instead, she simply sat, hands spread out before her, as if waiting.

"You know, don't you?" Dani asked.

En Dor did not have to ask her to explain. She nodded. "The lord of lust has returned. He seeks you for his next conquest."

"You could have warned me."

"The spirits tell me only what they wish to tell me. I knew not who would come for you, only that one would."

"They didn't help me stop him."

"I told you: they would reveal to you all you need to know. It is you who must divine their meaning." En Dor replied.

"You were able to take down the shade outside. Are you telling me you can't get spirits to give you a little more insight?"

"I choose not to demand of them any more than I am given." She told her. "A little knowledge can change the world. Too much knowledge can destroy it."

"That's a load of crap."

"History proves it. Those who understand something like bacteria have also created biological weapons capable of decimating an entire species. Do not think I have not learned from my time on Earth what danger knowledge can impart."

Dani shook her head. She suspected she wouldn't win any arguments with this woman, so she wasn't going to try. "The spirits showed me things, but I need help interpreting them."

"Interpretation of dreams and visions was never my skill. I knew of a man once in the land of Egypt who had this ability, but he has long since departed this world." Her hood moved as she looked pointedly at Dani. "But you do not need a talent to understand your visions. The spirits wish to show you the way. They fear the evil that has come and want you to stop it."

"Well, that's great, but until they draw me a roadmap, I'm a bit out of my depth. You can't help me?"

She shook her head. "I only play my part in this story, as I did when King Saul came to me; not to intervene, but to show. My part now is to give you these."

From beneath the table, the witch placed three boxes in front of them. Each one was made of a dark wood and engraved with symbols she recognized as angelic script. They were all about the size of a jewelry box and radiated energy unlike any Dani had ever felt. The boxes seemed to draw her forward; pulling her out of her seat. It was like she was supposed to somehow crawl inside them.

"A bane box." Kleos said, sliding his fingers along the lid of one. "They're hard to make."

"Bane box? What the hell is that?"

"They're made to contain magical artifacts or, in some cases, spirits. You put things inside you really don't want to get loose. They're like magical cloaking devices. I know of a cabinet that once held a malevolent spirit called a dybbuk. That cabinet is a bane box. The myth of Pandora's jar might be another." He flicked his eyes from the boxes to En Dor. "What are these for?"

"Your journey. The spirits say you would need them."

"I don't know where I'm going." Dani said. "That's why we came here. I don't know the first thing about stopping Asmodeus."

"I know not how to defeat the lord of lust," En Dor told her, "but there is one who does."

Dani thought she knew, "Raphael? You know where he is?"

"No, but I do know another. You must seek him through your visions. Listen for laughter and you may find him." She pushed the three boxes towards Dani. "You have not much time. The hallowed days are upon us soon."

Dani took the boxes, unsure exactly what to do with them. She tucked two into her bag and Kleos took the third.

"*Um, Dani,*" Caesar said from her perch near the curtain, "*we got a problem.*"

"What is it?" She went to the curtain where Caesar perched.

Down on the dance floor, the crowd parted as a new group arrived from the backdoor: armored Numen Powers, with purple raiments and full adamantine armor. They pushed their way into the club. There was a dozen of them.

"What is it?" asked Kleos.

"Looks like Empyrean's hunting party caught up with us and it's a party I don't want to join." She returned to En Dor, pleading, "Please, I am almost on my own with this. Is there any way you can help? Anything else you can tell me?"

"Only two things: first, the spirits have already shown you where to go, so trust your visions. And second, that you and only you can defeat the monster that hunts you."

"Why?"

"Because, by marking you, he created his own enemy: a woman who can rival his power. You must realize that if you are to defeat him."

Great. It didn't help them now and Dani had no idea if it would help her later.

With a glimmer, Idunn appeared at the curtain. She wore a long, flowing white dress emblazoned with a symbol of a golden apple. The dress practically radiated with her inner light.

"Dani? Hey. What's up? When the homunculus told me you were here, I didn't believe it."

"Thank God you're here."

"Well," she smirked, "thank *goddess*, actually. What's wrong?"

"We're in trouble."

"Trouble?" She spotted Kleos. "Uh-huh. *Riiiiiiight.* Would that have anything to do with the small platoon of soldiers that just broke into my bar?"

"Kind of."

"Kind of?" she folded her arms.

"Okay, yes, they're here looking for us. But I promise, we didn't do anything wrong." The goddess gave them a suspicious glance. Dani asked, "Are you going to turn us in?"

"To them? No." She huffed. "I've been around Numen before. Most of them are jerks. No offense." She said to Kleos.

"None taken."

"So, what's going on?"

Dani filled her in quickly, giving only the basics.

"And what's the plan to stop this Asmodeus demon?"

"There isn't one."

"Oh, well, I'm glad you thought this through." Idunn checked out through the curtain, warning her. "Those Powers are talking to Judah. I don't think he can stall them for long."

"I only have these visions. That's it." Dani was at a loss.

"But you said they came true before?"

"Yeah, but only after the fact."

"Well, maybe you need figure out what they mean *before* the fact."

"You think I haven't thought of that?"

"Well, in about fifteen minutes or less, you're going to be out of time to think. Just say what you saw out loud and maybe we can figure something out."

With a disgruntled groan, Dani poured back over her visions. "Okay, so it starts with shadow people, but we already know those are shades. There's a golden medallion, but I don't know where it is. The fish in the river is the same way; no clue. Then there's a building with a neon tree decorated with mouths and a man sitting on a bench—."

"Wait, wait. Stop. What did you just say?"

"Which part?"

"You said you saw a neon tree sign with mouths?"

"Yeah. You know it?"

"I think I might. I'll need to look it up to be sure."

"What? Is it in some magic scroll or something?"

"No," she fished in her pocket, "there's this thing called the internet. It's on everyone's phones."

It was weird to watch a goddess surf the internet, but very quickly, she found what she was looking for and showed Dani.

"It's call the Glee Tree. It's a comedy club."

"How did you know about that?"

"My husband one time tried his hand at stand up. Trust me, he should stick to poetry and songs."

Dani cradled the phone. The picture looked exactly like her vision. "We have to get there. Can you write these directions down?"

She waved it off. "Take the phone. I'm in need of an upgrade, anyway."

Dani felt strange putting it into her pocket, considering she hadn't held anything modern in about a year. "Is there any way you could help us out with one more thing?"

"Like?"

"Can you get us out of here before the Powers see us?"

Idunn glanced over her shoulder again, then back at Dani. "There are way too many of them and they have every entrance blocked."

Dani frowned. "We could try some sort of distraction to open up an exit, but I'm not sure what we could do that wouldn't get us caught."

The goddess grinned toothily.

Dani noticed. "What?"

"I got an idea."

"What is it?"

"Oh," she said innocently, "something that might get me fired."

Idunn told them to wait. For what, Dani had no idea. She asked Idunn where she was going as she departed.

Idunn winked, "To make a mess."

The goddess descended the stairs to the ground floor and made her way towards the bar. Judah was arguing with the Powers' commander, or at least it looked that way from up here.

"What do you think she'll do?" Kleos asked from beside her.

"Nothing reckless." Dani assured him. "She's pretty level-headed."

Idunn strode across the main floor, making a bee-line right for them. A Powers soldier stepped in her way. "Halt!"

Idunn grabbed him and chucked him across the room into three of his fellow soldiers.

"Uh," Dani said, "I meant she's mostly level-headed."

Screams erupted; some in surprise, some in fear, and some in laughter. A good ol' fashioned bar fight was always entertaining. A soldier drew his sword and swung at Idunn's neck. She blocked it, glaring fiercely at him over the blade. A cut in her skin dribbled something like liquid gold from her cheek.

Idunn's punch knocked the man unconscious, despite the helmet he wore.

"Idunn! Stop!" Judah cried. "What are you doing?"

The commander drew his own sword. "Seize her!"

Idunn snatched an elixir bottle from the nearby tabletop and hurtled it across the room. It smashed into the commander's face, sending him to the floor.

The Powers surrounded her. Idunn was outnumbered. But as they attacked, she thrashed each one of them. One soldier got his leg snapped at the knee. Another took a punch so hard it dented his helmet. Idunn threw another into a wall hard enough to cave-in the plaster.

It was just the distraction they needed.

As the club-goers erupted in uproar, Kleos and Dani took off from the booth through the crowd. Shoving people and creatures aside, they descended the steps as soldiers left their posts to help their comrades.

Idunn launched another soldier into the ceiling and smashed one of the overhead lights. A second crashed through the stage where a similarly-glowing god had been setting up for his poetry slam.

"Idunn!" He chastised. "Idunn! My beloved! What are you doing?"

Idunn screamed at the crowd of Numen, who now second-guessed attacking her. "Thor's thunderous balls! Are you men or mice? Give me a real fight!"

"Idunn!" Her husband screamed. "Stop it! You're ruining everything!"

"Forseti," Idunn kicked a soldier, took his sword and hurled it at another Power, "will you please, for once, just support me?"

"There!" Someone screamed over the commotion. As Kleos and Dani reached an exit, one soldier pointed at them. "It's the Novice! She's—!"

He didn't finish. Idunn hit him with a table.

Dani, Kleos and Caesar crammed through the door and ran to the front exit. They burst out the front doors. The air was cool and clear of clouds.

They flew off into the setting sun.

Dani had forgotten how loud L.A. was at night. And how it smelled. A year living in a celestial city magnified every sensation on Earth. And, despite how most would hate the noise and the odor, Dani loved it all.

The sun finally set. The lights of Los Angeles made for a multicolored starscape below her.

They flew far enough to put some distance between them and the Powers. Idunn gave them plenty of time. No one followed and Caesar hung back to keep an eye out.

They settled down back on terra firma after twenty minutes. L.A. had a lot of parks. This time of night, the one they chose was mostly clear.

"How the hell did they find us?" Dani asked as soon as they dropped down. "We weren't even there an hour!"

"I don't think they did." Kleos said, settling down on a picnic table. "I think they guessed."

"Guessed?"

"You are a known friend of Judah's. I guess they figured you go there eventually."

She shook her head miserably, "I got him in so much trouble."

"Trust me: Judah can take it. He may look like a jovial sort of fellow, but he is by and far one of the most powerful men I have ever encountered. Empyrean will hesitate before they seek to punish him."

That made her feel only a little bit better.

Kleos unwrapped a piece of cloth from his bag full of dried meat. He tore off a chunk and chewed, then offered it to her, "Keresh jerky?"

"*Oooooo*, you know what I want? A fish taco!"

"A fish taco?"

Dani grinned. "Uh-huh. There's this one food truck in downtown L.A. called Peter and Simon's, where we'd always go to when my mom had money to spare. Best fish tacos I've ever had. Think we could grab one on the go?"

"You mean as we're getting chased by Empyrean soldiers and specters raised by an ancient evil?"

"Kleos, it's fish tacos. Anything is worth fish tacos."

But they didn't go and instead ate jerky in silence. The meat was enough to fill her up, even though she ate very little. Magical creature-meat like keresh could do that, she guessed. As they ate, she scrolled through Idunn's phone.

"You know how to use that?" He asked.

"I'm sixteen and from Los Angeles. What do you think?"

Again, Dani was struck by how odd it was to hold the phone; both because of who owned it—a goddess of all people—and by handling one in so long.

"Looks like the Glee Tree is in," she frowned, "Long Beach."

"Is there something wrong with Long Beach?"

"You mean other than the crappy air and grab-happy surfers? No." She grinned. "Actually, the air isn't that bad."

"We should go then." He hopped down.

"Wait." Dani told him. "We need to talk."

"About?"

"About Nazir. And Michael. And all of them."

Kleos frowned. "What do you mean?"

"Don't play dumb." Dani hopped off the table, too. "Nazir is a shade. So is Michael."

"We knew Asmodeus could raise the dead."

"Yeah, and then sick them on us! Kleos, Nazir was out for blood. Yeah, he might be some undead-jerk now, but he's an undead-jerk who wants you dead. I don't think it's just because some all-consuming evil made him do it." She looked him squarely in the eye. "Why does Nazir hate you? Even before he was a shade, he despised you. Back there, he brought up Titus and—."

Kleos cut her off angrily. "I don't want to talk about it."

"Tough."

"I can have my own secrets, Dani."

"If they concern me, then secrets-secrets are no fun, you better tell everyone."

His jaw tensed under his beard. Kleos was always so zen, so it was odd to see him upset. "It's personal. Besides, you don't have to worry about it. He's gone."

"Not for good."

"What do you mean?"

"One of those ghosts back there? It was from Beri'ah."

"And?"

"And Michael already killed it."

"You mean it came back? Even after it was killed?"

"Uh-huh. I'm thinking that it's not unique, either. Care to explain how you can kill something and it doesn't stay dead?"

His frown deepened. "Shades are souls."

"Uh-huh. You explained that part. They're stitched together like a Rainbow Quilt of Nightmares. And?"

"Souls are immortal." He explained. "They may be the shadow-aspects of the psyche, but they're still human. They're still souls. When humans die, they can't be obliterated from existence."

"Which means Asmodeus has an undead, unstoppable army?" Dani folded her arms. "*Madre de Díos.*"

"We need to stop Asmodeus as quickly as possible." Kleos confirmed. "If you're right and he arrives on Allhallowtide, he'll have an even larger army than he did before."

"Long Beach it is, then. And I have a feeling I know who we are looking for."

"Who?"

Listen for laughter and you may find him.

Gabriel did say Raphael's bannerman was the angel of laughter.

Chapter Twenty-Two

Long Beach wasn't far by air. From the night sky, it was just as pretty as Los Angeles; all grab-happy surfers aside. Downtown along the water was a rainbow of hotels, night-clubs, and hot spots. The Walter Pyramid, the LBSU campus stadium with its dark blue aluminum siding, lit up with its own back lights in the distance. Out on the water, the beautiful profile of the Queen Mary drifted in its moors.

Using Idunn's phone, she guided the three of them down towards the waterfront off Ocean Avenue.

The Glee Tree wasn't a glitzy hotspot like some of the clubs and bars in the area. Snuggled between two mega-hotels, the ramshackle place looked like it had just dropped out of Satan's butt crack. The place was filthy-looking, lit up with its green neon tree sign covered with laughing mouths; just like her vision. This was where they needed to be.

They landed under the power of the veil and crossed the street.

"Caesar, keep an eye out for us?"

"*Sure thing, chica. I'm hungry anyway. I wonder if there are any seagulls to eat around here.*" Then she was gone.

"This is where we need to be?" Kleos didn't look like he believed her, following Dani up the ramp outside the comedy club. "Angels are mystical beings that helped forge the universe and all of Creation. What kind of angel would be in a place like a comedy club?"

"One who had a hand in inventing comedy."

The inside was dark, gloomy, and stank of beer and bar food. Perfect. Dani wrapped herself up in the veil, going for total invisibility. The club was a wide-open layout, with a stage up front, a bar and tables littering the main floor. Dani scanned the crowd.

"Gabriel told me the angel of laughter was Raphael's bannerman, right?" They wove through the different patrons, who all watched as a comedian took the stage. "They called him Sechoquel. If Asmodeus was defeated by Raphael, and this angel is his...whatever a bannerman is...then he may know how to stop Asmodeus."

On stage, a comedian was getting a round of laughter. He looked like a lot of comics: everyday clothes, cap over his brow, and mike in hand.

"I used to teach." He said, shaking his head. "God that makes me scared for the future of our country." A few chuckles filtered through the crowd. "I was once reading this article with the kids about bears. Exciting, I know. So, we're reading it and the article says that 'bears kill on average two to three people per year.' Anyway, this punk in my class raises his hand and I swear to God asks me, 'Um, sir, how do bears know to only kill two to three people per year?'" A few of the audience members chuckled. "I know, right? And

I'm sitting there like, 'Oh dear sweet Jesus, does this kid actually think bears _try_ to only kill two or three people? Like they're holding back?' Does he imagine there's some bear out there sitting at a computer, typing emails out to other bears, like 'Yo, Frank, quit killing people. You're throwing off the national average. We talked about this after that Goldilocks incident.'"

They took seats at a table next to a larger guy in a Hawaiian shirt. Kleos glanced around. "I don't see anyone who screams 'angel' to me."

"Me neither, but then again, how would we know?"

"What was Gabriel like?"

"Tall, muscular, sort of...I don't know...neutral."

"Neutral?"

"Not male or female. He didn't seem to fit the whole 'human' thing."

"Yeah, definitely don't see anyone like that."

Up front, the teacher comedian finished up with one last joke. "And I was like, 'Hey, this is a test. You need to have a pencil.' And the girl tells me, 'Mister, I didn't bring one.' And I point to the pencil on her desk and say, 'there's one.' And she tells me, 'Um, that's a pencil for my eyebrows.'" Laughter erupted. "And at this point, I can only ask, 'So you brought a pencil for your eyebrows and not your test?' Which, of course, she answers by telling me, 'Um, yeah. Duh. My eyebrows got to be looking fresh.'"

Even Dani laughed.

"That's my time ladies and gentlemen!" The comedian waved. "You've been great!" And he left to another round of applause.

As he stepped down, headed for the back, something occurred to Dani. "Oh my God."

"What?"

He disappeared out the back door. She jumped to her feet. "It's him."

"Who?"

"The comedian. He's the angel of laughter, right?"

"Yeah. So?" Then Kleos caught on. "If he's here, he'd want people to laugh. You're saying that was him?"

"Could be. Come on." They wove away from the table, the only other occupant not even aware they'd been there.

They burst out the back door. The comedian was waiting there. Dani and Kleos slowed, still behind the veil. They waited for him to turn. If he could see them, then he definitely wasn't what he appeared to be.

The man slowly turned. It had to be him. He was waiting for them, like he knew...

He turned around and held a cell phone to ear. "Yeah." He said to the person on the other end of the line. "It went great. Yeah...yeah, totally killed it. Uh-huh."

He looked up to where they were, but Dani could tell he was looking through them. He didn't see them.

He was mundani.

"Thanks. Bye." He hung up, picked up a cigarette nearby, and took a final puff. Then he snuffed it out and walked past them back inside.

Dani frowned in disappointment. "I could have sworn it was him."

"Maybe he isn't here." Kleos offered.

"My visions brought me here. He's the angel of laughter. He would want people to laugh."

"Or be attracted to any place that is full of laughter."

The last wasn't from Kleos, but a voice behind them. The two turned around. Standing behind them was the guy in the Hawaiian shirt; the one from their table. Except he wasn't just a guy. Dani recognized him from his stand-up and signature Hawaiian attire. His skin tone was similar to hers and he grinned widely.

He also looked right at them. Humans wouldn't be able to do that.

"You—You're—!"

"Dude, I know, right?" He asked giddily. "At first, I was like: *screeeeech!* Pump the brakes. This is the guy I appear as here?"

He even did the sound effects like him. She stared at the rather "fluffy" individual.

"But you...you look like..." she was having a hard time wrapping her brain around it. "You look like him. Are you him?"

The big man shook his head, grinning. "No. He's on tour right now. I'm just borrowing his appearance for a little bit."

Kleos looked the most stunned of the two of them. By instinct, he reached for where his sword would be, but not only could the man—er, angel—see through their invisibility, he could see through their disguises as well. With a wave of his hand, Kleos' adamantine xiphos appeared in the angel's hand.

"I wouldn't do that, bro." His face was serious; more so than the comic he pretended to be.

"You're Sechoquel?"

He nodded.

"Why do you look like that?"

"What else am I supposed to look like?"

"I don't know...angel-y?"

"Oh, you mean like this?"

The overhead orange streetlight flickered and died, but a new orange glow burst from the man's back and formed a pair of translucent ginger wings.

Dani and Kleos backed up a step, awed.

179

The glow faded. The angel said, "But, if you're asking why I look like this dude, well, that's because since I invented laughter, I take the form of anyone who brings laughter. It's kind of my thing."

Dani couldn't help but ask, "Even women?"

The angel's large form blurred, like vibrating at a high speed. Instead of a fluffy Mexican, he (or was it she?) now transformed into a blonde with perfect skin, pink lipstick and a penchant for sex jokes.

"Laughter has no gender." The angel said in her voice. She crossed her arms. "Now, what are you two doing here? I've never had a Numen seek me out, especially," he/she glanced at Dani, "one like you."

"I'm Dani. This is Kleos. We're—."

"Earthborn. Uh-huh." The angel tossed the sword back to him. "I know what Numen are. I haven't been living under a rock. But I asked why *you* two are here; you specifically?"

"Well, Sechoquel—."

She held up a hand. "Please, I dropped that name a long time ago. It's too hard to pronounce and when I Google it, all that comes up is an anti-depressant, which is totally ironic."

"So, you changed your name? Can you do that?"

Sechoquel shrugged. "It worked for Katy Perry."

"Who's Katy Perry?" Kleos asked.

Dani ignored him. "So, what do we call you?"

"Haniel." The angel answered. "It was Anael for a while, but you can guess why I don't use that anymore." She blushed. "Sorry, that was crude. I sometimes take on the traits of the person I embody. You were saying about why you were here?"

"We need your help."

"With what?"

"With who." Kleos told her. "Asmodeus."

"Ugh! I'm familiar with that cling-on from the butt crack of Hell. I didn't think he'd ever get out."

"Get out? You mean out of Hell?"

"No, out of his—." She paused, narrowing her eyes. "Wait. How did that thing escape? My master bound that trash for all eternity. There's no way he got out unless something or someone helped him."

"A Fury named Alecto released him."

"With what?"

"The Horn of Gabriel."

The blonde grunted in disgust. "Leave it to *that* phallic symbol to screw the universe. Gabriel loves that stupid thing. It's 'his truth' or whatever. He could never get rid of it, even though it had the potential to mess up everything. So why are you here to talk to me?"

"We have no idea." Kleos confessed.

"Come again?"

Before Dani could answer, Sechoquel— or Haniel,—changed form again. Now, instead of a tall, leggy blonde, he was a short, black man.

"That's creepy, you know." Dani told him.

He glanced at himself. "Oh, thank God! I thought it would be the guy with the puppets."

"We're here," Dani said, trying to keep her anger under control and stay on track, "because my visions brought me here. And since you're here, you're supposed to help us."

"Well, I can't help you. I don't know the first thing about what to do."

Kleos removed a bane box from his bag. "We were given these. Does that help?"

Haniel stared at the boxes. He may not have been human, but he had a very human expression: fear.

"You know what those are?" Dani pressed. "I'm thinking you know what's supposed to go in them."

"You have three of them?"

She nodded.

"Then I may know."

"You know the story of Tobias, right?"

Haniel changed form yet again and this was a weird one. He was a hard-drinking Texan. After four stiff Scotches and a full cigar burnt to a snub, Dani understood what Haniel meant by "taking on the traits" of a comedian.

"We know the story." Kleos confirmed.

"Then you know my master helped Tobias defeat Asmodeus?"

"They saved a woman Tobias married. Sarah, I think."

He puffed out a long trail of smoke. "You know Sarah was Tobias' cousin, right?"

"What?" Dani shook herself. "Eww!"

He shrugged, finished with the cigar. "Ancient times. Humans are weird. Doesn't matter. What does matter is how my master stopped Asmodeus. Or rather, how he helped Tobias stop him."

"Yeah. The legend is fuzzy on the details about that." Dani said. "I thought angels don't intervene with humans anymore."

"I see you've been talking to Gabriel. So, you know why?"

She nodded. Kleos shook his head. "I don't."

"Trust me, you don't want to know." She assured Kleos. "Haniel, how did Raphael stop him?"

"Short answer: he didn't." Haniel dabbed his cigar into the ash tray, "Raphael gave Tobias the weapons to defeat the demon on his own."

"Weapons?"

"Magical artifacts," he held up his thick fingers, "three of them."

Dani glanced down at the bane boxes in their bags. "The boxes are for those things?"

He nodded. "My master knew of three things that could be used to stop such a powerful creature. He helped Tobias find them and with them, Tobias could drive away the demon and bind him forever. I think, if you have those boxes, that you're supposed to find them as well."

"What are these artifacts?"

Haniel sat back, frowning, "Well, there's a fish's guts."

"What?"

"Then a ring and a seal."

"Seal?"

"A medallion. It's what my master sealed Asmodeus in the first time." He explained. "Asmodeus was never banished to Hell. He survived the War in Heaven. When Prince Raphael defeated him, he instead bound him in a gold seal."

Something clicked in Dani's brain. *A golden medallion, engraved with a symbol, laid in fiery coals.* It was the same picture she saw in the tome about Asmodeus. "I've seen it. Do you know where it is?"

"Last I saw, Raphael buried it in upper Egypt, in the middle of a desolate desert."

"Wait, wait, wait, you mean *Egypt*, Egypt?"

"Well, that's not helpful." Kleos grumbled. "Egypt is a big country."

"And on the other side of the globe!" Dani pointed out, as if he forgot.

"Well, can't help you there." Haniel shrugged.

"How the hell are we supposed to get to Egypt, let alone find this medallion, before Allhallowtide?"

Haniel blurred and changed form. Now he was a thin, elderly man with a beard. Dani didn't know the comedian, since he died over a decade ago.

"Will you stop doing that?!" She snapped.

"Allhallowtide?" Haniel asked. "What about Allhallowtide?"

Kleos told him, "That is when Asmodeus comes to Los Angeles. He has an army of shades and we think he's going to attack Empyrean. He did it to Beri'ah."

"My master's city?" Haniel looked surprised. "That's impossible. The city is protected by—!" And then he stopped.

"Protected by what?" Dani asked. Her eyes narrowed. "You know something. Spit it out."

Haniel sighed. "Every celestial city was once a fortress to an archangel."

"And?"

"And each city has an artifact of the archangel within it."

"In the Fane, you mean."

"Or somewhere." He shrugged. "But the artifact also controls the magical border around the city—the firmament. No demon could break through unless allowed in, or unless the artifact was removed."

"What was in Beri'ah?"

"My master's ring; one of the artifacts you need." He shook his head. "No one should know of its existence."

"Well, someone did, and they took it." Dani remembered the arm of the statue, ripped off at the wrist. "Haniel, please, we need to know more. You have to help us."

"We aren't supposed to interfere."

"Then help us the way Raphael helped Tobias. We'll stop him. You just tell us where to go."

The angel frowned, lacing his fingers together on the table. He was silent; his eyes closed.

A long silence passed between them.

"Haniel?" Dani asked, irked.

His eyes snapped open. "Berkeley."

"Excuse me?"

"You need to go to Berkeley."

"Why?"

"One of the artifacts is there."

"In ancient times, Raphael hid one of these weapons in California?"

He shrugged. "All I know is that one of them is there. These things are special to my master. I can...I don't know...feel them when they are nearby."

Dani sort of understood. Gabriel didn't know who betrayed Empyrean, but he "felt" them when they were in the city.

"Go there. Find whatever it is. In the meantime, I'll look for the next one."

Kleos and Dani exchanged a look. What else could they do? "How do we get there?"

"Take Interstate Five. It's the fastest. There's a bus leaving in the next ten minutes."

"How do you know?"

"I'm an angel. We know things." Two tickets appeared in is hand. "You should get going. If you flew here, I'm pretty sure Empyrean is tracking you."

Dani took the tickets. "Thanks."

"One more thing: Asmodeus is not stupid. He knows you'll be coming for him and those artifacts wherever they may be. He may even want you to do it." He looked pointedly at Dani. "Expect him to try to stop you."

His form changed one last time. This one wasn't a standup comedian. He was from a show. Blonde, trim, and in a suit, he held one hand aloft. "High-five!"

Shaking her head, she left him hanging.

Chapter Twenty-Three

They made it to the bus on time. It was headed for Oakland, California; just south of Berkeley and San Francisco. They settled down onto the bus as it drove through the night.

But neither of them could sleep. Since this afternoon, they'd been on the run. Sitting still helped calm them down, but not enough to sleep.

Dani removed the black, obsidian mirror Bouden gave her. She used them once before. She whispered the angelic incantation, then said, "Show me Mastema."

She was concerned for her Guardian first. The mirror shimmered and showed her home. Mastema sat in the middle of the pavilion, as if in meditation, but he wasn't alone.

"We know you helped her escape." A voice said.

Dani realized Mastema's mirror lay off to one side of the pavilion; whether by design or by accident, it faced him. Someone stepped into the frame.

"We cannot prove it," Elder Maalik said, arms folded, "but when we do, you will suffer."

"I have nothing to tell you," Mastema opened his eyes, feigning boredom, "just as I had nothing for Elder Heman."

"Someone caused a diversion that allowed her to slip through the East Gate. Do not pretend you know nothing."

"I do not pretend. I know not where she has gone or what she is doing, but I believe what she is doing is right."

Maalik turned, disgusted, and left.

"Ethan." Dani whispered.

The mirror changed. Nothing. She stared at the ceiling; probably of Ethan's room. He wasn't there. She prayed he was alright.

"Bouden."

The mirror changed. At first, she didn't understand what she saw. The image shook and swung, as if moving in someone's hand. Dani saw it sometimes when people walked and FaceTimed. Then, Bouden's image floated into view.

"Dani?"

"Hey."

"I can't believe the mirrors worked! Is Kleos with you?"

She showed him. "We're fine. We're on our way—."

"Don't." he warned, glancing around. "I shouldn't know where you are."

"Why?"

"Because we're all being watched. The Council has declared you both fugitives for escaping. They sent a small battalion of soldiers to capture you."

"Yeah. We ran into them at Judah's club." Dani grumbled. "How bad is it?"

"Bad."

"Are they at least preparing for Asmodeus?"

He frowned. "Sort of."

"Sort of?"

"I don't know all the details, but you know how rumors go. From what I gathered, some want to while others don't think it's going to happen; like it's a conspiracy you concocted. Want to guess which Elders think you're lying?"

"I don't have to guess." Dani said.

"But there's a few. Elder Jeduthun seems to think it will happen. He's ordered what Powers he can to return to the city. But Heman, from what I hear, is fighting him on that."

"Great."

"Weirdly, you got one person who believes you most."

"Who?"

"Asaph."

That surprised her. "But he hates me."

"He also cares about the city. He's increased patrols. He's tightened security. Of course, that may be because you slipped out."

"If he's protecting the city, I don't care either way." Dani didn't like how defenseless the city was, especially knowing what was coming. "Where is Empyrean searching for us? Do you know?"

"I overheard some Powers talking about south of Los Angeles. Long Beach? You're not there, are you?"

"No, but you're right. We shouldn't tell you where we are."

"We'll keep the mirrors hidden for as long as we can. Look, there's something you should know: a storm is coming."

"Is that a metaphor?"

"No, an actual storm. Empyrean monitors the weather on Earth; looking for omens. A few hours ago, they picked up something weird. I spent some of my time up in the Citadel's Tower—you know, the one above the Armory?"

Dani knew it. The Armory took up several floors, but the Tower also held an observatory where they could send aerwhispers over long distances and, apparently, monitor other things.

"We know it." She confirmed. "And? They found a storm?"

"In the middle of the Pacific; coming this way." He looked worried. "Dani, the way they talk about it, it's not a normal storm. Something is driving it. It's not following any kind of weather patterns. And it's headed for L.A."

A massive storm of black clouds and shapes darting between them. A dark beast standing on a sandy beach, the same terrible storm behind it.

"Well, looks like another one of my visions is coming true."

"Officially, the Council says we shouldn't worry about it."

"Heman, you mean. Is he brainless or does he _want_ Empyrean to be destroyed?"

"You said the demons had an inside man."

That was true. But as much of a jerk as Heman could be, she didn't see him as traitorous. Still...

"Thanks Bouden. I need you to do something for me."

"Okay."

"Those monsters you researched? Shades? I need you to find a way to tell Elder Jeduthun, or anyone who will listen, that they're immortal."

"Immortal?"

"They can't be killed; permanently, anyway. Make it sound likes it's your own research, but let them know it's impossible to kill them. And tell them," she paused, hating to tell him, "tell them that anyone who died in Beri'ah is one of them; including our people."

Bouden's face fell. "They are?"

"I'm sorry, but we saw it ourselves. A group of them is hunting us."

He nodded solemnly. "I'll do what I can."

"Thanks."

"Just look out for yourself, *chica fuerte.*"

"I really hate that nickname."

"Tell that to Nathaniel. He's made it his mission to make sure we all call you that."

"I'll get Nate back for that later."

Bouden signed off. Dani put the mirror back and slumped down. She was worried, but now she was worried for her friends as well as herself.

"They'll be okay." Kleos assured her.

"Yeah. And pigs will fly."

"In our world, they sometimes do."

Halfway into their trip down Interstate Five, they pulled over at a rest area. The bus driver told them they had a few minutes to stretch their legs and use the bathroom. Dani needed to do the latter.

"Don't go far." Kleos called after her as she hopped off the bus and headed for the lavatories.

"What the hell is going to happen to me in the john?" She called back.

"You'd be surprised what lurks in there!"

"How would you know? Do you go into the women's toilets?"

The restroom was empty when she walked into the fluorescent-lit commode. Unfortunately, as Dani's senses were heightened by living in Empyrean, it worked against her now. She could sense things dozens of feet away, which was helpful with demons, but not helpful when going to the bathroom. The woman's lavatory stunk of disinfectant, soap and— underneath it all—the smell every bathroom couldn't eradicate.

Great. Demon-hunting senses now make it impossible to use the can. The place stunk.

Dani did her business quickly. After leaving the stall, her sword-belt over one shoulder since she took it off to use the facilities, she washed her hands under the cold spray from the faucet.

The lavatory was quiet, but the buzz of the florescent lights hummed and filled the space. The water rushing got a little louder. Dani didn't notice it at first, but her toilet hadn't stopped draining.

Then a second faucet came on by itself. Then a third. Then all of them.

The light flickered overhead. The buzzing got louder. Her toilet flushed again. Then all the toilets went off.

Okaaaaay. She grabbed a paper towel, drying her hands. The toilets were automatic flushers, sure, but all of them going off at once? That was too weird.

The hand-dryers roared to life. Dani belted her swords and drew Pointyend.

One of the stainless-steel toilets, the farthest down the line, rumbled and shook. The tile cracked underneath. Dani crouched cautiously, peering under the stalls. The steel bowl jiggled back and forth, continuing to flush. Dani knew she needed to leave. She backed towards the door.

The toilet exploded off the floor and crashed through the stall, spewing water and a lot of other things against the walls in a sick, putrid spray.

Dani's hand flew over her nose and gagged. The whole room turned into a toxic dump.

But as Dani crouched back from the smell, the stall door of the Amazing Exploding Toilet blew out and something shambled free; slithering from the depths of the hole it just blew in the floor.

She almost didn't see the human-looking part of it; a full-bodied man with a bare upper chest. She was more distracted by the slimy, putrid locks of sickly, stringy hair that were slathered about its face. It reminded her of dreadlocks, if someone made dreadlocks from sewage. Its hands were claws that scraped on the tile as it hoisted itself to its feet.

He was a nauseating mixture of a lot of colors Dani didn't want to see. Nothing should be brown, green and yellow. Ever.

"Oh God!" She groaned, covering her mouth. "What the hell?"

The creature coughed, hacking out a wad of yellow phlegm onto the floor. Dani literally tasted the bile in the back of her throat. The creature turned towards her. The two stared at one another for a minute.

"Hello." It croaked.

"Uh...hi."

"I didn't think I'd catch you in time."

"Who are you?"

It grinned, inhaling a loud ball of snot from its sinuses. "My name is Cholera."

"Cholera?" She glanced at the door behind her. "What, was something normal like Frank taken?"

"Don't run." The demon warned.

"Yeah, well, sorry, but I don't take advice from sewer monsters."

"If you run, it'll be more difficult for us to not hurt you."

"Us?"

More toilets exploded. Dani turned to run but one commode nearly took her head off. She had to roll out of the way. More sewage creatures crawled their way out.

"Get her!" The first croaked.

The sewer monster spit a wad of slime into its sickly hand—a loogie the size of a baseball—and then chucked it across the room at her. Dani dove sideways as the wretched ball of phlegm struck the wall behind her and cracked the tile on impact. When she looked back, the thick slime congealed into a hardened, calcified shell.

The other monsters began hurling up their own ammunition.

"Oh crap..."

She ran for the door and felt, rather than saw, another slime-ball coming. Dani ducked and it hit the door, smashing it off its hinges.

"You have a price on you!" The leader, Cholera, warned. "We're here to collect! Don't run!"

"Yeah, like I'm going to listen to you, Pooper-Scooper!"

She dodged through the door and heard the monsters coming after her; their scrambling sounding wet and slippery. Dani kicked the door closed right in the face of the lead creature. It bought her a few seconds and she ran for it.

She crossed into the open. She inhaled fresh air gratefully, but she could still smell the pursuing monsters. Her empyreal sword lit the darkness ahead.

Then she was hit.

A slime-ball caught her left leg. The slug of sewage exploded and Dani fell, rolling onto the pavement just outside the bathroom. The sewer creatures fanned out, all carrying large, gooey projectiles that dribbled onto the sidewalk.

"I told you," Cholera said, "to not run."

Dani tried to move her leg, but it couldn't. The slime congealed, turning into a hardened case.

It threw another. Dani cut it in half in mid-air.

The wad exploded. She moaned in disgust as the blast threw her backwards into a tree, sticking her to it. The stuff was revolting! Her arms, sword, torso, even her hair were all splattered with the foulest smell imaginable. The sludge hardened. The muck turned into a casing that locked up both her arms. Her neck was braced in place and stuck to the trunk.

The creatures shambled towards her, their putrid bodies shimmering in the light of the street lamp. Dani heard screams; people seeing the creatures for what they were, if only briefly.

"What," she choked, "what do you want?"

"Asmodeus pays well. He hired us to keep a look out for you."

"Hired...?"

Cholera grinned through twisted teeth. "Me and my people," it gestured to the group around it, "are going to make it big with the boss by bringing you to him. My kind doesn't usually get much respect."

"I wonder why. Bet you all are treated like the crap."

This was how she would die: making jokes. Fitting.

"I hear he wants you bad." Cholera growled. "Bad enough to work with us, anyway. Whatever he plans to do to you, I bet it's going to be slow and painful."

"Screw you."

It raised its hand, slime-ball ready. So did several of its buddies.

Then something flashed through the air and struck one between the eyes. The creature's mouth dropped open right before it dropped onto its back and dissolved into shapeless sewage.

"HEY! ŠULAK!"

Kleos appeared from the veil, xiphos in hand. There were five of the things left. He cut the head off one, and then launched several adamantine throwing knives into the chest of another.

"Kill him!"

The remaining two hurled their phlegm projectiles. Kleos ducked them, summoning Aer and launching up. As he came down towards them, the tree above Dani moved. Using Erthe, he forced a branch down that lashed the face of an unsuspecting monster. He landed a kick on the other.

When they ended up on their backs, Kleos stabbed both right through their hearts.

Cholera, the last surviving of the toilet-terrors, grabbed Kleos around the throat and knocked his blade from his hand. But Dani, summoning the warmth of her lightbringing, blasted through the vile casing around her hand and hit it in the shoulder.

Kleos snatched up his sword, spun, and decapitated the final one. It exploded into putrid slush.

Slime splattered outwards. Kleos staggered back, his raiments covered in sewer sludge. Dani had turned her head away, but that did little to stop the vile shower of monster parts as it died.

And the smell? Ugh!

Kleos flicked his sword, cleaning the silvery surface. He winced apologetically at Dani. "Sorry."

She felt the smallest trickle of something running down her forehead. She did *not* want to know what it was.

Chapter Twenty-Four

"A šulak?" She asked as Kleos freed her from the demon's slime trap. "What the hell is a šulak?"

The bathroom was destroyed. Water spewed out all over the floor from the ruined toilets and muck covered almost every surface. Police arrived. Dani could overhear bits of conversation from on-lookers; all of whom saw what happened. They were talking about M-80s in the toilets and not creatures crawling out of them. The veil already convinced them what they saw was wrong. The Aether was strong.

Kleos used an elixir called azoth on the slime. It dissolved and he cleaned it off harmlessly.

"A šulak is a demon of the privy."

"Privy?"

"Toilet. We call them lurkers or hitters."

"There's seriously such a thing as a demon of the toilet?"

"There's a demon for everything."

"Yeah, like phone apps." She grumbled.

Kleos removed another vial that Dani recognized panacea. "These demons were very common in Babylonian times; spreading disease, causing ailments, things like that. Now they're basically bottom feeders in most major cities. They rarely, if ever, come above ground. They mostly feed on waste."

"What's the panacea for?"

"Well, šulaks are vile creatures. Even other demons avoid them. Since they spend all their time in sewers, there's no telling what diseases he might have given you; Hepatitis A, typhoid, or who knows what else. I'd be willing to bet you got at least one enterovirus. You should take this before you get sick."

Dani gladly downed half the bottle. "Asmodeus," She coughed, despising the awful taste of the elixir, "Asmodeus sent them. He said they were 'hired,' whatever the hell that means."

"We call them hitters, not just because they hit you with all kinds of nasty stuff, but because other demons only hire them collect a contract on someone. They're like demonic hitmen. Šulaks are so gross even hellspawn despise them."

"No argument here."

He helped her up. "What were they doing here?"

"My guess: lookouts." Dani shook her head. "Something tells me we're on the right track if these things were waiting for us."

"You think whatever's in Berkeley, Asmodeus wants to protect?"

"I'm betting that, yeah."

"I got Caesar overhead on watch, but we should get going. Hopefully, if there's no more stops, we won't run into any more of these things."

They returned to the bus. As they did, Dani swore when she looked back that she saw shadows at the edges of the parking lot move. Inky shapes peeled away and stepped into the light.

Shades.

She ducked inside the bus and it rumbled off. Hopefully, they wouldn't be followed.

They passed Bakersfield in the middle of the night and tried to get some sleep. The azoth did enough to wash off the slime and not make them stink, but the whole encounter was unsettling.

Šulaks. She could add that to the list of demons she never wanted to see again.

As morning came, Dani was on Idunn's phone. She borrowed a charger—stole it, actually—and used it to look up Berkeley. She was still searching when they got off the bus at the Oakland terminal.

"Anything?" Kleos asked.

"Maybe. I'm thinking we need to go to UC Berkeley."

"Why?"

She showed him. "The Phoebe A. Hearst Museum of Anthropology." They passed through the crowd towards the street. "It's a museum known for a lot of things, but among them: an exhibit of rare Egyptian artifacts from the upper Nile."

"You think the medallion is there?"

"It makes sense. Haniel said Raphael buried Asmodeus in a gold medallion or seal or whatever in upper Egypt. What if it got accidentally excavated?"

"Anything about it online?"

"Nope, but this is the best bet."

Kleos grabbed her arm and stopped her, then shoved her behind a passing couple. She almost asked what he was doing, but he hissed, "Keep your head down."

"What is it?"

"Wraiths."

She spotted them ahead. A squad car had two officers standing next to it, watching the crowd. But when Dani peered close, she could see the cops had milky-white eyes.

Wraiths. Demonic beasts.

"Keep close to the people in front of us." Kleos whispered. "The woman's perfume is strong. Let their smell mask ours."

The wraiths sniffed the air, looking in their direction, but they were already past them by the time the couple ahead peeled off. By then, they were too far away to smell the Numen.

"Jeez, wraith cops?" Dani asked as they hurried towards the taxis ahead. "I thought they only picked on homeless people."

"Port cities are lousy with wraiths." Kleos told her. "The high transient population and the comings and goings of shore men and dock workers make them ideal for their kind. They can hunt without attracting attention." He shuddered. "Not to mention some of them are in human trafficking."

Dani did not want to think about that. It only pissed her off more. "That can't be happening."

"A lot of developed countries like the U.S. think their cities are safe, but in reality, they aren't. Human governments leave their people to nearly third-world conditions more than they care to admit. It's inconvenient for people in authority to acknowledge they suck at it. When they don't do something about the problems, wraiths move in. And it's not just port cities. Empyrean has been fighting a non-stop war for decades: Detroit, Houston, Baltimore...any place they don't address rampant drugs, poverty or human trafficking, the wraiths find a home. And that is just in this country. If it's this bad here, imagine how dad it is in the lesser developed countries."

They caught a cab and headed out of Oakland in the direction of the college.

Berkeley was a beautiful city. Dani had never been there. She rarely, if ever, went outside Los Angeles. Named for some bishop in the early eighteenth century, according to a pamphlet in the cab, it sat on the east shore of the San Francisco Bay. At times, when they could see the Bay, they could spot the rolling hills and the central tower of the more famous sister city. But Berkeley was just as beautiful. A lot of modern deco mixed with studio buildings and old mid-nineties style, the city was that kind of pretty that came with both age and modernity.

The town was just waking up when they arrived at the UC campus. Dani was exhausted, but they had a task in front of them.

"The Hearst Museum is on campus." She said as they exited the cab. It pulled away, the driver convinced by the veil that they had paid. "We'll need to find..."

She trailed off. The campus was already swarming with people; college students, professors, campus maintenance staff. But all Dani could stare at was the buildings. She'd never been to college. She didn't even visit one when she was on Earth.

"Are you okay?" Kleos asked, joining her on the sidewalk.

"Yeah. Sorry. It's just...wow. I never thought I'd be on a college campus. Even before I became an Earthborn, I never really saw it in my future. Mom could barely afford to send me to high school, let alone a four-year university. And besides, without me," she muttered, "who would buy her cigarettes and beer?"

"And now?"

"I definitely don't see it. I'm pretty sure I can't major in anything but demon-fighting. Something tells me most universities don't offer that."

They followed Idunn's phone GPS up the street to the museum.

"Colleges weren't around when I became a Numen." Kleos said. "Education wasn't public or widely accepted. There was one man, Socrates, who was big at the time, but I never got a chance to meet him."

"Is that a joke?"

He shrugged cryptically. "Maybe."

They walked up the street past tennis courts and then cut into campus. Overhead, Caesar kept an eye out for any more surprises.

The museum, like many on campus, was made from a soft, off-white colored stone and hung with banners advertising different exhibits. Part of it was under construction. A new expansion was advertised on a big billboard. Unfortunately, there was one part of scoping out the museum that Dani didn't consider: it could be closed. According to the sign, it was under construction for the new exhibit.

"Crap." The door was locked. "Sneak in?"

"There's a problem with that." He pointed to the lock. "That's an electronic lock. You can't use the veil to bust it open."

"I could lightbring that sucker and turn it into sludge."

"And probably set off an alarm." He shook his head. "There's a lot of unknowns. We shouldn't break in, even if we can hide behind the veil. There could be other things guarding the medallion, if it's inside."

She grumbled, hating the fact they couldn't do this easily. Across the yard, an early-morning crowd was gathering in one of the wide-open spaces of the campus.

"So, what do we do?" Kleos asked.

But Dani already had an idea. As they spoke, a raven-haired girl exited from the museum. She carried a book bag, dressed in khakis and a polo; a student Dani guessed by her age. She waved back to someone inside and when she did, an ID tag flashed in the early morning light. Not just a student; an intern.

"What if we asked someone about the medallion?" She suggested.

"You'd have to find someone who works there."

"Like her?"

Kleos spotted the same girl, who now walked quickly down towards the road.

"Maybe she might let us in, or tell us where to find it in the museum." Dani suggested, following.

"And how do you plan to get her to do that? Use your feminine wiles?"

"First off, no one calls them 'feminine wiles.' Second, don't be sexist. Third," she grinned, "you're just jealous you didn't think of my brilliant plan first. Come on."

They followed the girl across the street. She ducked into one of those bookstore/café combo places called Manna. Kleos and Dani slipped out from behind the veil and followed her in.

Inside, the café was quiet; contemplative. The aroma of freshly ground coffee mixed with vanilla and other spices. Dani craved java. You could only go so long in a Heavenly city without missing coffee. The open windows faced the campus, flooding the room with light. College students huddled around electronics or coffee or one another. More than one philosophical conversation was going on. Maybe it was cynical of her, especially since she never got past high school, but it seemed like every college student she saw thought their ideas were somehow inspired by God.

Still, she couldn't completely tease them. She liked their optimism. At least they were hopeful about the future.

The girl stood ahead of them, grabbing a cup of coffee from across the counter.

"So how do you want to approach her?" Kleos asked.

Dani grinned, "Oh, I'll think of something."

Then she shoved him right into her.

Kleos stumbled face first into the girl's back and spilled the steaming hot contents of it all over him and her as they crashed into the counter.

Dani ran forward. "Oh my God! Kleos! Would you watch where you're going? Jeez! What a klutz!"

Her friend sat up, his beard and clothes bespeckled with coffee; the girl even more so.

"I'm so sorry for my brother!" Dani told her, reaching down and helping her up. "My brother is such an idiot! Kleos! Watch where you're going!"

His glare was hotter than the coffee he spilled.

"I'm sorry. Here. Let me help you clean up." Dani grabbed some napkins and dabbed her clothes. "I really am just so sorry."

"It's okay." The girl said. "It was an accident."

Dani's smile stuck in place. "Please. Let me buy you another coffee. It's the least we can do."

Her plan worked. Kleos wasn't happy about it, but she didn't care. He went to get her another cup while Dani went to work with her 'feminine wiles.'

"I'm Dani."

"Miriam."

"Good to meet you." They took a seat at one of the tables and Dani poured on the charm. "I'm sorry about my brother Kleos. He can't go five feet without knocking something or someone over."

She waved at him. He silently gave her the stink eye from the coffee line.

"Seriously. It's totally okay." The good-natured girl giggled. "It's not the first time I ended up with a lap full of vanilla bean."

Dani used something else besides her best lies. She wasn't an expert with Aether, but she was good enough to use it when she needed it. She willed herself to appear as the over-eager college prospect. To this Miriam girl, she would be decked out in Berkeley gift-shop chic and be nothing but the quintessential potential future-student. Everyone took pity on visitors. She used it to her advantage.

"Well, I'm just visiting the college. My brother and I, I mean. I'm thinking about attending here next year and, you know, I'm getting a jump start on college visits."

"That's good. Hey, do you have a mirror I could borrow?"

Dani didn't, except for the obsidian one. She handed it over anyway.

"Thanks." Miriam checked her hair to ensure there was no more coffee. "What got you interested in UC Berkeley?"

"Oh, I just love the campus!" Dani gushed, doing her best eager-beaver imitation of the people from Lightpoint. "I mean, I just love it! Don't you?"

"Of course." Miriam responded politely.

"And the museum is amazing. I just love all the history."

"Really? I work there."

Even to her, Dani sounded way too fake. "You do?! I had no idea!"

"Yeah." Miriam giggled. "I'm an intern. I want to get an anthropology doctorate here, so I'm studying folklore for my thesis; hopefully to be used later for my dissertation."

"Really?"

"Uh-huh. I know what you're thinking: nerdy. But Berkeley has a great anthropology program. Like," she picked up Dani's mirror, "did you know that obsidian, like your mirror, was used in multiple cultures across the world for mystical purposes? In fact, they made mirrors like this to scry with. They used to believe you could see things in these if you knew the right spell or magical enchantment. Weird, right?"

"Totally."

She handed the mirror back. "Sorry. I just sort of nerd out when it comes to anthropology. The Hearst Museum has a lot of artifacts from all over the world. I go there a lot. It's pretty spectacular."

"Well, my brother and I came a long way to see it. We heard it has some of the best artifacts in the country."

Miriam shrugged. "Some, yeah. It's a great place to study; even better to visit."

Kleos arrived. He had two coffees and two muffins.

"Hi. Sorry again for the mess." He apologized. "I don't know what happened. It's like someone tripped me or something." He kept his tone innocent, but Dani could feel his sideways glare.

"That's totally fine." Miriam assured him. "Kleos is a cool name. Doesn't it mean 'renown' or 'glory' in battle? And you two don't look like siblings."

"She's adopted."

Dani kicked him under the table. *Adopted?! You little—!*

"Adopted huh? Well, everyone deserves a place and a family."

Kleos grinned politely back. "Well, what can I say? Dani is a special kind of girl."

"You were saying about the museum?" Dani asked, steering the conversation. "I'd love to see the inside."

"It's closed right now. They're setting up a new exhibit. You could stop by later next week."

"That would be too late." Which was true. She lied quickly. "I was kind of hoping just to pop inside. I heard all about the artifacts from Egypt. Is it true there's, like, a ton in there?"

Like a ton? Who am I? Some blonde bimbo from the suburbs?

Miriam smiled warmly the same way she did with explaining obsidian. Nerding out, she called it. "Yeah. There's some stuff that was brought over in the early nineteen-hundreds. Why?"

Dani tried to be nonchalant; casual. But she failed miserably. She was too desperate to get in that she sucked at lying. *Try to be casual*, she said to herself. "Well, I heard they have this medallion or something made of gold? It's inscribed with a dragon around the edges and had three faces in the middle." *Casual alright; casual as an elephant in a china shop.* "I mean, I don't know much about it. I just heard of it. But is there something like that?"

"You just heard about it?" Miriam looked suspiciously at her. But she answered. "Well, sure, medallions—or what we call seals—are rare. They're emblems of different nations, or people, or gods. Usually they're wax or something like that, but a few are known to be made from precious metals."

"But the one I'm asking about? Is it in there?"

She thought again. "I think I might know what you're talking about."

198

She tried her luck. "Could we...I don't know...see it?"

"See it? The medallion, you mean?"

"Yeah."

"A medallion you only slightly heard about but don't know if it's actually there: you want to see it?" she was definitely suspicious now.

Dani blushed, hoping she didn't just give herself away. "Yeah."

Miriam shook her head. "I don't have any authority to let you in. You'd have to talk to Dr. Trauco. He's one of the anthropology professors here. I'm on my way to go see him in his office."

"Can I come?"

She glanced between her and Kleos. "I'm not sure. It's a private meeting."

"Please?" It didn't hurt to ask.

Chapter Twenty-Five

Dani had Kleos hang back. She figured she could get more out of Miriam if it was just the two of them.

They walked across campus to the anthropology building and then up to the faculty offices. Miriam walked into one, where each faculty member shared a common area. She made herself right at home at one of the desks.

"Oh, it's fine." She assured Dani when she hesitated to step inside. "Interns are allowed in here any time they want and my professor is okay with it, so long as you're with me."

"That so?" Asked a deep voice.

A tall, muscular professor appeared from one of the offices. He had long hair, a deep, natural skin-tone and strong jaw. He had that rugged look a lot of girls went for; stubble-chin, air of confidence. Dressed in a blazer and jeans, he had all the machismo and sexuality of a telenovela star.

He extended a hand to Dani. "Dr. Trauco. Most call just call me Emmanuel."

Then he turned and without a word, kissed Miriam deeply. He pressed her against the desk, his hands doing things that made Dani instantly turn around. *Whoa!*

"Stop it!" Miriam slapped his broad chest playfully. "Sorry, Dani. He's not supposed to do that in front of people."

Dr. Trauco laughed.

"Faculty and students aren't supposed to...mingle." Miriam blushed. "Emmanuel, this is Dani. She's a potential student."

"That so? Well, I apologize. I guess I gave you more of a preview to the school than you'd like."

Dani tried not to show her uncomfortability. This wasn't what she expected by far.

"Oh, you." Miriam teased. "Let me get something from down the hall. Be right back!" she kissed him and departed.

That left Dani with Dr. Trauco.

"So," Dani said, "isn't it a little...I don't know...weird to date your student?" Dani asked him.

He shrugged. "Why would it?"

He looked to be in his forties, at least. Miriam was, what, twenty at most?

"So," he leaned against the desk, all suave, "you're here to look at the school, huh?"

"Yeah." She shifted uncomfortably.

"It would be a great opportunity for you." He said. "Berkeley would be a good fit. And I wouldn't mind see you walking around campus."

Did he just hit on me?

Miriam reappeared. "Okay. All done. Emmanuel, Dani wants to see inside the museum. Would that be okay?"

"Really?" He grinned. "Unfortunately, it's closed."

"That's why I brought her to you." Miriam chided her professor/boyfriend.

"Hmm," he rubbed his jaw, "I think I might able to do something. You would owe me." He told her. Then he shifted his eyes to Dani lustfully. "And, of course, you would, too."

Miriam kissed his cheek, oblivious to his gaze on Dani. "Please?"

He kissed her back. "Let me see what I can do." Then he disappeared into his office.

Dani took a seat in a chair while they waited. Miriam leaned against the desk with a look like butterflies were taking flight in her stomach.

When they caught eyes, Miriam blushed. "I know what you're thinking."

Doubtful, she thought. "I don't judge." *Out loud, anyway.*

"He's handsome. He's sweet. He really cares about me. Besides, I'll admit, it's also kind of fun sneaking around."

"Are you two serious?"

"We are." Dani heard hope, not truth, in that statement. Miriam only wanted it to be true. She added on, as if she needed to justify it, "We've been seeing each other for about a year. You know how things go."

"Gone on any dates?" Dani asked innocently.

"We can't." She said, apologetically. "You know: university rules."

"So how do you spend any time together? You know, normal couple stuff?"

That was the thing Dani didn't understand about relationships; especially ones like this. She wasn't judgmental, but if couples couldn't do normal couple stuff, what was the point? And if he hit on Dani behind her back...

If it was doomed, what was the point?

Of course, part of it was that he was handsome and she was cute. It was physical; not emotional. But that sure as hell wasn't enough to keep things going long-term.

"It'll work out." Miriam brushed Dani's unspoken criticism aside, instead asking her, "Do you have anyone?"

"Anyone?"

"Boyfriend?" She asked, then added. "Girlfriend?"

"No. I," she paused, "I work too much to have a boyfriend."

"You sound like you've got somebody, though."

"Let's just say it's like the Facebook status: it's complicated."

Dr. Trauco called Miriam into his office. Dani looked over the desk. It was Miriam's, it seemed. It had a picture of her on the desk, plus some knick-knacks and other assorted things. It was clear how the two of them started their secret, workplace romance. She worked five feet from him.

Still, Dani didn't like it. The way he acted, the student/teacher thing, necessarily; Miriam clearly thought more about their relationship he did. There was a picture of the two of them on Miriam's desk. Spying inside his office, there didn't seem to be any similar photos of them on his.

Dani spotted something in the trash as she looked around. It only stuck out to her because it was purple-tipped. She retrieved it and held it up. When she did, she caught Miriam coming out of her boss/boyfriend's office. She looked horrified.

"Is this...?" Dani asked.

Miriam snatched it from her. "What are you doing?"

"I'm sorry. I just saw it." Dani stood. "Is that a pregnancy test?"

Miriam hissed, "Please," she dropped it into the drawer of her desk, "don't tell anyone."

"Why?" It didn't take a genius to figure out who would be the baby-daddy. "Does he know?"

"No."

"Have you told him?"

"Not yet." Miriam folded her arms uncomfortably.

"I'm sorry. I didn't mean to snoop."

"I'm not mad at you. I just don't want him to see."

"Why not? Aren't you two dating?"

"Yes."

"And you think...what? He'll be upset?"

Miriam didn't have to say it for Dani to know. She never grew up in a bubble. She'd seen a lot of intense relationships—like the one they had; all excitement, but no real substance—fall apart the moment the girl got pregnant. It wasn't like the movies. Pregnancy didn't fix everything.

"I won't tell." Dani said. It wasn't her place. "I take it that it wasn't planned?"

"No. I don't know how it happened."

"How far along?"

"Not far. I just found out yesterday."

Dr. Trauco appeared from his office and shut the door. Miriam shoved the drawer with the test closed.

"So," he said, "I've secured us some time in the museum."

"Really? That's amazing. Thank you." Dani said.

"Only because it's Miriam here asking. Come on, I'll show you the way."

They followed the professor down and out of the building and back towards the museum.

Dani hung back and silently whispered, "Caesar?"

"*Yeah, honey?*" Her friend called back from overhead.

"Glad you're still up there. Can you get Kleos for me and tell him to meet us at the museum?"

"*How am I supposed to do that? We can't talk, remember?*"

"Charades?"

"*You think you're so funny, don't you?*" But Caesar agreed. "*I'll get him. Don't get into trouble.*"

"I won't."

"Dani?" Trauco asked, interrupting them. "Where are you from?"

"L.A. Sun Valley. You?"

"Chile. *Has montado alguna vez a Chile?*"

Dani shook her head. "*No. He vivido toda mi vida en Los Angeles.*"

"*Yo debería llevarte algún dia.*" *I should take you sometime.*

Dani did not like the way he said that.

"What are you two talking about?" Miriam asked lightly.

"She never learned Spanish." Trauco explained to Dani. "I'm from an island off the coast of Chile. I studied anthropology there. That's how we met. Miriam was one of my students."

"And she never learned Spanish?"

"I don't normally speak it around her. We keep no secrets from one another."

"No secrets, you say?" She doubted that.

Miriam frowned slightly.

Three student-interns waited for them outside the building. Dr. Trauco used a key-card to disable the alarm and a lock-key to open the front door.

"Miriam says you have a brother with you?"

"Kleos. He should be here soon."

"I'll have one of my interns let him in. Come on. You can tell me what part of the museum you want to see."

Trauco, Miriam, Dani and two interns went into the museum. Inside, the floors were polished wood paneling. The ceilings and walls were white, with in-built lighting for exhibits and general lighting. The museum was under construction, so they were off now and some scaffolding took up part of the entryway. But only a few seconds in, the impressive artifacts and exhibits began.

"What would you like to see?" Dr. Trauco asked as they walked. "Miriam mentioned Egyptian?"

"Yeah. There's this medallion thing I saw online; gold, I think."

He nodded. "I know what you're talking about. This way."

He led them through the museum. It was empty of people save for a construction crew, who they passed.

The Egyptian exhibits were in another part of the building. It had the same lighting and structure, but the artifacts were all from around the Nile. There were things in glass cases; some standing on their own pedestals while others sat on shelves in the wall. There was even a sarcophagus.

But when they stepped into one exhibit room, Dani felt the air change. It was like electricity on her skin. The more she walked into the room, the more she felt it. It radiated from the opposite end of the room. And as Dani approached, she recognized something on the far glass shelf.

The gold medallion was the size of her palm from fingertip to wrist and as thick as half a stack of quarters. It rested against the back of the case, so everyone could see the three faces engraved on its surface. Just like her vision and, a dragon wove its way around the edge in a sinister circle.

Dani stopped before it. The thing made her chest hurt.

"It was found in the early nineteen-hundreds," Dr. Trauco explained, "on a dig far from the Nile. Strange, since it wasn't anywhere near any known civilization. They stumbled upon it; like it wanted to be found."

"I'm sure." Dani didn't doubt it. The magic pulled on her, and at the same time, made her skin crawl.

It was right there, but how was she supposed to take it? Smash and grab? Go behind the veil and make a run for it once she had it? It seemed like the only plan.

"What's your interest in it?" Dr. Trauco asked from behind her. "It's far from the most ornate thing in the room."

"It stuck out to me." She shrugged. "Not sure why."

"It could be because it's beautiful."

"Maybe."

"It could be because as a Numen, you feel its power."

Miriam glanced sideways at him, confused, but then Dr. Trauco backhanded her hard enough to send her sprawling across the floor.

Dani drew her empyreal sword, spinning to face him and realizing her mistake. How could she have been so stupid? Dr. Trauco and his two interns created a semi-circle that backed her into the wall. And slowly, they transformed.

The interns sprouted hooked, bat-like wings that ripped their university polos, while horns grew from their eyebrows. Dani recognized them. Other than being men, they looked just like the succubae she fought before.

But Trauco changed the most. His lower legs rotted and collapsed. He dropped to the floor on new, shorter legs that ripped out of the ones he already had; these were grotesque, with hooked toenails on the end like claws. His handsome face transformed, too. Still strong-jawed with horns sprouting from his chin, he had other horns jutting from his eyebrows and along his jaw, and his skin peeled away in places to reveal sickly, discolored flesh underneath. His arms remained the same length, giving him a dwarfish, ape-like form with his own set of wings.

"We figured you would come for his seal eventually, Numen." The dwarf-doctor snarled.

"Who the hell are you?" Dani asked. "Really, I mean?"

"Trauco is my real name." He bowed a little, his once model-good-looking locks falling off in clumps. "Of course, you probably don't know Chilean demons, so you don't know me. But you know the father of all incubae and succubae, I'm sure. He has an intense interest in you."

Incubae. Male forms of the succubae. And, if the lore was believed, Asmodeus's offspring

Miriam sat up slowly; dazed. She starred in horror at the good doctor, who in the span of seconds, changed into Mr. Hyde. "Emmanuel? You...!"

He knuckle-walked over to her, running his clawed fingers playfully over his own cheek. "What? Do I have something on my face?" He smacked her again. Miriam hit the floor and passed out. "Shut up, cow."

"Don't you dare touch her again!" Dani shrieked.

"What? Her? Don't worry. I won't do anything to her." He grinned impishly. "After all, she's carrying my spawn. Why would I want to harm her?"

The horror of that idea dawned on Dani.

"Yes, I know all about her pregnancy. I wanted it. I made it happen. Just as my master wants you to bear his children, she will bear mine. After all, what else are women good for except breeding?"

"So, what? You care about her?"

"Of course not." Trauco waved it off. "That's like a farmer caring about cattle. She serves a purpose. Right now, she carries my child. Until that's over, she lives. After that..." he shrugged.

"You're disgusting."

"Thank you." He turned over his shoulder to his minions. "Capture her. Alive, if you can."

The incubae moved to take her.

One of the demonic interns flapped his wings and leapt off the ground, claws exploding from his tennis shoes. Dani spun under and sliced with her sword, but these demons were smarter than the ones at Lightpoint. Her blades missed. The other kicked hard and caught her in the ribs.

Trauco leapt onto her back and flipped backwards, carrying Dani with him. He tossed her head over heels, through the air, and through an exhibit. She shattered the glass and pedestal under her when she landed.

"My, my, that was expensive." Trauco sneered.

Dani groaned. She could feel some fresh cuts to her face and hands from the glass shards, but getting the wind knocked out of her hurt worse.

The incubae came at her again.

This time, Dani was ready. The first one ran right at her, claws extended. Instead of a dodge, she took his charge. She feinted with Pointyend, and when he moved to come around her blade, she stabbed up with Pigsticker right through the ribcage.

He disintegrated.

Through the ash, the second demon howled and slashed with its claws. Dani dodged away from it, swinging her swords; fending it off. Her swords finally found their mark and sliced off the end of one of the creature's hands. It howled in pain.

Dani cut its head off.

"Your turn." She threatened, glaring at the demonic imp.

"That so?" Trauco asked.

"You don't have any more lackeys."

"Not true."

Hungry growls turned her towards the door. The crewmen she passed earlier fanned into the room; four of them. And they were no longer human.

More of them. Great.

"You need henchmen to fight your battles?" Dani bluffed, hoping for time. She wasn't a master. Even with others' help, she sometimes barely got out of these kinds of situations. She had her lightbringing. She could use that.

But Trauco had surprises of his own.

"No." he said. "I don't. I just wanted to see how skilled you were."

Then Dani felt it. She tried to move away from the incubae coming towards her, but her feet wouldn't budge. She was frozen in place.

Then she dropped to her knees.

"You really should read the Chilean legends about me." Trauco sauntered forward, his gaze unwavering and, somehow, keeping her in place. "Some of us have powers you should know before you try to take us on."

Blackness pulled at the edge of Dani's vision and slowly, everything went blank.

The icy-prick told her she was chained with stygian, even before she woke. Her wrists were bound over her head. Each ankle was splayed apart. The chains looped into latches in the floor. Her swords were gone. Someone cut her backpack off.

"Glad you're awake." Trauco hovered over her. "I was worried we hurt you too much."

"What did you do to me?"

"Paralyzed you. It's a gift of mine, though it takes complete concentration. These," he touched the chains, "work better for keeping you in place."

"Someone will eventually wander in here, you know. I think tying a girl to the floor might be a little suspicious."

He laughed. "You think this museum is under construction because of a new exhibit?" He gestured to the crewmen standing around her. "We need a convenient way to station guards nearby. The interns are mine, too. Unfortunately, you killed two of them."

"Why the hell do you need that many guards?"

"It's why you're here, right? It's why you carry these?" He held up a bane box. "You want to take the medallion and put Lord Asmodeus back in it?"

She went with sarcasm; always a safe bet instead of letting on about their goal. "No. I just think it's a great place to keep my jewelry. You know us girls."

He hit her. Hard. Dani tasted blood.

"Humans found my master's medallion over a century ago." Trauco said. "It wasn't a coincidence. Once the incubae and succubae knew where our master was buried, it wasn't hard to convince mortals to go looking for it. After all: demons have whispered in the ear of humanity for centuries."

"And when," Dani painfully rose, "Alecto blew the Horn, it let him out."

"I was already here by that time. There was no way to free my master from the powerful angelic spell. So, I became its protector. Once he was released, it was important no one should ever find it again. After all, my master fears returning to the confines of that lonesome hell worse than all others. So, I was tasked to look after it, which," he glanced down at Miriam who still lay unmoving nearby, "gave me an ample supply of coeds to prey on. Trust me, there's nothing like being a hot, young college professor on a campus full of hormonal girls. I've done it for decades."

"You know what? I was wrong. You're not disgusting. You're repulsive."

"A lot of women have said that over centuries. And many of them have borne my seed."

"Borne your...you have kids?"

"Many." He smiled. "Demons learned long ago that humans could provide ample ways of reproducing. Our brood is much stronger than other demons'. Why do you think we do it? Humans are nauseating. And stupid. The only thing they're good for is having kids."

Dani knew the lore about incubae and succubae. It only said they were demons of lust; not anything about this.

"That's what I don't understand about you Earthborn. You think you're winning this war. Demons have barely been fighting it, and yet I have children all over the world that you'll never find. And eventually, one day, I and others will command those children to hunt you down. We're winning. You will one day bow to us," he smiled cruelly, "just like you'll bow to Asmodeus."

"Never."

"Brave," he commended, "but stupid. Allhallowtide is a week away. You won't stop him."

He had Dani's swords and tossed them across the room. When he did, one of his interns—the one left outside—arrived. In his arms, he had someone else.

Kleos. He was unconscious.

"What's this?" Trauco demanded.

"He's with her." The incubus dumped Kleos onto the floor. "I surprised him before he could put up a fight."

"Why didn't you kill him?"

"I thought you might want to interrogate him."

Trauco fumed. "Why would I want to do that?! The girl is the only one we need!"

"What should I do with him, then?"

"You stupid idiot! Kill him! Lideric," he called another incubus, "help him with the body."

"Yes sir." One of the crewman said, going to join him. "Now, where was I? Oh, yes, summoning my master's minions. I believe a group of shades was following you. I'm sure they'll be here soon to take you to him."

Dani struggled against her bindings. The idea of Michael and Nazir catching them was worse than anything this demon could do.

Lideric, the demon crew member assigned to kill Kleos, drew a stygian knife and knelt. "Maybe we should eat part of him? Numen taste delicious."

The intern snorted. "Might as well. He was pathetically easy to take down."

Trauco closed his eyes and began to chant, but paused. "What did you say?"

The intern glanced up. "Sir? All I said was that he was easy to take down. I've never known a Numen to be so weak—."

Kleos snapped awake, seized Lideric's wrist and shoved the knife in his hand forward into the intern's heart. With a blast of Aer, he then hurtled Lideric across the room into Trauco while the intern disintegrated.

He spun to his feet, grinning. "Easy. Yeah, sure, you putrid hellspawn."

The nearest incubus lunged, but Kleos drew a concealed adamantine knife from his wrist and shoved it under the beast's chin. Two dead, three left. He flipped the knife to a throwing position and hurled it across the room, striking another incubus.

Two left.

"Dani! Get up!" He called, using the Aer to propel an ancient statue into Trauco, Lideric and the final incubus.

"I can't!"

"Lightbringing!"

Dani had never used it on herself. She destroyed stygian shackles before, but they were on Ethan, not her. It never occurred to her that she could do that to herself.

She closed her eyes and willed her power into her hands. Her palms burned. White light flowed over her fingertips. Using her anger hurt her hands, but as Trauco shoved his two minions off, her anger for him was more than the pain she would endure.

Using Miriam for nothing but bearing children.

Threatening her life.

She had plenty of ammunition.

The white light flowed over the stygian chains. Her skin heated. Dani focused on what she wanted it to do. She saw the chains melting in her mind. She saw the black iron burn hot and peel away from her skin.

With a yank, it they snapped.

"No!" Trauco screamed.

One incubus charged. Dani extended her hand and blasted him with light that tore a hole through his chest and reduced him to ashes. She turned the light on her ankles and blew apart the bindings to free herself.

Kleos grabbed for his weapons, drew his sword and swung just in time towards to Lideric the incubus, which forced him back. He kept swinging, keeping the creature at bay.

Dani went for her own swords.

Lideric tried to break through Kleos' guard, but the Guardian was two quick. He flipped his sword into reverse, ducked and brought him in with a fake feint as he spun around. He buried the blade right through the demon's chest. Lideric disintegrated.

Dani snatched up her sword, summoned her lightbringing, and prepared to kill the college professor.

"That is enough!"

Trauco summoned that strange power of paralysis and froze Kleos where he stood. Paralyzed, the Guardian dropped to his knees. With a wave of his hand, his demonic magic knocked Kleos' blade away.

He didn't move his gaze off him. "Now where is that girl?"

"Here."

Dani cut his head off from behind.

Chapter Twenty-Six

Trauco came to an abrupt end. His body disintegrated like the rest of his evil kind. All that remained was his mangled suit.

Dani sheathed her sword. Her hands sizzled. She ignored the pain and knelt next to Miriam. "Miriam?"

Woozy, Miriam slowly came to and sat up, "What happened?"

Kleos knelt next to her, too. "You're fine."

"Emmanuel?"

"He's gone."

"He...he..." she shook her head, and then nodded. "He went to go get help, didn't he? I fainted?"

The veil. It was a powerful thing.

"Yeah." Dani lied. "Why don't you stay here with my brother for a sec?"

She stood, grabbing the bane box and walking over the medallion's display case. Up close, the magic radiated off it like sound off a subwoofer. She broke the casing with her elbow, her Arachne-weave stopping any glass from cutting her. She reached inside and grabbed the seal.

It was like touching a live wire. A voice in her head screamed. She staggered a bit.

"Dani!" Kleos caught her elbow. "Dani, are you alright?"

And then another sensation passed through her, but this time, it didn't come from the medallion. It came from Kleos. And something darted across her vision.

Kleos and another Numen—one she didn't recognize—sparring playfully. Laughing. Beyond them, up the hill, she could see Nazir watching them. Angry.

Then it was gone. The medallion lay in her glowing hand, her lightbringing coursing to the surface without her wanting it to. She shoved the medallion into the box and slapped the lid closed. The magic from it cut off. Her lightbringing dissipated. She could breathe again.

"What was that?" Kleos asked.

"It was..." she shuddered, swallowing to stop herself from vomiting. "Wow."

"You felt something?"

"Oh yeah."

"What?"

"Fear." She smiled a little. "I felt his fear."

"Whose? Asmodeus?"

She nodded. "It was like some part of him was still attached to that thing." She shoved the bane box back into her retrieved bag. "It was like feeling what he felt when he was inside it. Empty. Alone. Trauco said he didn't want to go back inside this thing. I can understand why."

"Are you alright?"

"I'm better than alright." She grinned wider. "I felt his fear."

It wasn't exactly something to get giddy about, but Dani couldn't help it. It gave her confidence.

She looked up at Kleos, aware it wasn't just Asmodeus she felt. The visions of Kleos was still there, in the back of her mind. She knew she saw something real, but couldn't make anything of it. What did that? The medallion? She glanced down at her hand. Her lightbringing?

Miriam slowly got to her feet. Dani ran to her. "You need to take it easy."

"Why does my head hurt?"

"You had a nasty fall. Come on. Let's get you outside. Fresh air will do you some good."

A few minutes later, they exited the building. Dani had her sit on a bench while Kleos went to get her water.

"I don't know what happened." She confessed.

Dani lied. "You just got woozy and fainted is all."

"Do you think it's because of the baby?"

Dani had forgotten all about that. Miriam was pregnant with Trauco's child. She literally had the spawn of a demon inside her. That made her shudder.

"Maybe."

Kleos arrived with a cup of water. "Here."

She drank it and thanked him. "You think Emmanuel's coming back?"

Dani and Kleos were both silent on that point. "Maybe." Dani said, since she had no other lie. "But I wouldn't worry about that. It's not like you and him had a healthy relationship anyway."

"No, he was good to me." She drank some more. "I mean, yeah, he didn't want to be exclusive or anything. I knew he had something going on with another girl on campus but..." She stopped herself and blushed. As if realizing how stupid she sounded, she shook her head. "I was an idiot, wasn't I?"

"You were human."

"Emmanuel doesn't really love me like I love him. God, I was stupid."

Maybe it was the veil. Maybe it was that Trauco was gone. But she didn't have her head in the clouds.

Dani wasn't about to make the girl feel bad. That was the one thing she detested: when someone finally saw the light and then someone put them down anyway.

"Like I said: human."

"I guess I wasn't a very good host." Miriam apologized. "I hope I didn't turn you off from Berkeley."

"To tell the truth, I'm not sure college is in my future."

"You never know."

"Trust me, I do." She stood up. "Look, I hate to run out on you, but my brother and I need to go." Trauco tried to mystically contact Asmodeus' shades. No telling how close they already were, considering they had to know where Dani and Kleos were going if they traveled in this direction. "Like I said, don't think too much about this. You'll be fine."

She shook her head. "Yeah. I got pretty loopy there. I could have sworn Emmanuel turned into a monster or something. I must have imagined it."

"Must have."

Kleos frowned.

"It felt real."

"Well, who said it wasn't?" She offered, then quickly chided. "I mean, maybe your brain made you see something because you realized what a jerk he really was."

"That must be it."

"Bye, Miriam."

"Bye Dani."

They walked away. Kleos glanced back. "Strange."

"What is?"

"The veil helped her forget, or at least think that what she saw wasn't real, but she remembered it any way. Normally, humans ignore the truth. They believe it's fiction. She didn't."

"So?"

"So, she's a mundanus. That doesn't normally happen."

"At least she escaped before that Trauco demon did what all incubae want."

"And that is?"

"Impregnate her." He shook his head. "If that happened, it would be awful."

"How so?"

"Empyrean won't allow a human to give birth to a demonic baby. They would stop it."

"They'd kill the baby?"

"They'd kill the mother before she had a chance to have a baby."

Dani felt a chill run through her bones. "Tell me you're joking."

"The baby would be part-demon, Dani."

"And part human."

"It's not just that. Exposure like that to demonic energy is dangerous. It would weaken the veil so she could see the demons. It would alter her."

"Would she die?" She tried not to sound worried.

"No. From what I know, demonic children don't kill the mother. The pregnancy isn't easy, but they're in no more danger than any woman with a normal baby. Of course, if any demon knew she was having one, they would come looking for her." He glanced sidelong at Dani. "It's good she isn't with child, isn't it?"

Dani faked a smile. "It is."

She glanced one last time back at Miriam. The veil hadn't completely affected her like other people. Dani thought briefly about telling Kleos the truth. He wouldn't be like everyone else in Empyrean, right? After all, he sided with her.

But she wasn't sure, so she wouldn't tell him.

And after this was all over, Dani would come back to find Miriam. What she would do, she didn't know. But killing her would never be an option.

They didn't stay in Berkeley. She didn't trust that the city was safe. They crossed the bay into San Francisco. Dani worried that the shades, or whatever Asmodeus sent when Trauco called, would follow them by tracking the seal. Kleos, however, wasn't worried. Bane boxes, it seemed, were so powerful that they kept anything inside them hidden. His thinking was that if the seal stayed in the box, no demonic creature could track it.

Staying in San Francisco was Dani's idea. Demons expected them to flee. If they stayed nearby, they might go unnoticed when the search went out of the city after them. They found a hotel and got a nice room, took turns showering off the last of the demonic sewer-sludge, and then spent the day resting.

She slept. No bad dreams. No visits from her demon stalker. She was finally able to rest.

The following day, they stayed put. With no leads, it made no sense to go out. Their use of the veil meant they could stay at the hotel as long as needed.

"What are you doing?" Kleos asked when he came out of the bathroom and spotted Dani reading from Idunn's phone.

"Research."

"On what?"

"Shades."

He frowned, sitting on the other bed that occupied the room. On the TV, some show about housewives played in the background. He was strangely interested in it.

"You're researching creatures on the internet? There are no human libraries on Earth that have the knowledge of the ancient scrolls and tomes of the Athenaeum."

"No, but there is Wikipedia." She showed him. "I want to figure out if there is a way to stop shades. Permanently."

"We already know they're immortal. Besides, what would the internet have that libraries don't?"

"Have you read anything on the internet? There are all kinds of things." She showed him. "There's talk of shades popping up everywhere. They appear in classical mythology like the Odyssey. They appear in the Bible. Almost every culture around the world has some kind of mythology or theology about them."

"We know all of this."

"But there's modern sightings of them, too." She pointed out. "And maybe a more modern source might have ways to combat them that older cultures don't. Now, most people think they're a hoax since the veil makes people believe that, but there's stuff from late night talk shows and even Native American parapsychologists who think they can be repelled. Even killed."

"How?"

"Varying ideas. Some say you can use special weapons or amulets or incantations. Others say they're ghosts that have unfinished business, or have some internal conflict that needs to be resolved."

They were interrupted by a knock at the door.

"Did you order any food?" Kleos asked her.

"No. You expecting anyone?"

"No."

Kleos retrieved his xiphos and Dani got her empyreal blades. After the events at UC Berkeley, neither of them wanted to face any more unexpected surprises.

"Who is it?" Kleos called out, taking position near the door.

A familiar man's voice called back from the other side. "America!"

Kleos glanced sideways at Dani. America? *What the hell did that mean?*

"Caesar?" Dani asked.

Caesar, who roosted on top of a dresser last night, glared at the door. *"Definitely something non-human out in the hallway, but it's weird. It's like whoever it is, they're there, but not there."*

Dani tilted her chin to the door. Kleos went to open it.

When he threw open the door, they came face-to-face with a man Dani had only seen on late night television. His brown hair was perfectly set in place. He had a slim suit, wide grin and strode in completely unafraid of their weapons.

"Hello." He greeted, taking in his surroundings. "I see we are living the lavish lifestyle."

Dani relaxed. "Haniel." How else did she explain such a famous face coming to see them?

"In the flesh!" He looked down at himself. "Well, in someone's flesh, anyway."

"You look like..." she couldn't even believe it. "I haven't watched him since he was on that comedy channel pretending to be a conservative."

"I know." Haniel smirked. "I was so glad he left that show. Channeling him in that fake conservative character is weird; taking on the persona of a man putting on the persona of another man. It's very meta. I miss the eagle, though."

Kleos shut the door. "What are you doing here?"

"What I told you I would." The angel said. "I came as soon as I heard you found his seal."

"You forgot to mention it was protected by incubae, and the road was watched by šulaks."

"Oh, it was protected by more than that, but you made it through the demonic dragnet just fine. And you did it before his shades caught up with you."

"The shades were here?"

"They just left Berkeley. That's why I came to see you."

"They might go after the next artifact." Kleos worried.

"I doubt that."

"Why?"

"Because I only just found it myself."

Dani perked up. "You did?"

"I came to give you these." He produced a pair of plane tickets. "Two tickets to St. Louis, Missouri."

"Missouri?" She took them. "What's in Missouri?"

"I haven't the faintest clue."

Haniel shimmered, changing from the late-night talk-show host into a different persona; still a talk-show comedian, but much different. His skin turned a shade of brown, his hair disappeared and he got a pair of thick, black glasses.

"Hmm," he inspected himself, "I must be channeling hosts today. They're always trending."

"Trending? What, is your form determined by Twitter?"

"Would it be weird if it was?"

"Very." She shook her head. "You were saying? How do you know we need to go to Missouri if you have no idea what's there?"

"It's hard to explain."

"Try me."

"Do you have a working knowledge of quantum entanglements?"

Dani frowned. "Let's pretend I don't."

The angel shook his head, making an odd chuckle-giggle. "Um, well, how about this: it's like sounds. I can hear things. I know where things are when I hear them. I just don't know what those things are."

Shockingly, Dani understood. "You're an angel. Angels sing things into existence. It's the way you communicate. Gabriel told me once."

"Exactly. The world sings back. It's how we hear it."

"So, you know something is in Missouri, but not what it is?"

"That's for you to figure out, I assume."

Kleos sighed. "Well, that's annoying."

"Hey, at least you don't have the magical slide show in your head." She told him. "En Dor left clues but not a clue what they are."

She got no argument back.

"Your visions should tell you where to go." Haniel reminded her. "After all, that's what led you to the medallion you've got stashed in the box over there."

She asked hopefully, "Any other help you can give us?"

The angel frowned. "Possibly. I can't be sure."

"Try us."

"I heard something when I searched for the object. It was...old. Really old."

"Demon?"

"It's a resonance different than demons. It's powerful, whatever it is, and feels like nature. Be careful." Haniel smiled his bravest. "I'm going to get going before I turn into another host. Heaven forbid if it's the redhead or the guy with the guitar." He shivered. "I wouldn't mind the British guy, though. The accent is interesting."

Haniel left through the door he came. Kleos shut it behind him. "Well, that was weird."

"Super-weird." She held up the tickets. "We got a flight to catch, apparently."

The flight had one problem: Caesar. The caladrius wasn't exactly carry on and, as she put it, *"trying to keep up with a 747 is like a turtle racing a Greyhound. And I'm the turtle."*

Dani had to ask if she meant the dog or the bus.

"Bus."

Ask a silly question...

In the end, Caesar hid out in the cargo bay after promising not to snack on any pets that might be making the flight from California to Missouri. They flew into St. Louis. Dani had to admit, the Arch was cool to see from the air. And the view wasn't bad either. She'd never been outside California, much less L.A. Seeing the wide expanse of green, brown and golden farmland, even in late October, was so different and beautiful than the arid, drought-filled state she was from.

While in flight, she did another check-in on Empyrean. Mastema remained imprisoned at her house under armed guard. Bouden's and Ethan's mirrors were in their rooms.

It was Nathaniel she contacted.

"Hey!" She caught him after a training session. He found a quiet spot to talk. "Bouden said you might be in touch. Are you okay?"

"We're fine."

"I heard what happened in Berkeley."

"You know about Berkeley?"

"The Elders tracked some demonic activity there and the Powers ran into a group of those shade-ghost-things. What were you doing there?"

Dani explained about the three artifacts of Raphael and how, somehow, they could be used against Asmodeus again.

"Any way I can help?"

"You read the Book of Tobit with Bouden, right?"

He nodded.

"Was there any mention of a ring in it?"

He shook his head. "Not that I'm aware. I can look again."

"What about a fish?"

That sparked his interest. "Yeah, actually. Why do you ask?"

"It was something someone said about fish guts."

Nathaniel thought. "According to the legend, Tobias—Sarah's husband—was on the way the town Sarah lived in when he stopped by a river to wash. When he was there, a fish tried to swallow his foot."

"His foot?"

"It was a big fish. Anyway, Raphael appeared in the guise of a cousin or something to Tobias, tells him to capture the fish. Later, when Asmodeus appeared on his wedding night, he cut the fish open and spilled the guts out onto a fire. It drove Asmodeus out."

"Out? What does that mean?"

"No idea. That's the phrasing: 'drove him out.' Whatever it means, the fish's guts repelled him. Why?"

Dani had a vision about a fish. *A fish in a murky river.* "It might be something."

"I'll look into it. Bouden and I..." he trailed off, frowning.

"What is it?"

"Something's wrong."

And then his image disappeared. Dani didn't know what was happening until a new image appeared. It was a face Dani didn't want to see.

"Novice Daniella." The face of Elder Heman swam into view. He looked, as always, disgusted with her. "We knew you were communicating with someone. Once we find out who it was, they will suffer your punishment."

"Screw you."

"Come back. You are in violation of the law."

"I am trying to stop Asmodeus; something you don't seem so concerned with."

He brushed it off. "You attempt to scare your fellow Numen with your conspiracy about this ancient evil. It is a fantasy that places you in the heroic role."

"You really believe that?"

"Yes."

"Then you're an idiot."

Dani undid the spell and the mirror surface went black. She chucked it into the bag.

"You okay?" Kleos asked.

"Our mirrors won't work anymore, now that Heman knows about them."

"Do you think he knows how to track Bouden's spell?"

"Not sure. I hope not."

They landed. Kleos went to find some kind of transportation while Dani went to wash up in the bathroom. She checked every stall this time. Her experience with the toilet-demons gave her a complex about public restrooms. She was glad no one else was in there, saving her from explaining why she pushed open every stall door like a crazed lunatic.

After finishing, she went to wash her hands. She was toweling off when she looked up into the mirror and saw Bouden's face.

"AH!" she tripped and fell back. "Bouden!"

"Hey." He said from the mirror. "I was hoping this would work."

"What the hell are you doing?" she scrambled back up. "You creeper! This is a girl's bathroom!"

"I know." He wagged his eyebrows.

"You're gross." And she meant that. "Have you been there the whole time?"

"Um, would you believe 'no?'"

"It's not safe. The mirrors—."

"Are compromised. I know. Nathaniel told me. I knew it wouldn't be too long before Heman figured it out. Don't worry. I changed the spell. This time, I can communicate with you anywhere you are, so long as you're near a mirrored surface."

"Can't Empyrean do that, too?"

"Well, yeah, but first they'd have to find you the first time, attach a tracking spell, and blah blah blah. I won't bore you. Basically, all you need to know is that I'm awesome and now we can talk."

"Aren't you worried they could...I don't know...hack the signal?"

"I think we're okay for now. Nathaniel said you have a way to stop Asmodeus?"

Dani re-explained the three artifacts to him, and suggested she might be on her way to find a fish.

"Sheatfish." Bouden corrected.

"Excuse me?"

"That's what you're probably looking for: something in the siluridae family. They're a type of catfish native to the Middle East. It makes sense. Raphael is the angel of healing and this whole thing is about a Raphael legend. The element of healing is water. It stands to reason one of the artifacts he would use to stop a demon would be a fish."

"And I'm going to find a fish from the Middle East in the United States?"

"You never told me where you were." He held up a hand. "And let's keep it that way. Any other clues?"

"Well, maybe something about nature..." *A rickety sign above a gravel-and-dirt path.* Dani tried to remember the words written on it. "Bouden, you are a genius!"

"Yup. Me and Kanye. Any reason why I am a genius?"

There was. He jogged her memory.

And Dani remembered what was on the sign.

"The House of the Star Ranch."

"What?"

Dani slid into the passenger seat of a car. Kleos sat behind the wheel. Dani looked around. "Where did you get this? Rental?"

"I borrowed it."

"You stole it?"

"Borrowed." He corrected. "Borrowed without the intent to return."

She rolled her eyes. "Right. And where did you learn to drive?"

"I didn't. You said a name. Why?"

"It's from my vision. I just remembered." The name on the rickety sign, the one from her vision above a dusty dirt road, floated to the forefront of her mind. "I think that's where we need to go next."

She took out the phone. They charged it at the hotel, but it was running low on battery. She did a search: House of the Star Ranch.

Kleos drove. He wasn't terrible, but his road rage left something to be desired. How did a Numen get so frustrated with city drivers if he never drove before? Once out of the city, Dani found what she was looking for.

"House of the Star Ranch." She announced, finding the link. "It's not far outside St. Louis." She plugged the address into the GPS. "It says here that it's a dude ranch. What the hell is a dude ranch? A place where they raise dudes?"

Kleos smirked. "It's a tourist trap. Dude ranches are where people go to stay for a weekend; ride horses, things like that."

"Uh-huh. And 'dude' comes from...?"

He chuckled. "It's a really old term meaning someone who has no idea what they're doing in the countryside. City slickers, basically." He saw Dani's sarcastic eye-brow rise. "What? It's old slang. Your generation doesn't have the market cornered on slang."

"Dude, seriously?"

"Cut that out."

"Dude, what? I'm not doing anything."

"Dani."

"I'm serious dude."

"Dani!"

She giggled. "Fine, fine, I'll stop."

Silenced passed through the car.

"But seriously dude—"

"DANI!"

They left St. Louis behind. As they drove, Caesar soaring overhead, Dani checked the date. It was October 25th. They'd been away from Empyrean for three days. In less than a week, Halloween would begin Allhallowtide. Asmodeus would have his chance to attack the city.

Following state roads into the backwoods of Missouri, civilization fell away and more small towns cropped up to break the endless forest and fields. Missouri was actually quite pretty. The leaves had changed. The air was cooler. As they drove out into the plains, the flats were bare from recently harvested crops or allowed to grow into straw-colored mazes. They passed more than one pumpkin-patch-slash-corn-maze on their way. Most of the farmers seemed to be readying for the winter months.

But as they neared their destination, things seemed to reverse. For the most part, it was overcast since they arrived. There were even thunderclouds on the horizon. But as they came down to the last two miles, the clouds broke. The air warmed. Flowery scents bloomed. Kleos turned off the heat and flipped on the AC. As if hitting a wall, they crossed over a threshold where the grass was spring-green again and there were crops still in season. The rolling hills of brown, grey or straw turned to emerald.

A single farm loomed in the distance. Sitting back on a hill, its bright red barn dominated the view. Stretched around in every direction were fields of fresh crops, cow pastures and even a vineyard. Just beyond that, teams of horses galloped around free-roaming meadowland. Farm hands were out, tending the fields.

The farm itself sat back with a large river just in sight from the main house. The house itself was a large ranch-style home, sprawling across the grounds with multiple rooms. It was like an idyllic spring getaway popped up in the middle of autumn.

Nothing did that. Nothing natural, anyway.

"So," Kleos said casually, slowing, "that's not weird at all."

"Uh-huh." Dani couldn't believe what she was seeing.

"I think we're in the right place."

He came to a stop just outside the gates. Just ahead, a wooden fence lined the perimeter of the farm and above a gravel-and-dirt path leading up to the house hung beat-up wooden sign with gold lettering.

House of the Star Ranch.

Chapter Twenty-Seven

"That's the sign from my vision." Dani said. "So, what now?"

"Go in?"

"To a place that's obviously enchanted with strong magic, and that an angel warned us is guarded by an old, ancient power?"

"I didn't mean go in the front door."

Kleos pulled away and drove up the road, hopefully to not alert anyone at the farm. Once far enough out of sight of the main house, they abandoned the stolen vehicle and set off on foot.

"Caesar," Dani called, "can you see anything?"

"*Uh, I don't know what to tell you, toots. Something is weird about this place.*"

"What do you mean?"

"*I mean my bird-sight isn't working; or something is messing with it. I can see everything, but everything I see...glimmers.*"

"Glimmers?"

"*It's like a mirage. I know whatever I am seeing isn't real, but I can't see what's underneath it, either. I'm not sure how helpful I'm going to be.*"

To Kleos, Dani translated. "Caesar says that she's seeing some kind of mirage or illusion."

"It's an enchantment." Kleos frowned, hopping the fence at the far end; far down and out of sight from the farm. "It's probably the same power that's making the weather stay springtime. Whatever is there, it can manipulate the veil; even against us."

"Which means?"

"Which means it's very powerful."

Dani hopped the fence after him. The sun was dipping past noon and headed towards sunset. They only had a few hours of daylight. They skirted the farthest field, using the woods for cover. Dani drew her sword. The last thing she needed was a monster sneaking up on them; especially if they couldn't see it through this illusion.

Once the barn was between them and the main house, they moved into the fields of tall, lush grass. Kleos withdrew something from his pack.

"What is that?" she asked.

It was a simple, smooth rock about the size of a baseball, but flat and glossy as if from a riverbed. In the middle was a single hole. It didn't look man-made, but worn through naturally.

"Adder stone." He explained. "They call them witch stones. They're naturally occurring talismans. Very rare. They can protect against demonic magic, cure snakebites, but they're best for seeing through enchantments." He held it up to his eye.

"And?"

"And," he passed it to her, pointing towards the barn, "see for yourself."

Two men appeared from the barn, leading two horses by the reins. They didn't look any different than the average person and the horses were beautiful. Dani closed one eye and put the hole up to her open one.

Things changed. The two men morphed from simple ranch-hands in jeans, T-shirts and cowboy hats, into something that was definitely not simple; or human, for that matter. They had goat legs, with scraggily, dirty hair. Their shirts covered boil-ridden torsos that had sores extending down their arms, across their necks, and over their faces. They looked diseased and malformed. Even their heads seemed misshapen. Each of them had gnarled teeth, stout sharp horns protruding under their cowboy hats, and rotting skin blotched slimy with fur. They carried axes on their belts; not tools, but deadly, stygian battle weapons which gleamed green-yellow.

"Should I even ask?"

"Se'irim." Kleos warned. "Se'ir if you want to talk about them individually. Think of them like demonic satyrs. We call them 'the hairy ones.'"

"Yeah. Hairy is a pretty good description." She snorted. "They remind me of this guy I saw at the pool once. The dude looked like a walking carpet."

"They were monsters of the field from ancient times." He took back the stone, taking another look. "People used to make human sacrifices to appease them." He started rummaging around in his pack.

"They're demons?"

"Some of the worst kind, yeah. I don't know why we didn't see them for what they were right off the bat. This whole farm is bathed in some level of magic I've never felt."

"Demonic?"

"It doesn't feel that way."

He took out a second stone, plus two lengths of line. He quickly fashioned necklaces from the Adder stones and put one over his head. She put on the other. Dani could still see through the enchantment this way.

"Look at the horses." Kleos pointed.

Dani did, this time looking past the beasts posing as ranchers. The first stallion, a black one, had a shiny coat that looked glossy to the touch. It pranced along next to the demon, braying loudly. But as the demon rancher pulled, it turned and snapped its teeth over the se'ir's arm. The demon squealed in pain as the horse bit off a chunk of its shoulder, gobbling the flesh greedily.

Dani's eyes widened.

"Mares of Diomedes." Kleos told her. "They're from my home country. Most were wiped out long ago, but I guess a few more have been bred."

"Cannibalistic horses? Seriously? With all the magical crap in the world, why isn't there real life My Little Ponies something? Instead, there's carnivorous livestock?"

She watched as the mare chewed on demon flesh, swallowing it and calming down. The satyr demon whined loudly like a billy-goat, holding onto its mangled arm. But it kept dutifully pulling it along.

Then she looked at the other horse. This one was grey and spotted when Dani first looked at it, but then the horse transformed into nothing but a grey-white skeleton. No muscle except for a few dried tendons that visibly moved as it trotted along. As it walked, it breathed fire from its nostrils and the empty eye-sockets ignited with flames.

Dani did a double take. "Aren't those...?"

"The Steeds of Abigor." Kleos nodded. "A team of them pulled Alecto's chariot. I thought they were the only ones left in existence."

Dani had seen them when the Fury came to Empyrean. "Demonic horses?"

"Sort of. They're horses of the underworld, but I'm not exactly sure 'demonic' is the right word. They come from Hell, but aren't demons themselves."

"What the hell is this place?"

"No idea. Come on. We should get closer." Kleos stood and crept through the tall grass downhill towards the barn. Dani followed.

They made it to the barn and sidled up next to it, stealthily following the infernal ranchers around the corner. The two demons led the horses down the slope towards the main house. Since they could see the four creatures for what they really were, when two people—two mundani—stepped out onto the porch, Dani almost screamed for them to run.

Kleos smacked a hand over her mouth. "Don't." he warned.

She fought him off, hissing. "Those are humans!"

"I know."

"Then you know they don't see what these things actually are!"

"And you don't see the dozen or so se'irim walking around." He pointed.

The field was full of them. Like with the two horse wranglers, she first assumed they were humans harvesting crops, but when she looked again, she could see a few of them were the goat-like monsters. They carried stygian spears, which they held like guns as they patrolled rows of workers. Dani noticed that the ones doing the actual picking were not demonic at all. They, too, were mundani.

"The workers in the fields are migrants." She said. Every one of them had a tan complexion like her. "And look what's around their necks."

Around the neck of each man and woman was a stygian choke collar. Some of the workers were old enough to be grandparents and some younger than her. The metal bands clamped around their throats painfully.

Kleos' jaw tensed. "Slaves. More than likely, they're illegal immigrants that demons smuggled into the country. Demons prey on all kinds of the weak and the helpless, including those desperate to cross borders illegally."

Dani felt sick.

The mundani at the house greeted the demons with smiles. As she watched from the barn, they helped the humans up into the saddles. They were going on a ride.

"Dear God," she whispered, "they're...they're dudes!"

"What?"

"Those two are paying customers! They're on vacation." What the hell was this place? A demonic bed-and-breakfast?

A newcomer joined them. He looked human, but for some reason, Dani got a strange vibe off him. He had a clean-shaven, all-American face with a strong jaw and dark eyes. He was dressed like a rancher; white hat, cowboy boots, denims and plaid button up, but it was like it was all for show. He seemed inauthentic. Fake.

He greeted the couple, shaking their hands and wishing them well. The pair began trotting their demonic steeds down the slope towards the road and the riding trails beyond.

As the couple passed the workers, one of the migrants stood. He was a little older than Dani; maybe only eighteen. He waved his hands furiously and shouted to them. Even from here, she could hear his Spanish clearly and understood the desperation in his voice. He was warning them.

But before he could get their attention, he collapsed. He dropped to the ground, strangled under the power of the demonic choke-collar. As the couple rode past, paying no attention, he struggled to breathe; legs kicking, arms thrashing. One of the demons strode over, point of the spear placed against the man's neck. He glanced over at a second demon; an overseer satyr in a cowboy hat and flannel. It barely nodded.

The se'ir lanced the point of stygian blade into the back of his head. The migrant stopped flailing.

"Oh my God!" She whispered. "They just killed him!"

Kleos swallowed his disgust, pulling her back. "Come on. We can't stay here."

"But—But those people!"

"Dani," he said seriously, "we have to go. There's nothing we can do for them right now."

Looking back, two other workers were forced to pick up the dead man and drag him away. It hurt to leave, but she snuck off. There were too many demons and too few of them. They wouldn't be able to do anything for them.

They crept around the far side of the barn. The whole farm crawled with demons. There were more in the back fields. One of them milked a cow. In another part of the field, a few were eating a cow. The horse fields were full of flesh-eating mares and fire-spouting steeds.

As they passed the double doors, she paused. *What is that?*

"Kleos!" she called out in a hushed whisper.

He stopped. "What?"

"Do you hear that?"

He listened. She did, too. It was soft, barely audible. But as they stood there, they could both hear it.

"...help us..."

"Please, is someone there...?"

"We're in here..."

"...is anyone out there...?"

Dani crept to the doors and pressed her ear against them. The voices were coming from inside.

"They must have people in there!" She hissed. "We have to get them out!"

A stygian lock and chain barred the double-door entry. They couldn't break it open, even with adamantine or empyreal steel, but Dani had something else.

She raised her palm, calling on her power. Kleos snatched her hand away. "Don't."

"Kleos, what are you doing?"

"Dani, we are surrounded by demons. We can't help anyone right now; even them."

"There are people in there! Do you hear them?"

"I do, but if someone hears you, we can't help anyone. The people in the fields, the people in the barn; they'll all die, regardless."

"I'm not leaving them."

"Dani—!"

She raised her hand again and fired a blast of powerful light. The lock exploded into red-orange shards. She flung off the chain and threw open the doors.

Sunlight washed in, illuminating the windowless dark space. At first, all she saw were horses. Steeds of Abigor, Mares of Diomedes; they took up the first few stalls. The monstrous mounts gnashed their teeth, straining to bite her or blow fire as she passed. But from farther in, the voices got louder.

She made her way past the monsters. Further down, the stalls became cages. And the cages held a different type of animal.

"*Por favor! Ayúdanos! Ayúdanos!*" The first stall had a woman of about thirty with her child. Their clothes were dingy and stained. They looked like they'd been in there for weeks. She came to the bars of her cage.

"Get us out of here!" A man in the stall across from her said in English. He looked homeless, but underneath his sweat-stained outfit and appearance, his bright blue eyes called out pleadingly in the dark. "Please! Get us out of here!"

"Be quiet!" Kleos shushed.

But more people joined the chorus. There were about ten or twelve cages, filling up the rest of the barn; a holding pen for human beings.

"*Por favor! Te suplico!*" Another man called from down the line. "*No quiero a morir!*"

"*Tranquilo!*" Dani told them all. "We'll get you out."

The mares brayed, their hooves striking the stalls that kept them penned in. The people screamed louder.

"We have to get them out." She told Kleos.

"Dani—!"

"We're doing this." She said firmly. "You either help or leave."

He hesitated, glancing around the room, and then nodded. "Alright."

She was about to start opening locks when, out of the corner of her eye, she spotted a pair of raiments. They were so dirty and covered in grime—a muted green color that didn't exist in Empyrean—but they were unmistakably Arachne-weave. Their owner, a sandy-haired boy of about eighteen, brightened when he saw her looking his way.

He stood. "You're—You're Numen!" He ran to the bars, grabbing them and then doubling back in pain. "Ugh! The cages are all made of stygian! Don't touch them!"

It was true. The cages had indeed been made from the hellish metal; midnight black. The cold could be felt even from a distance.

"Who are you?" Kleos asked him.

"My name is Liam. Please, get us the bloody hell out of here!"

Kleos was resolved to help now, as if it took an Earthborn to make him act. Dani didn't care. She was freeing these people, Numen or not.

"Find something to pry open the bars." She said. "I'll start getting them open on my own."

Dani started with the first cage, the one containing the woman and her daughter. "We're going to get you out, okay?" They didn't dare to touch the bars, since the icy coldness would sting painfully. Chains and locks kept them sealed in. "Tell me what they're doing here. What do they want with you? *Qué lo quieres con usted?*"

"*No se. No se.*" She murmured miserably, holding onto her daughter tightly. Her Spanish was shaky as she spoke, but she told her:

They were workers. Undocumented. Mexican or Central American, mostly. They weren't smuggled across the border, though. Most were already here and were either picked up in what they thought were ICE raids or detained by other means. From what the woman told her, they'd been kept at a deportation checkpoint before these "people" brought them here.

Dani's power poured from her fingertips. Like miniature, palm-flashlights, her hands lit up and the metal lock began to dissolve. She had to be careful not to blow it apart and send shards of metal everywhere.

"*Ellos tomaron mi esposo.*"

"What did she say?" Kleos asked.

The lock almost dissolved, but despite the warmth of her hands, she felt cold. "She said they took her husband." The woman kept speaking and Dani kept translating. "They take a lot of people; to work in the fields, or to fight. If they can't do either," the woman finished, crying, "they feed them to the horses."

"Who runs this place?" Kleos asked Liam.

"I don't know his name."

"Is he a demon?"

"I don't know. He's powerful. Everyone fears him, but no one says his name. He and his helper, a big man, run the whole ranch. They're—." he stopped.

Dani felt the cold chill of shadow across her back.

She turned, going first for her knife, since it was faster to draw. A large shadow was suddenly at her back and a thick hand seized around her wrist, twisting. She cried out, flung around by the intruder who spun and chucked her across the room into the bars of one of the cages. She slammed into them and landed painfully.

Kleos launched an adamantine chain at their attacker. Dani only briefly saw the man. He was gigantic. But for a guy his size, he moved fast. She barely glimpsed the wide shoulders, thick neck, and square jawline covered by a heavy black beard.

The six-foot tall guard ducked sideways as the whip passed by harmlessly and he flung himself at Kleos. Wrapping his arms around his mid-section, he hoisted her friend up and threw him to the ground in one motion. Kleos slammed hard into the floor and stopped moving. Unconscious.

Dani was up. The man turned to face her as she drew both Pointyend and Pigsticker. The blades flared to life in the gloom, illuminating her in a halo of gold.

The man looked normal enough, except that he was the size of a golem. Judah's staff were the biggest creatures Dani ever met; at least, until now. This guy dwarfed them. He was all muscle, which rippled underneath his red-and-black plaid shirt and threatened to shred the sleeves. He crouched into a combat stance, completely unarmed, but he kept his hands up like he knew how to fight.

"Come on, big boy." She prodded. "Come and get it."

He charged, but he didn't run straight at her like some did. He jounced from one foot to another in a slow lope, testing her balance as he came. When he got about two feet from her, she swung with her sword and he sidestepped it easily. He jumped and struck to her jaw with his bare fist. She took the brunt of it across the left side that was exposed from her missed strike. He delivered a kick to her leg, which made it go numb and forced her to stagger back.

Dani slashed with her knife. She felt a surge of satisfaction as the blade sunk into his arm and stabbed through to the other side.

But even though she just bisected his bicep, he didn't slow. He forced her hand back, still on the grip of her blade. No blood poured from the wound. The man glared down at her. With a yank of his arm, the blade came free.

He didn't wait. Even as Dani sloppily stabbed with her knife again, this time to his stomach, he turned his body sideways so the dagger shot by harmlessly. His forearm wrapped hers and pulled her forward, off-balance. The moment she lurched, he flipped her wrist and threw her onto her back. Both knife and sword dropped from her grip.

Pain shot up her arm as the joint-lock nearly tore the ligament in her elbow and wrist. She screamed, kicking at his face, but the blow didn't even landed before he grabbed her under her body and picked her up. He hoisted her above her head and then slammed her down again.

Dani didn't even remember landing.

Chapter Twenty-Eight

Dani crawled her way back to consciousness and her eyes drifted open. When she woke, she was tied, with both wrists above her head, to a tractor wheel. Kleos sat next to her, similarly bound.

"Dani, are you okay?" He asked.

"Kleos, what happened?"

"Well, now I know y'all's names."

The man who attacked them stood a few feet away. In the fading afternoon light, he was even scarier. Everything about him screamed steroid-junkie. His muscles had muscles. He folded his arms over his broad chest, not saying a word.

The one who spoke, however, was the man next to him; the one who greeted the couple at the main house. He was small by comparison to his enormous henchman, but by no means weak. Confident, thumbs hooked into the belt-loops of his jeans, he was utterly unafraid of the se'irim around him. In fact, the demons cowered in fear of him. They went through Dani's and Kleos' packs under his orders.

The lanky cowboy ambled forward with that Southern-gait that Dani despised in old, spaghetti Westerns. He looked the part of a good ol' boy, but Dani bet money there was nothing good about him.

"You broke in-tah my barn." He drawled. "I don't take kindly to trespass-ahs."

"Well Texas Pete, you had two dozen people locked up in there." She stared him down. "I'm not sure if you've heard, but slavery is illegal these days."

He smirked. "Numen. I didn't expect to see anymore of ya', other than the one in that there barn. Anyone else with yeh?"

Caesar was above, somewhere, but didn't attack when the big man surprised them. Dani didn't see her now, either. Hopefully, she was smart and stayed back.

"We've got a whole army of Powers about to descend on this place." Dani lied. "I'd let us go if I were you."

He hiked up on his pants and knelt, grinning, "Female, smart-mouthed and an accomplished liar; you must be that Daniella girl I heard rumors about."

"I hate being famous." She muttered. "All the paparazzi, party invitations, evil codpieces plotting to capture you. It's a whole big thing, really." She glared at him. "So, who are you? Or I guess I should ask *what* are you? Demon? Jinn? Because I can tell human isn't on that list."

"I'mma simple man of the field." He tipped back his hat. "Let's start with why you're really here alone. And I emphasize _alone_ because I doubt you've got any 'army of Powers' at your back, sweetheart."

Dani considered telling the truth.

For about five seconds. His 'sweetheart' brought out of the worst side of her. "Well, I'm Ryan Seacrest and we're looking for the next American Idol."

His smile flickered and then he backhanded her. Hard. She tasted blood.

"Do not get smart with me." He warned her, his tone changing darkly. His southern accent disappeared; replaced by something more Middle Eastern. Old world. "Do not take me for some fool, little girl. I survived the rise and fall of the Roman Empire, every plague from the Biblical to the Black, and every natural disaster from Vesuvius to the Dust Bowl. I have been around longer than the very idea of humanity. I am not to be tested."

Dani licked her lower, split lip and said nothing.

He sighed and the relaxed demeanor came back like a flick of a switch. When he spoke, his southernness returned. "I apal-ah-gize. It's just with so much to do around this here farm, dealing with snide remarks wastes my time and gets my fires stoked. Now, I assume y'all being here has something to do with these bane boxes." He took one from his muscled helper. "These are used for very special thingamajigs. What's in them?"

He attempted to open the one, but couldn't.

"Hmm. Must be enchanted pretty strongly. You gonna to tell me what's in 'em or am I gonna need to torture you?"

"Go to hell, demon." Kleos spat at his feet. "Just kill us and get it over with."

He glanced from the spittle, to Kleos, to Dani. Finally, he stood with a sigh and handed the box back to his lieutenant. "Take 'em up to the main house and prepare 'em a room."

The big man grunted. It wasn't a sentence. It wasn't even a word. But the ranch owner understood anyway.

"Yes, yes, I know. Go get them newlyweds from room five. We'll put our new guests in there."

He grunted again.

"What do ya' mean, what do we do with 'em? Feed 'em to the horses. They need to be well fed or they'll keep killing the ranch hands." Some of the se'irim whined. "You see? I can't have skittish hands. Go get the mundani! Hop to it!"

The giant headed off around the barn. The farm owner barked orders and his satyr-demons quickly untied Dani and Kleos, pulling them to their feet.

"You're a monster." She told him. "Even for a demon, you're sick."

"Well, that's the thing, sweetheart," he smiled, "I'm not a demon. I'm a god. My name is Dagon. Welcome to my ranch."

They took them to the main house. As their demonic escorts led them through the front door, Dagon's humungous assistant hauled the two people out the side, one in each arm. The couple that just returned from their ride.

They fought, but the giant was impossible to escape. He pulled the two kicking and screaming down to the barn. Seconds later, horse brays and bloody screams floated uphill. They lasted only seconds, and then there was silence. Dani's stomach turned.

The house was massive. Just inside the door was a wide-open living room converted into a lobby for guests, with hallways on either side leading to bedrooms. It was rustic, quaint and everything someone would want for a ranch getaway.

Minus the demons.

They shoved her and Kleos down the hall to the last room on the right. Once deposited inside, the demons shut and locked the door. Kleos jiggled the handle, but it wouldn't budge.

"I'll try." She said, raising her hand. Her lightbringing could turn it to splinters.

"Don't!" He stopped her, pressing his hand against the door, as if sensing it for something. "It's magically warded. I'm betting the windows are too. Your lightbringing might blow it open or blow us up."

Dani cursed. Wards. Great.

"I wonder if Caesar is alright." She said worriedly.

"She stayed out of the fight," he said, "so she's still out there. She's safe. It would have been nice if she helped, though."

"No." Dani shook her head. "The big man might have killed her too. At least now we have someone close by on the outside."

"Can you communicate with her?"

She stepped close to the window. "Caesar? Caesar, are you there?"

She knew Caesar could hear her voice for miles, even at a whisper, but no answer came.

"I can't reach her. Is it more magical warding?"

Kleos shook his head, running his fingers along the windowsill. "No. Something more mundane: soundproofing. They probably use it to hide the screaming."

Dani shuddered. "Great. We're in a Rob Zombie flick now. Who the hell is this guy, Kleos? Who is Dagon?"

He looked around outside the window. "He's a god."

"Yeah, I got that, but is like Hermes? Is he a psychopomp? Or is he some kind of false god?"

"No. He's an actual god." The room had a single queen-size bed, on which he sat down resignedly. "He's a pagan god, anyway."

"Pagan god? As in, from a polytheistic religion or something?"

He nodded. "Think of it like this: other than *God* God, there are two other types of gods. There's false gods—demons—who were worshipped and feared in ancient times. They usually got their followers to do things like child sacrifice in order to fuel their power. But the second type of gods are the pagans. 'Pagan' comes from the word 'countryside'. It means the gods of a particular region, as opposed to a supreme deity. Gods like Dagon were the deities of ancient civilizations. They were worshiped long ago. They're in almost every culture; Greeks, Romans, Norse—like Idunn—and those Wicca people; even Native Americans. Every continent in the known world has pagan gods. They were 'other powers' of the world. A lot of them have disappeared, while some work for us."

"Like Hermes and Idunn?"

"Yes. They became allies, or helpers, or psychopomps. Any others usually stick to the shadows, now; living immortal lives amongst humans. Even we don't know where most of them are now."

"Do we know why they disappeared?"

"Until you found Gabriel, we didn't even know where angels went; so no, not really."

"Great. But that guy?" She thumbed over her shoulder. "Dagon? I've never heard of him."

"He's a type of pagan god known as a *ba'al*; a Semetic god. He was worshipped all over the world back in the day: Babylon, Mesopotamia, Assyria, Canaan, but he's most known for being the national god of the Philistines."

"Philistines? You mean the guys who had a grudge match with Israel that nearly wiped them both out?"

"The same ones. Dagon was a major player in their pantheon. He was mostly known for being a god of the fields. And judging by this ranch, his power hasn't faded much."

"You mean the fact that its summer here in the middle of freaking autumn?"

He nodded.

Dani thought she'd seen power before, but control over nature like that? Even she knew that meant major juice. Haniel's words rung true:

An old, powerful force of nature. Dagon certainly was that.

"What about his helper, Muscley McMuscleton? Is he a god? He's enormous, but he's definitely not human. I cut him with my sword and he didn't bleed."

"He's not a god, at least as far as I can tell. I think he's a revenant."

"A what?"

"A returned soul."

"Like a shade?"

He shrugged. "Sort of. They're spirits, but really old spirits. It takes thousands of years for a soul trapped on Earth to become a revenant. In that time, they take corporeal form—a physical body. That's why we call them revenants, or 'the returned.' They return to life."

She shook her head, whistling lowly. "Wow. If I knew coming back from the dead was so easy, I wouldn't worry so much about dying. Being a revenant sounds great."

"Trust me, it's not." Kleos told her. "Yes, revenants come back from the dead, but it's not in a good way. Nothing in this world can ever fully live again; nothing gets a true second chance. With revenants, they get another body and can live a long time, but there's always something wrong with them. They come back broken."

The big man couldn't talk. Was that because he was a revenant?

"As far as the one with Dagon, I have no idea who he is, but he's helping him run this demonic ranch. Chances are, he'll be just as dangerous as his employer."

She shook her head. "Great. A pagan farm god with Gigantor as his bodyguard and they locked us up in a room in his House of a Thousand Corpses; I can't wait to see what comes next." She sat next to him on the bed. "What is he doing working for demons?"

"I don't know. The pagans despise demons about as much as we do. I mean, come on, they're demons. No one likes demons."

"Well, they're buddy-buddy now and he's got our bane boxes with Asmodeus's medallion."

"Yeah." Kleos looked up, thinking. "About that: I noticed he didn't know what was in them, so I don't think he's one of Asmodeus's lackeys. That could be a good thing. So as long as we don't tell him what's inside, he won't know why we're here."

It was a plan about as solid as water, but what other choice did they have?

A few minutes passed, but eventually Dagon himself appeared. He opened the door, smiling cordially. It creeped her out.

"Supper is ready in the dining room." He announced.

"I'd rather starve." Dani told him.

"I insist that you don't. My last guests just became meals themselves. I'd like the pleasure of y'all's company."

Dani asked, "You don't have any other guests?"

"No, just you."

"Then you didn't need to kill the couple staying here!"

He tipped his head to the side as if considering it. "I guess that's true, but then again if they saw you, there'd be questions. Also," he stepped back, holding out his hand to the hall, "I don't really care. So, supper?"

"I'd rather die."

"If you feel that way," his drawl slipped and his real accent shone through, "I could arrange to have both your legs broken and then impale you on a spike as a scarecrow in my fields. Eventually, death would honor that request. Or, you could come to supper."

It was hard to argue with that.

He led them to the dining hall at the back of the house. It was quiet. A dozen round tables covered in southern-plaid tablecloths decorated the room, each with festive centerpieces and laid out with empty dishes. It would have been a quaint place to stay if she liked B-and-Bs or antiquing like an old lady. The quiet, though, unnerved her.

Dagon, the god in the guise of a man, gestured them to a table. An imp hobbled out of the kitchen. Dani recognized the creature by the stench alone. The exposed, rotting gums and shark-like teeth, the upturn nose and black eyes were also a dead giveaway. It came to the table, barely as tall as she was sitting down. Unlike her last encounter, it wasn't here to kill her, but to take her dinner request.

"Bring them each a fresh ear of corn, the steak and collard greens." Dagon ordered for them. "Unless you two want anything else?"

They didn't.

The demon left and Dagon, leaning on his elbows, smiled at them. "Well, now, isn't this nice? It's so wonderful to have a meal with a small, intimate group. This time of year is our slow season, but as you can see outside, we do quite well year-round."

"Your power keeps this place in season." She said, not asked.

"Yes. I am a field god, after all. Farming is my domain."

"Someone will come looking for us. You won't survive if Empyrean's armies tear this place apart."

"Ah, yes, well that would require them to know you are here. From what I hear-tell, they're still California way. I imagine your fortress-city is also preparing for the arrival of Asmodeus, so I sus'pect they're pretty busy."

Dani glanced sideways at Kleos.

"Yes. I heard the lord of lust returned. It's not every day a master of Hell declares outright war on the Numen." Dagon rubbed one of his eyes, bored.

235

"Personally, I found him boring as all Hell. Blah, blah, blah, women are for service to the men, not having opinions, blah, blah, blah. Even for me, who values the strength of a man's arm over the weakness of a female, I find him tiresome."

"So you're not a fan?" Kleos asked. "Strange company you keep, then."

"The demons I hire?" he smirked. "Those are gifts from another power."

"Another power?"

"Yes. I'm sure you've heard of him." His eyes fell on Dani. "They call him Belial. He's mentioned you. You're quite the topic of discussion amongst the beings of Hell and he is very interested in meeting you."

The name was an ice trickle down her spine. "You work for Belial?"

His smile twitched with glee. "Yes. I know what you may be thinking: Belial hasn't shown himself. It's been months but the one demon Alecto wanted most of all hasn't even bothered to appear. Why do you think that is?"

"I don't know." She tried to turn it back on him to answer. "Why would you work for him?"

"*With* him." He corrected. "We're partners."

"Partners in what?"

"In this." He gestured to the ranch.

"Belial is into the agricultural business? What, did he pick up Home and Garden and just *had* to know more?" There went her mouth again; loose as ever.

Dagon didn't seem to find it as entertaining. "No. And if you're half as smart as you appear to be, you won't goad me. Doing that is likely to get you twenty lashes." His smile snapped into an ugly look of disgust. It was creepy how fast it happened; like a switch. And his other, ancient accent returned. "My mundani workers outside know the lash very well."

"Slaveholder." She snarled, not one to back down from a fight.

"Watch your tone," he cautioned, "but yes. Save the judgmental attitude, though. Slave labor is the foundation of modern America. It gave rise to this country; gave you and so many others the privilege of not living in a third world. It was built on the bones of black slaves, immigrants and Native Americans. Anyone who pretends otherwise is just plain stupid."

"*Escoria.*" She cursed. Some things just sounded better in Spanish.

"As with the masters of old, I do not speak the language of slaves. It is beneath me."

Their meal arrived. Covered in warm, steaming food, even Dani had to admit the platters set before them looked delicious. The corn was bright yellow. The steak was cooked to an even medium, already sliced in half. Even the collard greens, which she hated, smelled amazing.

Kleos and Dani didn't touch any of it.

"It's not poisoned." He assured them.

Dani folded her arms. "I still don't want it."

The god looked slightly offended. "As it stands, you two are living better than most of my workers and demons. You could be out in that barn with the others if I willed it. I think there is still one surviving Numen out there, if I do not mistake myself. But here you are, enjoying a nice meal courtesy of my good will. So, I advise that you take my hospitality."

Both Kleos and Dani resigned themselves and picked up forks and knives. Damn if it wasn't the best food Dani ever had.

They ate in silence for a few minutes. She tried not to shovel it down like a caveman, since she hadn't eaten since they got off the plane. And the food was delicious.

After a few minutes, Dagon continued in his southern drawl. "As I was sayin' about my relationship with Belial: we're partners. We speak often and he talks about you all the time, sweetheart." She could tell he meant to piss her off with that 'sweetheart' comment. "He's very interested in meeting you."

"Yeah, well, that's not high on my to-do list." She looked around. "Why would Belial help you anyway? What is all of this?" She played it cool, though. "I mean, feed us a nice meal and for what? Are you going to tell us your master plan like some stupid Bond villain?"

The god chuckled. "You're one funny little beaner, aren't you?"

Dani ignored the racial slur.

"Well, I might as well tell you. There ain't many sparklin' conversationalists here, is there? And besides, you assume you'll leave here alive to tell anyone about it. I can assure you, you will not. Which," he smiled, pressing a finger to his lips, "I think most Bond villains believe anyway. Still—."

"Cut the crap. What's with the funny farm?"

"It's purpose?" Dagon shrugged. "As you can see, breeding is the most important thing. You saw our steeds and mares outside. You could say supernatural husbandry is my specialty."

"Why breed those animals?" Kleos asked, sipping his water.

"Simple: every army needs cavalry."

The two of them stopped eating. The pagan god grinned widely.

"An army? Who's army?" Dani asked.

"Belial's, o'course." He told them. "You think Asmodeus is the only archdemon ready to strike? He is the opening salvo in a much wider war. There are many demon lords and princes and dukes and presidents out there. They have all returned with vengeance on their minds. And they're organizing, but their leader has yet to be chosen. Anyway," he waved it off, "I won't bore y'all with the details. Mainly, all you need to know is that you and the rest of humanity are going to die horrible, painful deaths full of blood, fire and brimstone. Would you like desert?"

He ordered ice cream for them. They didn't touch it.

"Don't be rude." Dagon chided.

"I'm lactose intolerant." Kleos lied.

Dani just said, "I'm too disgusted to eat anything else."

"Ah, yes, well talking about the human race's extinction will do that."

"Why are you doing this?" Kleos asked. "I know pagan gods. Some of them work for us. They're our allies. I'd even call them friends."

"And the problem lies in the middle of that statement." Dagon told him. "They 'work for you.' They're gods. They're not servants. Any god who speaks of servitude is a god who is weak."

"And you thought demons were better because...?" she trailed off, doing exactly what he warned her not to do: tease him.

But he didn't take the bait. "Better? Of course, they're better. I prefer them to humans."

"Is it the rancid garbage smell or the putrid sores all over their bodies?"

Dagon didn't hit her, but his face fell into a scowl. "You believe humanity is somehow superior?"

"We don't kill for the joy of it."

"You clearly never watch the news." The old god shook his head. "Humanity has always been a vicious killer. You think demons are bad? They kill, what, a couple dozen a year? Maybe more? Humans on average slaughter each other by the hundreds; sometimes in one day. You need examples? Search human history: Yangzhou, the Reign of Terror, the Batak Massacre, the thousands under Pol Pot, the millions who died in Holocaust or millions more under Stalin; they killed with a passion. And you think that's only in the past? Ethnic cleansings in the Balkans, cartels in South America, the Sudan," he shook his head, "the endless slaughter in Aleppo. Humanity's bloodlust is rampant and disgusting."

He leaned in, his eyes darkening, his voice thick with hatred and empty of southern charm.

"Do you know where all the old gods went? We did not die. We did not leave this existence like the cowardly angels. We stayed on this Earth. The only reason you have not heard from us is because we wish you not to; because we find you repulsive."

He tapped the table. "We are immortal. We carved out a little slice of paradise for ourselves and we ruled over humanity as benevolent protectors. We cared just as much for our worshippers as the One who forged Heaven—maybe even more, since we were not so distant! And then, when monotheism came around, do you know what we did? We did not protest. We did not fight back. We retired."

Dani's eyebrows shot up. "Retired?"

"Being a god is time consuming." He explained. "You have to answer prayers, payback sacrifices, smite individuals who dishonor your temples. The red tape alone would drive you insane. But it was our place in the world. So, when God decided He wanted to take over full-time, we were okay with it. Many of us wanted less to do, anyway."

"I know some of us are still out there, doing what they have always done. The Hindus never really stopped. The Norse have started up some of the old temples in Europe, but that's more for show. But for the most part, us Semitics from Assyria, Babylon, and all the old gods from ancient nations called it quits. Retirement suits us. We want the quiet life; free of distraction and responsibility."

"Then why are you working for Hell?" Dani had to ask.

"Because humanity is the devil." He snarled. "Have you heard of the Temple of Bel?"

"No."

"Of course you have not. In a world so interconnected by media, humans still do not care about what happens around the world, even though it is instantly at their fingertips. The world believes the internet age is the next Enlightenment. It is not. It is the new Dark Age."

"The Temple of Bel," he continued, "was one of the few centers of worship left for the old gods. We did not care that no one worshipped within it anymore, but at least it was held in reverence. Tombs, idols, shrines; it would stand as a testament to us for ages to come and for the new world to remember us. Then along comes a crazed group of humans who obliterates it in the name of their God."

"And what others have fallen into ruin?" Dagon kept going. "The Temple of the Baalshamin, the Lion of Allat, Apamea, Mari, the Nergal Gate, and all the sites of Nimrud and Palmyra; they're gone now, or sold to the highest bidder like trinkets for rich men to own. Most of the Western pagans care very little about their sites. They got other things to keep their names alive. The Romans are still honored in movies and TV. The Greeks have that book series. The Norse do not complain because they have a movie deal for their gods." He shook his head. "But us? Some of the first gods? Our places of worship are destroyed by vile, ignorant humans the way they destroy everything else! Nineveh, once the proudest city in the Assyrian empire, has lost its once wonderful statues. Mosul's libraries, with their rich heritage, have been wiped out. And here in America? The ancient lands of the indigenous people, the sacred areas left for their gods, have been taken over by lobbyists of the human government; greedy for precious metals and oil underneath their surfaces, or are at best used for some pipeline. Many humans gladly follow along, as if heritage means nothing.

My own temple of E-Mul, the original House of the Star, is gone. All knowledge of us is fading. And we," he pointed to himself, "we are angry."

He turned on Dani. "You ask me if I prefer demons over humans? I do. At least demons do not pretend to be something they are not. Humans are repulsive. Their hatred, their two-faced nature, and their self-destruction makes them what they are: evil. Your species is the only one on the planet that invents new ways to murder. How you are God's favorite creation, I have no idea. If you saw humanity the way that I have over the centuries, you would be disgusted, too."

Dani shuddered in either insult, anger or fear. She wasn't sure which. "So, you serve demons now? Is that it?

"I partner with them." He argued. "As I said before, I found a very satisfactory relationship with their kind. I live a comfortable life because of it. I am investing in the future."

"Helping them build an army, you mean."

"Yes. Belial is a very busy demon. Since his release from Hell's dungeons, he has been working. Meeting. Gathering. He has quite a host at his disposal already." Dagon sat back in his chair. "In fact, that is why I am very glad you are here."

"Us? Why?"

"I didn't tell you?" He grinned excitedly, his southern accent creating a disturbing façade of gleeful and hateful. "Well darling, in my partnership with the Wicked One, I set up treaties for him. You see, demons have gone so long without a structured peckin' order, they're more like tribes of savages than an actual army. There's warlords fighting over who should be in control, as opposed to working together. It's only recently that they began rallying around one potential candidate to lead 'em. O'course, organizing a demonic rebellion is tasking, so for Belial to gather forces, he needs a go-between."

"You, you mean?"

He nodded. "I have connections in the ancient world and amongst the beings of Hell. You don't become a god without 'em. Tomorrow, I have one such meeting. Two guests will arrive. I'm hoping to wine, dine and entertain 'em so they agree to give to the cause."

She didn't like the sound of that. "Entertain them with what?"

"Oh, a little exhibition." Dagon assured her. "A display of fightin' skill that might persuade 'em to side with us."

"Who's in this exhibition?"

Dagon's smile widened a fraction and slowly, with all charm of the southern good ol' boy, he said. "You two, o'course. Y'all will fight to the death for their entertainment. Now are you sure you don't want to eat your ice cream?"

Chapter Twenty-Nine

"I must say," said Dagon from his porch, the overhead lamp backlighting him in the dusk and casting shadows over his face, "it was quite an enlightening conversation at dinner. I thank ya' kindly for your pleasant company."

Dani and Kleos stood at the bottom of the steps, hands cuffed behind their backs in stygian bindings—black-metal bracers connected by chains that covered their palms. They stole the heat out of Dani's hands. There would be no lightbringing with them on.

"You can shove the pleasant company." She told him.

Behind her, the se'irim guards stirred anxiously. The undead hulk that worked for Dagon held her shoulder firmly. She wouldn't be flying, either.

"You shouldn't be so rude." Dagon warned, sauntering down the steps. "It's impolite of a lady. I could kill you with a simple order."

"But you won't." Kleos pointed out.

"True. Your deaths will be a fine spectacle for my guests."

Dani wanted to hit him. Even with her hands tied, she could put a shoulder into his gut. It wouldn't do much, but it would make her feel better.

She almost got an inch before the massive hand of the revenant squeezed her shoulder, nearly breaking the collarbone. She muffled a scream.

Dagon grinned, "I assume you remember my loyal servant."

"We've met." She growled.

"And tomorrow, you will again. He was my signing bonus from Belial. My most devout follower: Goliath."

She recognized the name. She didn't need her Studies in Empyrean to know him. He was a household name in the modern world. Hell, he was a freaking metaphor by now.

"The Philistine warrior?"

"Yes. When Belial asked me to aid him, I told him I wanted back what Israel's king took from me."

She smirked. "Yeah. Took with a rock, if I remember correctly. How does a pebble kill the greatest warrior of the Philistines, by the way?"

Goliath growled.

"What? No words? Is he some kind of mute? Or is he stupid?" She teased. "What's the word I'm looking for? Oh yeah! A *philistine!*"

One of Goliath's large hands caught her throat and lifted her clear off the ground. Her toes barely brushed the grass as they flailed. He might not be able to speak, but his hearing was just fine.

241

Dani gasped. Her hands were still tied back. He could choke her to death and there was nothing she could do about it.

"Goliath!" Dagon warned.

He let her go and she dropped to her knees, sucking wind.

"Not an intelligent choice, darlin'. One of these days, your mouth is gonna get you in trouble."

She croaked, "Yeah, well, you're a little late to that party."

He knelt in front of her. "For someone with so much fire, I find it odd that you side with the Numen. I can't imagine that the Earthborn treat you as an equal. Most of them are idiots. You don't seem stupid to me. Have you ever noticed they're on the losing side?"

"Have you ever noticed," she asked back, "that people who talk about others' faults don't see the problem with themselves?"

"I am simply pointing out the splinter in the eye of the beholder."

"Yeah, well, it's better than the plank sticking out of yours." She shook her head. "I wouldn't side with demons if my life depended on it. I don't side with Numen or anyone else because I'm blind. I do it because it protects the people I care about. So," she slowly stood, "go sard yourself."

A smile curled on his lips and he stood, too. "I see that my hospitality is lost on you both. You want to choose the losing side? Fine. You belong with the slaves. The barn cages suit you better. Take 'em away."

Goliath grabbed Dani and Kleos by the elbows, pulling them away. The god called out, "What? No witty comeback?"

Dani had nothing.

The lights of the main house faded as the demons led them to the barn. The night was alive with crickets, even now in the middle of autumn. It was so alive and yet, so very dead. Slaves built this place. No matter how beautiful it was, it was cold and lifeless to her.

In the distance, she could see a dark void in the back fields; a pit taking up a good portion of the ranch grounds. Bleachers shone in the moonlight around the rim of it.

Goliath opened the doors to the barn. A chorus of shrieks greeted them. The nostril-flare of the steeds illuminated the gloom as the demons dragged Dani and Kleos back to the cells. The mother and daughter cowered in the corner of their cage. Liam, the Numen, shrunk back as well. No one made eye contact with Goliath.

They threw Dani and Kleos in and slammed the cages. They left the braces on their hands, which ached painfully. The stygian sapped the strength from them, replacing it with searingly-painful cold.

Goliath left, whistling a tune to himself: Gershwin's *Summertime*. The living was easy for him, apparently.

He left the door ajar to flood the interior with dim moonlight.

242

Kleos kicked the stygian cage angrily. "Are you okay, Dani?"

"Peachy." She sat, moving her hands down and under her legs, until she got them over her ankles. At least now, she had them in front of her. "This is the second time during this trip that demons captured me. That's not a good track record."

"Got any ideas of how to get out of here?" Kleos asked, doing the same with his hands.

"Do I look like a lady with a plan?"

He shrugged. "Kind of."

"Really?"

He shrugged again, smirking a little. "Well, the way you mouth off to gods and demons, either you've got a plan or you've got serious lady-balls."

"Lady-balls?"

"Do you prefer *cojones*?"

"I prefer no references to male genitalia, thank you very much." She shook her head. "And no, I don't have a plan. I wish I did. This is first time someone asked me to take charge and I got nothing."

"Can you melt off the stygian cuffs like you did with the lock on the barn door?"

She tried, but with the stygian so close to her palms, the cold stole away her lightbringing before it could do anything. She kept her hands glowing just to keep the hellish metal from giving her frostbite.

"No." She answered glumly.

Dani tested the door, just to see if she could somehow pull it off its hinges, but the bars wouldn't budge. Across the way, the woman held her daughter close, stroking her hair. The fear in their eyes told Dani all she needed to know. They needed to get out of here.

How long had they been here? Days? Weeks? Months? The little girl sobbed. Her mother shushed her.

Her husband was gone. She was locked in a cell. Her daughter was in danger. Dani kicked the bars in frustration, but told her, "*Te liberamos.*" *We'll get you free.*

She hoped that wasn't a lie.

"*Psst!* Hey!"

Liam, the Numen from before, crawled over to the bars in the adjourning cage. Dani almost forgot he was there.

Kleos, who sat cross-legged on the floor, didn't open his eyes. Dani had plenty of experience with Mastema's mediation. She didn't disturb him, but she was restless and, apparently, so was her neighbor.

"Liam, right?"

He nodded.

"I'm Dani. That's Kleos."

"You're a girl."

It was an odd opening line, but she was used to it. "Great observation."

He spoke with an accent. It sounded Australian. "You're an Earthborn. How?"

"I'm complicated. I'm from Empyrean. Maybe we're just weird there. You?"

"Ber'iah."

Her heart skipped a beat. "Ber'iah?"

He nodded, turning to show her the emblem on the back of his dark, green tunic: the Pentalpha, symbol of Raphael.

"You're from Ber'iah? You survived?"

"Yeah. How do you know about Beri'ah?"

"We went there. We saw..." Dani didn't want to relive that. "How did you escape?"

His voice cracked. "I was working as a messenger. I arrived when," he bit back his words, "when it happened. I and a few others barely escaped."

"A few others? There are more of you?"

"Yes."

"Here?"

He paused. "There used to be."

Dani remembered Dagon talking about 'at least one Numen left.' "I'm sorry, Liam. What happened? How did Ber'iah fall? Was it demons?"

"No." he told her. "It was us."

"Us?"

"When I arrived, everyone had gone crazy. People killed each other in the streets; swords, spears, some just bashing in each other's heads. It was Numen against Numen; Gifted against Gifted." His voice cracked again. Tears shimmered at the edges of his eyes. "I don't know what they were doing! So many people...they just died. And when they died, they didn't stay dead. These things, these black shadows, came out of them. They began killing anyone in sight. They weren't just shadows. They were—were—!"

"Shades." She already knew. "The souls of the people who died."

"What could make anything, even a soul, do something like that?"

Kleos opened his eyes, flicking them back and forth between the two of them. "Dani? Maybe we shouldn't talk too much."

"Why?"

"The walls have ears."

Liam tensed, biting his lower lip. "I'm in here same as you. I'd like to know what killed my city."

"He has a right to know." Dani told Kleos. "Liam, what attacked your city was an archdemon; one of the first demons in Creation. His name is Asmodeus."

244

"Asmodeus?"

"He's a demon from legend and very powerful."

"And he can turn people into murderous monsters?"

"Yes. We're trying to stop him. That's why we're here."

"How do you plan to stop him?"

She thought for a moment. Could he help them? Maybe. "Liam, you've been here awhile, right? Since the attack?"

"About two weeks. My friends and I fled the city and were on the run for a while. We tried to get to one of the other celestial cities. We were almost to Empyrean when we landed here, looking for food. This place...it seemed like a paradise. We thought we could scavenge for supplies. Then that thing running the farm captured us."

"Dagon. He's a god." She brushed right past his next question, even before he asked it. "He's not important. What is important is if you've seen anything Dagon or his demons might be protecting?"

"Like?"

"A fish."

She knew the question was odd, but somehow she knew the vision of the fish in murky water was connected to this place. She could feel it.

"A fish? Any kind of fish in particular?"

"A big one?" *Yeah, that's helpful Dani.*

"Not that I know of," Liam confessed, "but Dagon doesn't allow fishing in the river behind the ranch. Some of the demons eat cattle or people, but he doesn't let them near the river. Does that help?"

"Liam, that actually does help." The river bordered the ranch. It wasn't too far away from the barn; just beyond the back field.

"They've been digging in the back field," he told her, "making some kind of arena. That big guy who works for Dagon? He's his number one warrior. He pulls one or two of us out at a time. Usually, if they come back, they're beaten nearly to death. Most don't come back at all."

So it was a pit in the field, she thought. Now she understood the bleachers: it would be a full spectacle like Dagon promised. "What about who's coming? Dagon mentioned a meeting with powerful demons tomorrow. Do you know who?"

"No idea. He doesn't talk much to me or any of us, but he seems nervous about it. He's been taking more people to fight his thug recently and he works the people in the field almost to death to get the ranch ready."

"Have they taken you?"

He grew pale, looking sick. "Me? Well, I've never been chosen—"

"*Mentiroso!*" A man across the aisle shouted, slamming his hand on his cage, even though it hurt him to touch the stygian.

"Am not!" Liam shouted back.

Kleos was up now. "Calm down!" He ordered the man. "Dani, what did he say?"

"He called him a liar. Liam, what is he talking about?"

The Ber'iah Earthborn couldn't look either of them in the eye. He stepped away from the cage. "When we first got here, there were four of us. We fled Ber'iah together. When Dagon captured us, he made us his bodyguard's special training tools."

"Training tools?" Kleos glanced sideways at Dani. "You mean, he gave you to Goliath to spar?"

"Sure, you could call it 'sparring' or you could call it what it was: an execution by beating. He fights whoever he takes and if you survive, you go back the next day and fight again. And the day after that. And the day after that. Eventually, everyone takes too much and they don't come back. Then, they feed their bodies to the horses. When he first came for us, they made us choose. The first one of us? He volunteered. He kept fighting, but they kept taking him back. The next one they came for, we all kept pointing fingers until he chose one of us. He only fought a handful of times before Goliath killed him. The one before me? He only went once, after a coin toss. He got the quickest death. I think he just couldn't bear to prolong the torture."

"Then they came for me and there was no one left. I'm not a fighter." He insisted. "I was a messenger because I can fly faster than anyone else, but I've never been adept at combat. I knew I wouldn't last one minute with him—."

"*Cobarde!*" The man yelled again, pointing to the little girl and her mother. "*El traicioné el padre de esta chica! Tu eres un cobarde! Pudrete en el infierno!*"

"*Cálmate.*" Dani told him. "Liam, he just told me—."

"I know what he told you." Liam said. "He told you I betrayed the father of that girl. I had to do something! I told the man, Goliath or whoever he is, not to take me. I told him I wouldn't stand a chance."

Dani and Kleos stared wordlessly at him. They both knew what came next, but couldn't believe it was true.

"I," he stuttered, "I was begging for my life when I said the man in the other cell was stronger than me. You have to believe me!" He insisted hurriedly. "I didn't think he would take him! I didn't know what he would do! He took the girl's father and he never came back."

Dani felt sick just looking at him. Maybe a year ago, she wouldn't be so brave, but even the old her wouldn't betray the little girl and her mother. She wasn't sympathetic to Liam's fear.

"We have to get out of here." She said to Kleos, ignoring him. "I'm pretty sure anyone in that exhibition tomorrow isn't going to make it out."

Liam's eyes widened. "But—But he won't make all of us fight, will he?"

"Looks like you didn't avoid your death after all." Her upper lip curled in disgust. "That girl's father died for no reason."

His head bowed in shame and he sat sullenly on the floor.

"We're still trapped in a cage." Kleos reminded her. "Any idea how to get past the bars?"

Dani was about to answer when she heard something. At first, she thought it was just her imagination, but the two se'irim on guard turned towards the open barn door. A shadow flashed across the full-moon. The steeds and mares brayed loudly, spewing fire and bloody spittle. The two demons, armed with crossbows and stygian bolts, quickly took position next to the doors with weapons raised.

Liam jumped to his feet. "What the hell was that?"

Dani smiled knowingly. "A friend."

The guards stepped into the moonlight outside, back to back. As soon as they did, something white shot out of the sky and took off the left satyr's head. The demon vanished in a cascade of dirty ash. It's crossbow dropped to the grass. The other turned, wailing in alarm. His call cut off when another blur of white removed his head from his shoulders.

The deadly, snowy shape shot in through the door. Caesar spread her wings, zipping down with a flutter in front of Dani's cage.

"*Dani!*"

"Caesar! You came!"

"*You know it, sister.*" She ruffled her feathers. "*I'm so sorry. When the demons swarmed you, I wanted to get you both out of there, but there were too many of them. I stayed back and waited until I got an opportunity.*" She fluttered closer. "*Dani, I'm so sorry I left you.*"

"It's okay, Caesar." Dani cried joyfully. "I'm just glad you're here."

"*I'm going to get you out of that cage.*" She fluttered up towards the lock.

"Wait, Caesar—!"

Her friend's talons latched onto the cage and she screeched in pain. She shot backwards away from it, flailing. When she landed on the floor, she thrashed.

"*Oh my God!*" She wailed. "*Oh God! Oh God, it hurts! It hurts!*"

"It's stygian!" Dani moaned. "Caesar, I'm sorry! I tried to warn you!"

Caesar mewled. Her feet were blackened, as if from frostbite. She could barely stand.

"Are you alright?" Dani asked her.

Her friend squealed in pain. "*Oh God, Dani! It hurts! It hurts so bad! My talons! What's happening?!*"

Kleos knelt, examining her claws through the bars. "Your friend has been hurt by the stygian."

"I can see that!" Dani snapped. "We need to help her!"

"You can't." He warned. "Stygian is hellish metal. It's cold literally steals the life from any creature it touches. This isn't just a wound. It's a death sentence. For us, our angelic side can heal its effects. She is a caladrius. It won't stop until it spreads to the rest of her body and kills her."

"I'll heal her, then."

But Dani's hands were bound in stygian. Her lightbringing wouldn't work. Dani's heart dropped as Caesar thrashed and wailed agony.

"I'm sorry, Caesar." Tears rolled down her cheeks. "I'm so sorry."

"*I have to get you out!*" Caesar moaned, trying to stand but unable.

The goat-whines of the se'irim filtered through the door. They must have heard the commotion. They were coming.

Caesar swallowed her pain. "*Dani, I'm going to get you out of here. I don't know how, but I am.*"

"No, Caesar, you can't."

"*Dani—!*"

"You need to go." She told her friend. "You need to go now."

"*I can't leave you!*"

"You have to! If they see you, they'll kill you." Dani told her. "Please, Caesar. I can't watch you die."

"*You'll die if you stay here.*"

"We'll be alright." It was a lie, but she said it anyway. She would not let her friend die for her, especially uselessly. "You go. Get back to Empyrean, or Judah, or someone. Have them heal your feet. Tell them where we are."

Caesar wavered. Everyone could hear footfalls, the clinking of armor and goat-whines. They were near.

"*Dani—!*"

"Go!" Dani screamed. "Now!"

Caesar flapped, taking off. The satyr monsters arrived at the door just as she shot out. They screamed. Two raised crossbows armed and fired, but they missed. Caesar disappeared into the night.

Goliath appeared. He knelt to retrieve the two fallen weapons of the dead demons. His eyes shifted to Dani, who glared from the other side of the cage.

"Eat me, big guy." She snarled.

A thin smile spread across his bearded lips. He pointed, grunting, and the demons followed his unintelligent orders to spread out. He grabbed the large double doors to the barn and closed them. Darkness enveloped the cages. A lock fell into place.

Dani sent a thought out the heavens where hopefully Caesar was headed. *Thank you for trying Caesar. Don't worry about me.*

"At least she'll be safe." Kleos said.

Liam cursed. "Ripper, there goes our only chance of getting out! Blasted bird didn't do a cursed thing to help us."

Dani kicked the cage hard enough to rattle them both. "Shut up!"

Liam flinched away.

"That 'blasted bird' is my friend you cowardly, stupid codpiece! So, listen up. We got no way out, which means we got one option: fight."

"Fight? Are you insane? Goliath, if that's his name, kills anyone he fights. Those demons are terrifying. And you want to fight them?"

"Yes, and you want to know why? Because I don't want to die a coward like you!"

Liam's face burned in shame. No one liked being called a coward.

"Let me tell you the same crap the people in Empyrean tell me: man up. You're a Numen. Act like it." Dani felt Mastema's words float back to her. She recited to Liam, "Fear is human. Fear immobilizes us. It defeats us. It takes from us the will to continue to live. It forges us into the worst version of ourselves. You have to master your fear."

"Master it? What the hell does that mean?"

"Stand up to it." She told him. "Stand up when everyone expects you to lie down."

"I can't."

"Then you'll die." How could a Numen be so spineless? She didn't know and she didn't care. "Liam, we stand together on this, got it? If we fight tomorrow, we fight together. We protect each other."

"What if—?"

"No what ifs." She cut him off. "You fight. Stand with me and we get through this together."

He bit back his next words and nodded. "Alright."

She left Liam as he went to sulk on the other side of his cage. Kleos took a seat on the floor, folding his legs. He gestured with his bound hands. "Join me?"

Dani sat across from him.

"You know there's a good chance we will die tomorrow." He told her softly. "You should not hold onto the fantasy we're going to survive."

"I'm not. If we die, we die."

"Do you mean that? Or are you pretending?"

"With all the crap that's happened, I can't pretend anymore." She told him truthfully. "A millennia old ancient evil wants me to his bride. It keeps trying to kill me. I'm scared, but I'm not going to curl up into a ball like a little girl afraid of the monster under her bed. I'm not going to lie down and take it, that much I can tell you. I'm going to fight like hell. And if I die, I'm going to die with my enemy's blood on my palm."

He nodded. "The Numen Creed."

"No. My creed. I'm taking as many of those monsters with me as I can."

Kleos' grin spread a tiny bit in admiration. "Mastema always said there was something incredibly fierce about you."

"Well it's not just my fashion sense."

She stood in the middle of a field of tawny grass, tickling around her waist. The air smelled sweet and clean. The sky overhead was sapphire blue, the bluest she'd ever seen. The grass was the color of gold and felt like silk on her fingers. The clouds were silver and the lake down the hill was a clear blue-green, as if made of the freshest waters. It was like paradise.

"Because it is paradise."

Ethan smiled. He walked towards her, dressed not in his Numen raiments, but in simple jeans and T-shirt; as if he weren't a warrior but an ordinary boy. His eyes glowed like amber. His smile was comforting.

She wasn't in her browns, either. She wore a light, breezy sundress. Her hair curled around her in the wind and her heart skipped several beats as he came near.

He slid his arms around her from behind, cradling her against him.

His heart raced to match hers. She could feel it. And yet his hands, as they slid down her arms, soothed her. Calm. Comforting. Safe.

"This is Heaven," he told her, "from before the War. This is paradise."

Just beyond the rolling hills was a forest so alive Dani could feel the vibrancy of the life within it. It was a harmony she never felt before and yet, though she never stepped foot inside, she could feel that harmony like wind against her skin. She connected with it; with the creatures inside the green wood as if their peace poured into her.

She looked up into the sky. Though it was bluer, clearer, more perfect than anything she'd ever seen with her own eyes, it was so much more. The heavens filled with planets and suns; some were as big as the moon, others as tiny as the stars at night. When she focused, she could see into thousands of galaxies, solar systems, and down onto the planets themselves; all she had to do was look. Some were blue, swirling with clouds and landmasses like Earth. Others were different, dazzling colors like gems; greens, purples, reds. But all of them were full of life. She could feel that life.

"How can I see this?" She asked. "How do I know it's real?"

"As anyone that believes in Heaven knows." He tipped her chin up to look into his golden-coffee irises. "You know it. You feel it. You have faith that it's real."

"I've never been good with faith."

"I have faith in you. Maybe that's enough?"

She blushed. "That's a good line."

"I thought so."

"Is it gone?" She asked. "Heaven? Is it all destroyed?"

"I don't know," he turned her around and took her hands in his, "but I know I see Heaven when I'm with you."

She blushed that much harder. "That's a cheesy line."

"Dani, I need to say this: you've been gone from Empyrean for days, but ever since you left, I haven't stopped thinking about you. And maybe this is a dream and you're not real, but I have to tell you. I was intimidated by you when we first met. I was in awe of you. You didn't stop fighting, or believing in yourself, for one second. And I couldn't help but fall for you." He held up her hands, kissing the knuckles. "All I wanted to do was be close to you. I needed to be with you. The most important part of it is you."

Behind him, the teeming world of Heaven moved and shifted. Stars shined brighter. Worlds filled with visible existences of beings unknown. The movement of the cosmos, of eons, changed in seconds.

He squeezed her hands gently. "I need you, Dani. I need to be with you. You're my world. I'd walk into the sun for you."

Dani looked into his eyes. They were the same ones she looked into the night of Alecto's attack. She knew then that he was someone important to her. When she kissed him, it felt right.

But now, so close to him here, her heart ached.

"Come back to me, Dani." He told her. "I need you. We'll face this thing and stop it the only way there is: together."

He leaned down and kissed her. His lips were moist, tender, and loving. She inhaled his scent, took in all that he was, and cupped his face to hers. Time seemed endless with him.

And when he pulled back, he whispered, "I love you."

Dani stared up into his eyes. It made her cry. It made her hurt. And she loved it. All the time spent making sure she was strong; unbreakable. It wore on her. No person was an island forever.

"Come back to me." He begged.

But she answered. "I can't."

Island or not, she couldn't. She knew it the moment he asked her to come back. Behind him, the sky turned a burnt orange. The sun began to set. Stars began to shimmer and fade.

"What?" He asked, dumbfounded.

"I can't Ethan. I can't come back."

"Why not?"

"I have to stop Asmodeus alone."

"You can't." He told her. "Dani, Asmodeus is too powerful. You're only one girl. The only way we can put an end to him is together. United. You need me."

"No, I don't." She pushed away from his embrace, suddenly wanting to be out of his arms. "I know you want to help, but you can't. Asmodeus is after me and there's a reason why. I'm the one who had those visions and I know where the things are that can defeat him. I have to be the one to end him."

More stars blinked out of existence. Planets dampened, becoming darker and colder. Life on them dwindled.

"But I need you Dani." Ethan pleaded. "Don't you need me, too?"

She bit her lower lip. "I love you, Ethan, but...no. I don't."

She always wanted what those other couples had; two people, entwined, totally absorbed in one another. It was like those pictures online of two people together; running their hands through each other's hair, sleeping together, totally in love. It was silly and she knew it wasn't realistic, but she sometimes craved closeness like that.

But wanting that now, to be that with Ethan, somehow felt wrong. She loved him. She cared for him in a way that defied words, but she didn't need him.

His face contorted in pain. "Dani..."

"That's not what love is, Ethan." She told him, backing away. "It's not about needing someone. It's not about walking into the sun for someone. It's about loving them. I know I love you, but that doesn't mean I can come back. That doesn't mean I will stop what I'm doing. I have to keep going."

A rumbling like thunder made her look up. Dark, thick black clouds crept into the sky. They flickered with lightning and cracks of thunder. Fiery embers began to rain from them. The wind picked up.

"Dani," Ethan moaned, "why are you doing this to me? Don't you care about me? I'd do anything for you."

"Then you shouldn't." She told him. "No one should. Because if that's what love is, then love isn't something I want."

His expression changed. His brow furrowed. His hands clenched into fists at his sides. Then, his chocolate brown eyes cracked with red.

When he spoke, a softer voice spoke with him. "You will love me, Daniella."

Dani's hands balled into fists, too. "Asmodeus."

The forest behind him smoldered; black smoke billowing into the sky as the trees caught fire. She could hear thousands of animals, all racing to escape the sudden blaze, even as they were consumed. She shielded her eyes as planets overhead cracked with molten flame and burst, killing billions in seconds. Others froze over into lifeless, icy spheres. Stars went nova. The lake below turned to sludge. The once golden fields faded and became grey. The storm overhead spit fire and lightning.

The archdemon smiled. "I thought I lost you. I know you have my medallion. I know what you're planning."

She snarled, "And I'll lock you away for all eternity. Or kill you. Either is fine with me."

"You will not reach them."

"Tough talk considering what I did to your little entourage in Berkeley."

"You think I care?" He asked. "You think that's the only place my children work? You think you've changed anything? Women are servants. There will always be those who learn that their place is satisfying men; giving them what they want. That's why, eventually, you'll give me what I demand: your undying devotion. Then you'll know where you belong."

"Go screw yourself."

"Without me, you are nothing. You will realize it. You will love me."

Planets collided, as if joining in some need for one another, but then cascading into destruction. The forest became an insatiable inferno. The fields were nothing but dead grass, ignited by the falling fire.

"This was what remains of Heaven." He told her as the sky turned red. "This is what remains of paradise. What you see is how the angels brought the cosmos to an end."

He stretched out his arms over the field. All around them, bones littered the ground. The dead strewn the hills; charred skeletons lying atop other charred skeletons. Gaping eye-sockets stared up at her. Open mouths hung wide in silent screams. Mounds of skulls laid testament to horrors.

"Heaven is a wasteland. Nothing remains pure. The waters are diseased. The air is poison. The earth is scorched and the ground salted. Nothing bears fruit in the land of milk and honey any longer."

"You won't win." She told him. "I'll see you dead first."

"You can't stop me. As I said, I know that you are seeking the artifacts of Raphael, but the Archangel of Healing abandoned you to the disease of the Earth. You will be mine before you reach the sacred fish or the corrupt king. It is foolish to try."

Overhead, the clouds opened. Above them, atop the mountain, was Empyrean. The city gleamed in the sunlight. But as she watched, black shadows flowed over the base and coursed up its cliffs. Shades, thousands upon thousands of shades, swarmed over the city walls. The sunlight turned black. Fires bloomed from within and Dani heard screams. Red shapes, Numen Gatekeepers, tumbled from the cliffs to their deaths.

"I come in five days' time." Asmodeus told her. "When the veil weakens, I will invade the city of angels. I will break through the barrier and I will slaughter every living thing within." He stalked towards her as Empyrean's mountain crack and broke. The peak tumbled. The city was swallowed in the falling rock. "And as each one of your beloved companions dies, they will become one of my immortal slaves. And you," he reached for her, "will be mine as well; not be by my side, but under my thumb."

He caught her, grabbing her around the back of the neck.

"You will be mine, Dani."

Chapter Thirty

Morning came. Dani was awake long before the sun peeked through the cracks in the barn doors. Nightmares never really made for a good-night's sleep. The demon guards made a shift change. Dani's hands ached, but she was okay with that; at least that meant she still had feeling left in them.

Kleos spent the night meditating. At some point, he fell asleep sitting up, but came to shortly after her.

The sound of people screaming in their cells announced Dagon's and Goliath's arrival, along with a host of demons dressed in plaid. The hellish creatures carried bowls of what looked like puke, which they deposited into the cells. The stuff smelled awful, but people ate. Food was food.

"I know it's not the exceptional meal I gave to you last night, darlin'," Dagon said, dressed in a fine white suit with string tie to go with his snow-white cowboy hat, "but I can't show favoritism to any of my contenders. It'll throw off the betting."

"Betting?"

"Yes." He grinned wider. "My demons use the matches with Goliath and my slaves for entertainment. Naturally, some wagering happens. 'Course, usually the wagers are on how long they survive, not win. But, I guess no one expects to win against my champ."

She said nothing, nor did she touch the food.

"What? No witty comeback? You were filled with a'lotta hate-fire last night. I hope one night in the barn didn't take all your defiance. You'll need it today." He leaned down, teasing. "Come on, no jokes?"

She leaned forward. "You mean something along the lines of how you look like Colonel Sanders' stupid, inbred cousin?" But she didn't smile. Not yet. "All I got for you is a promise."

"And what's that, sweetheart?"

"I am going to kill you." Then she smiled. "And I'm really, _really_ going to enjoy it."

Dagon's smile stayed, unwavering. "Girl, I'm a god. I've lived longer than almost anything in this world. I highly doubt you'll kill me. But, if you think you can escape what I got going on in the back fields, you're more than welcome to try." He straightened up. "Eat your mush. You'll need it. I'll fetch you when it's time."

The immortal ranch owner ambled off proudly. His demons followed.

Liam stared at her. "Are you crazy? Why do you mouth off like that?"

"Because cowering isn't in my nature."

She ate the mush. It tasted like oatmeal and sawdust, but she was hungry and she knew she needed the strength. The sun was high when a small platoon of armored se'irim came back for them. They took Dani and

Kleos out of their cages, but dragged Liam out, too. The demons also dragged out a few more people, but they were led off into the back fields while Dani and her friends were marched towards the front of the house.

The last thing she saw was the woman and her daughter, watching fearfully as the demons took Dani away.

As they trekked to the main house, Liam wouldn't shut up. He kept babbling about how he didn't deserve this; how he wasn't a fighter and how the man who died in his place wasn't his fault.

"Shut up." Dani told him. "It won't change anything."

"What if we make a deal with Dagon?" He suggested. "We tell him how we're better as bargaining chips than gladiators. He could use us in a prisoner exchange."

Dani spun around to glare at him. "Look, whatever deal you think you can get, you can't. He doesn't care, so don't try. Even if he does spare you, eventually, he'll kill you anyway." She grabbed him by the front of his tunic and made him look her in the eye. "You want to survive? Stick with us. Do your job and protect as many people back in that barn as you can."

"Why?"

"Because," she started walking again, "it's the right thing to do."

Dagon, Goliath and an entourage of demons awaited them at the top of the drive.

"So good to see y'all." The god grinned. "You're just in time. Our first guest should be arriving shortly."

"How? By car?"

Thunderclouds formed on the horizon. A funnel erupted between the earth and the sky and swirled across the open plains, churning up dirt and vegetation as it came. Dani closed her eyes to the wind and debris. When she peered through slits, the tornado crossed onto Dagon's ranch and died as swarmed up the road. It dissolved and a demon emerged.

He looked like a mixture of lion, man and bird. He had four separate, feathered wings; two folded up while two folded down. His feet were like lion claws, with shaggy fur running up the length of his body to a thankfully well-placed loin cloth. But his chest and arms were that of a man. Only his face and head didn't fit.

He wore a crown or headdress, which fanned up into plumage like a Roman centurion's helmet. His face looked vaguely human, except for the wide snout and twin fangs protruding from his mouth.

His wings folded back to reveal four other demons Dani hadn't seen before, flanking him. They took shape from the first demon's dust cloud; four-foot-tall women with raven-black bird wings and claws for hands. When they smiled, they too had fangs.

Dagon bowed reverently. "Pazuzu, demon of the southwestern wind, bringer of storms, drought and famine. Welcome. It has been too long."

"Since the ancient times, Dagon." The demon named Pazuzu looked at the three shackled prisoners. "Who are they?" He spoke with an accent similar to Dagon's; the one that came out when he was angry.

"Some of our contenders for today." Dagon drawled. "Numen."

"Does Belial believe I will be swayed by three deaths?" Pazuzu asked.

"No, of course not. But to watch them spectacularly fall and feasting upon their corpses I'm sure will go a long way in warming you to the idea."

Pazuzu grinned toothily. "Maybe."

"And you have brought what with you?" Dagon asked, indicating the other demons.

"Alé." He gestured to the creatures. "Storm demons of hail and drought from the Balkans. I rescued them from some summoners who used them to control the local populace. They flocked to me upon my arrival from Babylonia."

Dagon smiled at Dani and her friends. "Do you have nothing to say to our guest?"

Dani was halfway through coming up with a comeback when Kleos said, "Hopefully you've heard Babylon is gone, Pazuzu. And so is any who worshipped your pitiful hide."

A look somewhere between amusement and anger crossed Pazuzu's face. "I correct myself, Dagon. This one I will gladly watch die."

"Very well. My servant Goliath will take you into the main dining room, where we have a feast of varying flesh for you to enjoy. We'll conduct business once our other honored guest arrives."

Pazuzu left, followed by his four storm demons.

Dani glanced sideways at Kleos. "What the hell was that about?"

"I thought I'd try my hand at smack-talk."

"Smack-talk? First off, no one calls it 'smack-talk' anymore, except people who can't let go of the Nineties. And second, I'm the one that gets to be sarcastic and snippy because it makes me cute and fabulous."

Kleos shook his head in amusement.

Liam stared at them. "You both are insane."

Dani chuckled. "Yeah. I get that a lot."

She hoped the joking would keep their minds off their impending doom for a little while longer.

A rumbling under their feet announced the second demonic guest. At first, Dani thought it was just a mild tremor. She was used to them in California. Earthquakes were like boy bands; every few years, there was a new one and they were annoying. But the ground split open and from beneath, some*things* climbed their way out.

They looked like golems or gnomes, but these things were hideously ugly. They smelled like something laid out to rot and looked like they were made of different types of rock. One was composed of quartz, another of sandstone, and a third seemed to be made purely of flint; with a total of eight, each one was different. A swamp-like sludge dribbled from their bodies, causing the smell. Each monster was a good six feet tall. They formed a ring around the final creature, the one that led them, as it emerged out last.

He wore a long cowl so Dani couldn't see his face or body, but his hands were a mixture between lizard claws and human fingers; long, scaly, grey, and tipped with razor-sharp nails. He pulled his covering around his face and hobbled forward like a hunched old man.

"Dagon." He hissed with a horribly dry, scratchy voice. He extended a hand. Even Dagon choked down disgust so he could shake it. "How good of you to invite me."

"Asag." Dagon bowed. "Thank you for covering yourself."

The demon motioned to himself almost proudly. "The fish boil alive in the rivers at the very sight of me while men bleed from every orifice. I wished not to kill anyone."

"Of course."

He turned towards one satyr-demon, who did its best not to stare. But when he looked at Asag, the demon pulled back his hood enough to show only him his face. The se'ir shrieked, honking, covering its eyes. Black goo burst across its palms as they exploded in their sockets. Tar-like blood spewed from its mouth, out the ears and from its nose. The demon dropped to the ground, screaming before finally disintegrating to dust.

"Well, at least not anyone important." Asag hissed cruelly with the same raspy jeer.

Dani stared. Asag was a demon so hideous it killed people _on sight_?

Dagon hesitated. "I see you brought your offspring."

"Yes, products of my conquests: the terrene." Asag waved to them. "Beautiful, are they not? Of course, no woman could bear my seed, much less look upon my face, which forced me to mate with the mountains. Each one I copulate with produces my brood."

Mate with the mountains? Dani felt like she might throw up. This thing had sex with mountains? She stared at his demonic children. Earth demons? They were as disgusting as the story of their birth.

"They are," Dagon swallowed his revulsion, "so lovely."

"Yes. And these humans? Are they the Numen you spoke of who will do battle for us?"

"They are newer; just arrived this past evening. The others expired."

Asag turned towards them. A tongue slithered around under the hood, but he didn't show her his face. Remembering the dead demon, she looked away. The others did likewise.

"I wish you not reveal yourself to them." Dagon told him. "They make better gladiators than corpses. At least as gladiators, they will have to fight first."

"Yes. Indeed. But please," he patted Dagon's arm, limping past him, "leave one to look upon me. The horror in their eyes before they die is," he let out a savory rasp, "intoxicating."

"Of course."

"Do you have entertainment for my children? We have traveled many miles and they need some enjoyment. Perhaps a few of your workers would make nice playthings?"

"Certainly, but please don't kill too many. I still have a farm to run. If you will follow my guards, they will escort you."

"Thank you. Sagarmāthā, Denali, Tacoma," he called to his nearest children, "accompany me. The rest of you," he waved to the fields of workers, "have fun."

The mountain demons and their progenitor followed the remaining satyrs up to the house. The vile stench off them made Dani gag. The others walked towards the fields and the migrant workers.

"So, you brought us out just for show?" She asked Dagon. "Because if so, tell a girl next time so she can *not* pretty herself up. I really like to ug-out for demons and gods who are as worthless as glass sleeping bags."

"You're a funny girl, Daniella," the god drawled like a strum on a guitar, brushing off her insult, "but it don't change your fate. 'Sides, only two of you are here for show. And since there are three, I could use a servant who speaks English."

"We want nothing to do with you." Kleos snarled.

"My, my. It's obvious that you, Kleos, are the older and wiser one, but you allow some girl to tell you how to act." His accent switched. "She rebukes me and you follow suit. How odd you would follow a woman."

"I follow a warrior." He shot back.

"You follow a fool." He switched to drawl again. "No matter. On to my offer: I want to give one of you three Numen a role in today's exhibition; unlike them others that'll die bloody. I need'a singer for today's ceremony."

""A servant?" Dani asked. "You've got to be kidding me. None of us would do that." Dani snarled.

"Not one? They wouldn't die in that pit back there. They'd live. I promise."

"No." Dani told him. "Go screw off. We'd never—."

"I'll do it!"

Before she could finish, Liam jumped forward.

"I'll do it!" he said. "I'll serve! Take me!"

"Oh, you little *cobarde!*"

"Very well." Dagon nodded. "As humans say: the early bird gets the worm."

"He is a worm!" Dani spat. She tried jumping him, but the demons held her back.

"I'm sorry." He told her, but didn't sound the least bit that way. "I'm not a fighter."

"He'll kill you." Kleos reminded him. "If not today, one day."

"I'll live longer than you."

Dagon summoned another two guards and they took Liam away. He didn't dare look back at Dani and Kleos.

Dagon chuckled.

"You knew he'd do that." Dani accused him.

"O'course. Cowards always wear the stench of fear."

"What's your deal?" She asked him.

"Deal?"

"Why do all of this? Are mind games how you get your kicks?"

Dagon's smirk held an edge of contempt. "I am the god of the Philistines. My worshippers had one of the most sophisticated societies in the Ancient Lands, but now are synonymous with stupidity. They were refined and cultured, unlike the invading savages who believed themselves chosen by God. Your God destroyed my people. I would have let them pass to Him, but instead his zealots obliterated everything remotely associated with the other ba'als and I. My deal, as you put it—what I want— is for you to realize who you are dealing with, girl." He leaned down to her. His smile was cruel now; bitter. "I am much, much smarter and powerful than you will ever be."

Dani didn't flinch.

"Now," his face snapped into good ol' boy mode, "onto the last piece of business. An old friend contacted me last night 'bout you. Apparently, when you pitched your hissy fit last night, you forgot to tell me something."

"What?"

"How important you are to the Lord of Lust."

Before she could answer, Kleos tapped her arm and pointed. "Dani."

Downhill, a large oak tree that cast its shadow across the driveway began to sway and toss in the wind. Except there was no wind. The branches shook. Its shadows melted and, as if the absence of light under them became physical, the shadows solidified into a semi-transparent silhouette of a person.

A shade stepped from the gloom cast by the branches and walked uphill. Others appeared behind him; five in all. As the leader neared, his face became clearer.

"Hello again, Daniella. Kleos." Nazir sneered. "I thought we lost you in California."

"I thought we killed you. I guess we're both disappointed." Dani's heart went cold, knowing why he was here: to take her. Behind Nazir, Michael stood at attention, waiting. His black eyes filled with hate.

Dani still had her shadelight pendant. She only used it once. She could use it now.

Unfortunately, they were still cuffed and Dagon was probably more than a match for them.

"I love it when you speak all haughty. I'll enjoy it when Asmodeus wipes that smugness from your soul." Nazir's smile never faltered. He turned and bowed to Dagon. "My lord sends his regards."

"And I return 'em. He said to keep 'em alive."

"Yes. The girl, at the very least. She is precious to him. He thanks you for your cooperation."

"His thanks aren't necessary, because they ain't right." Dagon told him evenly, betraying nothing. "She competes in my competition today."

Nazir's whole body darkened to a deeper black. "Excuse me?"

"Lord Belial wants to recruit other demons for the war against the Numen. I promised these two as part of some entertainment. I won't change that to give one to you."

"Lord Asmodeus wills it."

"And he can speak with Lord Belial 'bout that, but I ain't giving her to you."

Nazir tensed. The shadowy blackness of his hands morphed into his hooked saber. Behind him, his fellow dark souls similarly armed themselves.

Dagon saw them, but only continued to smile. His un-American accent came out. "Your powers mean nothing to a god."

"The only god is the one who sent me."

"The powers of the lord of lust pale in comparison to Belial, shade. He gave me discretion to do as I please. He will destroy the Numen. He will burn this world to a cinder."

"He will not need to when my master destroys Empyrean within the next five days."

"You think some whining, misanthropic egotist can rule hordes of demonkind when he's obsessed with," he glanced at Dani, "menial matters? No. I made my pact. I am equal in the eyes of the demonic lords. Lord Belial has plans. Asmodeus wishes to slaughter and submit. Belial means to rule."

Dani allowed herself to smile. Nazir looked genuinely afraid of Dagon. Maybe he wouldn't take her after all. Of course, that meant staying with Dagon, which wasn't much better.

But the god sighed wearily and said, "However, I am a god of more than fields. I am one of business. You are here. You have come to demand what you seek. There may be a way in which both of us get what we want."

She didn't like the sound of that.

"How?" Nazir demanded.

"You wish to have the girl," he glanced sideways at Dani, "and you may have her for a price."

"What price?"

"The price all paid for centuries." Dagon told him. "Combat. Defeat an opponent, take their life to entertain my guests, and I will give you what your master wants."

Nazir's black eyes gleamed. He turned towards Dani at first, but then Kleos. "Do I get to choose my opponent?"

Dagon smiled. "It is only fair."

The arena was a hole dug nearly fifteen feet into the ground in the back field and was as wide as a house, edged with stygian spikes to ensure no one could climb out. For good measure, se'irim armed with crossbows and spears patrolled the rim.

Behind the spikes were bleachers, since every coliseum needed an audience. Satyr demons, imps, terrene and alé filled them alongside human workers forced to come watch the bloody deaths of friends and family.

Se'irim took Dani and Kleos to a holding bunker on the far end of the stadium, built into the ground with the exit to the arena. Shackles removed, the demons dropped them in through a manhole with the grace of a sack of potatoes. Dani's hands, thanks to her lightbringing, had almost no ill-effects from the stygian. They slowly warmed back up and healed.

Kleos' looked much worse.

She crawled over, taking them in hers. "Are you okay?"

"I'm pretty sure they're dead."

His hands were necrotic; black and sallow, sickly, decaying. Dani touched one and he winced in pain.

"How the hell are you not screaming in agony?"

He hissed. "Practice."

The walls were blank concrete. A gate forged of the same hellish metal as everything else in this God-forsaken place led into the arena. The bunker had ten other 'contestants.' Most of them looked like hardened warriors, or at least those who had seen too much. Dani looked for the little girl from before, but didn't see her.

Thank God. "Can I try to heal you?"

"Do you think you can?"

"I have to try. Otherwise, we'll have to cut them off." She did not like that idea. "I'm not a very good surgeon."

Every touch was painful, but he nodded and placed his hands into hers. Dani closed her eyes.

She tried to summon a good memory, or an emotion, or anything worthwhile. Unfortunately, she just spent the night in a cage owned by a god who wanted to drag from the back fender of a car. Not the most pleasant memory.

She tried to think back to her friends, but most of them were in trouble because of her. Others, like Izzy and Ethan, attacked her.

And Caesar. Poor Caesar.

"Having trouble?" Kleos hissed.

"It's not uncommon." She tried to joke. "One in five. I think I'm allowed a little leeway."

"What do you need?" he asked.

"A good memory." She told him. "Something purely positive."

"Like Ethan?"

She gave him her best scowl. "He's not the center of my world, you know."

"A lot of couples think that, though."

"We're not a couple." She shook her head. "Besides, I've never been the person to make someone my all-and-everything."

"You should try it sometime. It's kind of nice."

She tried to focus. "How do you know?"

"Because I had that. Once."

She cocked her head to the side. "Really?"

"Really."

"Who?"

"Titus."

It took a second for it to register, and when it did, she couldn't believe it took her that long. "You mean the other Guardian? The one who died the night I became a Numen?"

He nodded. "The same."

"He was a guy."

He nodded again, still managing a smile. "Yes."

Now that he said it, it made sense. Kleos had never been with any women during vespertide, which was most people's motivation for going. And he was immune to Asmodeus' power. Was that all because...?

"You're gay?"

"Does that bother you?"

She shrugged. "No. That's how you can be around me? Asmodeus can't warp any sort of attraction you have to me because—?"

"Because I have no attraction to you." He smirked. "You could say you're not my type. Kind of clever of Mastema to send me."

"He knows?"

"Of course. He, Ethan and a few others."

"So, not everyone?"

Kleos bared his teeth and hissed in pain. "I don't hide it, but I don't advertise it, either. I've never felt the need."

"Does the Council know?"

He chuckled. "I've never asked and don't need to ask. I don't really care either way. If they told me not to love who I love, I would love them anyway. That is how love works. I don't need someone's permission."

She shook her head. "You're different than other ones I've met."

Amused by that, he laid on thick with the sarcasm. "Other ones? You mean other gays? Because we are all *sooooo* alike."

"Well, no, it's not like that." She burned with embarrassment. "I'm sorry. That was rude. I'm trying to help you, but all I'm doing is insulting you."

"It's fine." He told her. "I don't make it my business to be 'out' or whatever humans call it now. I come from a time when that wasn't a thing. There are a few other Numen who are like me, but none who have ever admitted it to me. But like I said, I don't hide it." He smirked. "Don't worry. You're not the first to be surprised. There are a lot of people—both mundani and supernatural—who assume men like me are soft or feminine, but they forget hundreds of men and women that are soldiers, or police or a myriad of other 'manly' professions while also managing to be Other Than Hetero."

He shook his head and said, "I don't make a big deal about it because it's not all I am. You think straight people go around announcing that they're straight and making that the center of their lives? No. No one does because they don't have to; and there's a lot more to a person than who they find attractive. I play the fiddle. I write poetry. I'm an excellent swordsman. I'm your friend. And I'm gifted with enchantments. There is much more to me." It hurt him, but he squeezed her hands. "I'm more than gay the same way you're more than just a woman. We're here doing something important. In the grand scheme of things, I'm pretty sure our genitals and what we do with them don't matter that much in this moment."

Dani smiled, and then laughed.

"What?" he asked.

"I just realized that being gay makes you literally the only one who could help me do this. Asmodeus can get to everyone else, but not you. Without you, I'd be dead."

"You've done your fair share of saving me, too." He pointed out.

That warmed her. After so much doubt, someone having her back made her feel strong again. Supported. Able to do what she knew she could.

"So," she took his hands, "tell me about Titus. Is that why Nazir is so angry with you?"

He nodded. "Nazir was Titus's Novice. He grew close with his mentor."

"Is he gay, too?"

"No." He shook his head. "Nazir, like a lot of us, had no family before becoming a Numen. As you know, your Guardian becomes your family. He never knew about Titus and me, or what we were to each other. When I became a Numen, it was the same time as Nazir. He resented what he thought our relationship was because he felt abandoned by Titus. He never figured out what was going on and just assumed Titus wanted me as his Novice; that he wished to spend his time with me instead of him. I knew at the time I should give them space, but I was in love. So, I didn't care."

"It's not your fault."

"Trust me, I know," Kleos sighed heavily, "but Nazir took it personally. Titus and I were probably the best fighters amongst the Guardians. Nazir trained so he could best me in some quest to show his worth to Titus."

She remembered Nazir was well known for his skill. Now she knew why. "So that's why he's angry with you? That's why he wants revenge?"

"That is the anger Asmodeus twisted into his shade. Nazir would never try to kill me. His shade is not him. It's some perverse version of him."

"Yeah, well, one way or another, we're going to have to face him."

"I think we probably can."

"How's that?"

Kleos held up his hands, which faded to perfect from light. The black, necrotic flesh had healed. What remained were two regular hands, both fully whole.

"Look at that." She grinned. "At least something good came out of my curse."

"Your ability isn't a curse." He told her, standing. "You've got a power named after the Devil, but that doesn't make you the Devil."

"Tell that to a prophecy that says I may one day lead the forces of Hell to destroy the world."

Kleos seemed to understand. "So, your destiny, pardon the pun, is etched in stone?"

"You don't think it is?"

"Well, if Titus taught me anything, I think we make our own destinies and our own choices. I chose to be here. I still choose to fight alongside you. I think my destiny isn't made up yet."

The sound of demonic cheering outside caught their attention. Instinctively, every man in the cage backed away from the bars. They knew what it meant.

"You might want to hold that thought." She told him.

Chapter Thirty-One

Overhead, bleachers filled with a demonic crowd large enough to be Hell's version of March Madness. Across the way, three thrones made from hay and covered in cloth sat in the place of power. Dagon appeared and took the center throne to a round of uproarious applause. Pazuzu with his wide wings took the right; Asag the left. Dagon's undead henchman was nowhere to be seen.

"Well, the peanut gallery is here." She murmured.

"I never really liked sports." Kleos said, joining her side. "There was always something barbaric about them."

"We need a plan. This is basically a coliseum, right? We fight and whoever wins walks out alive, right?"

"Basically."

"So, what we need to know is what we're fighting."

"A good bet is se'irim or imps. Dagon has men to spare."

"Any advice on how to kill the goaty ones?"

"They're pretty stupid and not that fast," Kleos told her, "but if they send us out there unarmed, facing any demon with weapons, I'm going to bet it'll be a short fight."

"We have our *arche*."

"And your lightbringing, but don't use it." He warned. "I want to save that in case we need it."

Dani glanced up at the blue sky overhead. She wished Caesar were still here. They could use the backup. Fleeing that way wasn't an option; not with too many people still prisoner here and the demons on watch with their crossbows.

Seeing movement by the three seats, Dani looked and saw Liam, bowing to the three demons like a coward, serve them drinks and disgusting-looking hors d'oeuvres.

"Oh, look, it's that culus."

"Ignore him." Kleos told her. "Focus on escaping."

She nodded. "Well I see Asag's or Pazuzu's entourages up there, but not in the arena. You think they'll use them in the arena?"

"They weren't brought for hell of it. I'd bet my life on Goliath making an appearance, as well. I highly doubt Dagon brought him back from the dead to sit out on all the fun and games."

"He was beat before." She pointed out. "Didn't that king or something take him down with a rock?"

"King David. But that was a one-in-a-million shot and there aren't any rocks to throw."

True. Their prospects didn't look very good.

A trumpet sounded. The crowd cheered as Dagon stood. His voice boomed throughout the arena.

"Welcome! Welcome!" He gestured to his nearest seats. "Honored guests, demonic representatives, fellow ranchers, soon-to-be widows and orphans. Welcome!"

Demons clapped and made sounds like cheering, though it sounded more like smokers clearing their lungs.

"This is a momentous occasion!" Dagon boomed. "It is the beginning of an alliance that will forge a new power in this world. I have lived many lives. I have seen many nations. I have been the god to many peoples. But in that time, I have seen the depravity of humanity, which we will display here for you today! Not only will you see their depravity, but their insides as well!"

More cheering.

Well, Dani thought, *this is off to a great start.*

"Liam is a coward." She growled. "I should've killed him."

"You did what you thought was right." Kleos reassured her. "Besides, this won't end well."

Dani glanced sideways at him. "What do you mean?"

"They're demons, remember?"

Liam was speaking to Pazuzu, offering him a refill or some other nonsense. From his throne, Dagon leaned over to Asag. The hooded creature motioned to Liam for another drink, and as he approached, Asag lifted his head, making eye contact with Liam.

The demons cheered as Liam, frozen in horror, began to bleed out of his nose, ears, mouth, and eyes. Dani looked away. He uttered a soft sputter as he choked on his own blood, and dropped to the floor.

Dagon waved his hat to a loud applause. "And so it begins!"

Kleos bowed his head, praying softly in Greek.

"No one was ever leaving this arena alive." He told her. "Gods that make pacts with demons will always be dishonest."

A few minutes later, two imp guards opened the gates.

"Jorge Gutierrez. Rafael Rubio. Antonio Cruz." They read off the list.

No one moved. With a motion, the imp summoned several more demons to the cage and they pulled the three screaming men from the group, kicking and flailing. Their spearpoints leveled at Dani's and Kleos' throats. There was nothing they could do.

They shoved the men into the open and relocked the cage. Dani and Kleos got to the bars in time to see a mobile armory, a large cabinet full of adamantine and stygian weapons, wheeled into the arena.

"Our first challenge!" Dagon announced. "Three armed opponents against your one and only favorite gladiator! Put your claws together for Goliath!"

The gate below Dagon's throne opened again. Goliath himself strode out. Dani had only seen him in his rancher get up, but now he wore a much different attire: white tunic, with his legs bare, and armor composed of leather and steel covering him from his chest to his waist. Flaps hung to cover his thighs like Dani's raiments, except his had molded steel to protect him. He had no arm or shin coverings and carried no weapon.

"Is he fighting unarmed?" Dani asked Kleos.

"Appears to be."

"They might have a chance, then."

"You really believe that?"

The three mundani workers chose weapons; a little bolder now seeing Goliath unarmed. Two chose swords while a third chose a spear. The last one, at least, thought things through. You never wanted to get close to an opponent unless you had no choice.

The imps wheeled the armory from the arena. Goliath alone faced off against the three armed men.

"He'll defeat them in under a minute," Kleos predicted, "if he's merciful."

A trumpet sounded. Goliath fell into a combat stance. Just as in the barn, he was almost graceful in his movements. He charged towards the first gladiator as the man swung for the revenant's midsection. Goliath caught his arm and twisted, spinning him around and hurling him across the arena as if he weighed as much as a pillow.

The other man with a sword tried to use the distraction to his advantage. He stabbed at Goliath's back. He almost hit him, but Goliath avoided the blow. Unlike the movies, it wasn't that Goliath instinctively knew where his opponent was, but more like he was still moving and happened to feint around the sword-strike. True fighters never stopped long enough for their opponent to take advantage.

Goliath, in throwing the first man, kept spinning to avoid the second's blow. He seized the second man, finishing his spin behind him with an arm around the migrant's throat.

With a twist, he snapped the worker's neck.

The first man with the sword and the third with the spear circled around to keep their distance. Goliath dropped his dead victim to the ground as he moved to keep them in sight.

"Work together," Kleos murmured silently, half-praying for a miracle he knew wouldn't happen.

The remaining two men attacked at the same time; smarter than their first attempt. Goliath didn't wait. He turned towards the man with the sword, blocked his blow and then twisted his wrist back. The sword dropped from his hand with a snap and a scream from the wielder. Then the big revenant hurled him bodily into his companion.

He landed on the man's spear shaft.

The third and final gladiator staggered away, dropping his spear in horror. He looked up at Goliath as the revenant wound back and threw the dropped sword. The blade tumbled through the air and struck the stunned man point-first in the midsection. He dropped dead without a sound.

The demons cheered. Goliath grinned, fists raised in triumph.

"Did you see that?" Dani asked in awe. "That sword-throw was impossible! How did he do that?"

Kleos instead shook his head. "He was playing with them."

"He killed them in under a minute!"

"He could have killed them in seconds. He enjoyed himself." He walked away from the bars as the dead were cleared from the arena floor.

Goliath marched proudly away through the other side.

After a small interlude, Dagon announced, "Time for a display of true skill! Bring forth the Numen!"

The audience screamed for blood. The imps arrived, ready to drag Dani and Kleos out, but when they opened the cage, both were waiting. They walked out unescorted.

The dirt floor was still stained a black-red color where the three men died. Dani stepped around the stains, sticking by Kleos.

"They're going for the main event early." Dani gritted her teeth, eyeing the demons overhead.

"This isn't the main event." Kleos told her. "We're not facing Goliath. This will be a test to see what we can do."

They stopped at the middle of the arena. Above them, Dagon beamed. He was enjoying this.

"He's never seen us use our powers. He wants to know what we can do."

"Which means?"

"Don't use anything but the *arche*, and use them sparingly. We don't want him to gauge us right."

The trumpet sounded again. She was beginning to hate that thing. "If we get out of this, I'm gonna kill whoever keeps blowing that horn."

The gates on the other side began to open.

"Try to disarm them." Kleos advised. "If they have weapons, take them."

"And if they don't?"

270

"Don't use your lightbringing unless you have to."

The gates swung wide. The air coming out of the tunnel picked up. Dani shielded her eyes as dust, sand and dirt kicked up around them. From the tunnel, twin dust-twisters appeared.

"Alé!" Kleos warned.

Hailstones rained outward as the two mini-tornadoes broke from cover into the arena. Dani shielded herself, summoning her control over Erthe, Aer and Water to deflect the dust, wind and hail.

She backed away, but her foot caught and she fell. The ground closed around her ankle and something pulled her away screaming. A hand formed from the earth, and then a torso.

One of the terrene exploded from the ground with her in its grasp.

"Kleos! Watch out!"

As the thing rose from the ground, pulling her with it, she struck out with her foot. Her heel connected with its face and sent a shockwave of pain down through her heel. It was like kicking rocks. But it dropped her foot and she rolled back.

One of the alé leapt from its tornado, slashing with its claws. Kleos rolled, letting it land beside him. He lifted off on his hands, twisting acrobatically through the Aer back to standing. The demon charged, but he struck the demon with a low sweep-kick, taking out its foot.

The creature flailed with its wings to break its fall. Kleos summoned Aer, knocking out its break-fall and causing it to land hard on the ground. As it rose back to its feet, he seized it around the neck, pushed to angle the head down, and then jerked up hard sideways. With a snap of its spine, the thing fell limp and disintegrated to ash.

There was still one storm demon left and a terrene emerging from its hole. She backed towards the wall, remembering how she faced off against Michael, Andreas and Lester in Empyrean. She needed to minimize the ways they could hit her.

She pressed her back to the earthen wall.

"Dani! Watch it!"

She felt the wall shift. A stygian spike as long as her arm missed her head by inches as it exploded out of the wall. She rolled and another erupted in her path. She kept going, one spike after another attempting to spear her until she finally rolled away from the wall; too far for the barbs to hit, but unfortunately right into the path of the terrene demon.

The creature swung its rocky fist. Dani dodged and instinctively delivered a counter blow with her leg. Unfortunately, shin-striking a piece of rock hurt like hell. The demon back-armed her hard enough to possibly crack ribs. She landed and the air exploding from her lungs as she slid across the dirt floor.

The terrene came at her again, its heavy footfalls shaking the earth with each step. Kleos fought the other ala. She was on her own.

As the creature loomed over her, its rocky hand raised to pound her into oblivion. But as the fist came down, Dani rolled. The creature missed her by inches. Its fist cracked through the earth.

Sucking in wind, she rolled back onto its arm pinned it to the earth. She laced her legs around it, looped her heels behind its head, and locked it in an arm-bar. The creature screamed into her face. Its dank breath smelled something straight out of Hell, but Dani did not let go.

She pulled, using her strength and tumbled it sideways. She coursed her power over the Erthe down her arms, controlling the rock that the demon was composed of as she rolled on top of it. Leveraging her whole body, she forced it onto its face with its arm twisted up behind it. She rotated its wrist like a spigot until the tendons snapped and it howled in pain. Its arm turned in a way it shouldn't.

Thanks for the lesson Mastema, she silently acknowledged.

Dani leapt back to her feet. The demon's cries echoed off the walls. The ones overhead screamed louder for her blood.

"Come on, big boy." She goaded. "Get up. Are you going to let a girl beat you?"

The demon's rocky face twisted into pure fury. With an arm dangling uselessly by its side, it barreled towards her. She backpedaled.

"That's it! Come on!" She kept retreating, until the arena's wall cut off any more room to escape. "Come get it!"

Howling, the earth-demon charged with its remaining arm outstretched. Then, just as her back hit the wall, she turned away.

A stygian spike exploded outward and missed her by inches, but the demon charging at her didn't see it in time. The terrene impaled itself chest-first on the point. The collision launched a second spike through its gut and a third through its face.

It fragmented into small rocks. Dead.

The last ala snatched Kleos off his feet, claws digging into his tunic and hoisting him into the air. Dani ran to the fallen rock pile that once made up the terrene and grabbed the nearest baseball-sized piece.

The stone ignited in her hand from her lightbringing. She never used it like this before, but it worked. Turning, she hurled it like a fireball at the demon's back and struck it between the shoulder blades. It dropped its prey. Kleos fell while the demon dropped right in front of the god running the games.

The match was over.

Looking disappointed, Dagon waved his hand. Vines exploded from his feet and bound the demon to the ground in front of him. Wounded, it crumpled into a nearly-dead heap.

Despite defeating their three opponents, the demons above them cheered. Some of the migrants looked relieved. Dani ran to Kleos' side, helping him up.

"Are you okay?"

He smiled dizzily. "Did we win?"

She grinned, for the first time tasting the blood from her split lip. "Kind of. I doubt this is over, but right now, we're winning."

Dagon stood, arms raised. The crowd's cheers silenced.

"Ladies, gentlemen, and hellspawn alike," he gestured to Dani and Kleos, "I give you your victors!"

More cheering. Dani thought they should've been booing, but their appetite for violence was so strong that they didn't care who won. They just wanted to see death.

Dani was not comforted by their congratulations.

Dagon glanced down dismissively at the wounded ala, which mewled pitifully for its master. Pazuzu's twisted features snarled. His creature let him down.

"Lord Asag, if you will." Dagon asked, turning away.

Other demons in the crowd and even Pazuzu himself all turned their heads. Asag unfolded his scaly hands and took hold of his hood.

Dani and Kleos closed their eyes. She heard the ala scream, and then thrash. Its voice gargled and choked on its own blood. After a few seconds, it faded to nothing.

"Thank you!" Dagon's voice boomed. "You may all look again!"

When Dani opened her eyes, the demon was gone. Asag was once more covered. The ala was nothing more than dust and droppings of black goo at Pazuzu's feet.

"On to our next match!" Dagon beamed.

The crowd got to its feet, clamoring for more. The gates under Dagon opened and a column of armed-and-armored imps marched into the open, quickly fanning out with spears leveled.

"What now?" Dani grumbled.

"Daniella of Empyrean," Dagon called down, "step away from your companion. This next contest is his alone."

"Like hell I will!"

The imps advanced. Even if she didn't want to, spearpoints separated them and forced her aside. They herded Kleos one way, and her another. Dani could do nothing as they escorted her back to the cage. She thought briefly of calling on her powers again, but Kleos shook his head. They didn't notice her lightbringing the first time. That would be pushing it.

The bars slammed shut, leaving Kleos in the open.

One imp threw something to him. He caught his adamantine xiphos with one hand.

Then, from the shadows of Dagon's tunnel, something dark peeled away and formed into the shape of a man. He walked calmly into the open, hooked saber and dagger already drawn.

"Hello old friend." Nazir smiled. "Ready to die?"

Chapter Thirty-Two

More shades poured from the tunnel. The imps retreated. They swirled around the ring, cheering on Nazir as he and Kleos faced one another. One coalesced into full form on the other side of the gate in front of Dani, blocking her view of the arena.

Michael scowled. "You in a cage is something I've always wanted to see."

She backed away. "You've got weird fantasies, then."

He slipped past the stygian bars as if walking through a sieve. Now he was inside. "You're the reason I'm dead." His dark features shimmered and shifted. "I'm dead. Nazir is dead. All of us are dead because of you."

"It wasn't my fault Asmodeus attacked Ber'iah."

"Yes, it is!" Michael's scream echoed on the walls. The other migrant gladiators backed away. "He came there for you!"

Her eyes darted around, looking for a weapon. Unfortunately, there weren't any.

"You're the reason everything went wrong!"

"I didn't kill you. I didn't send you to Ber'iah. And I didn't ask you to save me."

Michael's shade—she had to remember this wasn't the real him—growled angrily. "He took me because he wanted you."

"Then don't follow his orders."

"I can't!" He roared in rage, but the anger was out of place. It sounded almost like pain. "I can't say no! He owns me! Don't you get it?"

Michael's sword formed in his hand. The deadly, gloomy shadow looked even more threatening up close.

"I tried to stop him. I'm still trying. But I can't say no. Everyone you love will die, just like me."

"I'll stop Asmodeus."

"Even if you do, others are coming. He is coming."

Belial. She knew that was who he was talking about.

"Well I don't see you standing up and doing something about it. Be a man!"

It was just a comeback; the first one she could think of and not all that clever. She hated the term "be a man" since she dealt with that misogynistic crap all day.

But the off-hand comment hit a nerve. She could see his expression change. Something besides the usual anger and loathing passed across his face. Was it shame? Could a spirit feel shame? And why was he feeling that now?

But it quickly disappeared. He took a threatening step forward.

She had the shadelight talisman. There were still two more uses in it. But to use it only on Michael would be a waste. Instead, she talked, hoping to buy time. "You tried to kill me once; before you died. Do you remember? I never understood why. I never once tried to hurt you. We fought," she remembered the first day she met Michael and the bout where she used her lightbringing unwittingly, "but why were you so angry? You don't like embarrassment?"

He growled. "None of your business."

"But if you hated me that much, why don't you fight Asmodeus now? You should hate him twice as much. He's a demon." She didn't know what else to do, so she appealed to his anger.

But he shook his head. "He allows me to hurt the one I hate the most: you."

"But you don't seem to want to fully." He hated her, sure, but she saw the same expression now: pain. Michael's shade was in pain.

"Nothing is my choice any longer." He told her. "That was taken from me when he took my life. I can only serve now. Kleos will die. You will die. You all deserve to die."

"Because you don't like women," she teased, "or because you don't like me personally?" She wanted to understand, but Michael pissed her off.

"Both. You're all the same."

"All? As in, all women?"

He ignored her. "You're coming with me. Nazir will kill Kleos. No need to wait for the death blow."

"I think you're a fool to doubt Kleos."

"And you're a fool if you think that if Nazir loses, Kleos will be spared." He sneered. "There are other shades out there."

They were going to kill Kleos no matter what. Dani's eyes flicked to the arena gate.

"You're unarmed." Michael reminded her. "Don't try it. Rule number one: don't enter a fight you can't win."

"Yeah, well," heat flowed down to her hand, "you must have forgotten rule number two: never underestimate your opponent."

She hit him with her lightbringing. Screw anyone finding out. She was not going to sit by and watch Kleos' murder. The blast hit Michael and his shade dissolved to smoke and screams.

Dani ran to the bars in time to see Kleos and Nazir clash swords. The two were evenly matched, if only because Kleos had the disadvantage. He parried and returned blows, but very quickly lost ground to his opponent.

"You can't kill me." Nazir sneered, striking quickly with his dark saber. "Even the witch could not destroy me. I will rise again and again until your death! A shade cannot die!"

276

Kleos dodged his slashes, moving backwards. His xiphos did not have the length to battle the shamshir saber and dagger. The adamantine steel clashed with the shadow blade, barely fending off his blows.

They circled, feinting and attacking and then coming in at another angle. Kleos chanced a hit, his sword slicing through Nazir's arm. Nazir dodged back, the inky blackness closing the wound in seconds.

"You were always the better swordsman," he said to Kleos, "but now I am immortal. You cannot kill that which is already dead."

The other half dozen shades cheered him on. They stayed away from the battle, allowing the two to fight, but every one of them carried a weapon; ready to kill Kleos if Nazir lost. Overhead, the three demonic lords watched.

"You were better than this, Nazir." Kleos told him, keeping his distance. "You weren't evil. You aren't now."

"No. I am dead now. I exist in constant pain. I died without a family because you took him from me!"

Titus. Nazir's anger visibly blurred his form.

"He was my Guardian! He was the only family I had!"

He slashed sideways, trying to bisect Kleos, but Kleos circled to keep away from Nazir.

"I had no one!" Nazir screamed. "No one! I was abandoned because of you! And the night Titus died, I was the one who found him! I rescued him when he was barely clinging to life! I carried him back to Empyrean! Did you know that, Kleos? Did you care?"

Kleos paused. Clearly, he didn't know.

"He died in my arms! Do you know his last words were about you? You! All he cared about was you!"

Kleos' sword lowered a fraction. Even from here, Dani could see tears in his eyes.

Nazir raised his saber. "You took him long before death took him. My family, my friend, only cared for you. And now, you'll spend the rest of eternity without him; like me, you will be a shade. You will serve Asmodeus and be denied the peace of death and reunion with him!"

Dani grabbed the lock of the cage, summoning her lightbringing. The stygian ignited bright orange. Her hands ached. She gritted her teeth.

"Time to die, Kleos!"

Nazir attacked, a long sweep of his saber aimed at Kleos' head. He brought his xiphos up and stopped it. Nazir's dagger came around. Dani melted the lock and tore it off. But she was too late.

Kleos saw the attack. His hand came down, seized his wrist and twisted himself and Nazir. The two wrenched around and Kleos tossed him to his back on the ground. Kleos flipped his xiphos and brought it point-down to his neck, ready to end Nazir.

But the blade stopped at his throat. Nazir stared up at Kleos. The tip hovered over his black skin.

The other shades swarmed forward. Dani burst from the cage and struck at random. She launched one bolt of light after another. Each shade screamed as they evaporated, the light scattering them into nothing.

The last shadow-person dissolved and Dani ran to help Kleos, but he stopped her with a single gesture of the hand.

"I didn't take Titus from you." He told Nazir. "We were not friends. Titus was my beloved. That's why we were together."

Nazir stared up at him, his black eyes wide. "Lies."

"It's the truth. Titus never abandoned you. He loved you, just not as he loved me. He was always your family."

Nazir wouldn't accept it. "You took the only thing I had! You had your own Guardian!"

"My Guardian was a cruel, merciless man who died long ago. I am glad he is gone. Titus showed me love. He helped me survive him! But because of that, you pushed him away!" Kleos screamed. "You became so angry with me that you distanced yourself from him and everyone else!"

"I was a child!"

"But you're not anymore!"

Kleos removed the blade and backed away. He could have killed Nazir; not permanently, but at least for now. Instead he allowed Nazir to get up. His shade-blades reformed in his hands.

"You know what I'm saying is true." Kleos told him. "You know it, but you can't bring yourself to believe it because you are not Nazir any longer. Asmodeus created you from Nazir's anger. You are not him. You are only a part of him. Giving up that anger would dispel your shade and put you to rest."

Dani's memory flickered back to what she found online: shades had 'unfinished business.' She realized Kleos was hoping that would stop him.

"I'll kill you." Nazir seethed.

Dani raised her hand to use her lightbringing, even through the pain, but Kleos waved her off again.

"You know it's true. You are not Nazir." Kleos dropped his xiphos. He raised his hands, unarmed. "You're his specter; a dark, twisted part of his soul that a demon turned into a monster. You're what Nazir couldn't let go of; his shadow. And the only way for you to stop the pain is not with a sword, but in accepting the truth: Titus loved you. I loved you, as any friend could. Give up your anger. Only then can you be at peace. If there is any part of the man who was my friend, you'll move on."

Nazir tensed, taking a threatening step towards Kleos. Kleos didn't pick up his weapon. Nazir took another. Kleos remained still.

"Let it go, Nazir." Kleos told him. "I will not fight you. You were Titus's Novice and you were his family, whether you believe it or not. All the anger, all the pain between you, and he still loved you. I miss him." Kleos' voice choked. "I miss him every day. What you told me about his last words gave me more peace than anything since his death."

Nazir growled angrily, but he didn't take another step.

"What was good in Titus is still inside you. I want you to be at peace. You died bravely. You died my friend. Be at rest and feel pain no longer."

Nazir's image distorted. Dani didn't know what was happening. His face shifted, blurring between anger and grief. What Kleos said broke through, but whatever Asmodeus created from the dark, empty anger tried to hold on.

Nazir screamed.

As if fighting himself, something broke. His expression softened. His anger faded. The sword and dagger dissipated. Smoke began to curl off him as he raised his hands to look at them, as if for the first time.

"I—I—!" He looked up at Kleos. "I am sorry. I am so sorry Kleos." His face blurred, the anger creeping back across his features. "I want to leave. It hurts so much. But he won't let me."

"I know."

Nazir groaned in pain again. A blast of shadow exploded off him as he fought. His imaged clouded. His anger flared back to life. "I'll kill you!"

"Fight it." Kleos told him. "Fight back, Nazir."

He screamed again, anger changing to pain. He doubled over.

"He's so strong!" He moaned. "I can't. I can't fight him!"

"You're stronger." Kleos knelt and took his hands. The moment they touched, Nazir collapsed to his knees. "This is not you. This is what Asmodeus summoned to torture you. Let go of your anger."

"I can't!"

"I know you can," Kleos gave him a soft smile, "my friend. I know because I see Titus's love in you. Accept it. Let him take you away."

Nazir wept, dark tear-like streams from his black eyes that flowed into black steam rising into the sky. He cried again, but not in anger. In defiance. He tilted back his head and screamed.

His body began to dissolve. And yet, when he looked down at Kleos, he smiled.

"Thank you." His voice was soft. His form began to disappear. "Thank you, my friend."

"Be at rest."

"I will see Titus on the other side. I will tell him you miss him."

Kleos smiled tearfully. "Thank you."

Nazir's eyes shifted to Dani. "For what I have done, I am sorry."

She nodded once, curtly, "I know."

"He's coming for you."

She nodded again, "I know."

"Kick his ass."

Then he gave in. Nazir, a man she hated for so long but couldn't bring to hate any longer, dissolved into nothing. His shadow blew apart and scattered into the wind, leaving Kleos' hands empty.

Silence settled over the arena.

"Is he," she almost hesitated to ask, "is he dead?"

"He's been dead since Ber'iah," Kleos told her, standing, "but his shade is gone."

"How did you know that would work?"

"I didn't." He retrieved his xiphos. "But what you said made sense: a shade has unfinished business here, so the soul can only leave this world if it allows itself to. Asmodeus created the shade from the part of Nazir's soul made of his anger. Then he sicked it on us like a dog. We wouldn't defeat him through torturing him further."

Before Dani could say anything else, the stereotypical, sardonic clapping—worthy of a B-movie villain—echoed through the silent arena. Dagon rose to his feet.

"Very well done!" Dagon commended. *Clap, clap, clap*; slow, sneering. "Very, very well done indeed! Although, that bout could have done without the melodrama."

"Sarcastic clapping? Really?" Dani turned her glare on him. "Get knotted, dipstick."

"Now, now, don't be so crass. That was an amazing display of skill, especially on your part. Ladies and gentlemen, we have a lightbringer amongst us!"

The chorus of shouts echoed as the demons got to their feet, gnashing teeth and screaming down at them. Or rather, at her.

"My, my, no wonder Asmodeus is so keen to have you. And now, with his servants gone, I don't need to hand you over. I believe you would be a prize much more suited for another!"

More cheering.

"What the hell is that supposed to mean?"

"Lord Asag, Lord Pazuzu, our arrangement should be amended." Dagon said to the two demons next to him. "Would you agree to pledge yourself to Belial, Lord of All Demons, if he had such a weapon in his arsenal; a lightbringer to challenge the Earthborn? Surely with such a powerful thing, no Numen army could stand against him."

"Hey! I'm not a 'thing,' creep!"

"We agree." Asag hissed. "My children will pledge themselves to Lord Belial, should he use such a girl against the Numen."

"As will I and all those who call upon the storms." Pazuzu echoed.

"Now wait one freaking minute!" Dani shouted. "Like hell I'm joining Belial. I'll die before I serve that putrid piece of scum!"

Dagon sighed, southern-accent all sympathetic and belittling. "Well, we'll see about that. Ladies and gentlemen, this fight is over!" Groans of disappointment surged up and down the bleachers. "Please, please, we have no contest left. Kill that there spare Numen and feed him to the horses. Audience, feel free to snack on your neighbor and thank'ya kindly for bein' such a wonderful crowd. Our show is ovah!"

The se'irim leveled their crossbows at Kleos.

"Grab the girl and drag her back in chains." Dagon said lastly. "Lord Asag, Lord Pazuzu, if you would follow me back to the house so we can draw up the agreement."

"WAIT!"

Everyone stopped and turned back to the pit.

They all looked at Dani.

"That's it?" She asked loudly. "That's all? This whole exhibition and all these demons get is one fight between us and bunch of random, Red-Shirt-Demons? I thought this exhibition was about giving them a show?"

If demons could give a vaudeville collective gasp, they would have. Instead they made a noise somewhere between a grunt and a loud fart, but the effect was the same. They all looked at Dagon.

"What the hell are you doing?" Kleos asked her softly.

"Saving your life. Again."

"Really? Because it looks like you're pissing him off."

"That's kind of the point. Follow my lead." She stepped up. "So, what gives, Dagon? You talk a big game but I don't see your star player. Afraid he's not up to snuff?"

"You want to challenge my champion, Goliath? You court death?" He asked, very much the old-world god of legend.

"Death can kiss my left butt cheek. He should fight real warriors. His best against ours."

"You would not last against the champion of the Philistines."

"Prove it. Give us our weapons and we'll see who's really the best."

It was weak line, but Dani quickly formed a plan. It wasn't a great plan, but it was better than watching Kleos get shot to death. She had a policy about not watching her friends die.

It would work, especially if they got the right chance.

"Our swords against your best. What do you say?"

Dagon looked to his companions, then around at the assembled crowd. Everyone waited.

His lips pulled back into a cruel smile. "Very well. If it is a match you want, then a match you shall have."

The demons cheered; louder than ever before. They got their encore. Everyone was happy.

Dagon yelled. "Bring out Goliath!"

And Dani prayed she knew what she was doing.

Dagon tossed Dani's swords and armor into the ring; Kleos' remaining weapons, too.

"You are a fool, Daniella of Empyrean." He snarled.

"I get that a lot; usually from people I kill."

"Bring forth my champion!"

The demonic screams crescendoed.

Dani and Kleos quickly latched on their armored gauntlets, bracers and greaves. Kleos knelt beside her, talking softly as he fitted his throwing blades on. "What the hell are you thinking?"

"I'm thinking I'd rather you not get riddled with arrows."

"You know Goliath is stronger and faster than either of us. We were armed last time and he wasn't, and he still nearly killed us both."

"Trust me. I got a plan."

"What plan?"

She glanced up at the three thrones. "A good one that doesn't entail you and every other person on this farm getting slaughtered."

She told him in hushed tones as they belted on their blades. It was nice to see Kleos surprised, especially since he automatically agreed to her idea. The only difficult part was surviving long enough for it to work.

The stygian gate below Dagon opened with a loud, slow creak. They stood, swords out. It felt good to have Pointyend back in her hand. The blade glowed softly.

But her confidence waned when Goliath appeared. He seemed bigger than before; taller, wider. He also added more armor. Stygian plates covered his tunic and he wore a different helmet; one with trailing black horsehair from the crown and covering his jaws and nose with guards. He added gauntlets and greaves, bathing his whole body in the hell-forged metal so dark it reflected black. In one hand, he carried a short javelin-like spear as well as a hooked khopesh blade twice the size of Mastema's on his hip. A square shield the length of his body cradled on his other arm.

"Are you rethinking this plan?" Kleos asked, tensing for battle.

"A little, but we're already down the rabbit hole."

Goliath stepped into the open and the imps closed the gate, locking them in. Dani and Kleos stood shoulder-to-shoulder, both practically naked next to a guy covered in that much steel.

"Use your speed." Kleos advised. "He'll be slow, but don't underestimate him. This is not a movie. The little guy doesn't always win against the big hulk."

"Yeah, well, at least he can't chase us."

The trumpet sounded.

Goliath roared.

She was wrong.

He hefted his javelin and launched it towards them. Dani ducked, but she wasn't fast enough. The stygian tip cut her shoulder and knocked her to the ground.

Then Goliath charged.

She could barely stay ahead of him. Even armored, Goliath was unbelievably fast. He went for her first. She got up, backing away to put some distance between them. When that didn't work, she jumped and pin-wheeled around, slashing with her sword.

It glanced harmlessly off his big shield.

The wall of metal smashed into her as he swept her aside. Dani flew a good three or four feet before she landed, breaking apart the dirt floor as she landed. She rolled backward onto her feet, but he came again. She'd never be able to keep this up.

How does he move that fast? She leapt up, kicking out with both feet to force him back.

Nope. All she did was bounce off and twist mid-air, landing back another two yards. This was a very one sided fight.

Kleos joined the fray. With Goliath distracted, he attacked from behind, stabbing into his back. The double-thick stygian armor stopped his sword point, which barely penetrated an inch. He withdrew to strike again, but Goliath elbowed back and struck Kleos in the face.

Then with one hand, he drew the impossibly long khopesh.

Like a demonic scythe, Goliath slashed around, backing both of them away. Dani summoned her power into her sword, igniting the blade and taking the stygian weapon full force across the edge. Her bones shook as their blades collided. A second blow nearly knocked her sword from her hand. She had to retreat, coming back to Kleos' side and drawing Pigsticker.

"So, any idea when we enact your plan?" Kleos asked her.

She glanced up at Dagon and the others over Goliath's helmet. She shook her head. "I need to get close and I need something I can throw. Goliath won't give us a chance."

"We need to kill him."

"Any ideas on that front?"

Goliath came at them and the two separated to give themselves the best chance. Usually in movies, the big guy was too slow and the little guy won by tiring him out. In fact, that trope came from the story of David and Goliath. Unfortunately, the real-life Goliath proved a lot harder to kill. He was super-fast, super-strong and super-pissed off.

Kleos dodged near the wall, the stygian spikes shooting out to kill him. He barely avoided them. As Goliath neared, Kleos called on Erthe and hurled rocks from the ground at him.

A rock once took him down, but Goliath's shield blocked these.

"You think I have not learned from history?" Dagon taunted from his throne. "His armor is twice as thick and he is twice as strong. No rock can kill him!"

Dani went to help Kleos, sheathing her dagger and summoning her power. She blasted Goliath with a good ol' fashioned brute attack. The light struck and he raised his shield, giving Kleos time to retreat. The searing pain forced Dani to pull it back after only a moment. His shield held up under the assault, smoldering.

"You cannot wield the power of the Lightbringer!" Dagon taunted.

"Shut your face!"

Goliath adjusted his shield, sword in his free hand. He kept behind his steel wall. Dani blasted him again, keeping him back. Unfortunately, she wouldn't be able to keep it up. It hurt too much.

"I'm out of ideas." Kleos told her.

Goliath took his time; walking instead of running, keeping the shield up. He knew they couldn't run forever, nor keep him at bay with her light. A smile played on his lips.

"He's armored everywhere." Kleos told her. "There isn't a weak spot."

Her eyes floated down to his legs, partially hidden behind the shield and greaves. Damn. Armored. But he was still exposed near his upper legs, a small enough area with the right shot to the inner thigh. Then she looked up to his eyes. Those weren't armored.

Could that work?

"Wherever we hit, it won't slow him down for long."

"I don't need him to slow. I need him to trip. Then we go for the eyes."

"What are you thinking?"

"I want him to fall on something sharp. Remember how the terrene went down on the stygian pikes from the wall?"

Goliath edged closer. Dani summoned another painful burst of light. He raised his shield, deflecting.

Kleos shook his head. "He's not stupid. He won't go near those spikes."

"I don't need him to. I need him to fall on something."

Kleos knelt, fingertips to the ground, as if sensing. "I think there might be a way. It'll take me time to mold it right."

"I'll give you as much time as I can." She drew Pigsticker in her damaged hand. "Give me the word when you're ready."

Dani charged Goliath. Unlike before, this wasn't about running away. This was about standing her ground. He swung the sword and she dodged, striking back but only hitting shield or armor. Each strike met metal with metal. She couldn't land a blow. Goliath, on the other hand, could. Even her swords with all her emotional power couldn't stand up against the force they carried. Her hands hurt. Her arms ached. But she fought back desperately.

Goliath feinted with his shield. She dodged. He stabbed with the khopesh and she moved, the blade glancing off her bracers. But then he pulled, using the hook to tear her guard apart. Her swords were flung from her hands.

He swung with his blade and she rolled back.

"Now, Dani!" Kleos warned.

Dani rolled up and jumped, summoning Aer under her. As she did, Kleos launched a throwing dagger. The blade lashed inside Goliath's leg under his shield and armor, burying into open a section of his inner thigh. It dropped him to his knees with a grunt.

Dani soared up over his head and kicked, connecting with the back of his skull. The helmet protected him, but that wasn't the point. The full-force of impact knocked him forward off balance.

She turned in midair and blasted with one last gush of light, propelling him forward onto his face. As he fell, Kleos extended his hand and pushed up with Erthe.

A sharp pike of quartz exploded from the ground and pierced Goliath through the right eye. The force of it coming up and him coming down sent the shard straight back through the socket into his skull. He landed, impaled on the rock as Dani dropped back onto her feet.

And the crowd went silent.

She strode over and retrieved her weapons. With her foot, she pushed him over onto his back, ready to stab him again. Goliath stared up blankly at the sky with his one good eye, the other nothing but a hole with a large piece of stone sticking out of it. Then, as she watched, his body withered and desiccated. His muscles shrunk. His skin turned to leather. Going through decomposition in fast-forward, after seconds only a skeleton remained, which crumbled to dust and blew away.

When she looked up at Dagon, the angry god glared down at them.

"Now," she said sarcastically, "normally I'd make a Dust in the Wind reference here, but that would be _way_ too easy."

Dagon shot to his feet. "You stupid little witch!"

"Aww, did I break your favorite boy toy?"

"I'll kill you! Guards! Shoot them! Shoot them both!"

The satyrs leveled their crossbows.

"Stop!" Asag snarled. "She belongs to Belial!"

"I care not!" Dagon began cursing in a language Dani guessed was native to the Philistines.

"Hold the order to fire!" Pazuzu shouted.

The god and the two demons burst into argument. The satyrs hesitated. Kleos knelt, retrieving Goliath's fallen javelin.

"Can you hit him from here?" She asked softly.

"With this thing? Definitely. My people invented the Olympic javelin throw."

"Then do it."

Dagon turned on them, pointing angrily. "I said kill them both!"

"Wait!" She held up her hands.

Everyone stopped. Dagon fumed. The demons paused. Dani stepped aside to give Kleos a clean shot.

"I have one thing to say." She warned.

"What's that?"

"*Todos cúbranse los ojos.*"

Dagon blinked. "What?"

"*Todos cúbranse los ojos!*"

"And that means?"

She smiled. She knew, of course, and so did anyone who spoke Spanish. *Everyone cover your eyes.*

Kleos took a step and launched the javelin.

Most of the demons were so shocked Kleos attacked, they didn't react. The stygian-tipped spear shot through the air, up and over the rim of the pit, and past the spikes; aimed directly at its target.

Dagon watched as the spear sliced right past him into Asag's hood. The blade yanked back the covering. Dani and Kleos had already turned away.

And then the demons began to scream.

Chapter Thirty-Three

As with the masters of old, I do not speak the language of slaves. It is beneath me. That was what Dagon told her over dinner.

Well screw you, then, she thought.

Her message got through. Every enslaved worker looked away, closed their eyes, or covered them with their hands. Even those who weren't Hispanic got the message and followed suit. The javelin knocked back Asag's hood and every demon watching, from the imps and se'irim in the crowd to the terrene and alé, started to scream.

The coliseum erupted in chaos.

Kleos and Dani ran blindly. The sound of many demons dying was horrendous. It was a chorus of unearthly cries suited for Hell. They didn't dare open their eyes until they knew they faced away. When they finally looked up, hellspawn exploded into ash or convulsed as black blood oozed from their eyes, ears and mouths; some all at once.

Demons dropped like flies. Some fell onto the stygian spikes while others dropped through them into the arena. One of the satyrs fell, crossbow tumbling from his hands as he turned into a shower of dust. Kleos snatched the weapon out of the air and aimed at an imp who survived the slaughter. He fired the arrow into its neck and charged through the gate back into their holding pen.

"*Qué está sucediendo?*" One of the men inside asked. *What is happening?*

"*Nos vamos ahora mismo.*" Dani told them, stepping into the middle of the room. She raised her hand. "No one is dying here!"

She launched a blast of light upward and obliterated the stygian bars that covered the manhole. Kleos and she quickly grabbed the men and one at a time, flew them up and out of the cage.

It was pandemonium above. With so many demons dying, others who weren't hit scrambled in panic. When Dani looked back, Asag covered himself once more, but there were tons of dead ash piles around him where demons used to be. Others only got a glimpse and survived, but they were black, bloody messes feebly trying to crawl away. The humans fled in all directions. Others picked up fallen weapons and killed the remaining monsters, or shoved them into the pit or onto the spikes that guarded it.

Pazuzu looked as if he'd taken the full brunt of Asag's revelation. The archdemon choked and sputtered, his wings fanning dirt clouds around him as he thrashed. His eyes were gone and he screamed as he fell, exploding into a large puff of dirt when he hit the ground.

Dagon was nowhere to be seen.

"Dani! Come on!" Kleos warned.

Asag rose to his feet, furious. He hobbled forward, climbing over the crumbled bodies of his terrene. Just ahead, the woman from the barn pulled her daughter away from the chaos now that they were freed from the demons. But Asag spotted them, scaly hands greedily flickering as he stalked after them . The little girl screamed.

Dani moved to head him off.

"Dani! No!" Kleos called.

Asag spotted her. He pointed one of his clawed fingers in her direction. "Tacoma! Kill her!"

One of the mountain demons lumbered towards her. In the pit, Dani wasn't a match for it. This time she was armed. Using her glowing blade, she sliced off one arm as it threw a punch. Her sword carved through its rocky flesh like butter. She hacked and slashed until it toppled to its knees. She kicked the remaining pieces into the pit as it fell apart, and then she kept going after its father.

"You killed my offspring!" Asag snarled. "You'll die the same death!"

He reached for his hood. Dani cast out her hand and blasted him with light. She was in so much pain, but her hate fueled her fire. The bolt struck Asag in the chest and knocked him back over his throne. He rolled to his hands and knees as she came forward.

"Look upon death, girl!"

She couldn't hit him in time. He pulled back his hood in front of her eyes.

The thing underneath was hideous. A long, forked tongue slithered through his smiling, rotten fangs that oozed yellow-green pus. Though the skin was the same grey, scaly color as his hands, it was rotten with mold. Slimy, wet, flesh fell off his diseased cheeks and lips. He was disgusting.

But nothing happened to Dani.

She stared at him, but no matter what happened to the demons and people who saw his face before, nothing happened to her now. Her blood didn't boil. She didn't have a seizure and keel over. Nothing.

Asag cowered back. "Impossible! No creature can look upon me!"

Dani shook out of her shock and raised her sword to kill him.

The ground beneath Asag opened and he pitched himself into the sinkhole. Dani ran to the edge and looked down. The chasm was deep; so far down that she couldn't see the bottom. The earth quickly knit itself together again behind him. Asag was gone.

Kleos ran to her side, his sword stained with black demon blood. "Dani! What happened?"

"I," she hesitated, "I don't know."

Someone released the Mares of Diomedes and the Steeds of Abigor from the barn. The creatures sprang into the open. Some of the skeletal horses took to the sky in freedom, galloping on invisible roads into the clouds. The mares took great pleasure in attacking their former captors. They ran down demons, teeth tearing into hellish flesh and trampling them underfoot.

The leaves on the trees began to change color and the grass started to die.

Dani, Kleos and a handful of refugees—including the girl and her mother—headed downhill towards the river. A small dock moored a pontoon boat and they quickly got everyone aboard.

"Get onto the boat!" Dani told them, repeating herself in Spanish.

Kleos helped some of the lesser able aboard, and then retrieved the keys and started it up. The boat was good-sized; a tour-craft Dagon must have used for his dude ranch. Everyone got into seats that lined the wide-open deck. Dani slashed the linings with her sword and hopped on as they pulled away.

The ranch burned. Someone started a fire that blazed into an inferno, consuming the barn and the main house. Even as she watched, Dagon's power waned. Green turned to brown, or red, or yellow as autumn reclaimed the springtime ranch. The air became cool.

They slowly left that hellhole behind.

"Is everyone okay?" Dani asked. "*Está todo bien?*"

She got a chorus of grateful yeses. Leaving them, she walked down to Kleos behind the controls. "Are you okay?"

"How did you say it last night? Peachy?"

She shook her head, glancing back. "Do you think he's dead?"

"Dagon?" Before he could answer, he looked past her. His face paled a little. "Uh, no, I don't think so."

Dani looked over her shoulder. Just on the shoreline, glaring at them from a circle of still-green river grass, was the god. His hat was missing and he tore off his tattered, burnt white coat. His shirt and pants were stained with black soot and demon blood. His hands clenched into fists at his sides.

"Oh man, he looks pissed."

They were a good dozen feet from the shoreline. The river was too wide and deep to cross. Dagon didn't move. He just glared.

"What's he waiting for?"

"He's a field god." Kleos reminded her. "The river isn't his domain."

"So?"

"So, pagan gods aren't people. For all their power, they can't go where they want. If it's not their domain, they can't enter it. He's not allowed into the river."

She smirked. It was the first good thing about gods she learned. Running to the railing, she yelled out to him. "What's wrong? A little scared of the water, Dagon? Maybe you should have spent some time in swim class instead of being a racist pain in the—!"

Dagon stepped down from the shore into the river before she finished. As he did, his appearance transformed. His white slacks and shoes disappeared, replaced by golden scales and webbed feet. His lower body molded together, forming a shark-fish merman body. Seething angry, he tumbled forward underneath the surface of the river and disappeared from sight.

She glanced back at Kleos. "Um, what the hell was that?"

Kleos bit his lower lip, his face paling even more. He looked around the side of the boat furtively.

"I thought you said he was a field god!" Dani reminded him. "He shouldn't be able to get into the water, right?"

"Technically, he's a field and fertility god."

"So?"

"Well, fertility is often associated with multiplying. The symbol of that," he swallowed, "is fishing."

"Fishing?" Dani groaned. "Meaning he's also a fishing god. Which makes him a river god, as well."

Kleos nervously nodded. "In some traditions."

"Well, lumme, why didn't you tell me that before I pissed him off!"

The river shuddered. The people onboard screamed. Something rocked the boat and Dani and Kleos braced. Then, another tremor shook the surface.

"Not good."

The water in front of the boat exploded. A funnel churned upward and from the top, Dagon appeared. The river swirled around his waist as he rose above them, blocking their path.

"You never learn!" The field and fish god roared. "You insignificant little wench! You dare mock me?"

His face was different. He was no longer a simple rancher. He had horn-spikes, like that of a crab shell, in lines down his cheeks. His eyes were large and lidless. His hands were webbed claws. His skin, like armored scales, glinted in the sunlight as he stretched his shark-like teeth wide.

Dani leapt to the front of the boat and drew both swords. "Back off Jaws, or I'll turn you into sushi!"

The boat rocked and swayed under her feet as the water started to chop. Some of the passengers tipped out of their seats, falling onto one another or onto the floor.

Dagon cackled. "This is my domain! It fuels my power, as the fields do! I cannot be killed by the likes of you!" He sneered. "I'm going to enjoy killing you!"

A wave curled from his funnel and smashed into the boat, nearly tossing Dani off her feet. She steadied herself. She and Kleos could fly, but then they'd leave the people behind. They couldn't do that.

Another wave crashed and someone almost went over the side.

"I can't move the boat!" Kleos warned. He throttled up, but the engine couldn't overpower the water Dagon controlled. It churned and churned, but didn't move them.

Dani summoned her light, but the pain was unbearable. She had used it too much.

Dagon grinned devilishly. "I know why you are here, Numen. I see it now." He funneled around to one side, nearly tipping the boat. "You came to this river for the fish of legend. I know you did."

Dani swallowed hard.

"I know it is in this river. It was called here by me. But this river will not be your salvation! It will be your tomb!"

He had her at her mercy and he knew it. Even though she wouldn't show it, she was afraid.

Fear is the true enemy of strength, Mastema taught her, just moments before he dangled her out on a tree trunk over a river. *It is the one darkness all things experience.*

He taught her to face fear. He sent her out without him, knowing she would have to face it. And, she realized, it wasn't just Asmodeus she feared.

She left the safety of her new home.

She left without knowing where to go or what to do.

She left, doubting she might be able to do what she had to.

She left, leaving behind everyone she loved.

The only thing to drive out darkness is light. Fear is one type darkness. And it can only be conquered by two powers, the most important of which is yourself. Knowing yourself is to know your enemy. It is the only one you control.

Dani gripped her swords tighter. She took a deep breath and without a second thought, rose defiantly up from the boat into the air to face the devilish god. "Well, if you're so confident about yourself, come and get it."

Dagon hurled himself at her. Dani slashed with her swords, hacking into his flesh. He howled in pain as they circled one another.

As Dani watched, the water coursed over his wounds and shut them.

He grinned. "You need to do better than that."

They collided again. And again. His claws cut her legs. Spikes along his forearms stabbed her in the side. Unlike the wounds she inflicted on him, hers didn't heal.

He smacked her back down to the boat. Towering above them, he gloated. "Time to die."

Dani stood again, ready.

Dagon descended, water and god crashing towards her. She braced one foot against the side and took the brunt of the assault. Waves blew her backwards and Dagon landed atop her, snarling animalistically. The people braced, stopping themselves from being washed overboard, but Dani and Dagon tumbled over the side into the river.

Water enveloped her, as if the god could make it choke her, too. The world went mute. As they descended under the surface, everyone she loved came to mind. Everyone she fought for, would die for, flashed before her eyes. She might die.

Dani sunk both sword and knife home into Dagon's sides. His eyes widened, so close to her face in the murky river she could see the surprise in them. He thrashed and cried, the blades slicing him up inside. She withdrew and stabbed again. Bubbles erupted around them. The weight of his body disappeared and with one last, loud moan, he dissolved into froth in the murky darkness around her.

He was gone.

Dani floated listlessly in the dank deep. She tried, but she couldn't bring herself to surface. Her lungs burned. Her limbs were weak and heavy. Dagon had forced her too far down. Her feet touched the bottom of the riverbed.

She would drown, but it didn't matter. Dagon was gone. The people were safe. The little girl and her mother and everyone he held captive were free. Dani closed her eyes, her chest burning for air.

It's okay, she thought. *They're safe. Belial lost. Asmodeus can't get to me.* She was free. Death could have her.

Dani opened her mouth and expelled the last the air from her lungs.

Chapter Thirty-Four

Something grabbed her underneath her arms. Dani came back to her body with a jolt. She shot upwards. The water peeled at her eyes. She had to close them as she rushed through the river. She couldn't see her rescuer and by the time she managed to open her eyes again, the surface of the water surged towards her.

She screamed as she flung free from the surface of the river onto land. Or rather, onto wooden planks. Dani landed on a small pier like a wet rag doll, flopping to the dry ground as a soggy, half-dead mess.

The landing hurt. She coughed up water and groaned. When she opened her eyes, her swords clattered to the feet of a man standing just beside her.

Dani blinked and wiped her face, looking up. The man knelt. Dani recognized him. Anyone who grew up with the Genie of *Aladdin* or *Mrs. Doubtfire* would.

"You're dead." She said lamely.

"Yes. And yet immortality exists for all who bring joy to this world." His smile was serene as he offered her a hand. "May I help you up?"

She took it, slowly climbing to her feet. "Haniel. What are you doing here?"

"You are here. Thus, I am." The angel said, more serious than his comedic visage typically was. "I've never been far from you."

"Never been far? How far?" She spit out river water. "Did you know we got kidnapped by a psychopathic pagan god?"

"Yes." He said it without noticing the problem.

"Are you kidding me?" She shoved him. "You knew we were in trouble and you did nothing?"

"Angels cannot interfere in the affairs of humanity or those of Numen. You know this."

"You mean you choose not to! And did you not know that Dagon kept a farm full of slaves? What is wrong with you people?"

"You people?"

"Angels! For God's sakes, I get that you nearly wiped out Creation or whatever, but have some balls! You could have saved us. You could have done something to help!"

"You did not need help, as it appears. Well, except for nearly drowning. I helped with that."

"And how did you—?" She turned towards the river and stopped.

Dozens of fish floated on the water's surface. At least, at first she thought they were fish. They looked like fish, except for the fact they were the size of human toddlers. These fish, however, also had arms and hands along with their fins. And at second glance, their upper wide 'fish bodies' were actually more like monks, with monk-caps and cowls about their shoulders.

"Mermaids?"

"Sea monks." He corrected. "Or rather, river-monks in this case. They are healers of those who dwell in the waters; priests of the deep. Normally, they reside in Europa, but I wanted their assistance looking for the artifact."

A boat horn pulled her attention upriver. Kleos spotted them and steered towards the dock.

"I see everyone made it safely." Haniel commented. "Very well done."

"No, not well done. Haniel, we lost the bane boxes. They were back at the ranch. I think they might have burned up in the fire."

"These bane boxes?"

All three appeared at his feet, along with Dani and Kleos' packs.

"When did you get those?"

"Just now." He opened one box and showed her Asmodeus's golden seal. He opened a second and walked past her with it, placing it at the end of the dock. "And if I am not mistaken, our second artifact should be close by." He gestured Dani to follow. When she did, he instructed, "Now, please, dip your hand into the river, palm open and it should come to you."

"Dip what?"

"Just do as I ask, please."

Dani knelt and extended her hand. The water was cold, but nothing happened.

"What am I—?"

Something swam into her palm and settled there. Dani stood and pulled it out. Thrashing around between her fingers was a large, scaly fish the size of a sea bass.

"How did you make that happen?"

Haniel held up the bane box in his hands. "In here, please."

Dani deposited the fish into the box. It flopped around, threatening to leap out but the angel snapped the lid shut and latched it. Then he held it out to her.

"The fish will stay preserved inside until the time is ready."

"Ready for what?"

"Gutting." He explained. "The fish is one of three components. Its heart and liver, once burned, can cast the demon Asmodeus from any vessel he inhabits."

"Cast out? You mean, like in the story? That's what it means?"

He nodded. "In ancient times, Asmodeus sought the young woman, Sarah. The legends may not speak of it, but she was a woman of passion and spirit. She refused the lord of lust. As he now is refused by you." The angel placed the box in her hands. "Asmodeus then sought to take her by possessing her husbands. On the night of their wedding, she would not invite her husbands into her bed. When they could not enter, she knew they were possessed. In anger, he killed them. Tobias was possessed as well. But before the wedding, he gave the fish to Sarah to save him."

"I thought Tobias burned the fish guts?"

"Ah, yes, well legends are written by men, aren't they?"

She shook her head, looking at the box. "Why this fish? Why does this one fish work?"

"Exactly why, I am not sure."

Dani shook her head. "You know, I think I liked it better when I thought angels were all-knowing, benevolent beings, and not jerks who know nothing."

"You must accept there are mysteries you will never know. It is the curse of joyous mortality. I may not know all, but what I do know is this fish is one amongst millions. As are you. For the fish to present itself to you, in this time and this place far from its natural habitat, means God chose it, as He chose you. It is no accident you are both here."

"It's coincidence." She said. "If God were behind it, He would have told me where it was."

"Are you sure He didn't?" He gave her a smile right out of her favorite movie. "Dagon is a god of fishing. His power attracted it here, where you could get to it. You received a vision that not only brought you here, but put you in a place to save the very people Dagon enslaved. And by doing so, you struck a blow against the demonic. That is not a coincidence. You are tools to defeat a great enemy."

"*You're* a tool," she returned the box to her bag, "and whoever is doing the choosing is a total douche. Seriously, a golden seal and a fish? What's next? A compass? A special wand? What other ridiculous piece of junk can stop the Lord of Douchenozzles?"

"That is not for me to say."

Kleos arrived at the dock, disembarking. Another person took the helm and continued on. The girl and her mother waved to them as they left. She looked happy. Hopefully, she would remain that way now that she was out of Dagon's clutches.

"You again." Kleos grumbled. "Did you find what you sent us here for?"

Dani held up her pack, now containing two bane boxes full of demon-fighting artifacts. "Get this: it's a special fish we have to gut."

"Gross."

"I agree." She turned back to Haniel. "So, what is next?"

"I am not sure. You are being sent to—."

"Oh save it already!" Dani interrupted irritably. "I'm tired, I'm completely soaked and I have had it up to here with lying."

"I don't understand." The angel said evasively.

"Back in California, you pretended not to know what was there. Yet, you knew about Asmodeus's seal. I saw you make a face when I mentioned my vision at the club. For an angel, you're a terrible liar. You sent us here with the same BS story, yet just now you knew a ton about that fish. So, either you got memory issues that solve themselves when we finally find what we're looking for, or you've been yanking our chain. And I'm done getting yanked around. Cut it out."

Haniel's face, once something she watched hilariously *Live on Broadway*, was now blank. Careful. He was thinking of what to say next.

"If you lie to me, I swear to God I'll punch you. I don't know what punching an angel can do, but I'll punch you right in the suckhole."

He opened his mouth to speak, but stopped. Haniel tipped his head to the side, as if listening. There weren't any sounds except the usual woodland noises, but he seemed to be listening for something. Or to something.

Kleos leaned in to Dani's ear. "What's going on?"

"I'm not sure."

Haniel interrupted them, asking out loud. "Are you sure?"

"Is he talking to us?" Dani asked.

Haniel didn't seem to. No response came that Dani could hear, but he got an answer. "Yes sir. I will tell them."

"Tell us what?"

"I'm sorry." Haniel said, now actually talking to Kleos and Dani. "I wasn't able to tell you before. I was forbidden."

"Forbidden from what? By who?"

"I know what you seek." He confessed. "I've known since before you arrived at the club in Long Beach. I was ordered to be there and to give only little assistance in your quest, as all my kind has agreed to do over the centuries. Since the War, it was our agreement. But the situation has changed. He wishes to speak to you in person."

"Who?"

"My master, for whom I serve."

"Who? God?"

"No."

He reached out and touched them both. Then the world fell apart.

Part III
King

Chapter Thirty-Five

It was like someone smeared a painting and then very quickly redrew it. Dani, Kleos and Haniel were no longer on the dock.

Instead, they stood beside a different body of water; a pond. A sprinkling of fall-colored trees bordered its waters and dropped little leaf-boats onto the tranquil surface. The crunchy, brown coating of autumn covered the ground. Just beyond, a house overlooked the mirror-green waters. A bench waited nearby; a seat to admire the beautiful quiet.

"What the hell happened?" Dani glanced around. "What did you just do?"

"I needed to take you far and fast." Haniel explained. "It was easier this way."

Dani saw that Haniel no longer looked like the comedian; in fact, he didn't look like any comedian. Instead, he appeared as a young boy; maybe twelve at most. His skin was the color of hazelnut, his hair completely shaven and he had a face so beautiful it made her want to cry. He was an Adonis, with sharp features and dazzling eyes. His irises mixed with every color, as if it held the Milky Way Galaxy in them.

He looked like a true angel.

"Are we in Heaven?" Kleos marveled.

"No."

His face fell.

"Where are we then?" Dani asked.

Haniel turned and began to walk. "Bethesda, Maryland."

"Maryland? What the hell is so special about Maryland?"

"Nothing, but someone wishes to speak to you and he spends his days here."

As they walked around the pond, Dani spotted someone sitting on the bench by the water. She hadn't noticed him before, or he hadn't been there before now.

It didn't matter. Either way, she knew he was an angel.

He had a long walking stick laid over his shoulder and wore a simple brown robe like a monk. As they approached, he looked up. His hair was long, shaggy and black. It hung in loose curls about his thin face. He wasn't beautiful like the other angels she met; or rather, he was once beautiful, but now wasn't. His features were sunken. He had a gaunt, solemn face with eyes that held no joy. Dani once saw a picture of a famous musician— Lennon something. This angel reminded her of him, except that his eyes— for lack of any better description—looked like they had seen too much. No mirth. No joy. He looked haunted by memories she could only guess. He was the opposite of Haniel and the very opposite of the musician he appeared so similar to.

He stood. The brown leaves around him swirled in the invisible, twirling upward to form a pair of wings across his back, which flared weakly before falling again on the ground.

Kleos marveled in a whisper, "It's another angel!"

"Don't get too excited." Dani grumbled. "The dog and pony show gets old really fast."

They approached and Haniel dropped to one knee, bowing in reverence. The angel in the brown smock touched his head lightly as he stepped past.

"Hello." He greeted softly. "Daniella del Lucio. Alexi Patera, now known as Kleos. Greetings to you both."

Dani glanced sidelong as Kleos. "Alexi?"

"It was my name before joining the Numen. Titus gave me Kleos because it means 'renown.' It was his," he blushed, "pet name for me. Everyone began to call me Kleos after that."

Dani turned her attention back to the angel. "And you must be Raphael the Archangel, right? Gabriel's brother?"

He nodded. "The same."

"Well, then, where the _hell_ have you been?"

He wasn't shocked by her anger. Maybe he wasn't as easy to startle; however, Haniel rose to his feet with fists clenched. It was the first time she saw anything serious in him. His eyes grew dark; hooded. His irises, once beautiful pools that reflected the galaxy, now glowed hot like fire.

"Calm." The archangel told him, nodding to her as if he understood. "You are angry."

"You're right I'm angry!" She barked. "Do you know who just attacked your city? Who's threatening me? Who has tried to kill me or enslave me half a dozen times through his lackeys?"

"I am aware Asmodeus returned, if that is what you suggest."

"Trust me, there's no suggestion. I'm saying it. Where the hell have you been to stop the guy you had a throw-down with centuries ago?"

"Dani!" Kleos looked mortified. "Lord Raphael, I'm sure that she does not mean any offense."

"Yes, she does." Raphael said. "And she has every right to be angry."

The way he spoke lacked any kind of emotion except pain. It was soft, slow, and empty of anger. There was almost nothing to his voice and it took the wind out of Dani's sails.

"You can be angry. Anger is natural. Anyone who denies that, hurts themselves." Raphael told her. "Your kind has been the victims of the brutality that Asmodeus embodies."

"My kind?"

"Women." He said simply. "And others whom society deemed less important. I have heard their cries and felt their pain. Those who have endured so much have souls that cry out to the universe. It echoes with their pain."

"Nice words." Dani snorted. "It should go on a Hallmark card."

"You need to let go of your anger. It is a poison that will not help you."

"Yeah, well, while you've been sitting back on your laurels, people I know are dying. So, no offense, I'm not exactly in the mood to let things go."

"Dani, consarn it, stop!" Kleos scolded. "He's an archangel!"

"What is he going to do? Smite me?"

"I could." The angel offered.

That got Dani to stop. It wasn't a threat. He simply stated a fact. She swallowed her next words, as there was no need to piss of an archangel.

"But I will not." Raphael told her. "My days as a warrior are over. I do not seek war and death any longer." He turned to Haniel. "My servant, go with my thanks. I will seek you out when you are needed."

"Yes, my lord."

Haniel vanished in the blink of an eye.

Raphael turned back to them with the same saddened expression. "You have questions and concerns, I am sure."

"Oh, only a few." Dani grumbled.

The angel sighed, sitting down on the bench again. He nodded to the surrounding country. "Bethesda. Do you know the name?"

"I've never been to Maryland."

"I do not simply mean this city, Daniella del Lucio of Empyrean. I mean the name Bethesda."

She shook her head.

"It comes from an ancient human language: *beth hesda*. It means 'house of mercy.' I find there are few true places of mercy in the world these days. I visit them, few as there are. Society has become so enamored with conflict that mercy is a forgotten concept. Even amongst nations that say they stand for peace and freedom, mercy is very seldom given; even to one's own people. Of course, mercy has always been a rare emotion, but it seems so much less now."

Dani and Kleos exchanged a look. Both shrugged.

"You know why I did not intervene with Asmodeus." Raphael said. She wasn't sure if he was talking to either of them or himself, since he stared out over the water instead of at them. "You know why Haniel—though he could smite every demon and god you faced—was forbidden to interfere directly."

"Your brother Gabriel told me about what happened the angels and," she bit her lower lip nervously, "about what God did to you. He forced you to grow up, right? You were so horrified that you and the other angels left."

She shook her head. "God doesn't seem to do very well with His creations, does he?"

Raphael frowned. "What do you know of God?"

"Not a whole lot."

"An honest answer for a human; very few have learned such humility. Most prefer to tell one another about the Creator, instead of listening to one another's beliefs." He shifted in his seat. "Yes. We were once children; impudent, rash, given unlimited power but not unlimited in sight. Some of my brothers and sisters questioned God's plan for us, though they never questioned His plan for you. They wondered why He would punish us for defending His name against Lucifer; why He opened our eyes to the true horrors of what we did. Do you know why?"

"I'll bite. Why?"

"Because the reality is that our actions have never had meaning." He said. "It is our outcomes, how we affect others, which matters most. We went to war, but it didn't matter why we did. The loss of the universe was the only thing that mattered to Him."

"I don't understand." Dani said.

"Very few do." The archangel said with the slightest of smiles. "What I mean, is that the only thing that matters in this world is what you do to better it; not to destroy it. When the War was over, my kind fled in shame. Our legacy was nothing but death and destruction. You could say, as humans do, that the path to hell is paved with good intentions. In this case, that was literally."

"When angels departed, we left behind such devastation that the universe has been echoing its pain for the eons. The universe is no longer a place that reflects God's beauty. Most of it is dead. There is more in the galaxy that will kill life than nurture it."

"But you aren't all bad. You still decided to help." Dani challenged. "You may not have directly interfered with Tobias or me, but you still helped; just like your brother Gabriel. If everything is awful and hopeless, why do that?"

"I am a healer." He stood, stepping over to admire the tranquil waters of the pond's edge at his feet. He swirled the bottom of his staff on the surface. "I was the original physician. During the War, you could say I was both a soldier and a field medic. I treated the wounds of my brothers and sisters on the battlefield. I held them in my arms as they died. When the War was over, I remained here. I was lost and in need of a new purpose. So, I found a different group to heal and care for."

"Humans." Kleos said.

"Yes. I have appeared to many throughout time. I once came on the waters in another Bethesda; a healing pool to treat the sick and the dying so that I could offer some to become whole again, while others—which few relay in this miracle—I released from this life to go to something greater. Many believe angels have control of their powers. We do not. The pool healed some and helped others to die. There is as much healing in death as there is in life. After that, I walked through the world, granting healing where I could and helped others move on to the next life."

"But I realized that what I did was in vain. I could not heal the wound in the universe. The damage was not physical. An angel could do no more than a human to treat the disease plaguing this existence, even with such miraculous power in my hands." He held one up, almost pleadingly. "Humanity followed in our footsteps; mighty, and yet destructive. They created more death. Humanity could never be truly healed. They—and you—will continue to cause suffering despite your good natures, just as we did. I could work miracles every day, before the eyes of every human on Earth, and your kind would never stop its wars."

"You ask why we no longer interfere in the affairs of humanity directly? Because it would be futile. It would change nothing. We would only cause more suffering. I learned this. Humanity one day will, too."

"We're fighting demons," Dani reminded him, "not other humans."

"You assume they are not connected."

"What is that supposed to mean?"

"Demonkind was born out of our war." Raphael said. "It was borne out of our ignorance. Asmodeus was created to embody what is broken with humanity and angelic alike. Lucifer created a mockery of what it means to coexist." His eyes fell on Dani, leaning his cheek against his staff. "Asmodeus's power is fed by the very nature of what humanity denies: its dark side. Asmodeus creates shades and turns humans against one another because he knows they can never accept their dark nature. Their pain, their anger, their lust, their—."

"Fear." Dani finished, echoing Mastema. "So, what, demons can't be stopped? They're just the crappy byproduct and we're fighting a losing war?"

Raphael said nothing.

"Then how do we stop them?"

The angel sighed heavily. He tipped his chin towards the house overlooking the pond. "I once appeared to a man of God; a soldier, like I. He chose to give up his life of war and turned to helping others. It is an order dedicated to taking care of those with disabilities. The Order runs the home you see there."

Dani was getting tired of the cryptic crap. "What is it?"

"A house for helping the mentally ill." He smiled softly. "There are many like it around the world. There is one here in Bethesda I come to often: Walter Reed. It is for veterans broken physically and mentally by war; like my kind millennia ago. I visit these places; these shelters run by the religious and non-religious, all caring for those turned away by society. The sick. The friendless. The needy. The reasons vary for why some embrace them in such radical ways of love, but in these places, true healing happens. They are true houses of mercy. True *beth hesda*."

He turned back to her. "Do you know the original word for the soul, Daniella?"

She shook her head.

"*Psyche*." Kleos said. "It's Greek."

"Like psyche, the mind?" Dani asked.

"Yes." Raphael bowed his head. "It is amazing that when humanity wishes to heal its soul, they do not seek to mend their minds; their way of thinking. A man or woman with a broken psyche is one with a damaged soul. And many in humanity seek to hurt one another's soul, just as the demons you fight. You wish to stop Asmodeus when he comes in three days' time? Part of it is healing your soul and the souls of others he wishes to corrupt."

"That doesn't make sense."

"It will when it matters. Asmodeus will not be stopped by might alone, nor by the artifacts you seek. They are tools and tools are only as good as the person who wields them. You and others must stand against the darkness with souls of light. Asmodeus was not stopped by me in ancient times, I remind you."

"Yeah, I know. He was stopped by Tobias."

"Tobias was a great man. The legends do not do him justice. He did not seek Sarah to stop Asmodeus, nor did he seek her for her physical beauty. He loved Sarah in both heart and soul. What attracted Asmodeus to her was the same that birthed such pure love in Tobias's heart. She was as fierce as she was strong. Many sought to marry her simply to tame her. Her father found suitors to control her. Their weakness allowed Asmodeus such control over them, which is why they perished. But it was Tobias and Sarah together that defeated Asmodeus. Did you know that he allowed himself to be controlled, so Sarah could stop the monster. It was Sarah who developed the plan in the first place."

"I didn't know that."

"Very few do. She had a will of iron. If you wish to defeat Asmodeus, your will must be equally strong."

Dani wanted to say she had it. She wanted to put on the bravado she had on Dagon's ranch. She wanted to say she would face Asmodeus and defeat him.

But she was silent. More than water tried to drown her in that river.

"He hurt you." Raphael said knowingly. "He wishes to taint your soul; your psyche. He wants to control your mind and make you doubt yourself. Do not let him. I can see your bright soul. He wishes to put out that light. When the time comes, you will know what to do and you will change the fates of more than yourself. Much rests on your shoulders, but it is yours alone that can bear it."

"As for the last artifact you will need," he held out his walking stick, "it is like this staff. It was once carried by a great man, given to him by me to part the waters and save his people. He returned it upon his death. I once also held a ring that was used by Tobias to stop Asmodeus. It bears the mark of my city; the mark of healing, wholeness and strength of will."

"The Pentalpha." Dani realized. "Haniel said a ring was the last artifact. You left that on your statue in Ber'iah?"

"Yes. It was ripped from the hand of my visage within the Fane."

"By Asmodeus?"

He shook his head. "No. The demon could not enter my city so long as the ring resided there. It was taken by another."

"Who?"

"My brother, Michael, once gave the ring to a very wise king. He was a great ruler. In his time, he was known as the wisest of all men. He sought to stop demonic kind from harming his people, but he turned the ring into a weapon; not of self-control and healing, but of power. He sought to use it to bind demons instead of destroying them and enslave everything he touched. He did not relinquish the ring until his death and because of his lust for power, he did not stay dead."

"You mean, he's a revenant?"

Raphael nodded. "He is a broken man. His psyche is fractured. He is not the man he was in life. He returned, and stole the ring. He removed its protection from the city. That was why Asmodeus could destroy Ber'iah."

"Where is he now? This man you're talking about?"

"He fled to a land called Serbia. It is there he attempts to forge a new empire using the Pentalpha."

"Can you take us there?"

"I can," he nodded, "but I cannot be the one to stop him. Only you can. The corrupt king has many under his sway and not just demons. He will not relinquish the ring to you. He did not before his death, and in his maddened state, he will not now."

"I'll stop him any way I can." She promised. "Who is he?"

"In life, his name was Solomon." Raphael told her. "King Solomon."

Chapter Thirty-Six

"King Solomon?" Kleos stepped forward. "The former king of Israel?" Raphael nodded. "The same."

"Dani," for the first time, Kleos looked terrified, "King Solomon was the ruler of Israel after David. He was his son."

Dani nodded. "Yeah. I may not be the biggest church girl, but I know that much. He was all smart and stuff."

"King Solomon wasn't just wise. He was one of the wisest men who ever lived."

"He usurped his throne from his legitimate brothers." Raphael told them.

"And while he was alive," Kleos continued, "he founded the most powerful system of magic ever created."

"Come again?" Dani asked.

"Goetia. The act of summoning demons, spirits, and angels. Solomon was the most powerful summoner who ever lived. There are dozens of occult sources and grimoires dedicated to him. There's a whole story centered around his power over the demonic."

"And he's the one who has the ring?" Dani couldn't believe it. "So, the most powerful—and pardon me I'm just assuming here—and most dangerous practitioner of magic ever to walk the face of the Earth just so happens to have the last artifact we need to stop Asmodeus?"

"Yes."

"Awesome." She turned to Raphael. "He's in Serbia, you say?"

"Yes."

"Can you narrow it down? I am not that familiar with foreign countries."

"I will send you to where I feel his presence most." Raphael said. "But I warn you: those who pursue you will follow closely. You will have only a day at most to find him."

"Yeah, well, if we take longer than that, we may not get back in time to stop Asmodeus from attacking Empyrean. I'm ready to go."

Kleos and Dani stood next to one another. Raphael bowed, fingertips to forehead. They returned the gesture.

"Go in peace." The archangel said. "May the light guide you and keep you."

Then he extended his hand. The wind blew harder. Leaves leapt off the ground, swirling around them. The angel disappeared behind a torrent of brown, crackling debris and a small funnel enveloped the pair in a powerful gust.

The wind died. The leaves fell. A new world appeared. They were on a hill of wild grass. The air was cooler; crisper. The sun had set and darkness enveloped them.

"Damnation." Dani cussed, pulling leaves from her hair, which became a rat's nest in the wind. "I look like Bride of Frankenstein."

"Never saw it." Kleos mused.

Dani undid her braids, smoothed her hair into a ponytail and checked the phone. "It says it's three p.m. Why is it dark?"

"Time zone difference. It must be closer to midnight here."

"I can't see anything."

Kleos pointed downhill. "I see lights. It looks like a town."

"That won't help us if we can't see how to get there." She drew her sword. Pouring her energy into the empyreal-steel blade, it glowed to lamp-like illumination. She held it aloft. "Well, that's better. Come on."

They trudged downhill in the dark and into the outskirts of the town. In the middle of the night, it was cold. Dani was thankful their Arachne-weave raiments protected them from the chill. They slipped up their hoods, hid behind the veil and walked down the street.

It was a small village by American standards; a lot of tiny houses that weren't so much 'run down' as 'old.' Narrow streets. Cobble stones. Since this town predated America by a good few centuries, their tile roofs, brick buildings and walkways all looked old-world, and yet electric lamps and modern neon signs dotted the roadway.

Dani slid her sword into its sheath. "Where do we start looking?"

Kleos chuckled. "Where everyone starts: a bar and a hotel."

They slipped out from behind the veil outside a hotel. Dani did better with Spanish while Kleos seemed adept with European languages. He read the sign easily and she followed him in to register for a room.

Once that was done and their packs were left in their two-bed hotel room, they headed back out and across the street to a local bar.

"Won't I stick out?" she asked. "I don't exactly look twenty-one."

"In some places, the drinking age is whatever looks old enough. Don't worry. Come on."

The bar they entered was similarly old-world. The wood had a sagging look that came with age. The floorboards creaked as they stepped through the door. Even though it was midnight, the bar was alive. Dozens of patrons from age-lined bar rats to the younger crowd squeezed into booths, tables or at the bar.

Dani and Kleos slid up onto barstools.

The barkeep, an old guy with a shaved head and a plaid, wool shirt, put two glasses in front of them.

"Here." Kleos pulled something out of his raiments—a knotted bracelet—and slid it onto her wrist.

"What's this?"

"Can I help you?" The barkeep asked. Though he spoke some language that sounded vaguely Russian, in Dani's mind it came out English.

Kleos grinned. "Language charm. You won't be able to speak it, but you'll understand it." He turned back to the man. "We're just passing through, but we're looking for someone."

"Is that so?"

"He might be local, he might not be, but we heard he lived around here."

"Who are you looking for?"

"He calls himself Solomon."

The faintest twitch pulled at the side of the man's face and his baby blues filled with the wide-eyed telltale of fear.

"Sorry." The barkeep lied. "I have never heard of him."

"Are you sure?"

"Are you going to order something or ask stupid questions?"

Kleos ordered a beer and Dani a soda with ice. He quickly placed them on the table. Using the veil, Kleos gave the bartender invisible money and he walked off.

Dani pointed at his pint. "That smells disgusting."

"It tastes amazing." Kleos sipped. "Did you see his expression when I asked about Solomon?"

"He did his best not to wet his pants. He's scared to death of him."

"Which means they know him around here."

She scanned the bar. "What can you tell me about him?"

"The occult sources say Solomon was a great man. He was wise and powerful. But his power over demons corrupted him."

"And apparently, he scares the pants off of our bartender."

"Do you think he's here in town?"

Dani scanned the room again. A smokey haze hung in the air; just enough to remind you that your lungs were important. As she looked around, she couldn't tell if anyone was a revenant. Other than his size, Goliath looked completely human. The bar patrons looked equally human.

But as the bartender came to the end of the bar, his head turned to one corner. He tipped his chin, and then subtly tipped his head back in Dani's direction. She followed his line of sight.

"Hey Kleos." She casually pointed towards the corner.

A man sat at a table, drinking a beer. The first thing Dani noticed was his fire-red hair. It was the kind of burnt-red that looked almost natural, but wasn't. He was tall, thin and wore some kind of uniform-tunic. Around his shoulders was a long white cape. The man saw the bartender's gesture and then saw them.

He left his beer and rose to his feet.

"Okay, here we go." Kleos said tightly. He took a swig of his drink and stood up, hand on his sword. Dani gripped Pointyend and followed suit, ready for a fight.

The man started across the bar. Dani and Kleos spread out, blocking his path. Some of the patrons noticed and moved away.

Dani drew her blade as he approached, stepping in his path. "Okay pignut, listen up. I've had a really long week, so let's all just calm down and—!"

The man wordlessly drew something from his waist. The cape hid it, but he tossed it at her; a sack of leather. The moment it hit Dani's chest, it exploded in a powerful, concussive blast that knocked her back through the window and out into the street.

Dani burst through the glass and skidded across the cobblestones. She felt like the Hulk put his fist through her chest. She landed, skipping like a stone and smacking into the opposite building.

She heard screams. The door to the bar blasted open and Kleos tumbled out, his sword falling from his hands. White Cape the Wonderful followed right after. He punched Kleos as he tried to stand, striking him across the jaw and sending him down again.

Dani slowly got to her feet. "Stop!"

The man turned in her direction. He tossed back his cape, revealing all manner of things on his belt; leather bags like the one he used before, a double-edged dagger, charms, ingredients and vials; all sorts of things she couldn't begin to guess. He held his hands up, fingers spread, and looked skyward.

Thunder rumbled. Overhead, black clouds swooped in as if summoned. Which, she didn't doubt, they were. They blocked out the once-starry, clear sky. Lightning danced between them.

"Not good."

With a crackle, lighting dropped. Dani cast out under Aer and darted away seconds before a lightning strike hit home, blowing a hole where she had just stood. When she landed, the man was walking away.

"Hey!" She shouted, running after him. "Stop you little freak!"

He saw her coming. A heavy rain started to fall, soaking the street. He turned, striding backwards. He wasn't angry or upset. He was calm. He removed a bottle from his waist and as casually as tossing the TV remote to someone, tossed it onto the ground between them. The bottle shattered.

Dani skidded to a stop. Something like dirt spilled from the inside of the bottle. The dirt, mixing with water, slowly oozed its way out and began to expand. It rose off the street, spreading and taking shape.

"Well...crap." She dropped into a combat stance.

What formed from the dirt looked something like a human boy, maybe all of ten years old or less. The dirt coalesced into a pale-skinned, dark-irised kid in filthy clothes and shoes.

Behind the boy, the red-haired man said something. It wasn't normal language. It sounded like a spell.

The boy, hands clenching to fists at his sides, started towards her.

"Whoa there, Damien." She raised her sword threateningly. "I've seen *The Omen*. You keep your creepy, child-demon self over there."

He ignored her and stalked forward. The boy bared his teeth, showing off a pair of fangs that slid out of his gums.

"Vampire? Are you serious? Vampires are a thing?"

The boy charged, hissing. He launched at Dani, jumping the short distance on top of her. As he came down, Dani stabbed up and buried her glowing blade through his stomach. She reflexively put an arm across his throat, keeping him back. He seized her in a two-handed choke, hissing, spitting and snapping his jaws. Despite the sword skewering him like kebab, he didn't die.

"Bad dog!"

She released her sword and grabbed at his face, using her thumb to gouge at his eye. At the same time, she kneed up and pushed him over, throwing the demonic child off her. As she rose, she grabbed her sword again and twisted, which should have shredded his heart. The boy put both feet into her chest and kicked. The blade yanked free and she hurtled backwards into the nearest wall.

Dani summoned her power, cushioning her fall and put her feet back to catch herself before smacking into the side of a house. She hovered back down to the ground as every babysitter's worst nightmare got to his feet.

"Alright." She swiped her sword, flicking blood off. "You're strong, I'll give you that."

Screaming, the kid ran at her again. She swung. Her sword cut clean through his swinging fist, severing it midway up his forearm. He swung with the other. She cut that off too.

"Ha! Try to grab me now!"

The creature staggered back. It looked down at its severed limbs, but then glowered up at her.

She held up her sword. "Back down or I'll go full Monty Python and chop off every limb you've got."

But to her horror, the ends of his arms began to flow with the same sludge that came out of the bottle. Two new hands formed.

"Oh come on! That's not fair!"

The boy kicked and struck her in the chest, once again flinging her back like a rag-doll. She'd gotten better at stopping that, summoning the Aer to halt her fall. She skidded back a few feet on her heels like she was doing reverse limbo and then shot back up to her feet.

"Fine." She seethed. "You can regrow limbs. How about a head?"

Screaming, the boy ran at her, hopefully for the final time. Dani tensed, judging the distance. She slipped one hand back to Pigsticker, waiting. Then, when he came in range, Dani dodged and buried her dagger into his gut. The kid-creature stuttered to a stop, growling but not dead.

Dani cut his head off.

That did the trick. The head hit the pavement with a wet thud and broke apart, dissolving back into sludge. Similarly, the body dissolved and flopped into a puddle of mud on the street.

Dani took a long breath, dropping her blades and put her hands on her knees. She hurt all over. Groaning, she looked up the street.

"And, of course, he's gone."

Whoever the redhead was, he wasn't there any longer. Kleos slowly got to his feet, staggering down towards Dani as she retrieved her weapons.

"Thanks for the assist." She grumbled, sheathing them.

"What happened?"

"Oh, nothing that won't haunt my nightmares for the next few weeks." The storm let up. "That guy, whoever he was, unleashed some kind of demon-child on me."

"Demon-child?"

She waved at her mouth. "It had fangs and hit like a gorilla; whole nine yards of pure evil. I had to cut its head off."

"Must have been a moroi."

"A what?"

"A Slavic vampire creature."

"You all really need to tell us newbies that things like vampires are real, you know." She paused. "They don't sparkle, do they?"

He shook his head. "I've never encountered one. They're not demons; just creatures. I've only heard about them in legends."

"Yeah, well, legend or not, I just had a Sunday Night Smackdown with one."

"We should get off the street." Kleos advised. People appeared out of their homes. A crowd was forming. "Whoever he was, people are afraid of him. And if he has a moroi on his leash, I don't want him finding us."

They disappeared behind the veil and got off the street.

Chapter Thirty-Seven

She knew she would have a dream. And when it came, she didn't understand it.

Dani stood on beach and looked out over the water as the sun was setting. In the distance, massive black thunderheads swirled and oozed their way across the sea as far as the horizon. The wind picked up. People abandoned their outings on the sand for their cars.

Dani shielded her eyes. Something was moving in the clouds. She couldn't see them clearly at first. The shapes were obscured as they darted in and out. But as the clouds got closer, and quickly, she could see them.

Shades.

Hundreds of them.

Thousands.

It was the storm from her vision. It had come.

As the storm clouds rolled overhead, she could see the storm was made of them. They moved like a frothing ocean in the sky. She watched as the storm wall stretched over Los Angeles.

Then something came walking out of the ocean. Even though it looked like a shade, it wasn't. For one, the human figure was at least seven or eight feet tall. And for another, it had horns. The inky shape dripped with ocean water as it strode onto land; a beast from the ocean.

Lightning and thunder clapped from overhead. Something else darted from the black clouds; not shades, but purple-clad Numen. Powers. They dropped in formation from cover, adamantine weapons spearing or slicing apart shadow-people in the sky.

One of them broke off and hurtled towards the ground.

Ethan, with Stormthrower in hand, dropped to the sand in front of the creature. He dropped the point of his Montante sword into the beach, holding it hilt up like a cross; a formal stance for a duel.

The creature continued up the beach towards him.

"You go no further." Ethan warned.

Something dark, like a laugh, rumbled from the beast of the sea "We will see."

Ethan kicked the blade, scattering sand and swinging Stormthrower up for his first strike.

Dani woke, staring at the ceiling fan spinning above her. Light spilled through the curtains of their room. Kleos was gone.

Swinging her feet down, she pulled on her boots and grabbed her swords. After the previous night, she wasn't going anywhere without them. Dani slipped on her shadelight pendant and went in search of her friend.

The hotel had two floors; B-and-B style. When she came downstairs, guests were eating breakfast in a small dining room, though more than a few looked in a rush. Kleos was among them, as was another woman across the table from him.

"Dani!" He waved her over. "I want you to meet someone."

The woman sitting next to him was elderly. She wore a simple dress, sipping her tea with an almost nonchalant attitude. Almost. Her age-lined and weathered face regarded Dani coolly over her cup. Her grey hair, pulled back into a neat bun, reminded Dani of Strega Nona; a kid's story her mom used to read to her about a witch who made food.

But what bothered Dani most was, as she approached, she felt something waver in the air around the woman; something unearthly and powerful.

"This is Adelina." He introduced, and then switched into the same language as the village. "Adelina, this is my companion: Dani."

"Good morning. How do you say, 'good morning' Kleos?"

"*Bună dimineața.*"

She repeated. "*Bună dimineața.*"

The lady replied in perfect, albeit accented, English. "I appreciate your attempt at my language, but you do not need to struggle. I can understand you." She finished her tea and set it down. "Though, I must say, I envy your ability to speak the language of birds. Even amongst my kind, such a gift is rare."

Dani's eyes flicked to Kleos. He held up his hands. "I didn't tell her."

"Then how does she know?"

"I know many things." Adelina said cryptically, with a soft but knowing smile.

"Who are you?"

Kleos answered. "Adelina is a strigoaică."

"A what?"

"A Romanian witch."

Dani tensed. She instinctively touched her swords; concealed from everyone else in the room by the veil. But when she did, Adelina's eyes followed. She could see them.

"I am not here to hurt you." Adelina assured her. "Please sit. You do not need to be afraid of me."

Dani sat, uncomfortably. "You're a Romanian witch? Like a gypsy?"

Kleos coughed. Adelina frowned.

"What did I say?"

"A gypsy is how you describe the <u>*Romani*</u> people." Kleos told her. "They're from India's northern region, not Romania. And that term is a racial slur."

"Oh." Dani burned with embarrassment. "I'm sorry. I didn't know."

"Most do not," Adelina told her, "but do not fear. When you live as long as I have, you tend to let people's mistakes be mistakes and not a reason to crucify them."

"How long have you lived?"

"Oh," she shrugged, smiling devilishly now, "a long time."

"Adelina saw what happened last night." Kleos explained to Dani. "She says she can help."

"Help how?"

"The man you faced last night is a solomonar; a summoner. He, like all his kind, is gifted in calling on the elements and the supernatural to do his bidding. They are a local legend; or rather, they used to be. Now they are a frightening reality for the people of this village."

"Adelina tells me the summoners were a secret society that existed here during the pagan ages." Kleos said. "Boys were chosen from the surrounding villages to join them; twelve at a time. They can harness the power of storms and learn magical secrets."

"That guy learned something alright." Dani took panacea when they got back to the hotel last night. Her ribs still ached.

"These boys would be taken," Adelina continued, "and trained under a master at a secret school."

"A school?"

"We call it Solomonanţă, or Scholomance. It is the school of the summoners."

"Where is it?"

"I know not. No one has ever seen it, except those who have been trained there."

"It is most likely a magically warded compound." Kleos suggested. "These people are basically a type of Gifted. There are Gifted enclaves all over the world. They use magic to keep themselves safe from demons and other creatures; sometimes, even humans."

Adelina nodded. "It is said to be in the mountains, next to a lake, but no such place has ever been found."

Dani smirked. "What? Is this place like Hogwarts?"

"That could be an inspiration," Kleos shook his head, "but this is a place of legend going back thousands of years."

"What do these summoners want?" Dani asked Adelina.

"Power." The witch told her. "My kind has always coexisted with them, as have many throughout Europe, but lately they have changed."

"Changed?"

"The summoners have become much more powerful. Creatures, such as the moroi you faced last night, as well as demons and even mortals, have come under their sway. Something is different now. They are more terrifying than they ever have been."

Dani remembered Pazuzu at Dagon's ranch. "A demon we met said that the alé, the storm demons, were being captured by summoners here."

"Yes. The alé have always existed in these parts, but now their powers are turned to much darker purposes."

Demons getting worse? How can demons get worse? "So, you don't know where they are?"

"No. But their leader is the man you sought out last night: Solomon. He is an evil man."

That was in line with what Raphael told them. "We knew him as a great man, once. In legends, I mean."

"Any man can change for the worse or better." Adelina finished her breakfast pastry. "I do not come to these villages anymore for fear of the solomonari. I will depart when we are finished."

"Is there anything you can tell us that would help?"

"Yes. They will return." The old lady rose. "The solomonari will not take an attack on one of their people lightly. They will retaliate. This is why the village is very much abandoned, if you have not already noticed. The people are frightened. They know they will come."

Dani glanced out the window. The street was deserted. It was around ten a.m. local time. The town should have been bustling.

"They will come with their magicks, their beasts and their demons. You should pray they kill you."

"Why?"

"Because capture would be a fate worse than death." She removed a rolled-up piece of paper, a papyrus scroll, and handed it to her. "This is a history of Scholomance. Read it."

"How does this help?"

"Just read. I wish you well."

The witch bade them good-bye and left. More than one of the patrons of the hotel checked out even before she made it to the door. Even the front desk clerk had a to-go bag as he helped customers vacate.

"Well this is nice." Dani said sarcastically. "I was hoping to have breakfast before taking on a group of sorcerers."

"So, do we run or do we stay?"

"Oh, we stay. No doubt about that. If we want to get to Solomon, they're the way." *Yeah*, she didn't say out loud, *like shocking yourself to find out if the light socket works.*

314

It took the guests all of ten minutes to finish breakfast and depart. Soon, the clerk was gone and the hotel—as well as the rest of the town—was either abandoned or shut up in their homes.

Kleos sipped his tea. He slid a plate with a single pastry over to her.

"What's this?" she asked.

"Baklava. It's good."

"Sweet." She picked it up and took a bite. "*Mmmm. They really need to learn to make this in Empyrean.*"

"Tea?"

"Please."

He filled a cup for her and added cream and sugar. Dani picked up a local newspaper and began skimming through. Might as well enjoy a nice meal. It wasn't like they had anything to do in the meantime but wait.

Finished with breakfast, Dani and Kleos exited the hotel onto the street bathed in the mid-morning sun. A small group already waited for them at the end of the road leading into the countryside.

"They don't waste time, do they?" Dani asked.

Five men, all with red hair and dressed in tunics, stood silently with their hands concealed by their white cloaks. Dani recognized the one from the night before in the middle. It was eerie how alike they were; not clones, but the red hair, pale skin and angry expressions made them eerily look like grown-up versions of the girls from The Shining—minus the braids and bows, but the same dead-eyed expression.

Dani read the history of Scholomance in the hotel. It didn't paint a pretty picture of what they faced. According to the legends, the summoners were trained by a pagan deity known as Zalmoxis. Whoever or whatever it was, Zalmoxis gave them strength and power.

Kleos glanced up and down the street. "Looks like they gave the townspeople time to flee."

"How nice of them." Dani drew her sword.

Kleos followed suit.

"Our beef isn't with you!" Dani called out to them. "It's with your master. Where is he?"

None of them spoke. *Of course not*, she grumbled to herself. *Why would they? It's much creepier to stand there silently.*

"Okay, look, you...solomon-whatevers...we don't want to have another go like last night. Now, you can be Solomon's flying-monkeys and try to capture us, or you can tell us where he is and avoid all of this."

Again, none of them spoke or moved.

"Okay, I'm out of ideas." Dani whispered to Kleos. "I can't goad them into talking. Maybe they didn't understand the flying-monkeys reference? Do they not get basic cable up here?"

"Doubtful. Besides, it looks like they're waiting for something."

"For Solomon? Maybe he had car trouble."

But as they spoke, a cold chill ran down Dani's spine. She shuddered, feeling something familiar behind her. Glancing over her shoulder, she discovered her instincts were spot on.

From the shadows of the buildings, gloom blended together into several dark shapes, which pulled their way free of the darkness. Shades stepped from concealment into the morning light; semi-transparent, faces pulled back into sneers as weapons of shadow formed in their hands.

"Well crap."

At the lead was Michael. He and about ten shadowmen blocked off the other end of the street.

"What are the chances?" The undead Empyrean Novice asked. "We feel your presence in this town and we arrive to find you waiting?"

"Please tell me you're not working with Solomon."

"Who?"

"Never mind." She glanced back at the summoners, who had yet to move. She asked Kleos, "So, what do you think they're going to do?"

"No idea," Kleos said, "but I'm not about to fight two armies at once. Maybe we should reconsider running."

"Not the worst idea."

One of the summoners pulled something from his belt. It was a string of bones on a cord, ending in a charm bag inscribed with markings. He touched his fingertips to it, mumbling a spell. The bag flashed, catching fire and he tossed it onto the road.

The air around them—above their heads, behind the summoners and all the way across the village to the other end of the road—shimmered faintly.

"Tell me that wasn't what I think it was." Dani said, pressing her back to Kleos'.

"I think he just cast a ward-spell over the entire town. We're trapped."

"Can he do that?"

"I've never seen anything like it. You'd have to have a lot of spirits chained to that charm to get that kind of juice."

"You mean like the father of all goetia could probably teach them to summon?"

"Good point."

They were trapped; summoners on one side, shades on the other, and now they couldn't fly.

Michael bared his teeth. "Well, I don't know who the boys in white are, but I thank them for keeping you here. It'll be easier to gut you now."

"Asmodeus needs me alive." Dani reminded him.

"He didn't say you needed to have all your limbs."

Dani balled energy into her hand. Kleos had his xiphos and a throwing knife in hand. They faced off against impossible odds.

"Kill Kleos, bring me the girl." Michael ordered.

The shades surged forward. Their shapes blurred as they shot through the air, skimming across the ground. At the same time, the summoners charged.

Dani spun, firing a blast of light over Kleos' shoulder. The blast struck the leader of the summoners and launched him backwards out of the town; however, when his body hit the invisible barrier it sparked to fire. Unlike the ward in Empyrean meant to only wound, this one shredded the man apart in a shower of embers that reduced him to nothing but a smoldering skeleton.

Don't pass the barrier. Got it, she thought.

Dani turned back and pulled her shadelight pendant from her tunic. She hadn't used it since Los Angeles. It worked like a charm then; no pun intended.

The moment the shades closed on her, the amethyst glowed and a bloom of violet energy burst forth. It struck the oncoming shadows. Some tried to brake in mid-air. Others ran headlong into it and turned to clouds of darkness. The wave of energy emanated out and seven of them disappeared.

One more use, Dani reminded herself.

"Dani! Watch out!"

Something struck her from behind and sent her sprawling. She landed hard, but had enough sense to put out her arms in an L break-fall. She landed and rolled, snatching back up her sword.

The summoner who tackled her drew a long, ceremonial knife from his waistband, raising it to strike as he leapt down on top of her. She swung her sword, but he caught it. She in turn caught his wrist.

He landed over her, baring his teeth. This close in the daylight, she could see a lot that she hadn't last night. Namely, what looked like a burn mark on the back of his hand; glowing as if rebranding on his skin from nothing but air.

A burn mark in the Pentalpha symbol.

Dani rolled, bringing him under her. His grip slipped and she sliced open his arm. He howled in pain, but fought. Dani was so shocked by the sight of actual blood—since her opponents usually weren't human—that his kick to her ribs stunned and knocked her back.

317

The summoner rose. Dani scrambled back, sword still in hand and leveraged herself into position to strike from the ground. Before she could, the summoner flew sideways as a dark shape tackled him. Together, he and the shade soared through the glass window of the hotel and disappeared.

Michael stalked towards her. Behind him, Kleos downed another summoner with the hilt of his throwing dagger sticking out of his chest. The remaining sorcerers summoned two moroi, who fought Kleos back down the street. The battle was very one sided and not in his favor.

Dani stood. "Back down, Michael."

"Or what?"

She removed the pendant again.

"Are you going to use your little trinket on me? You know it won't kill me. It didn't before."

"But it'll send you pretty far away and I'll settle for that."

"You wouldn't waste your hail-mary pass."

"First off, I don't play football. And if it hurls you across a few countries, I'll gladly do it. I know from watching your buddies that you may not die, but it hurts like hell."

Michael paused a few feet from her. His shadowsword wavered in his hands. He considered his options. They had a standoff.

It lasted all of ten seconds.

Something shook the air around them. A blast of sound louder than the trumpets of Empyrean shook the rocks beneath their feet. Both Dani and Michael gripped their ears, stumbling to their knees. It was like someone gave a dinosaur a megaphone the size of the Empire State Building. Dani prayed her eardrums didn't burst.

The sky blackened. Whatever it was shot overhead, blocked by the few clouds in the sky. It turned, dropping from cover and breaking through the barrier that surrounded the town. It landed behind the summoners and roared again.

Dani stared. She couldn't help it. The wide, leathery wings; the claws on the front and back legs; the wide snout with jaws rimmed by razor-sharp teeth; it even had horns.

She quickly learned that not only were vampires real, but so were dragons.

Chapter Thirty-Eight

A dragon.

An actual dragon.

An actual, full-on, for-real, M-Ffing dragon.

Dani couldn't even cuss in her head it was so surreal.

The dragon landed behind the downed summoner. It opened its jaws, roaring, staggering everyone. It wasn't as big as Dani expected one to be, but that didn't take away from the fact it was a dragon. Its wings were as long as a car in either direction and the creature stood about as tall as a horse. The tail, tipped with spikes, swung back and forth anxiously; about as long as one of its wings. It lowered itself to its stomach and she spotted two riders on its back.

The first dismounted. "My summoners! Hold!"

The man who dropped to the ground from the scaly steed was neither tall nor short. His skin was an even Middle Eastern shade of olive, with a thick beard and long black hair. Dressed like the solomonari, but much more extravagantly, he wore leather riding gloves he casually removed. His boots, his tunic, and his cloak were all of higher quality than his men and looked newer. His clothes weren't soiled by mud or grime. If his summoners appeared as servants, he was their master. Around his head, he sported some type of crown; not a Western one embedded with jewels, but a golden plate across his brow that tied on cords behind him. He grinned good-naturedly, as if everything was perfectly normal and everyone in the street wasn't trying to murder each other.

He strode over to the first solomonar, the one Kleos hit with the dagger. He tisked in the Romanian language. "Costicâ, what happened?"

"*Stăpân,*" the man groaned, the word translating as 'master' in Dani's head, "please... help me..."

"My boy," he said unsympathetically, "if you had not allowed yourself to be wounded, you would not need my help. Weakness cannot be helped except through learning from one's mistakes." The man stepped over the pitifully crying summoner and left him there to bleed.

He looked around. Pinned to a wall, the two summoned moroi held Kleos off his feet. Their summoners stood behind them, controlling the creatures. The remaining summoner staggered from the hotel, the shade who tackled him destroyed. Then there was Dani and Michael.

The man came to a stop in the middle of the street. Like a worry-stone, he rubbed something on his index finger and surveyed the damage. After a few seconds, he demanded of the summoner from the hotel, "Grigore, where is Mihail? Is he not with you?"

"He is dead, *stăpân.*"

The crowned master chewed the inside of his cheek in annoyance. "Hmmmm, pity." His eyes fell on Dani, then on her glowing sword. "Empyreal. Interesting. I have not seen a weapon forged of it in many millennia." Then his gaze traveled to Michael. "And a *rephaim!* Very interesting. Not since the days of my grandfather have I heard of one walking the Earth."

"You know about shades?" Dani asked.

He raised an eyebrow, chuckling. "English! What a wonderful language! It is so full of contradictions!" He spoke it fluently and giddily as a schoolboy. "My, my, well yes, my lady, I know quite a bit about resident souls of the underworld. Yes, I heard my grandfather, Saul, once asked the Witch of En Dor to bring back a shade. Not since then have I heard of a shade fully rising and in such," he seemed to admire Michael closer, "exquisite form. Exquisite is the term, correct? For such magnificence? I only learned English last week. It took much longer than the other languages. Five days, if you can believe it."

Is he bragging? Dani thought incredulously.

His eyes never left Michael. Michael growled at him. "Back away, sorcerer."

"And it speaks! Simply amazing!" The man gushed. "I must add you to my collection."

"Your collection?"

The man extended his hand and pressed his knuckles to Michael's arm. He screamed. Michael's shade blurred as he dropped to his knees. When the man withdrew his hand, the white-hot brand burned into his upper arm.

The Pentalpha.

Michael stood again. His shadowy form didn't heal the mark like the other wounds. He turned on the summoner. "You basta—!"

"Silence!" The man commanded.

Michael's mouth snapped closed, as if not under his own power. Fear crept into his dark eyes. He took a step forward, but the man held up a hand. He stiffened to a halt.

"Join my summoners and await my instructions."

Michael's eyes widened. He stayed in place, at least at first, but the Pentalpha mark hissed. He groaned in pain. Then, after only seconds, he staggered away as commanded.

The man admired the ring on his index finger, holding it up to the light. "How ever did I manage without such a gem?"

"Raphael's ring."

His head turned towards Dani and a gleeful smile spread across his lips again. "Why yes, it is. Given to me by the Archangel Michael. How did you know?"

Dani flicked her eyes to Kleos, who watched helplessly from where he was pinned.

"You attack my solomonari," the man said, turning on her, "and you wield such magnificent weapons. You must be very powerful. Who are you?"

"My name is Dani. That's Kleos." She eyed the ring cautiously, keeping out of his reach. "We're Numen from Empyrean."

His eyebrows shot up. "Numen? Earthborn, you mean?"

"Yes."

"Like the great Enoch?"

"Who?"

"The Metatron, as you call him; first of your kind." He clapped his hands happily. "He is my ancestor, you know; on my father's side. I've read all about him. I've even sought out his great book of spells, the—!" he paused. "I am sorry. You must excuse me. I have been remiss in introducing myself. All kings should. My name is—"

"Solomon. Former king of Israel. Father of goetia." Dani already knew.

Solomon looked very pleased. "Yes. I am glad my legend has spread far and wide. I once attracted the most powerful kings, the most beautiful queens, and the greatest advisors to my kingdom, but you would be surprised how few truly recognize my brilliance in these times. I am a master of the mystical and secret arts. I conquered death! I returned to the land of the living and still no one truly recognizes my lordship over the Earth." He waved dismissively to the wrecked village. "Save, of course, for these small yokel hovels."

"Lordship over the Earth?" Dani asked.

"Yes. Of course." He sighed. "Doesn't anyone understand? I was the king of the greatest kingdom on Earth. It is only fitting, now that I have returned, I should rule over the entirety of God's creation. Only I have the mind to govern the world. It is my right as the wisest man in existence."

Dear God, Dani thought, *he wants to take over the world?*

He turned away from her, calling out to the dragon, "Servant! Come forth! I have need of you!"

The second figure on the back of the dragon climbed down. They wore a long, white cape and hood over themselves, hiding them from sight. Stitched across the back, displayed in bright red, was the Pentalpha; a symbol Solomon took for himself, apparently.

They hurried to Solomon's side and knelt. "Yes, master?" They asked in English. It was a woman. The voice was soft, feminine and familiar.

"Attend to the wounded. Feed my dragon." He extended his ring hand to her. She took it and kissed it.

Then Dani saw her face. "Oh my God!"

For the first time, the girl looked up. Her mouth dropped open in shock, seeing Dani.

It was Roxelana.

Roxelana worked. The wounded man on the ground, Costicâ, moaned in agony as she applied an herbal salve to his chest wound. She fed Solomon's dragon, as well. She did everything she was asked. It was only when the summoners, using their captured creatures, rounded her and Kleos up that Dani saw why.

Burned into her cheek, just below her right eye, was the Pentalpha mark.

Solomon looked bored. He stroked his dragon's scaly chin while the summoners removed the skeletal remains of Mihail. His gruesome corpse made her shudder. Sure, he tried to kill her but these days, who hadn't? And he was human. Above everything else, that made his death more repugnant.

We're fighting demons, Dani told Raphael, *not other humans.*

You assume they are not connected.

The summoners seized Kleos and Dani's weapons without a fight. There wasn't much point resisting a fierce looking dragon and a man who could enslave them with a touch. Dani, however, didn't worry about them. She couldn't stop looking at her friend.

Roxelana was alive. Alive and, for the most part, unharmed. Until she could ensure she stayed that way, Dani wouldn't pick a fight.

Solomon wandered over, slapping his leather gloves in one hand into the other. "Are you well, Numen? You look pale."

She glowered a bit.

"Is something wrong?" He noticed Dani look over at Roxelana. "Do you know her? The vila?"

Dani caught Roxelana's eye. She worked, but she gave Dani a slight, imperceptible shake of her head.

"No." Dani told him, stammering for a lie. "I—I just didn't think you had so many working for you."

He nodded. "My domain is expanding every day. With every creature I take, I become more powerful. Creatures such as this one, for example."

Michael stood next to them at attention. The Pentalpha brand glowed on his skin. He tried to fight it, tried to move, but every time he did the brand grew hotter and brighter and he moaned in pain.

"What is your name, shade?" Solomon demanded.

"Michael."

"Who summoned you?"

Michael tried to resist, but the brand burned again. Raphael said the ring could control things, but Dani realized the control wasn't over the mind. These people—the summoners, Michael, Roxelana, anyone it touched—weren't turned into some kind of zombie-slaves. They were tortured by the ring, somehow, and Pavlov-ed into obedience.

"Asmodeus!" Michael groaned finally.

Solomon's eyes widened. "Truly? That beast has returned? Well, he will be dealt with in time. For now, you are mine, shade. Do you understand?"

Michael nodded.

"Good." He turned back to Dani and Kleos. "We will take you back to my school."

"Scholomance?"

"Yes. We have lost one of our number, so the other seven must be informed and we must begin looking for a replacement. It really is a pity. Mihail was the eldest of my solomonari. He was loved by many of his peers and I relied on him for my upcoming plans to subjugate the world, but," he shrugged, "such is life, as the French say."

"You don't feel bad that he's dead?"

"I did not kill him. He executed my orders faithfully."

"Like he had a choice!"

She instantly regretted that. Solomon frowned, toying with the ring on his finger. He stepped closer and Dani backed away.

"If you wish to say something, Numen, speak freely."

She didn't.

As if to defend himself, he said, "My subjects love me, as God's kingdom loved me during life. The mark of this ring only keeps their fealty." He said it like he didn't see the contradiction. "And I point out that they are destined to be my subjects. They are named after me: *solomon*ari. Summoners named for the greatest summoner of the ancient world. It is their destiny to serve me." Satisfied with his justification, he turned on his heel. "Now, we must away. Come. Be my guest."

Dani grumbled the *Beauty and the Beast* song under her breath. "Be our guests, be our guest, in our creepy cult of death." Slightly adapted, of course.

Roxelana waited, as did the other summoners. Solomon barked orders to his underlings. The summoners prepared to leave, the moroi returning to the vials from which they sprung. Solomon mounted his dragon.

"Will Costică live?" Solomon asked Roxelana in the Serbian language.

She answered fluently. "He is too injured to walk. I am afraid of moving him. If we could fly him back or give him—."

Solomon held up his hand for silence. His mark on her cheek didn't burn, but she stopped speaking anyway; whether because a verbal

323

command wasn't needed, or she was too afraid of his orders and their effect on the mark.

He leaned over and whispered to her. Roxelana nodded and whispered back. Then, Solomon straightened up. "Costicâ will be carried. If he cannot make the journey, spare him the pain of an agonizing death and kill him. I expect you back at the school by sundown regardless."

The Pentalpha marks glowed on his servants.

He turned to Roxelana. "I expect you to do all in your power to keep him alive. Your lives are linked. Should he perish, ensure you do as well."

Dani's eyes widened in horror. Roxelana bowed her head, nodding. She couldn't keep quiet and stepped forward. "Are you insane? You see him, the same as I do! He won't survive a journey anywhere and especially not if you expect everyone to get back by sundown!" The man groaned in pain behind her. "You basically sealed their deaths!"

Solomon shrugged, uncaring. "Death comes for us all. Only those, like I, wise enough to overcome it, will be spared. Costicâ made an unwise choice in battle. The outcome is his own."

"That's cruel." Kleos remarked.

"You are the one who wounded him."

"In my culture, there was a code of honor and compassion on the battlefield, especially for those who followed you. Have you no guilt for sending him into battle?"

"Guilt is altruism's stock in trade." Solomon said airily. It sounded like a quote. Dani had no idea what it meant and from the sound of it, neither did Solomon. "I have no altruistic delusions like the rest of humanity, so I am unburdened of guilt. I am more knowledgeable."

"Knowledge without wisdom is like water in sand." Kleos quoted back, though he sounded sure of its meaning.

"You call me unwise? The most knowledgeable man who ever lived?"

"I say there's a difference between knowledge and wisdom and you're lacking in one."

Solomon regarded Kleos with a frown and ordered to Michael, "Follow the instructions of my summoners. Do not allow either of these two to escape, even if it means your death. If they resist, kill them."

Michael's black sword grew from his hand, but his usual blood-lust to kill Dani wasn't there in his eyes.

"To the rest of you, return before nightfall! If you do not, kill yourselves immediately!"

With that, he urged his dragon and the creature flapped its wings, taking off into the clouds. Everyone else started on foot; Dani and Kleos prisoners once again.

The summoners led them out of town; one with a blade in hand, two carrying their wounded fellow between them and Roxelana helping, and Michael following with his sword. As they left the town, Dani spied more than one fearful face behind curtains or at the edges of windows. Frightened townspeople didn't dare come out until they were outside the limits. Dani didn't know what the mundani saw through the veil, but whatever it was, it scared them.

They trudged uphill into the boonies, but all Dani could think about was Roxelana. There she was, alive, and yet she didn't dare speak to her. She tended to the man, Costicâ, and said nothing.

They tramped through tall grass, up rolling hills and into the woods. Going was slow. Not only did they walk uphill but Costicâ cried or moaned with every wrong move as they bore him over the rough terrain. His chest-wound seeped blood through the bandage. Sweaty and pale, he didn't look good, but they continued. None of the summoners would allow him to slow them down.

Dani fell back with Kleos.

"Are you alright?" he asked quietly.

"Why do you ask?"

"Are you kidding? One of your best friends, who you've been looking for, is right there."

"She can't talk to us."

"I see that." He glanced around. "I have a feeling she doesn't want Solomon to know that you know her."

"Uh-huh. And I bet we can't let these summoners know, either. They might tell him."

"You could rescue her, you know." He pointed out. "Use your lightbringing. You could take these guys if you surprised them."

"I know, but I don't know what that ring will do to Roxelana. I won't risk it."

They walked in silence for a bit.

Dani sighed. "So, Solomon is a bit of...oh, what's the phrase... a cruel, narcissistic piece of pond scum."

Kleos tried to cheer her up. "Narcissistic? That's a big word for you."

"I have a word of the day calendar." Dani joked back.

"However, Raphael was correct: Solomon is corrupt. As I said, if someone comes back as a revenant, they come back broken."

"At least he can talk."

He shook his head. "Each revenant is different. Maybe whatever was their best quality in life, it's broken when they return. He was once the wisest of men. He settled disputes from nations to widows with a mind greater than any before him. But now, that man back there," he shook his head, "he's nothing but a shadow."

"He's still plenty intelligent and dangerous."

"Intelligent, yes. Wise, no."

She could hear something in his voice. "Care to share with the rest of the class?"

"There is a difference between intelligence and wisdom, Dani. I said as much to him. If someone were to, say, memorize an entire book, would that make them wise?"

"No. They'd be boring with WAY too much time on their hands."

"Exactly. Solomon can speak several languages, obviously knows magic and turned everyone around him into slaves. He's smart. He's intelligent. But he's not wise."

"'Knowledge without wisdom is like water in sand?'" She quoted.

"A truly wise man sees value in all things—in all life. Every life, every bit of creation, is precious. Solomon sees no value in life beyond his own."

"He's a jerk, you mean?"

Kleos smirked. "Sure."

"We knew there'd be something wrong with him. He wasn't perfect before his death, I'm sure."

"King Solomon was human, like everyone else. He made mistakes. It was because of him the kingdom of Israel eventually fell. He spent lavishly and worshipped many gods; some of whom were not actually gods."

"Demons, you mean?"

He nodded. "And his use of that ring is the reason he never departed this life. He clung to it and its power corrupted him."

"Well, we have to deal with him now and we need that ring. We've got two days left before Allhallowtide begins." She pulled him close. "Last night I had a dream."

"A dream?"

"I've had them off and on since this whole thing started. Usually, it's Asmodeus trying to mess with me, but last night, it was different."

"Different how?"

"I saw an army of shades make landfall in Los Angeles." She said. "They're like some kind of biblical storm. I saw Ethan. He and the Powers attempted to stop them." She shuddered, remembering the beast from the water. "And I think I saw Asmodeus. Ethan confronted him on the beach."

"What happened?"

"I don't know. I woke up. But if Asmodeus is on land, he'll attack Empyrean when the barrier weakens. We need that ring."

One of the summoners shoved them forward. "Keep going."

Kleos turned. "Your friend does not look well." He said in the Slavic language. "We should rest."

"We cannot rest. We must return by sundown."

"Why?"

"Master ordered us. We must walk."

"But why?"

"Because we must!" He raised his blade to Kleos' nose. "Now walk!"

"And if we don't make it in time?"

Dani watched the man's face. It twitched, only slightly, but the expression was unmistakable: pain. Whatever Solomon ordered them to do, they would do. They couldn't say no. And if they weren't mindless slaves, then he would kill someone he knew and be unable to stop himself.

Roxelana stepped between them, "We should rest." She said, making sure not to look at Dani and Kleos.

"We cannot."

"Costicâ is in pain." She told the summoner. "Moving hurts him. We can take a moment and I can give him something for the pain."

"If we do not make it—!"

"We will." She insisted. "But he needs rest."

The man frowned. He said something to his companions and they slowly lowered the man to the ground.

"If we must kill him, it is on you, vila." The summoner snarled and turned away.

"You should rest as well." Roxelana said, loudly enough that Dani expected it was for show. "I will check on you once my companion is secured."

They rested by a river. The sun was already beginning to dip. Roxelana applied more healing herbs and salve for pain, but the pain overpowered its effects. He was human. Dani and the other Earthborn healed quickly, and they had panacea to help. Unfortunately, Solomon took their packs and weapons. Watching this man—Gifted, but human—slowly die was unbearable.

Eventually, Roxelana wandered over. She extended something to the both of them. "Eat."

It was a loaf of bread, which Kleos cracked in half and gave partly to Dani. She took it and ate. While she did, Roxelana glanced over her shoulder. The summoners weren't paying attention to her.

She dropped quickly and wrapped Dani in a fierce hug.

"I'm so happy you're alive!" Dani choked back tears. "I was so worried."

"Me too." She stepped back from the hug. "I'm sorry. I didn't want Solomon to know that I knew you. You don't know what he's like. You don't know how it's been for the last few weeks—!"

"Roxelana, what happened? How did you get here?"

She sat, making sure to keep her voice down, but she couldn't keep it calm. "It started in Beri'ah after we arrived. Gifted, Numen; at first, it was a few incidents, but eventually, people were fighting everywhere. They began killing each other." She shook her head. "Akela...he tried to get us to leave, but..." she trailed off. "Is he alive?"

"I'm so sorry, Roxelana. No."

Her friend bit back tears. "He's dead?"

Dani only nodded. She wouldn't lie to her, but she wouldn't give any details about her husband's death. Some things she could still protect her friend from, at least for now. Roxelana let the tears flow and Dani let her grieve.

Eventually, Dani asked, "How did you meet Solomon?"

"Well," she sniffed hard, tears still streaming, "when the riots broke out, Akela disappeared. He told me he would be right back, but he never came. I was looking for him when," she scowled, "he appeared."

"Solomon?"

"I knew he wasn't Numen and I knew he wasn't Gifted. He wasn't even a man, really. He's—."

"A revenant. We know."

"You don't." she shook her head. "He's a monster, Dani. He has no soul; no compassion. He only cares about himself. How he got into Beri'ah, I don't know, but he took me with him when he left. He thought I was useful. I had skills, he said, that made me a good servant."

"He hasn't...you know...forced himself on you, has he?"

She shook her head. "He doesn't seem to care about that. He brought me here and he...he began gathering creatures."

"Creatures?"

"Demons. Monsters. Gifted. And then he heard the local legend of the solomonari. He sought them out." She glanced over her shoulder. "Solomon enslaved them. He turned them into his own personal army. Since then, he's sent them out all over the local countryside. He uses them for everything: extorting money, gathering more monsters, brow-beating local towns to give him what he wants. It's that ring. He took it from Beri'ah."

"We know." Dani told her. "Roxelana, that ring is why we're here."

"It is? I thought..." she trailed off, as if thinking better of what she was about to say.

Dani figured it out. "We didn't know where you were or if you were alive."

"Dani never stopped believing, though." Kleos added.

That made Roxelana smile. "What do you need the ring for?" Then she paused. "No, don't tell me. Dani, he can force me to tell him everything you say."

Dani understood. "You couldn't help us get to it?"

She shook her head. "You don't understand: Solomon compels all his followers using that thing. It's not just simple commands. He puts all of us through hell to break us." She shuddered. "The ring does things to you. It hurts you until you comply. The longer you resist, the worse it gets. It tortures you physically and mentally. Eventually, we fear what he might say so we do it before he asks." She began to cry again.

Dani took her hand. "We'll get you free. Is there anything you can tell us? What do you know?"

"Not much. Solomon keeps me in his quarters, in case he wants something; either to take messages to his servants, take care of his dragon or tend to his vessel."

"Vessel?" Kleos perked up. "A bronze vessel; looks like a gigantic egg or something similar? It rests on an altar?"

She nodded. "How do you know?"

"In the stories, Solomon trapped demons and monsters inside a vessel like that. I thought it was lost to history."

"He's reclaiming his history." Roxelana warned. "I'm terrified of him. He's not just dangerous. He's egotistical. He—."

A scream cut their conversation short. It came from Costicâ. Standing above him, one of the summoners drew his knife while the others held him down.

They were going to kill him.

Chapter Thirty-Nine

The three of them rushed over to them, but the main summoner commanded Michael to stop them. He jumped between them. Dani almost destroyed him with her light.

"What are you doing?" Dani demanded.

The summoner didn't understand until Kleos translated. Then he said, "We won't make it by nightfall. He is my friend. I won't let him die an agonizing death."

"But you'll kill him?" Roxelana demanded.

"We must. We cannot disobey."

In most stories, the brave soldier told his comrades to go on without him. In most stories, he accepted death. In reality, he cried long streams of tears and begged for his life.

"Please..." he pleaded. "Please...don't kill me...I don't want to die..."

The leader prepared to kill him. Dani made a decision. "Wait!" She jumped in front of them, kneeling over the fallen man with her hands up. "Wait! I can help him!"

Roxelana looked confused, but Kleos already knew what she would say. He knelt next to her. "Dani, don't."

"I can help him." She hissed. "Translate."

"Dani, if they discover what you can do—."

"Translate." She demanded.

Kleos did.

"No one can help him." The summoner with the knife shot back when Kleos told them what Dani said.

"I can. I have an ability."

"An ability?"

"Listen to her." Kleos urged. "Allow her to help and she can save your friend, if that is what you want."

"Unless that is not what your master wants." Dani pressed. "Unless he _wants_ you to kill him."

She and the lead summoner locked eyes. There was a knowing look there. Costicâ's death was exactly what Solomon wanted. For whatever reason—as punishment for his weakness or because Solomon was an awful person to the core—he wanted them to kill this man. And he wanted them to feel like it was their fault.

But the summoner said nothing. Yet, the solomonari all stepped back; a sign they were willing to let her try. Roxelana looked still confused.

Kleos whispered beside her. "You do this and they'll know. They'll tell Solomon."

Dani placed a hand on the man's bleeding side. "I'm not letting him die."

"He tried to kill you."

Costicâ stared up at her through teary eyes. "Please..."

To Kleos, she said, "It doesn't matter."

Dani closed her eyes. Summoning the power of Lucifer, she poured the energy down her arm and into her hand. It glowed to life. She pushed it into him.

The man groaned. His body arched up off the ground. Like a jolt of electricity, something came out of him and hit Dani. And like a switch, her vision blanked and filled with a place she'd never seen before.

There was a lake, surrounded by fog. Dani knew this fog wasn't normal. It was a magical barrier against intruders. She knew because she saw the memories of the man she healed.

And he was there; Costicâ, now a boy with red hair standing with his parents.

The three of them waited before the large double doors of a walled compound. The bricks radiated energy from within. Overhead, a dragon flapped its wings and soared in the distant sky. The parents and the boy did not cower in fear. Instead, they marveled at the creature. It wouldn't hurt them.

The boy was chosen.

The doors opened. A man stepped out; old, wizen. He wore the white garb of a summoner and bowed to them.

"By Zalmoxis, welcome Costicâ." He said. "We have waited for you."

Costicâ stepped forward, bowing. "Am I to be trained, stăpân?"

"Yes."

The image changed. Dani shuddered.

Costicâ was years older; his current age. He and the summoners knelt in a circle in a courtyard. Stone-barracks buildings surrounded them; one for sleeping quarters, another for a dining hall, and a multitude of different storerooms. Beautiful flowers and vines sprawled along the walls, filling air with sweet scents. A dock led out onto the water. A statue, some kind of shrine, took up the middle of the courtyard. The gaze of a worshipped entity watched over them.

Between them, a miniature stormcloud formed inches above the ground and crackled with lightning. The boys smiled.

Their Stăpân smiled as well. "Very well done, my pupils."

Then, from overhead, the dragon roared in warning. Everyone shot to their feet.

"Stăpân? What is it?" One asked. Dani recognized him as Mihail, the summoner she killed.

"I do not know." The master summoner said. They could hear the worry in his voice. No one should be able to find Scholomance.

The double-doors to their walled school shuddered. The summoners turned. Something large slammed against them, bending the brace that lay across it. The master stepped forward, placing himself between his pupils and whatever attempted to come inside.

The door lurched. The brace cracked. A third slam and the beam shattered completely. The double doors swung inward.

What stepped through was something that Dani could only describe as a vampiric lion-bat. Nearly six-feet tall, its wide, bat-like wings fanned as it stepped through and roared; bearing two, long fangs. The face was slightly human, but had a mane of dark hair, matted as if it hadn't ever bathed, that circled about its face.

Then, behind it, several boys followed. Dani recognized them as moroi. Vampires. But with them were other creatures; cynocephali-looking wolves, beings that appeared from balls of light, demonic imps and wraiths—

—then Roxelana. She cowered in fear.

Finally, with a flourish of self-importance, Solomon appeared. He wore an oddly modern look; jeans, T-shirt, sneakers. But he had his crown. And as if the world owed him a parade for just being there, he stepped before the assembled group of summoners.

"Who are you?" The master demanded.

"Your lord." Solomon spoke back flawlessly in their language.

Mihail stepped forward to one side. Costicâ stood on the other. "You are not welcome here." Costicâ told him.

"I am. This is my school. You are my servants." Solomon cradled one hand in the other, fingers toying with his ring. "You are the solomonari. I am Solomon. You are named for me and I have come for what is mine."

The master didn't move or back down. Above him, the dragon circled lower. Dani could feel the master's power call it.

"This is an ancient school, dedicated to none other than Zalmoxis." Solomon frowned. "Who?"

"The god of this region." The master gestured to the statue; the image of a man holding an axe. "It was he that founded this school."

"He is only another demon I will conquer." Solomon told him dismissively. "The real god of the world will prevail."

"The real god?"

"Me." He gestured to the demons at his back. "I am lord of this land, and eventually, I will be lord of this earth."

The master raised his hand. The dragon swooped down. Solomon saw and only shrugged, removing his ring.

"Ornias," he said to the lion-bat-demon, "take my ring and bring that dragon to me."

It bowed, growling. "At once, master."

The demon launched into the sky, ring in hand. It flapped upward as the dragon descended. The sky-serpent spouted fire, but the demon shot away from the blaze and attacked. The two collided in midair and fell out of sight.

The master summoned a ball of lightning-clouds to his hand. Solomon pointed at him. "Kill him."

Two moroi ran forward, hissing with fangs bared. The master extended his hand and the clouds flowed from his fingers, enveloping the two creatures. Lightning streaks stabbed into their bodies. They screamed and the two vampires disintegrated to ash.

The master summoned the power back to his hand. "You will not prevail here."

With a roar, the dragon appeared again. It landed behind the summoners atop the roof of a barracks. Its cry shook Dani's bones. The summoners stepped away from their master.

"As I said," the master told Solomon, "you will not prevail."

The demon, Ornias, landed next to Solomon. Black blood seeped from his lip. One wing looked nearly ripped off and burns caked his chest. But Solomon didn't seem to care as the creature handed the ring back to him.

"Our dragon," the master told him, "is more powerful than your monsters of darkness."

"Is that so?"

"Yes."

"No, you misunderstand." Solomon said. "I was asking if you were sure it is your dragon anymore." Solomon pointed. "Destroy the shrine to the false god!"

The dragon turned, breaking the barrack's roof under its clawed feet, and spouted fire. The summoners screamed as they hurled themselves away. The fire from its jaws slammed into the axe-god and obliterated it. The master toppled over as debris shattered across him.

When the smoke cleared, the master slowly rose to his feet. The creature that once protected them now glared in his direction.

Solomon held up his ring. "The power of a false god is no match for the power of the true god."

"What have you done?" The stăpân demanded.

"I revealed the true god to your creature." He said, his voice oozing with joy. "Destroy him!"

The master turned back to the dragon. Just below its jaw, burning hot like a brand, the Pentalpha mark seared to life. The dragon lowered its maw toward the master. Teeth parted. Fire swirled in its throat.

The master didn't cower. He stood, unable to stop the flames, and waited for them as they churned down over him. He closed his eyes and his body disappeared in the inferno.

With the master gone, Solomon strode over the scorched earth where he once stood. The army of vampire children and monsters followed behind him. The summoners backed away.

He raised his hand lazily. "Bring them to me."

His creatures rushed past him.

Dani withdrew her hand. Costicâ inhaled with a groan. His hand landed over the wet spot where his wound used to be, but was no longer. When he sat up, he stared at Dani.

"You—You—!"

"Thank me later." She grumbled.

She rose to her feet. The summoners gathered around their friend. Every eye was on her. And the expressions were not ones she was used to:

Grateful.

Relieved.

And hopeful.

The hopeful ones scared her.

———————————

The men tended to Costicâ; if anything, just to be sure what she did to him was real.

Dani's hand didn't hurt. Healing someone never hurt, unlike destroying them, which caused pain. She left them to be by herself.

What was that vision? It happened with Kleos back in L.A. She knew it was real, but not what it meant. Could she see people's pasts through her powers?

A hand grabbed her elbow. "What was that?"

Roxelana looked pale; confused. Dani staggered away. "I'm sorry I didn't tell you."

"Tell me?" She shook her head. "Dani, I've only heard one legend about a being that healed with light and that was—."

"Lucifer. I know."

"Are you saying you have Lucifer's power?"

"She is." Kleos confirmed. "And you cannot tell anyone."

"I can't promise that. You know I can't."

"But you can _not_ offer it." Dani told her. "Unless Solomon asks, you can omit it."

She didn't look as sure, but nodded. "I can try."

"What happened back there?" Kleos asked. "It was like you went into a trance."

"I saw something; a vision, I guess." Her eyes flicked up to him. "Kleos, in LA, when I touched Asmodeus's seal and then you grabbed my elbow, I saw a vision of you and Titus."

"You did?" The mention of Titus caused the smallest flicker of grief across his face, but he pushed it aside. "What did you see?"

"I saw...I don't know...you two sparring or playing or something. Does that make sense?"

It took a moment, but he nodded. "Possibly. It was something we did often in our time together."

"How it is possible to see into your past?"

"You have the Lightbringer's power. There is no telling what you can do." His flicked over to the men. "What about with the summoner? Did you see something with him?"

She nodded. "I saw Costicâ's memories. I saw Solomon kill his master. Kleos, the summoners...they're not evil. He used the Pentalpha to enslave them."

"How will knowing that help us?"

"I don't know," she stared at her hands, "but with everything going on, I don't think it's a coincidence that this power suddenly can do more than heal or destroy. My powers are growing. Do you know if Lucifer could see into people's minds?"

"No one knows much about Lucifer at all. Study of him in Empyrean is forbidden. But if you can see into someone's memories, then it is possible."

She knelt by a stream, running her hands through it to wash them. Roxelana went to check on the summoner. Dani stared at herself in the mirror surface of the stream; her skin double-tinted brown by the color of the water. Even in the muddy surface, she looked pale.

She nearly had a heart attack when the image changed and Bouden appeared.

Kleos flinched. "What the sarding—!"

Dani smacked a hand over his mouth. "Shh!" She glanced at the summoners, and then back at Bouden. She put a finger to her lips.

He stood at the water's edge in Empyrean, a stormy, wind-swept day appearing in the background. Bouden nodded in understanding and quietly held up his hand. He spoke across the palm and blew. The surface of the water rippled. A puff of air slipped off the water's edge and over Dani's ears; an aerwhisper.

"*Caesar back fine. Storm approaching. Empyrean preparing for battle.*"

Asmodeus had arrived, just like her dream suggested.

"I don't know aerwhispers." Dani said softly to Kleos. "Can you?"

"What do you want me to say?"

"Tell him where we are and what we're doing."

"Someone in Empyrean might discover our location."

"I'm not worried anymore. It's almost sundown. Allhallowtide is in a little over one day and that storm is in L.A."

He nodded, held up his hand and whispered. Dani felt Kleos' magic stir the air. The space over his palm shimmered. He blew it outward and the whisper hit the water, rippling the surface again.

Bouden nodded and gave a thumbs-up. He understood.

"We are leaving." The lead summoner approached.

Dani dashed her hand in the water, rippling the surface and eliminating Bouden's image. She slowly stood with Kleos' help.

"We must return to our school." The summoner said.

"We can make that trip easier." Dani told him. "We can fly you."

Kleos translated. The red-haired man shook his head. "So you can drop us out of the sky and kill us?"

"We wouldn't do that." Kleos said defensively. "Dani saved your friend's life. We obviously mean you no harm."

The man grimaced. "How can we trust you?"

"You can't, but I swear to you, we will not hurt you. I can only give you my word of honor."

The man hesitated, but finally nodded called to his friends.

They paired off. Kleos took the leader, one of his companions, and the third ordered Michael to fly him. Dani got Costicâ and Roxelana.

Costicâ looked different as she put her arm around him; happier, more alive than before. Dani looped her arm around his waist.

"Thank you." He said.

"You're welcome."

Kleos didn't translate, but he understood her just fine. Together, they took off into the sky.

They headed north into the mountains; the lead summoner giving directions to Kleos. Costicâ clung to her side fearfully as they followed

The sun was setting. As it dipped, so did they. Over the mountains now, they descended back to the ground and dropped through a fog-clouded tree-line, bristling past tree branches.

When they landed, the magic hit.

It was like a sudden panic. All Dani wanted to do was run. The magic twisted her stomach into anxious knots. She knew, if she wanted to feel good again, she should run. The magic ward nearly sent her and Kleos retreating into the wilds of Serbia.

Costicâ placed a hand on her shoulder and mumbled a spell. She staggered. The fog's ability lifted as quickly as it came like some physical weight. She gasped.

The mist rolled away, revealing the edge of a sloped clearing. It curled back until the walls of the compound from Costicâ's dreams appeared; the walls of Scholomance.

The school was breathtaking. Though not large, its ivy-covered stone structures echoed in that way only the oldest buildings could. History could be felt on them. Rooftops poked over the walls, with towers in the corners and grounds that once looked like they held gardens. The summoners started down the slope to the lake's edge, which peeked from beneath the magic fog. The tarn's deep, black waters lapped against the rocky shore of the school. The same heavy doors Costicâ walked through years ago greeted them.

And as they all approached, something lurked above; a creature Dani saw before.

The lion-demon crouched, gripping a stone figure above the archway of the door with one clawed hand while his wings cowled at his shoulders. He growled, dropping from his post in front of them.

"Is that—?" Kleos whispered.

"An archdemon. I saw him in my vision. His name is Ornias."

"The vampiric demon?"

"You know him?"

"He was the first demon Solomon enslaved in Israel."

Dani eyed it warily. A long tongue flapped his chops as he eyed her and Kleos, but the look wasn't one of hunger. It looked like disgust.

"Legend has it," Kleos continued, "he tortured young boys. Solomon enslaved him as punishment for attacking one of the young courtiers of his kingdom."

"Why does he attack young boys?"

"He prefers them."

She shuddered.

"Ornias." The lead summoner greeted.

The demon snorted, folding his arms. "Master said you would not make it before sundown, Dragan."

"We would never fail the master." Dragan bowed his head.

"I heard Mihail failed and paid with his life." He sneered. "What a pity. I guess we'll have to find some," he drooled a little, "new, young recruit."

Dani nearly threw up in her mouth.

"Are those the Numen?" He stepped past Dragan and the others. He reeked of brimstone, but what disgusted Dani most wasn't the matted fur, the sickly breath or the crude, disheveled tunic he wore; it was the small baby toys he wore around his waist. Dingy rattles, action figures, even a torn stuffed bear lined his hips; a gruesome collection.

"You like what you see, girl?"

She glared up at him. "Back off, Simba."

He chuckled, husking deep in his throat as he switched to English. "You must be that Daniella girl I heard about; sent Alecto down to the Furnace. You're the talk around the playground. A lot of demons want you dead."

"Tell them to get in line." She narrowed her eyes. "Are you one of the ones Alecto let out?"

"Me? No." He shook his great hairy head. "I've been on Earth a while. I tortured supple little village boys when Israel was the name of a man, not a country."

"And now you're some dead guy's lackey. You've moved up in the world."

His face dropped into a scowl. "I'd be careful, girl. The master wants you alive, but he didn't say how alive." His eyes shifted to Kleos. "Who are you?"

"Someone who hopefully gets to kill you."

Dani so badly wanted to give Kleos a fist bump for that one.

"Hope." The demon chuckled, waving his clawed hand to the school door. They unlocked and creaked open. "You should abandon all of that before you enter here."

Chapter Forty

Dani remembered Scholomance from her vision of Costicâ's; the ivy-covered walls, clean white stone, lush gardens, and birds chirping. What was inside the walls now wasn't the same. The ivy was dead; brown and brittle vines laced across the buildings and grimy stones. Dead leaves blew absently across the ground. Something like spiders moved among them and an unnatural moss that pulsated, as if breathing, clung to everything. The air had a wet, mildew smell.

In the center of the square, where the shrine once stood, was what looked like a large, bronze egg as large as a tub, supported between two standing holds. Dark energy radiated from within, like something supremely evil wanted to get out. As they neared, the air warmed sickly.

"Solomon's vessel?" Dani whispered to Kleos.

He nodded. "I hoped that thing would stay lost for all eternity. I don't want to know what he has trapped in there."

Other white-clad summoners looked up from their chores as they entered. Everyone avoided Ornias' gaze as he led Dani, Kleos and Roxelana across the square. She glanced back and caught eyes with Costicâ, who nodded appreciatively, but then he, too, quickly went to work, as if afraid to stand idle.

The archdemon led them to the newest building; one not from her vision. It looked less like living quarters and more like a temple; three stories and cleanly kept. Two summoners scrubbed the stones on hands and knees out front. Great, gilded stairs led up to a perfectly manicured porch decorated with hanging gardens and vine-covered columns of sweet-smelling flowers. Lanterns glowed brightly in the dim sunlight. Ornias led them through the open double-doors and they stepped into a lavishly furnished apartment of expensive oak furniture, a warm fire, and a table of food and drink.

Solomon lounged inside, casually draped across a plush chair while reading. Dani hadn't noticed how young he looked before, even with the beard. He looked like a child playing king.

He glanced up. "Ornias?"

"The Numen are here." Dani noticed the tremor in the demon's voice. He may have threatened her, but Solomon made him shake with fear. He was terrified of him.

"My summoners returned?" The king snapped the book shut and tossed it away as he stood.

"Yes, master." The demon bowed. "All of them."

"All? Really? Costicâ lives?"

"Yes, master."

"Interesting." His eyes shifted to them. "No doubt thanks to their prisoners. Very well: all is well when my subjects live. Have the men begin cleaning out my dragon's stable. Have a feast prepared, as well; for me and my guests. Remind the men that they do not eat until their chores are done. Then send a few into the mountains to capture more moroi. We lost some in our battle."

"Yes, master."

"Your men have just returned." Kleos pointed out. "They are exhausted and evening has fallen."

"They serve at my pleasure." Solomon retorted, as if that somehow argued against Kleos' point. To Ornias, he commanded, "Summon the shade as well."

"Yes, master." The demon left.

He turned his eyes on Roxelana. "You kept Costică alive as you were told. Well done. I am unsure how you could do such a thing."

Roxelana tensed, prepared for him to ask.

Instead, Solomon sighed. "For your service, you are rewarded: you will not have to do your usual duties tonight. I can draw my own bath and cut my own food."

Dani blinked. *As in, before that, Roxelana did all those things?*

He dismissed her. "Return to your quarters."

She bowed and left.

But then, he called out, "I did not hear a thank you."

Roxelana paused in his doorway, turned back, and bowed again. "Thank you, master."

"Very good." He commended her, and then cryptically added. "Remember what I told you before in the village."

Her eyes widened, but she nodded and left in a hurry.

Solomon grinned. "I love my subjects, as they love me."

Solomon waved his hand. The book he read leapt from the table, sailed through the air and inserted itself into a shelf above their heads. When Dani looked up, she realized why Solomon's home was so large. The apartment was nearly three stories tall and besides the main floor, every story was hollowed and rimmed with bookshelves. Stepping into the room, a railing ran the rim of the main floor revealing it was nothing more than a platform. Below them, tunneled into the ground, were three more stories with even more shelves. Solomon not only lived in the newest quarters of the school—

—he lived in a library.

"I call it my temple of information. Here, I worship the god of knowledge. Here, I commune with the spirit of intellect." Solomon sighed happily, pouring himself a cup of tea, as well as two others. He offered them to Kleos and Dani. "Please, come sit. We have much to discuss."

"Like what?"

"This is a war council. I need my counselors to counsel me." He retreated to the chair, gesturing to a couch. Dani and Kleos sat, not knowing what else to do.

"What do you mean 'counselors?'" Dani demanded.

"Is it not obvious?"

"Let's pretend it's not."

He smiled, sipping his tea. "You are here to advise me. I do not think it a coincidence that you appeared in my lands. It is fate. You have come because a true leader has emerged. What I am doing here—my work in this wilderness—is all for a great, single purpose."

He paused for dramatic effect. The effect was lost on them.

"To save the world." He clarified, a little dourly when they didn't guess. "Don't you see? The solomonari are the greatest summoners in existence. It is why they are named for me. Their ability to control the demonic, the natural, and dare I say even the angelic, make them the perfect lieutenants. They are just the beginning. With them at my side, we will forge a great force."

"A force to do what?"

"To save the world, as I said."

Neither Dani nor Kleos touched their tea. Whatever this guy was drinking, they didn't want any.

"You want to save the world," Dani asked, confused, "with an army of monsters?"

"Yes."

"How does that make sense? You can't save the world using evil things."

Solomon frowned and finished his drink. "There is no question that this world is evil. There is no question it is in peril. Demons, humans; everything seeks to destroy it. Even God."

"God's going to destroy the world?"

"Through His apathy, He already has." Solomon stood. "When I first returned to Earth, my eyes opened." He gestured to the books around him. "I consumed all the knowledge this world had to offer; this library, the internet, I read it all in a matter of days."

"You read the entire internet?" *Is that possible?*

"Yes. Do you know what I found? Climate change. Endless war. Inventions of death. Purposeful creation of the Third World. Corporate greed. Why has God not stopped it? Why has God allowed it to continue?"

Kleos and Dani didn't have an answer.

"Because He is apathetic. Either that, or He is impotent. God is evil. Even worse, he may be useless." Solomon paced away from them, frowning and shaking his head. "God is no longer relevant. This world falls apart and He just watches. Demons are only part of it. Something needs to change."

"And that is?" Dani asked.

"This world needs a new God." He told them proudly. "Me."

"You?"

"It's logical." He said. "If the world sits on the brink of destruction and no human or God has the audacity to save it, then someone else must. Since humans cannot be trusted with their own fate, only I am fit to rule."

"So what do you plan to do?"

"Spread my mark." Solomon told them, holding up his ring. "This power allows me to control others; bring them to heel. Don't you see? If the freedom of humanity brought the world to where it is, then humans can no longer hold that freedom."

"Slavery, you mean." Dani realized. "You want to make everyone slaves? Trust me, I've seen a god try that. I ended up killing him."

"Not slavery." Solomon told her. "Just an absence of free will."

As if those aren't the same thing, Dani didn't say.

"The problem with God was His plan." Solomon told them. "Or lack of plan. He gave humans free will to oppose Him. Looking at it now, I wonder if He truly was all that intelligent. Only a fool would give people freedom. Have you heard of the rock that God cannot move?"

She shook her head.

"It was a paradox conceived by great thinkers of old: can God make a rock so large he cannot move it? If He cannot, He cannot do something and thus is not God. If He can, then He created something He cannot control, which makes Him not God either."

"I assume you have a point?"

"Humans are that rock." Solomon told her. "Free will; God's greatest mistake. God created creatures with the ability to make their own choices and since then, they have decimated the world. I, on the other hand, will not make that mistake. I will guide humanity with a steady hand. I will never allow them to destroy my creation."

"What I started here is a model for my new world order." Solomon gleefully grinned. "Soon, others will come to know the joy of being in my service."

"Are you high?" She asked. "These people you enslaved aren't happy. They're terrified. You nearly sent them to their death."

"Is that so?" Solomon asked slyly. "And why do you think I did that? How did you save Costică, hmm? You had no elixir and I sense the energy within you that you had upon our meeting has been weakened. And that foolish vila girl couldn't possibly have kept him alive. So, how did you do it? How did you pass my test?"

Dani's jaw clenched. "It was a test? You used one of your people's lives to test us?"

"Not 'us.' Just you. Clearly, your companion," he glanced at Kleos, "is older, but he looks to you to lead. So, yes, I tested you. A wise man uses all means at his disposal to get what he wants."

She jumped to her feet with her hands clenched at her sides. "You're not the new God, Solomon. You're the new Devil."

His smirk turned into a chuckle. "Is that so? And tell me: what do you know of the Devil?"

"What do you mean?"

The fallen king's smile didn't waver. "There are some secrets even the wisest men don't know. You think the Archangel Lucifer is the greatest of monsters? The father of evil? Do you know what it means to be a 'lightbringer,' Daniella del Lucio? Light represents knowledge."

"What does that mean?"

"It means you know nothing of the angels—of Michael, of Gabriel, or of Lucifer. You have been fed lies. You know nothing of the power of the Lightbringer."

Her hands balled into fists. He wanted to know the power of a lightbringer? She'd show him.

Before she could, Michael's shade swept into the room and put himself between Dani and Solomon. He materialized facing her; not angry, but something much worse. Fearful. A being created out of pure anger, but Solomon scared him.

He turned to Solomon. "I have come as you demanded."

"Excellent." Solomon clapped his hands. "I do enjoy studying such creatures. You are exquisite."

"...thank you?" Michael sounded sick.

"I must say: Asmodeus has gained such power since he was in my service. He could never have created a shade like you."

"The fact you used to work with that thing," Dani spat, "speaks a lot about you."

"It does." He acknowledged. "Someone as wise as I would be the only one to ask: why kill the Devil's minions when you can use them? Don't you understand my brilliance yet?"

"Oh shut up!"

Surprisingly, this came from Kleos, who until now had done nothing to anger the fallen king. But he very quickly dropped that.

"You're insane. You're nothing but a shadow of your former self."

"I conquered death."

"Really? How long ago did you return? A few months?"

A flicker of recognition passed across Solomon's face. "Yes. Why?"

"You came back around the same time as the archdemons; Asmodeus, Belial. You think that is a coincidence?"

"I do not understand what you mean."

Neither did Dani. "Kleos?"

"What brought you to Beri'ah? Because when you took that ring," he pointed at Solomon's hand, "from Raphael's statue, you allowed Asmodeus into the city. It's because of you that all the people who lived there died."

Solomon scoffed. "So what? I simply exercised my free will. So what if it harms others?"

"Have you ever considered that something else wanted you to take that ring so it could then enter the city?"

"You imply Asmodeus manipulated me?" Solomon asked incredulously. "Me, the smartest man alive?"

"I'm not implying it. I'm saying it. Asmodeus played you for a fool, because you are one."

"Be quiet." Solomon snapped threateningly. "That foul beast could never outwit me. I will bring him to heel, as I will all Creation!"

But Dani caught on. "And you've been hiding out here since then; keeping one of the things that can stop him safely away from us. Come on, even you can't be that stupid."

"I said be quiet! Shut them up, shade!"

Michael groaned and rushed forward, tackling her over the couch. As they did, light burst from Dani's hand and obliterated Michael. She landed and rolled to her feet.

When she came up, two alé flanked Solomon. Dani prepared to kill them, but Kleos warned her, "Dani! Stop!"

"Why?"

He pointed over her shoulder. When Dani turned, Roxelana stood in the doorway with a knife held to her own throat.

"You think I didn't know?" Solomon demanded haughtily. "You think I didn't see that you knew her? I put her life at risk, as well as my fool of servant Costicâ, to see what you would do to save the life of an innocent. And I gave her instructions should you attack me." He held up a hand threateningly. "Now, I will make her slit her own throat if you do not concede defeat."

Dani uncurled her fingers and extinguished them.

"My God." He marveled. The alé grabbed Kleos. Solomon walked around the overturned couch. "I knew it. I knew something was different about you. I sensed power, but I never imagined that you had the Light!" Solomon brushed his fingers against his lips in wonder. "You have the Power of the First Dawn! You have the power of Lucifer himself! You're a lightbringer!" Solomon clapped his hands happily. "Oh my! This is a sign!

344

An omen! My destiny as God of this world is ordained! His greatest power has come to me! Seize her!"

He waved his hand. Dani felt the Pentalpha ring send out a wave of energy and the air behind her coalesced. With a scream, Michael reformed, throwing his arms around her. Several moroi exploded through the front doors and surrounded them. Ornias swooped down from somewhere above. Even the summoners arrived, all painfully drawn by the Pentalpha.

"My time has come!" Solomon crowed, throwing a fist in the air. "I will be the Lord God!"

Her room was a prison; a lavish prison, but a prison. And her jailer was Roxelana.

Like Solomon's room, Dani's was extravagantly furnished with couches and chairs and a bed that felt like a pillow of clouds. According to Solomon, these quarters were constructed for his eventual wives and concubines when he conquered the world. He had plans to resurrect his dynasty. Dani didn't want to think about the poor women he would enslave here.

Ornias brought plates of fresh vegetables and fruit, which she ate guiltily. She doubted the summoners had such good food.

Solomon himself didn't see her to her new living quarters. He instead excused himself because he "had work to do." Dani painfully watched her friend watch over her, ready to kill herself if she resisted.

Roxelana lanced thin, stygian chains across her hands. Costicâ waited with her as extra security; ensuring Dani couldn't free her friend and stop them at the same time. Solomon may have been 'unwise' as Kleos said, but his lack of compassion didn't stop him from thinking everything through.

The stygian chains were as thick as a necklace and laced through her fingers, stealing her power away like the cuffs Dagon used. Roxelana's fingers blackened; frostbitten by the hellish metal. She wept in pain as she put them on.

"I'll get you out of this." She told her.

Roxelana said nothing. She wasn't commanded to be silent. Instead, it was shame that kept her quiet. She was complicit in Solomon's scheme to out Dani. Forced or not, she was humiliated.

Ornias sneered, "Those chains will keep the power of Lucifer at bay."

"Until?"

"Until my master decides how best to use you."

"I guess he uses everyone." She shot back. "Even you."

"Tell me, how does it feel to be an undead sard-nugget's lackey?"

Ornias didn't answer, but the mark glowed in the center of his forehead. He groaned. "He is a wise and just lord."

Any command Solomon gave to his branded-slaves made the mark burn. She smirked. "Really? He told you to talk him up if anyone insults him? How fragile *is* his ego?"

"Dani, don't." Roxelana pleaded.

"Listen to her, Numen." Ornias warned. "You'll feel my master's wrath soon enough. He has plans for you and when they're done, you're free game. You may not be my...predilection, but I'll enjoy your blood just the same. And when you're no longer useful, that is exactly what I will ask for. Your blood," he stroked Roxelana's hair, "or hers."

The demon left, slamming the door. Roxelana, finished with binding Dani's hand, moaned in pain. Costicâ applied panacea.

"*Da li boli?*" He asked her. Dani didn't have her translation charm anymore. She didn't understand, but Roxelana nodded. Apparently, he asked *Are you hurt?* Or something to that effect.

They spoke as Costicâ healed her hands. It broke Dani's heart to see her friend like this. She lost so much: her husband, her freedom. She needed to help her, but didn't know how.

Costicâ went to get something from a bag; another healing ointment. Dani, her hands aching from the stygian, knelt down next to her friend. "Are you okay?"

Tears streamed down her face. "I'm so sorry."

"This isn't your fault."

"It is." Roxelana told her. "You don't understand: I'm from here."

"Here? As in, Serbia?"

She nodded. "Vilas are native to this land. I grew up in a village not far from here. I'm the one who told Solomon where the school was and because of that, I helped enslave these people."

"He made you. That doesn't make it your fault."

"If I had died at Beri'ah—." She sobbed, choking on her words.

"Don't." Dani warned. She couldn't touch her, but she wouldn't let Roxelana blame herself. "We will get out of this."

"How do you know?"

"Because I didn't come all this way, and find you, only to lose you."

"It's my fault you're held here." Roxelana told her seriously, stifling the tears. "And tomorrow, if Allhallowtide occurs and this Asmodeus comes to our city, everyone we know will die."

"We'll stop him."

"You will." She insisted. "Me? I'm a failure."

Dani tried to think of what to say. "You know, I used to think the same way, but Mastema told me that only light can cast out darkness." She sat beside her on the floor. "He said it because he thought I was the only one that could stop Asmodeus and Belial and all these things like Solomon that stood in my way. But you know what? I found out that's not true. Kleos has helped me. My friends have helped me. If it wasn't for them, I wouldn't be here. I wouldn't have gotten this far. You aren't a failure. You survived. And I believe, just like everything else, that it's not a coincidence."

"You're trapped." Roxelana pointed out. "And Solomon wants your power. Right now, he's trying to work out a way to get it."

She said, "And I'll stop him," then insisted, "we'll stop him. Together. He thinks you're a slave? Well, Asmodeus thinks the same thing about me and I've hurt him already. I think these guys have to stop underestimating us."

Roxelana smiled sadly, but hopeful. It was the first time Dani saw something other than despair in her eyes; something close to the old her.

The mark on her cheek burned. She winced. "He's calling for me. I have to go. He told me I couldn't tell you what he wanted, but Dani," she touched her arm, "be careful."

"I will."

Roxelana got up and left. A few minutes later, the door opened and two demons hurled Kleos bodily into the room.

"Are you okay?" she asked.

He grunted as he got up, "I'm fine."

"What did they do to you?" She asked fearfully. "Did they—?"

"No. Solomon didn't brand me. He says I'm not important enough for that." Kleos straightened himself up. "Are you okay?"

"I'm fine. At least," she shrugged, "for now. I'm worried about Roxelana. I'm worried about you."

He chuckled good-naturedly. "You, always caring about others."

"I'm a saint. What can I say?" She shook her head. "We need to find a way out of here and get that ring."

"I'm not sure how. Solomon is a lot stronger and more cunning than I thought. He's already out there now, setting up for something. He's got monsters and demons and we don't have anything."

"After demons, shades and a psychopathic god, I think we've proven we're up to it."

Kleos smiled. "Always the optimist."

"Do you know what Solomon plans to do? You were with him when they brought me here. What's going on?"

Kleos shook his head. "He's gathering his people—well, monsters and people. As far as planning, I could only catch part of it. My Serbian isn't great. I think he wants to find a way to take your power."

"My power? You mean my lightbringing? Can he do that?"

"I don't know. Do you know a way he could?"

"As far as I know, no. I don't."

"Are you certain?" he pressed.

"Yeah. Trust me on that. I tried to find a way when I was in Empyrean. I never found anything about lightbringing, much less how to get rid of it. If I could, I would have a long time ago."

Kleos frowned. "Well, that's good. He won't try to hurt you."

"Hurt me _much_, you mean. I don't think Solomon is thinking clearly."

"He does appear to be a few cards short of a full hand." Kleos grinned jokingly.

"He's a turd I'd like to royally flush." She folded her arms. Her hands ached and keeping them close to her kept them warmer. "We still need to find a way out."

"I have no idea on that front." Then he glanced sidelong at Costicâ. "Do you think he does?"

"He's marked, remember. He wouldn't be able to help us, even given the chance."

"You saved his life. Even with the mark, he might try to help us. Maybe Solomon didn't think of every way to prevent us."

Dani doubted it. She looked over the summoner as he packed up his kit of elixirs and medical equipment. His hands were shaking as he put up his tools.

And it was then that Dani noticed something.

"Kleos..."

"Hm?"

"Look at his hand."

Kleos did. "I don't see anything."

Dani strode over to him and grabbed his right wrist. The summoner groaned in pain as the stygian sent icy spines through his skin. Dani let go, but yanked back his sleeve.

"Oh my God! Look!"

"What is it?" Kleos asked.

Dani stared up into his eyes. Every summoner had the Pentalpha brand on one of their hands or wrists. She checked both of his.

Costicâ didn't have the brand on either.

"The Pentalpha mark is gone!" She said. "He doesn't have it anymore!"

Chapter Forty-One

"*Ne! Ne!*" Costicâ cried in his native language, shoving his sleeve back down.

"He doesn't have the mark?" Kleos asked in disbelief. "As in, it's gone? How?"

Dani stared at her own hands. "When I healed him...Kleos, my lightbringing must have somehow removed it. My power is the power of Lucifer, right? Maybe one archangel's power can undo another's?"

"You can heal the mark! Bloody Nora, Dani! You can help them!"

"And he can help us. Costicâ, you don't have the mark." Kleos excitedly translated. "You can help us stop Solomon. He doesn't know you can disobey him!"

He shook his head. "*Ne!*" She could easily tell what that meant. *No.*

He spoke quickly, and Kleos translated. "He says he discovered the mark was gone when he got back. He didn't tell anyone because he feared what would happen."

"To him?"

"To his family." Kleos continued to translate. "He means the summoners. They're like his brother. It's why he hasn't left. If he stays, no one will know, but if he leaves, they may hunt him down or worse..." he trailed off as Costicâ finished, "...Solomon may harm them."

"Then he has to help us stop him and get that ring."

Costicâ already shook his head and babbled.

"He says he won't. He's terrified Solomon will find out."

"How?"

"He says Solomon is dangerously intelligent. He's a monster. He manipulates everyone around him until they beg for death from Zalmoxis."

"Zalmoxis?" Dani recognized the name, but from where?

Costicâ explained through Kleos. "It's the god that founded this school. According to the legends, he was a powerful summoner; so powerful than he eventually became a god. Those summoners who die, they say, become one with Zalmoxis."

"Is that true?"

He shrugged.

"You can trust us." Dani told Costicâ.

"*Ne!*" Costicâ told her. "*Ne mogu!*"

"He insists he can't."

The summoner was unwilling, but Dani wouldn't let this go. Her lightbringing could heal the mark. They already had one freed of Solomon's control; one Solomon didn't know anything about. They couldn't just leave;

not with the summoners and Roxelana still under Solomon's sway. They needed to do something. They needed to surprise him.

"What is Solomon planning?" Dani asked him, allowing Kleos to do the interpreting.

"He plans to force you to give up your power." Kleos explained as the summoner spoke. "He plans to test you again; get you to perform your power to better understand it."

"Great." Dani grumbled. "Just like Dagon."

"What do you want to do?" Kleos asked.

She sighed, but thought. Then, with a grim expression, she said, "Well, we have to go along with it; at least until we get the upper hand. Can you ask him this: if we get the chance to overpower Solomon, will he help us bring him down?"

Kleos did as she asked, but Costicâ still didn't agree.

"Remind him that I saved his life and I am the best chance of saving his friends."

Again, Kleos translated her words. With a coerced nod, Costicâ agreed.

"So, what's next?" Kleos asked.

"Next?" She asked. "'Next' is getting through whatever tests Solomon has planned."

They took Kleos out first and after a minute, Dani as well.

The courtyard outside was lit by torchlight. Every summoner held one, while more lamps and braziers burned in the darkness. The orange glow shimmered off Solomon's bronze container, which remained in the place of honor where the old god's statue once stood. Dani could feel its dark energy against her skin.

Solomon waited at the bottom of the stairs to his 'temple of knowledge.' Costicâ brought Dani to a halt, left her wrists unbound but kept the stygian chains across her palms. Then he took Kleos with him and joined the summoners at their master's back. She tried not to look at him. If he was going to help her, they had to be quiet about it.

She and Kleos exchanged furtive glances. From somewhere in the darkness of the stables beyond Solomon's temple, his dragon growled.

"I once settled a dispute between two women." Solomon told her. He had changed clothes into newer, finer, more kingly garb. He still wore the ring. "They both claimed a child for their own. The two women, it seemed, lived in the same house. One mother claimed the child was hers and that the other woman's child had died. She claimed the child was stolen from her and replaced with the dead baby. The other claimed the first woman was lying. There was no evidence to determine who the child belonged to and the keepers of the law, some of the most intelligent men in my kingdom, could not figure it out. I, of course, deciphered the truth easily. Do you know how?"

"No. Enlighten me."

He grinned. "I knew the woman who truly loved the child, the real mother, would not want him harmed, so I offered to cut the child in half with a sword. I told the women that they each could keep a half. Of course, one agreed, but the other wished to keep the child whole and give it up; preferring the baby live instead of being put to the sword. The story is quite famous. Have you not heard it?"

From within the stables, the dragon growled. Its snout poked out. Solomon strolled over, petting it affectionately.

"It was a marvel of genius," he bragged, "and since then it has taught me that humans—and Numen by extension—will do anything to protect those they love."

"It's what makes us human."

"It's what makes you weak. I didn't understand it then, but I do now. It is what will allow me to triumph." He seemed to straighten up taller; like trying to make himself look more kingly. "I will give you a choice: you can choose to give up your power, or you can watch the ones you love die."

With a wave of his hand, the bronze vessel creaked. Dani watched as layers of bronze slid around under their own magic and a hole appeared at the top. From within, dozens of expelling trails shot outward and fell around them, materializing into monsters and demons; moroi, the wisps of light, cynocephali, and demons of all manner. It was a small army; not as much as Dagon's, but more than she and Kleos could handle alone, even if they were armed.

"Servant! Come here!"

Roxelana walked into the open, standing between Dani and Solomon. "Face her." He ordered.

Roxelana did. She was shaking with fear. Tears streamed down her face.

"Tell the truth," Solomon commanded Roxelana, "do you wish to die?"

"N—No." She stuttered.

"If you give me your power, she will live." Solomon promised Dani. "I give you my word. You resist, she will die a very painful death."

"You're a monster." Dani spat.

"My absence of compassion is why I am fit to rule. Compassion leads to ruin. Now, choose."

"I don't know how to give you my power."

Dani noticed Costică move. He stepped right behind Solomon. He still held his summoner's dagger. She pleaded silently with him to do something.

351

"Very well." Solomon sighed, waving his hand. "Servant, will you please cut your arm?"

Roxelana's mark hissed painfully and she drew a knife out of her belt. She sliced open her arm, screaming. Dani ran towards her, but she held it up threateningly, keeping her back.

The monsters all moved closer, too.

"These creatures will consume her in seconds if I allow them. Do not touch her. Give me your powers."

"I told you I don't know how!"

"Do it!"

Again, she looked pleadingly at Costicâ. Kleos was with him. Together, the two of them could overpower Solomon. This time, she said out loud, "Please!"

Solomon thought it was directed at him. "Do not beg. I am above that. Last chance!"

"Please!" She begged again.

Costicâ flinched.

Solomon raised his hand. "She will die, Numen."

"I can't give it to you!"

Costicâ moved. He drew the dagger from his belt. He was behind Solomon, so he couldn't see him. Dani's heart leapt as he prepared to shove it through the revenant's back.

But then two things happened at once. Solomon turned and saw the blade. But he wasn't scared.

Instead, he said, "Stop him."

None of the summoners were close enough, but to Dani's horror, someone was. Kleos—who stood just behind Costicâ—removed a black, stygian dagger from concealment. He seized Costicâ by the shoulder and drove the point right through the summoner's spine.

It was so quick that it was over before the summoner hit the ground. The others cried out in alarm and grief. Costicâ barely had time to know what happened before he died.

Kleos moaned in pain. Even from where Dani stood, she could hear the soft hissing noise of a Pentalpha mark burning under his clothing; concealed from Dani's sight.

Solomon glanced down dispassionately at the dead summoner and then up at Kleos. "Thank you, servant."

Kleos dropped to his knees and wept.

"You continue to doubt my intellect." Solomon told Dani, turning back around. "I see much farther ahead than you."

Dani's hands painfully curled into fists at her sides. "You monster!"

"I knew that if you did have a way to give up your powers, you would never tell me. So, I had Kleos ask for me. He told me, like a good servant, before you came out here that you didn't know. But, just in case, I wanted to see if you held back from even him. Thus," he gestured to Roxelana, "this test. Clearly, you don't know how to give up your abilities. And, oh," he smirked, pursing his lips behind a single, mirthful finger, "he told me all about your plot with Costicâ. Hopefully, you now understand what you're up against."

She did. She understood that this man was more of a demon than the demons around him.

"So, now that we have that out of the way, Roxelana: you may put away your blade and rejoin me. A good servant would be such a waste to kill."

She put down her sleeve, still dripping blood, and returned to Solomon's side.

The leader of the summoners sighed, "We must come at this from a new direction. Kleos, it's time you served a purpose. Join here in the open like I told you."

Kleos stood, the stygian dagger frosted with red ice that he wiped off. He picked up a second blade, Pigsticker, and carried them both into the ring. He stagger-stepped, like he was fighting the mark, but it burned so much it spurred him on.

He tossed Dani the dagger, his watery eyes full of fear and pain. She caught it in its sheath.

"No." She shook her head. "I'm not fighting him."

"In your fight, maybe you will find a way give up your power."

"Consarn it, I told you I don't know how!"

"It is said that in the most desperate times, humans find strength they didn't know they had. Kleos, draw your weapon." He did. "Find the strength to give it up, Daniella."

"I won't fight him."

Solomon sighed and said to Kleos, "Do all in your power to force her to kill you; fight, but do not kill her. If it means throwing yourself on her dagger, do it. Just...make it hurt her, too. Do you understand?"

"Dani, please," Kleos pleaded, "I'm so sorry. I wanted to tell you what he was making me do, but I couldn't!"

"Kleos, it's okay." She told him, her own tears forming. "I won't kill you. Do you hear me, Solomon? I won't kill him! I'll disarm him first."

"You'll try. Kleos: attack!"

Dani drew Pigsticker and flipped it to hold the sheath as a guard across her forearm. Kleos swung for her mid-section, too quick to really block. But even as he swung, he groaned in pain and nearly toppled over. He fought the Pentalpha. It made him weak. Dani swung instinctively and cut open his upper arm, the glowing blade powerful enough to sear through his Archane-weave tunic.

He rolled to the ground, convulsing.

"Stop it!" Dani screamed.

Solomon shrugged. "He disobeyed. I didn't think he had the strength. When those under my ring's sway disobey direct orders, the pain is excruciating. The only thing to alieve it is to obey. Kleos! Attack!"

The hissing stopped and Kleos flipped onto his belly, leaping up and kicking into her mid-section. A blast of Aer exploded off his heel, launching her backwards across the stones. She skidded to a stop, groaning in pain.

He attacked again. Dani rolled up and sliced. Kleos deftly leapt over, cutting across her shoulder with the stygian blade. She screamed as cold stung through her body.

"Yes!" Solomon cheered. "Again! Keeping cutting her if she will not give me her power!"

Kleos straightened, begging, "Dani! Stop me! Kill me if you have to!"

"No!"

Kleos flipped the long dagger into underhand grip, something you did only if you were coming near. Dani kept hers hilt-forward and her right arm with the sheath up to block. They circled one another.

"Please!" He begged. "Please!"

"I won't kill you Kleos!"

"I can't keep fighting it!"

He swung, slicing backhand. Dani blocked with the sheath. He feinted back. The greatest warrior in Empyrean was pale, sweating, and in agony. Dani kept her blade ready.

"That's it! Keep going!" Solomon urged. "This can be over, girl, if you just give me Lucifer's light!" He gripped his ring-hand into a fist.

Kleos moaned and swung, full power, with the large blade. Dani blocked with the sheath, but the force of the blow knocked it out of her hand. She swung with her own, backing him up.

She stared at Kleos past her fingers, laced with the stygian.

He charged.

She got an idea.

Stupidly, her free hand shot out.

Kleos' stygian blade sliced along her palm. Dani screamed as the icy bite—like painful knives—shot down her wrist. She fell back, kicking at the side of his leg and connecting with his knee. The sacrifice move worked. He was too close to block. She heard a pop and both of them went down; her hand bleeding, his knee shot sideways out of place.

"Fight!" Solomon screamed at him manically.

Kleos rose; tortured into submission. He snatched up his dagger, ignoring the now out-of-place knee. But before he could hobble up, Dani rose as well and connected her heel with his temple. Once. Twice. He went down and didn't move.

She shot back to her feet, bleeding down one arm, and glared at Solomon.

Now, she was armed.

Solomon's frenzied, gleeful smile faded. His plan failed. He glanced down at Dani's blade, which he gave her, and though still surrounded with hostages and an army, he looked slightly worried.

"Very well. That didn't work. Apparently, knowing you were never in danger of dying isn't motivation enough. Ornias!"

From the bronze vessel, fire and black smoke swirled out and formed into the demon. He landed between her and her master.

"Kill her for me." Solomon commanded.

Dani stood her ground; unmoving. She squeezed her dagger comfortingly. "If he kills me, you won't get my powers."

"True, but you'll still be dead. It's self-preservation. You'll find a way to give up your power somehow. Ornias, kill her!"

The archdemon nodded and stalked towards her, wings out and claws extended.

Dani backpedaled. The demon half-floated/half-walked through the air, closing the distance between them. He bared his fangs. From his claws, putrid fluid leaked across the taloned ends.

"My touch tortures, girl." He growled. "It's so much fun to torment little kiddies, but you? I'll make you beg for death."

He swung. Dani ducked back and he missed. He swung again. The third swing and she sliced with her blade, the glowing edge carving off the clawed hand. Ornias howled in agony and withdrew the bloody stump, grabbing it just below the wrist.

Dani shoved the blade up into his chest.

The lion-creature's face dropped into a stare of disbelief. He looked into Dani's eyes as she twisted the molten empyreal steel through his black heart.

"No." She told him, her face inches from his. "No begging from me. And no more children for you." She grabbed his belt and ripped the baby trophies free.

The glowing steel melted out the back of his chest. Burnt, fiery charcoal dropped away. Dani yanked the blade away and Ornias began to dissolve.

Embers exploded from his mouth. Wide-eyed, staggering he managed to sputter, "Thank you. Anything is better than this; even Hell."

Dani kicked, shattering him in a smoldering shower that fell back to Solomon's feet and sent him back to the depths of the underworld he longed for so much.

Everyone went silent. Solomon's frown deepened.

Dani couldn't help but smile. "Next?"

Chapter Forty-Two

She had no idea what she was doing, but it was pissing Solomon off. That was something, at least.

With his demon-lackey deader than doornails, he barked out, "Shade!"

Inky blackness poured out of the receptacle, billowing up and forming into Michael; his midnight longsword already in hand.

"You can't kill that which is already dead." Solomon told her. "Same plan, different animal. Let us see how you fare against an immortal beast. Shade, kill this little witch!" He seemed more vengeful now that Dani appeared to be ruining his plans.

Michael turned on Dani.

She only had her knife. Michael had a sword. Dani glanced at the unmoving form of Kleos and backed off, leading him away. Michael followed.

"I'm going to enjoy this." He threatened.

"Being some kind of slave, you mean?" she taunted. "First Asmodeus, now Solomon; when are you ever going to have your own life?"

"I don't have a life, remember? You took it from me."

"Really?" she shook her head. "What made you like this, Michael? Nobody wakes up one morning hating someone. What did I do to you?"

"You embarrassed me," he seethed, "just like all the others."

"All the other what? Numen? Novices?" That didn't make sense. "Girls?"

His face twitched.

"Girls? What, some girl teased you or something? That's pathetic."

"You'd never understand!"

He swung. Dani rolled back out of reach of his blade. Michael summoned what appeared to be a black ball of shadow in one hand and hurled it. The blast struck Dani in the chest, knocking the wind out of her and sending her sprawling.

"I've learned a thing or two." He growled.

Dani sucked wind, trying to stand. Michael stalked towards her

Scrambling under her clothes, Dani yanked her necklace free; her mother's necklace containing the shadelight pendant. As Michael approached, she held it up.

Purple light exploded outward and struck Michael, scattering him like smoke in the wind. The final burst of power from Kleos' gift dissipated the shade and allowed her to sit up.

She sighed in relief.

But with a scream echoing off the hills, Michael reformed only a few feet away.

Solomon chuckled. "Yes. After your last attempted destruction of him, I took precautions. From what you friend Kleos told me, your amulet has no more power."

It was true. The shadelight pendant's amethyst changed from purple to clear crystal. It was over.

Dani tried to stand. Fully reformed, Michael shot towards her. Instead of a sword, he wrapped his grip around her throat, lifting her up and smacking her blade out of her hand. One hand on her neck, the other holding her by the front of her raiments, her feet dangled helplessly off the ground.

"You think you can kill me?" He demanded. "You think you can just turn me aside? Never speak to me? You think you can act like every other girl who ignored me?"

Dani choked. "Please...!"

"Shut up! SHUT UP!" His grip tightened. "Always saying stuff! Always putting me down! I'm not listening anymore!"

Her vision swam. Black leaked around the edges.

"I won't let you hurt me anymore!"

Dani grabbed his wrist with her bleeding hand. Kleos' blade sliced through the stygian chains around them. They fell away. Warmth returned to her palm. Dani clasped his wrist and light poured from her fingers.

Like Kleos, like Costicâ; she poured not anger and hatred, but something pure from within her into Michael. She could destroy him with lightbringing, but what would that do? The only thing she could think of was Nazir. Pain didn't stop him; only love did. Dani called on it.

And a vision hit her.

"You fat, little pig!" An older woman stood over a little boy, maybe eight. He was chunky. The woman held a spoon threateningly down at him. "Sneaking cookie dough? No wonder you're a fat, disgusting swine! You think any girl wants a fat man, Michael? You think any girl is ever gonna look at you!"

"Momma, please—!"

"Nothing but a hog! That's you!" She hit him with the spoon. Hard. "Be a man!"

The world swam. A new image appeared.

Michael was older; high school. She knew, because he did. It was a year before the eclipse; a year before he became a Numen. His mother was dead, having gone to the grave hating him because he reminded her of his father.

He held a rose out to a girl, no older than him; friendly face, nice eyes. Her light brown cheeks flushed happily, accepting it.

Some snickering from a group of boys and girls nearby turned their attention.

One of them, a girl with a mean face, sneered. "Looks like Abigail is a chubby chaser!"

The girl frowned. She stepped back from Michael and dropped the rose on the ground.

His mom's voice echoed in his mind. "You think any girl is ever gonna look at you?!"

Dani's eyes rolled back as a third image hit her.

She saw herself. She stood across the open training grounds, surrounded by Novices.

Nazir whispered into his year. "You have this. She is only one girl."

Michael stared at Dani, but in his mind it wasn't Dani. It was Esmerelda; the girl who never spoke to him again; the girl he still held that rose for.

"Nah." He shook his head.

"You gonna punk out?" Andreas asked behind him. "She's supposed to get treated just like us. So treat her like it."

But that wasn't treating her like them. They didn't want him to fight her. They wanted him to beat her. They knew he outweighed her.

"Are you gonna be soft or are you gonna be a man?"

His anger flared and he stepped into the ring.

Michael stumbled back and Dani dropped to the ground, choking. The shade looked horrified, staring at his hands. She summoned her power to her hand, ready to destroy him, but then she saw the tears. He cried and collapsed to his knees.

"Michael?" She croaked.

"I'm sorry!" He sobbed, his shadow-form shaking. "I'm so sorry Daniella..."

She stood warily, staying out of reach. He looked up from his hands, inky black lines of shadow-tears running down his cheeks.

"It was me." He moaned. "It was all me. All I did to you...everything that happened..."

"I saw." She understood; not excusing him, but she understood. "I saw your memories."

"It was all my fault." His head tilted back, as if praying. "Every time they said be a man—every time they teased me—I shouldn't have listened."

She said nothing. She knew so many like him: little boys, even when they were older; not men, but trying to be men. And the only way they could be was to attack someone they thought was weak. How many women suffered because of them?

But the thing looking back at her now wasn't a shade and wasn't the boy who tried to hurt her. It was the man Michael was supposed to be.

Acceptance, for lack of a better term, changed him.

"I'm so sorry." He told her.

She couldn't believe she was saying it, but Dani said, "It's...It's alright."

No matter why someone did what they did, it never excused their actions. It never made it okay. But seeing what Michael had become—some dark creature born out of pure anger—it didn't matter anymore. She wanted it to end. She couldn't keep holding onto the anger. All her anger, all the vengeance she wanted; she let it go. For him. For herself. She let it all go.

"Kleos forgave Nazir." She said. "I can forgive you."

"I don't deserve it."

"You might not, but I give it anyway."

A sad smile broke across his lips. In his eyes, there was something there Dani had never seen: humanity. Shade or not, he was more human now than before. A piece of who he was—before his mother, before everything he turned himself into to "be a man"—was there.

"I want you to be at peace." She echoed Kleos' words.

Michael shuddered. "My anger kept me here," he spoke sadly, "but your anger drew me to you. I followed it. I fed on it. It was part of the reason I couldn't move on, but now..." He shuddered once more. "Thank you. You freed me."

Michael began to dissolve into mist.

As he did, he warned, "He's coming for you. Asmodeus won't stop, but you can stop him. Only you." He turned and looked at Solomon. "You can stop all of them."

Michael's shade dissolved. In a wisp of wind, he broke apart and dissipated into nothing.

Dani retrieved her dagger, glaring at Solomon.

"What do you think you're going to do?" He demanded.

Her grip tightened. "Kill you. Again."

"With your knife?"

"With this."

She raised her hand. Light poured down her arm into her hand, igniting it.

"Stop." He ordered. "I forbid it."

She didn't care. She put every bit of anger behind the blast.

"Lower your hand."

Ready to strike, she was about to. Then, to her surprise—and horror—she did. Something inside her burned. Her hand dropped.

Then she saw it: on the back of her palm, in the bend of her thumb, the Pentalpha mark burned brightly.

Chapter Forty-Three

The ring lay where Michael vanished. Under Solomon's orders, he branded her, like Ornias branded the dragon.

The king of summoners extended his hand. "Bring it to me, servant."

Dani tried to stop, but her whole body burned. She wanted to pick it up and bring it to him. She _needed_ to pick it up! Retrieving it from the stones, she stutter-stepped towards him.

"Very good." He sneered condescendingly as she placed the ring in his hand and he slipped it onto his finger. "I knew that if I could not persuade you to give up your power, I would need to take it by force."

Dani hovered one hand over the other, summoning her light to obliterate the mark, but Solomon *tisked*. "No, no. No freeing yourself with lightbringing. Ever. I can't have the crowned jewel of my army disobeying me."

The light faded under the ring's command. Dani groaned in pain, unable to bring it forth again. It hurt all through her body. How did Kleos fight this?

"I won't serve you." She snarled.

"Quiet. Speak only when spoken to."

The muscles in Dani's jaws tensed and her mouth snapped shut. Instead, she moved to draw her blade, but Solomon stepped past her, touching her wrist.

"Never raise your blade to me."

Dani lowered her arm.

Solomon looked pleased as he strutted into the square, every creature and demons transfixed on him; either out of fear or command to do so. He raised his arms.

"My subjects, the time has come! The world must know the true God has returned! It is time to rid the world of freedom, so that true peace can be achieved!" He turned towards Dani. "The traitorous Costicâ is dead. My new weapon is now bent to my will. And in order for us to begin our work, the last vestiges of resistance must be stamped out!"

He turned on Kleos. "Rise!"

With a groan, Kleos came to; crawling up to a kneeling position. He raised his head and saw Dani—saw her powerless—and knew.

"Roxelana! Come and kneel!"

Roxelana peeled from the crowd and knelt next to Kleos.

Then Solomon extended his hand to Dani. "Lightbringer, come here."

More smoky/fiery trails burst from the bronze vessel, filling the square with even more demons and creatures; more of an audience to witness

Solomon's commands. They landed all around Dani as she was forced into the square with her friends.

"Her sword!" Solomon called.

A summoner stepped forward and offered Dani her blade, Pointyend.

"Take it!" Solomon commanded.

Dani grabbed the grip and drew her blade.

"You have questioned my authority!" Solomon commanded. "Of all the creatures I have bound with this mark," he gestured to the multitudes, "and those around you I imprisoned within my vessel and tied to its magic; only you have caused such regret. As a show of my dominance, I now command you: kill these two."

He pointed at Kleos and Roxelana kneeling side-by-side.

The suddenness of the command made her groan in pain. Her sword flinched, but she willed it to stay at her side. The pain made her collapse to the her knees.

"Do not fight my commands!" Solomon seethed. "I have had enough of that from you! Kill them now!"

Dani screamed; loud and long into the sky. The pain doubled her over, but she didn't kill her friends.

Solomon frowned. Those around him shifted uncomfortably, watching her fight. Her blood felt like it was boiling in her veins. Her skin reddened. She moaned in agony.

"Stop!" Solomon commanded, though probably trying to tell her not to fight, but she felt the pain subside as she took it to mean 'stop from killing her friends.'

"That is not what I meant!" Solomon roared. "I will not have anyone question me. You will kill these two. You will do as I demand so I may save this world!"

Dani wasn't having it. "For a savior, you sound a lot more like a conqueror."

Solomon fixed her with his steely gaze. "Wise men realize the only saviors are conquerors."

"Wise men realize those who say stuff like that aren't wise."

It was a pretty good quip, considering the pain returned as he clenched his fist around the ring. "Be silent!"

Dani felt her jaw tighten and lock again.

"Stand, take your sword, and kill these two!"

Screaming through clenched teeth, she leapt to her feet, sword raised, but she froze it in midair. Dani sweated through her raiments.

Then, unable to stop herself, she swung.

Her blade sliced over Kleos' head into the stones beside him.

"Did you not hear what I said?" Solomon demanded. "Do it now!"

"Dani shook her head furiously.

Roxelana was crying; thankful for Dani, but afraid. She knew she couldn't hold out forever.

"Very well." Solomon growled. "You won't kill them with a sword, then I have a better idea." He snarled in her ear. "Use your lightbringing."

Dani's eyes widened. Her swords dropped from her hands and clattered onto the stones. Solomon took the wrist of her freed hand and raised it, pointing her palm towards Roxelana.

"Use your lightbringing on her." He let her go. "Do it, or I will make it worse."

Tears stung in Dani's eyes. Tears flowed down Roxelana's cheeks. They stared at each other.

"Do it. If it'll make you feel better, you can say good-bye." Though it was more taunting than helpful.

"I—I'm so sorry!" Dani sobbed.

Roxelana swallowed down her fear, and nodded. "It's okay."

"Kill her!" Solomon commanded again.

Dani groaned in pain, gritting her teeth. And then, in the midst of the pain, something came to mind. Her lightbringing swelled down her arm and into her hand.

She moaned to Solomon, "You want me to use my lightbringing?"

"Yes!"

"You want me to use my lightbringing on her?"

"Yes! Do it!"

She had to obey the command, but once he gave it, her gritted teeth turned into a clenched smile.

Light erupted from her hand and hit Roxelana. The beam was bright. In enveloped her. Roxelana screamed.

Images rushed through Dani's mind; like Roxelana's life going in reverse.

Lying on the beach of Akela, feeling the love and warmth of safety.

Meeting Dani for the first time in Empyrean.

Shea, their friend, taking Roxelana from a vila village destroyed by demons; how she came to live in Empyrean.

Dani screamed and unleashed all of it, on both her and Kleos. But instead of the destructive light, she unleashed her love for her friends. And even though she couldn't see them, she knew what was happening:

The Pentalpha marks erased from their skin.

Dani closed her fist and the light haloed around them. Everyone shielded their eyes. Then, screaming, the pair darted from the halo and tackled Solomon.

Too shocked to speak, they landed on him. Kleos' hand flew over his mouth, stopping his next words.

Roxelana picked up Dani's sword and buried it through his stomach.

With a scream, the creatures all around them surged forward; probably commanded to protect Solomon at all costs. Dani snatched up her dagger, fueling it with her power, and cut the other stygian chain from her palm. Solomon told her she couldn't free herself using lightbringing. He said nothing about her blades.

She lashed the chains, dropped her sword and cast out her hands. Light exploded out in both directions. Dani spun, lancing it around. Moroi, demons and other creatures vanished in flashes of burning light. Those behind them still alive came to a halt.

Dani turned on the bronze container in the center square. *All those around you I imprisoned within my vessel and tied to its magic*, Solomon said. She threw out both hands and hit it with everything she had. Dani's lightbringing struck it like twin beams of pure sunfire.

The thing exploded in a blast of light.

The blast knocked everyone over, but as the magic basin exploded into nothing but emberish bronze flakes, a wave of energy erupted outwards. Dani felt the release of magic and the release of the creatures controlled by it.

Demons took to the skies or ran for their lives. Moroi screamed and fled over the walls. None of the creatures stayed to fight any longer. None of them would fight for Solomon.

Only the summoners remained.

Roxelana reared up over Solomon, sword still firmly stuck in his abdomen. His eyes were wide, staring up at the girl glaring down on him. No blood leaked from his wound; he was undead, after all. But he felt pain as she twisted the sword.

Solomon screamed past Kleos' hand and kicked, knocking her off. Using brute strength, Solomon dragged Kleos down and butted his head into his nose. Grunting in pain, Kleos lost balance and Solomon threw him off.

Then he hauled himself to his feet, pulling the sword from his gut.

"How dare you!" He screamed. "How dare you!"

He held the ring out threateningly towards them, but they were beyond his sway.

"You don't own me anymore!" Roxelana screamed back.

"It doesn't matter!" He pointed angrily at them. "Lightbringer! Kill them!"

But nothing happened. The square of Scholomance was silent, save for Solomon's heavy breathing and the crackle of his vessel's remains smoldering on the ground. Staggering, he turned towards Dani.

She lay, collapsed upon the ground. Both her hands were burnt black by her release of power and the blowback of the explosion.

"Dani!" Roxelana screamed.

"No!" Solomon echoed. "My weapon!"

Black-grey smoke furled through the square. The haze was so thick, the three of them couldn't see anything. But, before any of them could move towards her, something shook the ground.

Then again.

Then again.

Each shake felt like Godzilla's footfalls as he towards Tokyo. Roxelana and Kleos staggered. They stared past Dani. Something was coming through the smoke.

And it was big.

They saw it by its shoulders first—his shoulders, that is. He was wide, muscular, and he towered over them at nearly eight feet tall. As he came through the haze, his body shimmered. Other than a white, ceremonial battle dress around his waist, the giant wore nothing else, leaving his reddened skin bare as it glowed ethereally with light. His shaved head was square, strong, and his eyes pierced through the haze as he came to stand before Solomon. In both hands, he carried a massive two-sided battle axe.

When he appeared from the haze, he put the butt of the weapon down on the stones. The ground shook.

Solomon stared. "Impossible!"

Roxelana recognized him. She had seen his statue before Solomon destroyed it. "Zalmoxis…"

The large deity spoke with a voice that rumbled like thunder, "I am the god of Scholomance."

Solomon glared up defiantly at him. "I am the God of Creation!"

"I have met Him. You are not He."

"I am!" Solomon held up his hand with the ring on it. "I hold the power of angels on my finger!"

He reared back with his ring hand and punched his fist into the exposed thigh of the god. His knuckles collided with a *whack!*

But the god stared down with cold, black eyes that shone like obsidian. Unafraid. When Solomon withdrew his hand, no Pentalpha mark burned into the god's skin.

"I hold the power of angels within my body." He told him.

The light on his body looked very familiar; the same light that came from Dani's hand.

He picked up the axe. "It was lent to me by the brave girl behind you."

Solomon backed away. Zalmoxis slammed the butt of his axe into the ground. Lightbringing exploded outward, coursing through the ground and across the stones. The light flowed along the walls and the putrid mold and fungus burnt away. The vines turned from brown to green. Flowers bloomed to life again.

The smoke dissipated. The solomonari shielded their eyes and for the first time, they saw their god. Energy kept going, pouring up through the summoners and into the stable. The summoners dropped to their knees. The dragon crashed through the stable, thrashing.

Their Pentalpha marks disappeared.

Zalmoxis hefted his weapon in both hands. Solomon faced him alone.

"You accomplished your goal, King Solomon; king of nothing." Zalmoxis warned. Solomon backed away. "This brave girl did as you asked: she gave up her power to save her friends. It took only a cruel man like you to show her the way. Truly, in desperate times, humans show remarkable strength."

"You—You do not frighten me, you insignificant nothing!" Solomon raged. "You will serve me! I will bring you under my sway, as I will bring all!" He turned to where the bronze vessel used to stand. "I command more than enough demons—!"

But it was gone. Instead, all that remained was the reassembled statue of Zalmoxis.

"That's your problem." The god said. "You think power comes from ownership."

Solomon drew back his hand to strike the god again with his ring. Zalmoxis swung the mighty blade and sliced the hand from Solomon's wrist.

He stared at the stump and screamed.

"That's enough out of you." Zalmoxis reared back and swung again.

Using the flat of the axe, Zalmoxis connected with the smaller revenant square-on and thrashed him across the square. He bounced on the cobblestones past his quarters, down the dock and like a stone, he skipped across the water out of sight.

The sun poured through the haze, glinting rays of light off Dani's swords. She slowly opened her eyes and looked up. Every droplet in the air shimmered like diamonds. The first thing she saw was a massive, eight-foot-tall man standing over her. She nearly screamed, but he stepped back and her friends came into view.

Kleos knelt and helped her sit up. "Are you okay?"

"Did we win?" She murmured.

He laughed loudly; much louder than his usual reserved chuckle. "You could say that."

"Who's the beefcake?"

Zalmoxis rested his axe down as Dani slowly stood up. "A grateful deity." He said. "Solomon is gone. The countryside around us feels as if it rejoices."

The summoners knelt, once again at the service of their god, but in gratitude to Dani.

"These men you see here," the god gestured to them, "are those of devotion. Their task is to better the world here; not destroy or dominate it. You freed them. For that, I am grateful."

Dani's hands hurt. She winced in pain. "I think you did that."

"You gave selflessly." The god's skin glowed with the energy of Dani's lightbringing; the power she accidentally lent him. "Your power allowed me to physically manifest and take back my school. I thank you."

Dani stared warily up at him. "I didn't do it for you."

"No, you did it for others; a rare trait amongst humans. At your most desperate, your instinct was to act altruistically."

Dani warily regarded the eight-foot-tall man filled with her power. The god noticed.

"You may be at ease around me."

"No offense, but I've had a bad run-in with a pagan god recently."

"I have heard." Zalmoxis nodded. "The old ba'als and the regional gods; some have sided with the demons. I hope I can make some gesture to assure you that not all of us stand on the side of Hell."

"I doubt it."

The deity extended his hand, palm up, and offered to her the item in his hand: the Pentalpha.

Dani blinked. "Do you know what this can do?"

"Yes. I still wish to relinquish it. Such power should not be in the hands of anyone who wishes to use it."

"Then why give it to me?"

"Because you wish not to use it."

Dani took the ring, running her thumb over the symbol. It was an object that could enslave anyone it touched. She could feel the draw of it; the urge to use it.

And just as she thought to find the bane boxes, Zalmoxis extended one, lid open. Dani tossed that sucker in and snapped it shut. The power faded.

"Thank you." She said.

"You have a long journey in front of you, Daniella del Lucio of Empyrean." The large man looked saddened. "I do not envy the choices you must make."

"Asmodeus is still out there."

"I do not speak of only one demon, but the many in your future."

Dani was about to ask how he knew, but Kleos interrupted her. "Dani, it's the thirty-first. Hallowe'en. Allhallowtide begins."

Dani's eyes widened. "Asmodeus! We have to get back!"

Zalmoxis knelt and extended a finger towards her. "Then I believe you may be in need of this, Lightbringer."

The light poured from Zalmoxis into Dani. She shimmered for a second and then, she was herself again. She didn't have to ask. She knew he returned the power of Lucifer to her. She sensed it there, like a weight in her soul. Her hands were healed.

Strangely, she felt disappointed that it was once again her responsibility.

"I need not this power." The massive man stood, picking up his ax. Already, the god looked different; paler, becoming transparent. "Without it, my physical form will fade."

"I could use a god on my side right now."

"Who says you do not already have One?" He shook his massive head. The pagan deity's expression was solemn. "Daniella del Lucio, the matters of the Creator's messengers are not for us gods any longer. We gave up our power to live in peace, but peace will not come on its own. Only one can return it to this world."

"Somehow I think you're talking about me." She grumbled.

"The greatest of tasks have always fallen to those who wish not to undertake them." He put a large hand on her shoulder. "Do not let your fear rule you. Do not let it turn you from what needs to be done, for no one but you can now accomplish it."

Dani heard Mastema's words in his.

And with that, the god of Scholomance vanished as the sun crested the hills. And all around them, the flowering vines had retaken the walls from the decrepit fungus and the last of the mist escaped into the foothills.

The summoners returned their weapons. Dragan put the bane boxes into a pack for her.

"Thank you." He said, and not in his native language; in Dani's. "You saved us."

"Thank you." She said in reply. Kleos translated the rest. "We need to return to the United States. Something terrible is coming."

Dragan spoke quickly. Halfway through, Kleos' eyes widened.

"What did he say?"

"He wants to give us a ride back."

Dani heard a rumble. Two summoners approached, holding the reins of the dragon Solomon once rode. Dani thought the beast looked much happier now that the king of summoners was gone, but how a dragon could look happy to begin with? Still, it seemed much more content. She ran her hands along its scales.

"You want us to ride this? Seriously?"

"Dragan says the creature will take us where we want to go."

"It's a long flight."

Dragan spoke again. Kleos chuckled.

"What?"

"He says," Kleos' smile hid in his beard, "no beast of the air or machine of man can out-fly a dragon."

The summoners helped them mount the scaly steed; Kleos up front, Roxelana with the boxes in the middle, and Dani at the rear.

"Why do you get to drive?" She asked Kleos.

"You want to try to control a thousand year old dragon?"

"Not particularly, but it seems a little sexist that you just assumed."

"Shut up."

Roxelana looked bewilderedly between them. "We are about to go try to save the world, and you two act like this? What's wrong with you?"

"It's been a long two weeks." Dani grumbled.

The dragon turned towards the west, the rising sun at their backs. Its wings tucked back and then the dragon lumbered forward. With several powerful flaps, it kangarooed off the ground and then with one last strain, ascended into the sky. Up and up and up; each thrust of the wings sent them higher.

It wasn't the most graceful take off. It was no 747. Instead, it was like the world's most vomit-worthy rollercoaster, but they quickly left the school and the summoners behind.

Dani tried not to scream; in terror or delight. She just hung on for the ride.

Chapter Forty-Four

They reached the clouds as dawn fully broke. The air whipped by them. Dani's eyes watered, dried, and watered again from the wind. Kleos kept ahold of the reins, but it was doubtful he could control the dragon if it chose to do anything he didn't want. Roxelana hung on for dear life.

They rode a monster they couldn't control and prayed it didn't kill them.

Dani looked down. Through the clouds below, the world seemed to pass both slowly and quickly. She recognized the village they first encountered the solomonari in, but then quickly they were over a European city. Then they were over an island; Britain. Then they were over ocean.

They'd been flying less than an hour.

"How is it going so fast?" She screamed over the roar of the wind.

Kleos shrugged. "No idea! I've heard that dragons could ride with the dawn, but I didn't think that meant literally!" Some things even the Numen couldn't explain.

Within another hour or two, they were over land again. Dani spotted beaches, then flatlands, and then mountains. They were over the east coast of the U.S. and making good time. The sun was fully up.

Halloween was here. Allhallowtide had begun.

The dragon plummeted downward across another set of mountains; the Rockies. They were passing Colorado. As they arced over what had to be Utah several minutes later, she felt something odd. It was like the air changed. It was cool, yes, but charged. The hairs on her arms stood up on end.

"Do you feel that?" Kleos yelled.

"Uh-huh! Not good!"

Storm clouds began gathering around them. Lightning forked between the thunderheads. When Dani looked to their right, she noticed vaguely human shapes danced between them.

"Shades!" She pointed.

The storm, drizzling rain and hail and all matter of hell, swallowed the dragon and its riders. Lightning shot overhead. Dani instinctually ducked. When she looked back, four shades were flying after them.

"We got company!"

Roxelana saw them, too. "What do we do?"

"Hang onto those boxes at all costs!"

The shades gained on them; four black streaks furling right towards them. Dani snatched a throwing knife from Kleos' belt, turned and threw it. The adamant dagger tumbled end over end and smashed into the lead, obliterating it. Three more joined the three already in pursuit.

"More coming!"

That wasn't the half of it. From below, a shadow-person shot upwards across the dragon's back. It materialized into a full-grown woman, who screamed and grabbed at the boxes Roxelana held.

Her friend fought back, lashing out with her bare fist. The creature screamed something unholy and in its hand formed a shadow-knife.

But whatever powers vilas had, Roxelana called on it. It wasn't like Earthborn arche or Dani's lightbringing. Roxelana scooped some clouds into her hand and threw it in the creature's face. Unable to see, it dropped off and disappeared.

"Nice one!" Dani said.

"Can you stop these things? Do you still have that amulet?"

"It doesn't work anymore, but I got something better!"

Her hands gushed with light. As the dark souls closed around them, Dani threw them both out and blasted lightbringing in all directions. Screaming, the shadowmen shattered into nothing.

Kleos angled the dragon down and more of Asmodeus' creatures joined in the hunt. The California valley was right ahead.

"We can't get higher!" Kleos warned. "I don't know how we'll pass the barrier into Empyrean!"

Dani screamed back, "Then we don't!"

A shade shot down from overhead and hit the dragon's right wing. Screaming, they nearly fell but the beast pulled up and maintained altitude.

"What?" Kleos asked. "Go down? Are you sarding insane?"

"These things aren't going to let us up! So we go down!"

Los Angeles was awash in the worst storm Dani had ever seen. Thick, black clouds blanketed the sky. Lightning streaked down, even striking the ground in places.

It was apocalyptic. Literally. Whether or not the mundani below saw, the sky swarmed with shades. An army of thousands flew through the sky. Most Los Angelians already took shelter inside and very few were out, but how long would simple homes keep out the dead?

Dani drew Pointyend. Kleos drew his sword. Blades ignited, she swiped left and right, cutting through the shades and fighting in tandem with Kleos' strokes as they descended towards the streets. Roxelana kept down, putting her body between the artifacts and the ghosts. Hellfire loomed below.

A shade attacked the dragon, but its jaws bit through it and disintegrated the screaming soul. With a blast of fire, their ride blew a hole through an approaching swarm, but they were falling too fast.

"Coming in for a landing! It's going to be rough!"

Hellfire shot at them. The dragon, with shades now overrunning it, couldn't pull up. A 'rough landing' was putting it mildly.

Dani sliced through the bindings that kept them firmly on the creature's back. "Jump!"

The three dismounted the dragon as it collided with the back parking lot of the Hellfire Club, clawing up pavement. The three landed hard and rolled. It hurt, but they would live.

The shades abandoned the dragon and came at them like locusts. Dani summoned another burst of energy and lanced outward. Her hands hurt, but she swung the beam in an arc, killing about a dozen in a single stroke. Kleos, armed with his adamantine xiphos, cut them down in quick succession as they fought towards the building.

The dragon rolled to its feet and poured another intense wave of fire on them. Shades blasted apart.

Not paying attention behind her, a shade landed in Dani's path, shadow-blade extending from its hand. She turned in time to see it draw back.

A golden fist crushed its head.

"Get the hell away from my bar!" Idunn screamed as it turned to wisps of black smoke.

The goddess bartender stood like an island of golden light in the storm, fist clenched and bat over her shoulder. Taking it in both hands, she swung hard enough to hit a home-run across the city as well as crack open the head of another shade.

She held it up. "An amaranthine Louisville Slugger. I keep it behind the bar to beat up drunks. Come on!"

The four of them fought their way back towards the club. The dragon took off, its job done, and spread flames through the sky on its retreat. Another swarm of shades descended.

But just as quickly as they came, they curled off; repelled. The shades suddenly couldn't be near Dani and her friends. They screamed in pain, and she saw why.

Standing at the door with arms raised, the Witch of En Dor waited. "Welcome Daniella del Lucio. We meet again."

She couldn't see the witch's face beneath the cowl, but Dani sensed a smile as they slipped past her into the safe haven of the Hellfire Club. En Dor followed, closing the door behind them and the sounds of the storm faded. She followed into the gloom.

"Idunn!" Dani heard Judah before she saw him. "What in hellfires did you go outside for—?" He stopped mid-rant when he saw Dani. "Dani! My darling!"

The big man was dressed in a tattered suit that looked like it had just gone ten rounds with a weed-whacker, but he swept her up into his arms without a second thought.

"We thought we lost you!"

She smiled, hugging him back. "I'm okay!"

"My dear, you have no idea how good it is to see you." He dropped her back to her feet, then spotted Roxelana. "My dearest vila, you don't know how glad I am to see you alive and well."

She hugged him, too. "Alive, but not so well."

"I pray you both come with good tidings."

"Hopefully." Dani looked past the bar owner. The club was filled with guests; humans (maybe), cynocephali, jinn, and all other manner of creatures. Instead of partying, the guests huddled in groups. Each clap of thunder outside sent them cowering under tables. "What's going on?"

"I gave shelter from the storm. Unlike the mundani, my patrons see the monsters outside." He put a hand to her back, leading her to a corner. "I hope you have something to stop this. After you left the club, I feared your quest would be fruitless."

"Trust me, I've got plenty of fruit." Roxelana handed her the bag.

"That's the girl I know." He gave her a brave smile. "The Medium of En Dor and my staff have held the creatures at bay. They appear to leave the mundani alone for now, but the supernatural are at risk. These demons seem to have another goal in mind."

"They're about to attack Empyrean. Hallowe'en—."

"Begins Allhallowtide. Yes, I came to that conclusion." He shook his head. "Dani, the Earthborn made a stand when this storm first arrived. I saw some of it. Many of the Numen perished in battle. They withdrew to Empyrean. I didn't see Ethan or any of your friends, but I fear the worst."

"We can't think about that now. Judah, we need to get up to Empyrean. Can you help us?"

"I don't know how I can be of service. The only avenue to my club was the ladder, but that cannot be opened from the outside."

"We don't need it." Kleos cut in. "Dani, the barrier is weak. Even Numen can get through the firmament now; no ladders or psychopomps needed."

"Yeah, well, in case you forgot, there is an army in our way. And Empyrean will be on lockdown. We won't be able to get in without someone letting us in."

That gave Dani an idea. "I think I might have a way of getting someone on the inside to let us in. Do you think one of you might give us a way through the storm?"

"Possibly." Answered Judah. "What do you have in mind?"

"Realistically? Something insane."

Dani went to make a call, or whatever the equivalent was with obsidian mirrors. She summoned Bouden and prayed he still had his mirror on him.

"Dani?" His face floated into view. "Dani, is that you?"

"It's me." She assured him. "What's happening?"

"Armageddon, if I had to guess. Everyone's armed. The city is on lockdown and the Gifted are sheltered. The shade army took over Los Angeles."

"What about Asmodeus?"

"I haven't seen him." He shook his head. "The shades are swarming at the base of the mountain."

"I know. They're covering the skies here, too."

"'Here?' Where are you?"

"The Hellfire Club."

"You're in Los Angeles?" He grinned despite himself. "Does that mean you—?"

"We have the artifacts," she promised, "but we're stuck down here."

"What do you want me to do?"

"Nothing about that." She said. "Kleos and I are working on getting past the shades, but we still need a way into the city."

"I wouldn't know the first thing about how to get you in. Every Gate is shut and manned by soldiers. At least Asaph prepared for this."

"What about the river gate? The ladder?"

He shook his head. "The Elders shut that, remember? And you can't fly over it. They put a ward in place to stop the shades."

Dani frowned, trying to think. And then, "What about the East Gate?"

"What about it?"

"Is it any more protected than when I left?"

He thought for a moment. "They had more Gatekeepers there before, yeah. But they pulled most of them when the shades appeared. No one can find the Gate in all that fog and the fog itself is magical. It takes away powers, right?"

"That's true, but it's our best shot."

"That's insane, Dani."

"Well, right now, insane is what we have. Can you get someone to open it for us?"

"I don't know, Dani."

"Try, Bouden. We need to get in. If Asmodeus comes, these three things in my bag are the only way to stop him."

"How do they even work?"

"I have no idea."

He shook his head. "This is a horrible plan."

"Agreed."

But it was all they had. Bouden promised to get the Gate open at any cost. He prepared to leave, but Dani stopped him. "Wait, Bouden, what about Caesar or Mastema?"

"Mastema is still confined to quarters." Bouden said. "Caesar arrived at your home a few days ago. Some centaur brought her to us."

"Nessus?"

"No. He was younger. I've never met him—Orion, I think."

Dani's heart skipped a beat. "How is she?"

"Alive. Orion did what he could, but he brought her to us because he couldn't do anymore. We helped save her talons. She'll be fine."

Dani let out a sigh of relief, but was nervous to ask, "What about Ethan?"

"Ethan? He's fine. Why?"

"I saw," she paused, "never mind. As long as he's okay."

"I'll see if he can help us. I know Izzy will, maybe a few others."

"Good. Be ready. We're leaving soon."

The plan was set. Now all they needed to do was execute it.

Kleos waited for her when she returned to the main club. "Will he help?"

"He's going to try, but here's the kicker: we have to go in the East Gate."

"Can we do that?"

"We'll find out. What about getting us up there?"

"That will be our task." En Dor waited nearby. Behind her were Kleos, Roxelana, Idunn, Judah, and a handful of golem security guards with some homunculi. "You will need a way through the storm. We will provide it."

Dani nervously bit her lip. When she asked for a way through, she didn't think it would involve risking anyone else.

En Dor sensed her hesitance. "We offer to do this; we are not commanded. Your friends stand with you, Daniella del Lucio."

Dani looked at them all. "Are you sure?"

Leaning against the bar with her bat, Idunn knocked back two shots of elixir. "Well, I'm not getting any younger. Literally."

Judah folded his arms over his massive chest. "I'm tired of demons messing up my bar."

Dani nodded. "Then let's do this."

They gathered at the back entrance. The golems were unarmed, but needed no weapons, while the homunculi carried makeshift weapons like kitchen knives, pipes and—in the case of one—a meat cleaver. It wasn't the most stellar group to face a bunch of immortal dark souls, but you worked with what you had.

Idunn opened the back door. Shades swirled through the sky above. The wind picked up. The storm of the century covered Los Angeles.

"Here we go." Dani murmured and stepped out after her.

Blades glowing, she moved into the open with everyone close behind. The shades descended again. En Dor raised her hands, muttering a curse under her breath. Immediately, the black creatures turned and shot back into the sky, screaming.

A few got past, but Judah summoned some kind of electric spell to his hand. Lightning coursed between his fingers and he fired it at the nearest dark figure, blowing it apart.

His security and wait staff made a ring around Dani, Roxelana and Kleos.

"I will open a way." En Dor told her. "Give me a moment."

"Not sure if we have one!"

More shades dropped. Dani ducked back as one with a shadow-ax tried to take off her head. She swung her empyreal swords, slicing it apart. A homunculus leapt onto another, stabbing with the knife. The shadowman screamed, falling as more homunculi joined in. Their knives, though nothing special, pulsed with energy. Judah did say he could imbue them with spells.

The golems protected En Dor, using their fists to punch and tear into the shades, but as more inky creatures joined the fray, the golems began losing ground. More than one came down and tore them apart under black hands and blades.

This wouldn't last long.

"My fair En Dor, you may open it at any time!" Judah warned, firing another spell that shimmered in the air and reduced a handful of shades into nothing. He murmured under his breath, crafting spells as quickly as he could, but he looked like whatever he was doing was weakening. He sweated through his tattered suit. He looked pale.

These weren't warriors. They shouldn't be doing this.

Idunn swung the Slugger with two hands, breaking apart the skull of another shade. She screamed as one landed behind her and stabbed into her back. She grabbed it by its dark hair and jerked, taking the head off and turning it all to smoke. Limping, one of the golems helped her back towards the club.

Their line was crumbling. It was Beri'ah all over again.

And then, just above them, something happened. A hole of light appeared through the storm; a sunburst that bathed them in light.

"Go now, Daniella del Lucio!" En Dor commanded.

She didn't have to be asked twice. Grabbing Roxelana around the waist, Dani shot into the sky with Kleos right behind them. They soared upward away from the club. The shades turned to pursue them. Everyone else retreated back inside.

Up, up, up; the wind whipped past them. They closed on the storm ahead. Above them, the shades seemed unable to enter the light. The ones behind tried to swirl around them and attack, but couldn't.

They kept ascending until finally, they hit the cloud line. But instead of passing through into the sky above, they hit something that felt like a fuzzy barrier and broke through.

They entered the realm of Empyrean.

The city of light was dark. The blue sky was navy-black despite being clear of clouds overhead. The funnel around its base was black and stormy, sending bolts of lightning into the rocky sides of the mountain; blasting off chunks. As they ascended, red uniforms of the Gatekeepers and the purple of the Powers appeared along the battlements. Empyrean's crater was dotted with defenders as well. Fortifications usually never manned now had soldiers. Empyrean soldiers crowded the gate. Alchemists, Naturals, and even Guardians and Novices stood at the ready.

Dani, Roxelana and Kleos came up between the West and South Gates. She could see the river gate leading into the Vale, but that was closed. She turned, willing the Aer around her to keep up their speed. They shot parallel to the South Gate and kept going. The misty side of Empyrean lay ahead.

She chanced a look back and wished she hadn't.

The stormclouds surged and then, as if belching out, a large column of shades broke through into Empyrean. The mass of them was colossal; writhing with souls, funneling upwards towards the mountain. It looked as if the dead were climbing on top of each other as they flew. The thing was so wide around, it made a skyscraper look skinny. It reminded her of a hungry snake as it twisted through the sky.

Then it turned and began to follow the three of them.

"Go faster!" Kleos warned.

Dani put on a burst of speed, but the mass was much faster. As they passed the South Gate, though, Empyrean came to life.

From the West and South Gate, and all along the crater where the city had fortifications, a volley of death rained down. Ballistae with adamantine tips, flaming Fyreballs the size of sedans, catapulting rocks and volleys of arrows collided with the massive cloud from one end to the other. Stretched out like it was, they had a wide surface to hit.

Shades screamed as they disappeared; not dead, but it would take them time to reform. Distracted, some peeled off and tried to assault the celestial city, but the soldiers kept firing. The mass slowed its pursuit of Dani, Kleos and Roxelana.

They hit the fog and disappeared.

Dani's powers almost immediately began to fade. She stumbled through the air, regained her ability to fly, and it faltered again. Roxelana extended her hand and pushed on the mist with her own Gifted ability, but it wouldn't budge. They began to lose altitude.

"I can't stay up!" Dani warned.

Kleos was similarly struggling. But ahead, through the gloom, Dani saw the East Gate. Marked by flaming torches, the platform was in reach. She saw figures on it, waving to them.

"Roxelana! I'm going to throw you!" Dani warned.

"You're going to _what_?"

"Get these three artifacts to my friends! Stop Asmodeus!"

Dani surged Aer around them both, grabbed her friend by the back of her clothes and hurled her up. Roxelana, still gripping the bane boxes, was launched forward through the void and towards the gate.

Then Dani began to fall.

Her final push cut out her powers and she stumbled from the sky. Kleos grabbed onto her, but he too fell. The pair dropped into the mist, but this time, no aurora would take them to safety. They disappeared.

A second later, the pair emerged. Screaming, Dani flew upwards with Kleos holding onto her hands. And above them both, a large white bird strained to get altitude.

"*Not gonna let you down again, girlie!*"

"Caesar?"

"*Duh. Who else would it be?*"

They flapped upwards and the platform loomed ahead. Caesar was straining under both their weights. She wouldn't be able to carry them both much longer.

But just in time, she dropped the pair and they landed hard on the stone outcropping. Dani ended up face first on the stone in front of a pair of boots. Painfully, she sat up and looked up into the smiling face of Bouden.

"Welcome back." He said. "And for the record, this is still insane."

"Yeah," Dani blushed, "but it worked."

Then she spotted someone over his shoulder.

Ethan.

Chapter Forty-Five

Bouden, Izzy and Ethan managed to break through the Numen guards to get to Dani and her friends. With Caesar in tow, they rushed back through the East Gate and slammed it behind them, in case the shades followed.

Even from here, they could hear what sounded like explosions in the distance; a battle.

"How long can Empyrean hold out?" Dani asked Ethan.

"As long as it takes."

Everyone was armed. Hopefully, if it came to a fight, they had enough to take on whatever came their way.

"We need to find Asmodeus." Dani said as they emerged into the crater of Empyrean, shrouded in fog. "Then, we use these things to destroy him."

"How?" Ethan asked.

Dani hadn't actually thought about it until now. She only knew a little bit. "Not sure, exactly, but we can figure it out on the way."

Kleos ran ahead with Bouden and Izzy. That gave Dani and Ethan a pause she hadn't been sure she wanted.

Ethan slipped an arm around her. "I'm glad you're okay."

"Ethan, now isn't the time."

"It's never the time." He said. "Dani, I was worried about you. You were gone and I didn't know where. I know you had to go, but I couldn't help wishing I went with you."

She placed a hand on his chest. His arm around her felt good. She let herself relax, if only for a moment.

Then she kissed him deeply.

Roxelana pretended to be interested in the rocks at her feet.

Dani pulled back from Ethan, cradling his face. "When this is over, we need to talk."

"I understand." He said truthfully. "And I just want you to know: I believe you."

"About?"

"About the traitor in Empyrean." He took her hands and squeezed them. "I was an idiot for not believing you before. I need to trust you. And I will from now on."

Dani noticed a cut on his upper arm. Whether from the battle down below or breaking into the East Gate, he had a pretty bad gash.

"You're hurt." She raised her hand. "Do you mind?"

"Heal me? No, I don't mind. I need to be comfortable with what you do. I can't look at it as something to be scared of, if you're the one doing it."

She smiled, flowed her energy into her hand and pressed it to his arm.

A vision hit her.

Ethan strode down the hill towards Dani's house. He undid the ward that kept him in.

Mastema rose to his feet and came out into the square.

"Dani's coming." Ethan told him. He was already armed. "We're going to the East Gate to get her."

"That is good." Mastema said. "I have no weapon, but I will gladly accompany you. The shades will attack at any moment."

"Let's get going, then."

But neither of them moved. Ethan stood, hand on his sword, but Mastema didn't turn to leave, either.

A long silence passed between them.

"You need not lie to me, beast." Mastema told Ethan. "I know it is you."

Ethan said nothing.

"The guards to my prison here have mysteriously disappeared. And Ethan left to face the monsters below and returned alone. I am not as much as a fool as the Elders."

Ethan's smile cracked across his face, and his eyes cracked bloody as well. "You're smarter than I gave you credit for."

"And you are more disgusting than I once thought."

Ethan went to draw his sword, but Mastema struck out with his palm and hit the pommel, shoving it back into its scabbard. Ethan lashed out and backhanded her Guardian across the square into his own house. He landed hard.

"I was going to just stab you in the back." Ethan said, drawing his long blade and walking over. "Now, I think I'll just run you through. No need for her Guardian to get in the way. You already did when you sent that Kleos boy with her. I couldn't manipulate him."

"That," Mastema got painfully to his knees, dazed, "was the point."

Ethan had his sword in both hands. "I'm going to take her. And Ethan—who by the way, is still in here—is going to watch."

"She will kill you."

"She'll try."

Ethan reared back and struck, the point of his blade lancing towards Mastema's gut.

Her Guardian's hands slapped together to stop the blade, though the tip pierced through his raiments into his stomach. He grunted, holding back the sword, but staggered by the blow. Ethan kept pushing, but all he did was push Mastema to the edge of the cliff.

"Just die already!" the demon wearing Ethan growled. "You should have already been dead! Just like your last charge!"

Mastema's eyes widened. "What did you say?"

A sneering smile played across the archdemon's lips. "That's right. I know all about your failure; about the boy you didn't save. He left you alive to live with your guilt. No sense in ending the life of the great Mastema; the feared warrior of the Numen. Letting you live in shame was a better torture."

Mastema kept his hands tight on the blade, stopping its progress, but Ethan twisted. He groaned in pain. "What demon was it?"

"You'll never know."

Ethan kicked and knocked Mastema off his blade, but he also knocked him over the side. Wounded, dazed, her Guardian fell over the cliffside and out of sight.

Dani snapped out of her trance.

Ethan, who wasn't Ethan, stopped her from falling by grabbing her arm. "Are you okay?"

"I'm fine." She lied. She moved her arm away. "My powers are draining me. That's all."

"This mist doesn't help." He put an arm around her. "Dani? Can I tell you something before we go confront this evil monster?"

"What?"

"I love you."

It's not him, she knew. *It's Asmodeus*. As much as Dani would want to hear those words from Ethan, it wasn't Ethan who was talking.

He didn't know about her lightbringing's ability to see visions of someone's memories. He didn't know she knew. She prayed Mastema was still alive, but she couldn't do anything about it now. She had to play along.

Kleos and the others arrived back. "Time to go. The shade army is attacking the Citadel in full force. They can't get near yet, but if Asmodeus is going to show up, it'll be there. We can run to the edge of the fog and then fly the rest of the way."

"Let's go then." Dani said.

She stuck close to Roxelana and the objects. She needed to get to them. Maybe if she got the ring, she could bind Asmodeus and control him like Solomon did to her. Maybe the medallion would frighten him. Or, if the fish guts worked the way they were supposed to, she could get him out of Ethan. They just needed a fire.

They ran at full tilt. She needed to warn the others about Ethan. But how could she, without alerting him?

She got an idea. "Kleos!"

"Yeah?"

"Before this gets heavy, I wanted to thank you."

He glanced sidelong at her. "What?"

"You stuck by me through this whole thing. Thank you."

He shrugged, not understanding. "Sure."

"It wasn't just the fighting stuff. It was those vision-things as well. You know, like the one at Dagon's ranch?"

He blinked. He could tell she wanted to say something.

"I'm glad you helped me. I'd hate for it to come true." Her eyes flicked to Ethan.

Kleos glanced sideways at him. Recognition flickered on his face. Then he said, "Yeah." His run began to slow, dropping back closer. "It would be bad."

"I, for _one_, am glad that you're here."

He gave a slight nod. "That makes _two_ of us."

"Well, two's company, _three's_ a—!"

She stopped mid-sentence, went for her sword, and swung around. Ethan's longsword blocked the blow.

It happened too fast to warn the others. He spun and kicked hard enough to launch her backwards. Asmodeus swung and cut Bouden across the shoulder, spinning him to the ground. Izzy backed away, protecting Roxelana instinctively, but a wave of shadow erupted from Ethan's hand and hurled them both into the rocky crater-wall.

He faced off against Kleos.

"You really think I wouldn't pick up on that?" Asmodeus demanded. "You think you're so clever."

"Let my friend go." Kleos warned, xiphos held ready.

"Or you'll what? Kill me? Then you'd kill him."

They were at the edge of the fog leading across the torch-lit pathway. The arrival of the shades caused some kind of eclipse across the city. It was almost like night.

His eyes turned on Dani. "How did you find out?"

"I've got tricks." She bluffed. "Get out of him."

"Why? When I finally take you, it'll be nice for you to see his face. You'll invite me into your bed, give me the offspring I require; you'll cleave to me like the good girl you should be."

She held up her sword. "I'll show you the girl I am."

Izzy slowly got to his feet, hunga-munga in hand. Dani waved him down. Roxelana was doing something behind him. Bouden was the worst off; groaning, bleeding, and unable to get up.

"I'll kill all of them." Asmodeus warned. "My army will break through. You can't destroy it. They'll keep coming back, again and again, until they overwhelm the Numen. You can't stop me."

She heard something behind Asmodeus. Something was coming through the fog. And as it became clear, she gritted her teeth with a smile.

"You know, you're right." She said. "Everyone thought *I* could stop you, but you know what? I think it's better to say *we* can stop you."

Orion appeared from the fog, galloping hard with Caesar overhead. He drew back his bow and fired. The arrow lanced through the air into Asmodeus's shoulder; not a killing blow, but a painful one.

Asmodeus grunted. Izzy drew back and hurled his weapon. Dani and Kleos charged forward.

But Asmodeus was quicker than them. He dodged the hunga-munga as it sliced past, turned and hurled a blast of dark energy at Orion, who toppled over. He spewed the energy up as Caesar descended, screeching with her talons extended. The blast hit her too and knocked her from the sky. Izzy got the same treatment.

Then he spun, swung, and cut Kleos across the chest with Ethan's sword.

Dani's and Ethan's blades connected. Sparks flew from where the edges met. She made an X and shoved him backwards. Yanking Pigsticker away, she reared back to strike.

Asmodeus's hand came up and grabbed her by the throat, dropping Ethan's sword and knocking hers out of her hand. When she stabbed with Pigsticker, he snatched her wrist and forced her to drop it, as well.

"Just like before." He growled. "You were nothing then, and you are nothing now!" Ethan's eyes cracked and bled. His voice had that same soft tone, as if someone spoke at the same time he did. Soft, but creepy. "You exist for one reason: to please me. You're mine."

Dani choked. "...screw...you...!"

He turned and threw her across the pathway into the wall. Disarmed, she had nothing.

Except her lightbringing.

Dani curled the light into her hands. "Stop or I'll destroy you."

"You couldn't then and you can't now." Asmodeus taunted, stalking forward.

Dani whispered to Roxelana, who curled up protectively over Izzy. "I need the ring."

Asmodeus neared. "Try your little light trick. But when it fails, then you'll know you're mine!"

Dani stood, blocking Roxelana, and extended her hand.

But her lightbringing didn't come. It faded.

Asmodeus grinned cruelly with Ethan's face. He grabbed Dani's hand and twisted. She cried out in pain.

"Dani," he huffed, standing tall over her, "all I ever wanted to do was show you what love is; to show you how serving me would make you happy. I wanted a companion; to love and be loved by you. I wanted love, affection and adoration! But you think I am unworthy of it?" He bent her to her knees. "I'll show you. I'll show every woman like you!"

Dani grunted through the pain. "Your idea of love is pretty messed up!"

He shook his head. "Your defiance is crime that can never be forgiven. I will not be a kind master to you!"

"Oh yeah? How about we change that!"

Dani's other hand balled into a fist and she swung, but Asmodeus caught it. She was fast, but not fast enough. And staring him in the face, on one of her fingers, was the Pentalpha.

Asmodeus snarled in rage. "You dare try to enslave me with *that*?"

Howling in rage, he crushed the hand he already held. Dani screamed as her bones broke. He grabbed the ring and yanked it off her hand, then threw Dani aside.

She rolled to a stop.

"I would have been kind, Dani. I would have showed you love. But now, I'll make you beg!" Asmodeus cackled, slipping the ring onto Ethan's hand.

Dani slowly got to her knees, cradling her broken hand.

"I'll use this to control every part of you and take every part of you!" He started forward again. "Then there will be no way of saying no!"

Dani was afraid, but she would not give him the satisfaction of showing it. "I'll never say yes to you."

"Who's going to stop me?"

But Dani didn't answer. Instead, another voice did, "Me."

Asmodeus turned towards Roxelana. She stood over one of the blazing braziers that lined the pathway. In one hand, she held Dani's dagger. In the other, she held the sheatfish over the flames.

She stuck the blade in, slit it open and spilled the guts onto the flames.

Asmodeus screamed. A waft of air exploded outward as the fire extinguished in a gush of foul stench. The blast hit the archdemon and, with a scream, black energy curled off Ethan's body. He collapsed to his knees as the dark mist blew off him and formed into another person.

The beast Dani saw in her vision appeared; a tall, horned man ugly as sin and staggered on his cloven-hooved feet.

Asmodeus was out of Ethan.

The beast opened its eyes and roared. Yet, when he spoke, the voice didn't match the monster. It was soft; child-like.

"You'll pay for that."

Dani stood, extended her unbroken palm and said, "Bite me."

Dani blasted him with light and staggered him back. Unlike the other demon, he didn't disintegrate, but the light burned him. He howled in pain and bowed under it as Dani pressed forward. She scorched his skin.

Groaning, he tried to stand. Dani pressed him down with her light.

"You can't kill me!" Asmodeus screamed.

Dani finally relented. Both her hands hurt. When the light vanished, the demon stood tall. He smoldered from where her power burnt his black skin.

Bearing broken, twisted teeth, he laughed. "I am stronger than most demons. You can't use Lucifer's power to kill me." He straightened up. "No woman could ever kill me."

One of Dani's hands was crushed, but her other was just fine. With her sword in hand, she raised the edge towards the monster.

"Well, this one's gonna try."

With a scream that echoed all her pent-up rage, Dani charged right at him. Asmodeus extended long, black claws and lumbered forward, too.

Dani struck with her sword, slicing the air in front of him and spinning at the same time. Her glowing blade carved through the darkness. Her first strike forced him back, and the second aimed to open his chest.

Asmodeus was quick. He dodged away from her blows and swiped with his claws. Dani felt them kiss her shoulder, but not cut through her Archne-weave tunic.

She dodged under his next blow and struck upward, slicing open his bicep. He howled in pain.

Dani the cut his exposed, unprotected leg and staggered him.

In her fury, she went on the attack; not a balanced, calm attack, but instead one fueled by pure anger. And every blow she landed, in her mind, was payback for something he did to her or those she loved.

When she opened his side with a single stroke, it was for his hands on her; violating her. Taking her dignity.

When she swung her leg and struck to the back of his knee, it was for turning her friends against her; making them into monsters. Terrifying her.

When she slashed him again and again with her blade and drove him back to his knees, it was for invading her dreams; her private thoughts. Her safety.

And when, as he knelt mewling in pain, she smashed the pommel of her blade into his face—once, twice, three times—and cracked the bones beneath, it was for everyone he killed; everyone she was forced to kill. Everyone who suffered or died because of him.

Akela.

The Empyrean Numen in Beri'ah.

The Gatekeeper he made her murder.

Miriam.

The migrants at Dagon's ranch.

Costicâ and the summoners.

She hit him again and again, her screams unleashing every painful emotion she had bottled inside, until Asmodeus was dripping black blood from his hellish mouth and nose.

Dani raised her sword to take off his head.

"ENOUGH!" He backhanded her, knocking Dani away.

In her rage, she'd been too rash. She let down her guard and allowed him a chance to hit her. Bloody as he was, Asmodeus staggered back to his feet.

"HOW DARE YOU?" He demanded. "HOW DARE YOU RAISE YOUR HAND TO ME?"

Dani steadied herself, ready hit him again if he came near her.

"You want to kill me?" He demanded. "You think you can? Well, you can't! You're weak! You're pathetic! And I will make you pay for what you just did!" He raised a clawed hand and pointed threateningly at her. "When I get my hands on you—!"

She cut him off. "You're never touching me again!"

"And how do you plan to stop me?"

Dani spotted something behind him.

"Simple: you won't have a choice."

He must have heard it in his voice and spotted her looking over his shoulder. While Asmodeus wasn't looking, Ethan got to his feet. When the demon turned, Ethan punched him in the gut. Ethan's fist barely moved the monster, but the archdemon grunted as he felt a brand burn into his skin.

He staggered back, screaming when he saw the Pentalpha mark on his abdomen.

"No! No! No! No! Not again! Not again!"

"Be QUIET!" Ethan commanded.

The mark glowed and Asmodeus quickly suddenly stopped screaming. "Stand still. Don't move."

Frozen in place, Asmodeus looked on in terror. Ethan pulled the ring off and handed it to Dani, who slipped it onto her hand. The archdemon's eyes widened.

She held it up in front of his eyes. "Feel pain."

The mark hissed and Asmodeus screamed past clenched teeth. He wavered on his feet, unable to fall to his knees because Ethan commanded him to stand. Dani had no sympathy.

"Talk." Dani commanded.

He immediately answered. "Please stop!" He screamed. "No more!"

Dani didn't listen.

All of what he did to her, all he put her through; she hoped he felt that now. It felt good to make him feel pain, but even as she enjoyed it, Roxelana spoke.

386

"Dani..."

She turned towards her friend, who shook her head. They both knew what it felt like to be under that ring's control. Asmodeus may have been a demon, but Dani wasn't. She wouldn't torture something out of pure spite. She was better than that.

Only light could drive out darkness.

"Stop feeling pain." She commanded.

Asmodeus' screams turned to whimpers.

"Your shade army: destroy it. Release those souls so they can be at rest."

He resisted, gritting his teeth. "No!"

"Do it!"

Groaning, he raised his face to the sky and Dani felt a weight in the air lift. The skies lightened. The sounds of battle faded to nothing.

Extending her hand, she touched Asmodeus with her lightbringing and saw through him.

The hundreds of dark souls attacking the city began to vanish. Released by the archdemon, they evaporated even as they almost broke through into Empyrean's battlements. She could see Asaph amongst the defenders, looking around, puzzled, as their enemy evaporated.

Dani withdrew her hand. "It's done. The city is safe."

Kleos groaned and Ethan went to him. Orion, Caesar and Izzy were coming to, as well. Izzy ran to Bouden's side. He would live, but she was still worried for one of them.

"Is my Guardian alive?" She demanded.

He nodded solemnly, broken. "I could only wound him."

"The centaurs found him." Orion told her, climbing to his feet. "He is being healed in our village."

She smiled gratefully. "Thank you."

He bowed, "You said that I could trust you and that you were a friend. It is what friends do."

Dani turned back to the demon. "Kneel."

He did without question, but defiantly stared into her eyes. "I am not afraid to die. Kill me. I will be at peace." There was a glint of the old Asmodeus there; smug, triumphant. "You will never fix what I broke inside you. You are weak."

Dani leaned down into his face. "You know, I probably once was, but I have to thank you. You made me stronger." The words were not what the demon expected, and fear crept into those soulless, black eyes. "In fact, you helped me see that killing you would be wrong. Roxelana?"

Her friend stepped forward with the last bane box and opened it. Asmodeus screamed. Lying inside was the medallion; the one Asmodeus feared to return to.

"I think you need a different punishment." Dani took it and held it up. "Return."

"No!" Asmodeus screamed, over and over repeating, "No! No! No!"

But, too weak to resist her commands anymore, his body began to break apart into the same black shadow-smoke as his shades. He screamed in agony. He came apart, swirling around her and back into the medallion—

—trapped forever, once again, inside his personal hell. Alone.

It was quiet. Everyone looked to Dani; waiting for her to say something. Instead, she took the ring and pressed it against the medallion. She burned the mark into it, like Solomon with his books. She knew she could make inanimate objects do what she wanted, just as much as living ones. She inspected the star at the center of the gold seal.

"I think no one needs to find this again." She said and flung it into the air. "Turn to dust!"

The medallion exploded into gold-tinted sand, which picked up in the wind and blew into the sky; over Empyrean's walls, over into the valley below; scattered to the wind for eternity.

With Kleos propped up on him, Ethan asked, "What did you do?"

"The medallion holds him. But, unless someone finds every grain of that thing and puts it back together, he won't be coming back."

Trapped and gone forever. Alone for all eternity.

Dani was satisfied with that.

Chapter Forty-Six

Empyrean was saved. Again.

Dani saved it. Again.

She wasn't thanked by a single member of the Elder Council. Again.

The mood of the Council wasn't a happy one. She went before them the following day and to her satisfaction, Heman was mute. His lack of preparation almost cost the city and he was no longer a favorite amongst the Elders. But that didn't stop her from getting in trouble.

"You broke the law, Novice Daniella." Castus proclaimed from his seat. "Because of you, this city was at risk."

"To be fair," she pointed out, "I also saved it."

"Yes." He conceded. That was a close to appreciation as she would get. "For that, you will not be punished for breaking our laws."

"Well, thanks." It was only a half-assed thank you.

"With no other business to discuss, should we adjourn? Does the rest of the Council wish to say anything?"

Dani specifically looked at Heman, who said nothing. Maalik was likewise silent.

Jeduthun spoke up, though. "Novice Daniella, what of the ring? The Pentalpha? That was the artifact of Raphael stolen from the Fane of Beri'ah, correct?"

She nodded. "Yes, Elder, it was."

"Where is it now?"

She sighed. "Destroyed. When I used it on the medallion, I guess the two powers canceled each other out. It broke into shards."

"And those shards?"

She shrugged. "I dunno. I guess you'd have to search the Vale."

"Perhaps we will."

She shrugged again and did her best not to make any expression. Mastema would have been proud.

Jeduthun regarded her behind his clasped hands. He didn't believe her, but she didn't care. They didn't trust each other, no matter what happened. And she wasn't about to start now.

Some things never changed.

Mastema healed from his gut-wound, though it took time. He landed in a tree that broke his fall; it broke his ankle, too. Now he knew how it felt. And since he would live, Dani decided to remind him of it every hour of the following day.

He less than enthusiastic.

Ethan came by the day after Halloween. Dani was cooking dinner for her and her Guardian, since Mastema couldn't walk yet.

"Hey." He greeted.

"Hey." *Awesome start*, Dani didn't say. "What's up?"

"I wanted to talk."

"About?"

"About what Asmodeus said...you know...when he was controlling me."

She kept her eyes on the cooking fire and tried not to give anything away. "What do you mean?"

"He took control of me," he hesitated, "but he couldn't completely shut me out. I remember most of it. I know when he was pretending to be me, he told you that I loved you."

Dani's heart ached. After everything that happened and all she went through, this wasn't something she was ready for. "Ethan..."

"I do." He cut her off. "Love you, I mean."

She didn't know what to say. Did she love him? She considered it in her dream with Asmodeus. She knew she had deep feelings for him. But love? What did that feel like? How would she know?

Her silence pained Ethan. "I'm sorry to put this on you. If you don't feel the same way, I understand."

"Ethan." She took his hand. She stepped close, got up on her tip-toes, and kissed him. It was long, deep, and fully what she wanted. Then she dropped back to her heels and said, "I don't...I don't know what love is. I really don't. I wish I did. I know I have feelings for you, I know I care about you, and maybe it is love..."

He smiled hopefully.

"...but," she said, before he could speak, "this thing with us...I don't know how it could work. Ever."

He frowned.

"We don't exactly live normal lives." She hated the words even as she said them. She sounded like some teenage drama queen. She despised that. But at the same time, what was the alternative? How were you supposed to have a relationship in a situation like theirs? It didn't change her feelings. It just made what to do about them difficult.

He let go of her nodded. "I guess I should expect that. So, what now?"

"No idea." She rubbed her hands up and down on her arms like she was cold, but it was just nerves. "There's still a lot to figure out."

"Well, there is one thing I don't need to figure out anymore." He told her. "The person who betrayed us to Alecto: I'm with you on that now."

Really?" She smiled. "I thought that was Asmodeus talking."

"He may have been lying, but I'm not. We'll find him, Dani. Whoever it is, we'll find them and make them pay. And as for everything else," all he could do was give her a brave smile, "we'll figure it out, like you said."

He stayed for a bit longer, those feelings still there but easier deal with, and eventually he left. Afterwards, she got one more visitor; one she called for specifically.

"What's up?" Nathaniel asked, arriving from the air. "Your aerwhisper said you needed me?"

"I did."

"What is it?"

From underneath her raiments, Dani removed her mother's necklace. Now, however, a second ring hung on the chain. "Do you know what this is?"

His eyes widened. "Is that the Pentalpha?"

She nodded. Solomon's ring, the gift of the archangels, dangled on the loop. She withdrew it, leaving only her ring around her neck. She held it out. "I need to hide this."

She placed it into his hand. Nathaniel shook his head. "I don't understand. Shouldn't we give this to Council?"

"I don't trust the Council. Hell, I don't trust half the people in this city; not with that thing, at least. But I trust you. This ring has the power to enslave people. It needs to be kept out of anyone's hands, including our own."

"Until when?"

"Until I find a way to destroy it." She handed him a necklace chain she bought. "Keep it hidden. Maybe we can find a place to hide it where no one will find it, but for now, I want you to keep it."

"Why me?"

"You won't use it. The Council suspects I still have the ring, but I'm hoping they won't go looking into any of my friends; especially one that wasn't at the battle."

Nathaniel had been on the front lines when the shade army attacked. Dani was betting that would make him less suspicious.

He put the necklace on and tucked the ring out of sight. "I'll do my best."

"Thanks."

"So what now?" He asked. "You saved the world. Again. What are you going to do now?"

She smirked. "I'm going to Disneyland."

He rolled his eyes. "Why did I expect you to be serious?"

"I'm just all kinds of fun, Nate."

"Uh-huh. Sure you are *chica fuerte*." He smirked.

"Please stop calling me that."

His smirk widened. "See how annoying it is?"

More good news came in on the last day of Allhallowtide: some of the Numen and Gifted survived the attack in Beri'ah and fled into the mountains. It wasn't many, but Beri'ah would survive. And with the next eclipse, they would replenish their forces, if only slightly.

And, for more than any, it gave Roxelana something to smile about. She lost her husband, friends she made in the city, and her home; but something would survive. She chose to stay in Empyrean and find her own home among Sanctuary Hills.

The final day of Allhallowtide was *Día de los Muertos*; the Day of the Dead. Dani and her friends went to honor Dink, while Dani also took Roxelana, Shea and Airlea to honor Korë and Akela; both of them taken in a war that they shouldn't have been a part of.

But to her own surprise, Dani didn't just light candles for them. She took one to the empty grave of Nazir—a man she used to hate with a passion—and his Novice, Michael. They both did horrible things to her, but letting go of her anger towards them was the best thing she ever did. It didn't weigh on her soul. And because of that, she was able to forgive them. Like the others, she was glad they were at peace.

She spotted Kleos hovering before a grave she knew as Titus's. They exchanged only silent, understanding nods, but said nothing else.

When she returned to her village, Mastema was waiting.

"You know," she said, joining him in the pavilion, "I don't understand something."

"I assume there are many things you do not understand."

She gave him a sarcastic, ugly look. "Keep talking. I killed a Fury and imprisoned an ancient evil, not to mention defeated a bunch of demons and a god. I can kick your sarding butt. Just remember that."

He shrugged and asked, "What is it you do not understand?"

"Allhallowtide. Why is the veil so thin then?"

"It is a time for the dead to return to life. The supernatural barriers of the world are weakened."

"But why *that* time?" she asked. "And how do mundani, who supposedly can't see the supernatural, know it's that time to honor the dead?"

Her Guardian shrugged. "You assume one preceded the other, when in fact, it may be the other way around."

"Huh?"

"Allhallowtide is one of many celebrations of the dead around the world. Mundani believe that the dead return to life. What's to say that because of their belief, it comes true?"

She blinked. "You can't be serious."

"Belief is very powerful."

"That's BS."

"You believed you could stop Asmodeus, and you did."

"I had help."

"And your belief in your friends helped them to help you do it."

She opened her mouth to retort, but didn't have anything to come back with.

"My belief in you," Mastema continued, "helped redeem me. I told you that light drives out darkness. That light," he pointed to her chest, "comes from within and spreads to others. It is the single greatest force in the universe."

She hesitated before saying, "Mastema, there's something you should know about my powers. Something's changed..."

She told him about her visions; all of them, including the one where he was stabbed. Mastema's face was once again the blank, emotionless mask.

He said nothing as Dani finished, so she reminded him, "I told you I would help you find whatever killed your charge. I mean that. I still do."

He shook his head. "My life cannot be about revenge, Dani. I won't let it consume me."

"Trust me, coming from someone who got revenge on the thing that abused her, it does help you sleep better."

"I have never seen the demon that killed my charge since that night." He told her truthfully. Usually, he was mute on this subject. "I don't expect to again."

"Is there anything you could tell me about it?"

He hesitated. She was prepared for him to keep whatever it was to himself, but after a moment, he spoke, "The creature looked like a man. He did not appear demonic, and that was why I did not think him a monster. When he did attack, he was vicious. He could not be killed, even when I ran him through with my sword. He defeated me in single combat, and then killed my charge."

"How did you escape?"

"I did not. He let me go."

That surprised her. "Really?" She never knew of a demon to leave any Numen alive.

"The archdemon Asmodeus told me that he did so in order to make me suffer." He said. "I have suspected the same thing for many decades."

"Anything else you can tell me?" Dani asked. "Anything else that you remember may tell us who or what it was?"

He thought for a moment, and then nodded. "Its eyes."

"Its eyes? What about them?"

"They looked different than that of a demon or a human. They were unnaturally bright and the color of rubies. I remember them because when I wounded it, though I could not kill it, I did hurt the beast. The creature cried. It cried crystal tears."

Something flickered at the back of Dani's brain. "Crystal tears?"

"Yes. I have never seen anything in creation do that."

"Mastema, this thing: did it look...I don't know...beautiful? Like, not man or woman, but still unearthly pretty?"

He nodded. "It was the most beautiful creature I have ever seen."

A shiver went down Dani's spine. The beauty of it, the crystal tears, the unearthly eyes; she'd seen that before. What Mastema described wasn't a demon.

It was an angel.

Chapter Forty-Seven

That night, with Allhallowtide ending, Dani took advantage of the thin barrier between the worlds and slipped down to Earth. She could pass through it on her own and planned to return before midnight when it became solid again.

Floating from the Heavens, Dani passed over Los Angeles into Sun Valley dropped quickly to the street in front of Ricky's house.

The bungalow was dark; nobody home, which she wanted. Dani grabbed the doorknob, poured her lightbringing into it, and twisted. The lock shattered and she let herself in.

The house was empty of life. It had always been empty in other ways for Dani, but she didn't dwell on that now. She went to her mother's and Ricky's room. The place still stunk of cigarettes and beer. It wasn't somewhere she wanted to be, but something made her pause just inside the door on the dresser; a picture. It was of the two of them, smiling and happy; long before Ricky, the drinking, and everything else that happened. Dani touched the photo lightly with her fingertips, but didn't dwell. She had something to do.

She found something to write on in the living room, along with a pen and an envelope. Dani quickly wrote a note to her mother. Most of it was true: she loved her, she missed her, and she was alive. Dani didn't tell her where she was; just that she was safe.

She also said she knew Ricky was still hitting her and begged her mom to leave him. She couldn't make her mom leave, but she could try her best to save her.

Before sealing the envelope, Dani took her necklace off and coiled it inside. Hopefully, it would do as much for her mom as it did for her.

A car pulled up outside, flashing headlights through the window as it turned into the driveway. Dani peeked out. Ricky got out of his beat up old sedan and walked toward the house. Dani knew she needed to slip out the back. She couldn't let him see her.

But when he stepped into the living room, already taking his tie off from work, Dani was waiting for him.

"What the hell happened to the door...?" He paused, keys still out. Then he spotted her. "What the hell are you doing here? Did you break into my house?"

Dani folded her arms. "I came to talk, Ricky."

He slammed the door. "You here for your mom? She's still at work."

"No. You don't need to tell mom I was here. I'm here to talk to you."

Dani remembered her visions from En Dor. Everything in them had a purpose, right down to Roxelana and Ethan helping her to defeat

Asmodeus. But the last vision—the last face she saw—was her mother's. Dani didn't know what it meant, but she knew one thing:

She couldn't abandon her mother to this creep anymore.

Ricky stepped past her without concern. "What'dya want from me?"

"For you to leave my mother alone."

He grabbed a beer from the fridge and cracked the can open before taking deep, long gulps. "Leave her alone?"

"I know you're hitting her." Dani told him. "I know it's probably worse since I left. You're going to stop."

He crushed the can and tossed it on the floor, walking right over to her. "Or what?"

Dani hit him. Hard. Her fist connected with his gut and he groaned, dropping right to his knees. Then she grabbed him by the throat and got her face right up in front of his.

"Or I'll come back, Ricky. And you don't want me to." Grabbing him by the front of his shirt, she hoisted him up off his feet and threw him onto the couch. "Kick my mom out, or leave her the house and skip town. I don't care which. But you don't live with her anymore, got it you *idioto feo?*"

Ricky stared at her in horror. All his usual bluster was gone.

"Do it and do it soon." She warned. "I won't be so nice if I come back, understand?"

He nodded quickly.

"Good." Dani turned to leave. "Bye Ricky."

She felt amazing. Like when she imprisoned Asmodeus, she felt like a weight lifted off her chest. She conquered a part of herself she never thought she could. En Dor's visions led her here for this purpose. This had to be why.

She was almost to the door when Ricky spoke again behind her. "Tell me something: what does your Elder Council think about you coming here?"

She froze. The voice he spoke with sounded like the usual Ricky, except the inflection was wrong. The tone was calm and collected; not something he was known for. And the Elder Council remark stopped her.

When she turned around, he was standing, but not quivering in fear. He seemed...different.

"They would never allow you to see your mother, which means they do not know you are here." He said.

Something was wrong. "How do you know about...?"

A smile spread across Ricky's face; not his abusive, drunken sneer, but something closer to what she saw on Asmodeus's face. What was smiling back at her wasn't Ricky.

It wasn't human.

396

Dani summoned her lightbringing to her hand, but something invisible slammed her back against the door. She saw stars. The invisible force then yanked her up and threw her into another wall, cracking the drywall inward on impact. She groaned in pain, pinned and unable to move.

Ricky calmly stepped around the coffee table and walked over to her. "I wondered how long it would take you to come for your mom. All I had to do was wait."

Dani choked, the air unable to get into her lungs. She felt as if something pressed on her chest, stopping her from breathing!

Ricky came closer. "I am very patient, Daniella. Or is it Dani?"

"You—!" She choked. "You can't be here! You're imprisoned in the seal!"

The Ricky-Monster blinked questioningly. "What? You mean Asmodeus? I am not him. He's nothing compared to me." He stepped closer, looking up with eyes she knew, but not recognizing the creature behind them. "No, I have much more composure than my foolishly-rash brother. He made a mistake and it cost him. His imprisonment is his own doing."

"I don't know who you are, but I will never tell you where he is!"

He shrugged. "No matter. I am not here for him. I am here because you destroyed my ranch and interfered with my plans."

To Dani's horror, she realized who she was looking at. "Belial."

He nodded. "It's good to finally meet you." He stepped back, indicating his appearance. "I figured coming to you as this waste of a man would make it easier. After all, you already hate him, as I am sure you will hate me. It should drive home the point that you should not expect mercy from me. But take solace in this, at least: Ricky is gone. I saw to that. You may sleep well knowing he is dead."

"How?" Dani managed to ask.

"I came to him. I promised him wealth, women, anything his heart desired, so long as he was my vessel. I needed one for the time being, but in order for me to possess him, I needed his permission. He agreed almost immediately. Ricky was quite the greedy, self-serving monster. It took very little to win him over. Then, once I was inside him, I took his body and sent his soul where it belongs: Hell."

She shook her head. "Doesn't make a difference what you look like. I'll still kill you!"

"I heard you are boastful. Of course, after killing Alecto, Dagon, all of Asmodeus's loyalists, I guess you have something to be boastful about."

She gritted her teeth. "What do you want?"

"It is not obvious?"

"Let's say it's not."

He chuckled. "I guess it might not be. I'm here for the Ring of Raphael, the Pentalpha."

Dani didn't speak right away. She was too shocked to answer with anything snippy.

"Do not pretend you don't have it." He warned. "I know you do. I want it."

She twisted, trying to free herself from her invisible bonds. "What do you want with it?"

"A weapon that can enslave anyone it touches? Why would I not want it?"

"How do you even know about it?"

"Solomon told me, of course. He spoke of only it when I brought him back from the dead."

She was stunned. "You brought him back?"

"You think Asmodeus would want to bring back that narcissist? The one who imprisoned him in the first place? No, I brought him back. Neither he nor I could enter the city on our own. I needed him to retrieve the weapon for me and keep it from my brother. And, of course, I had to wait."

"Wait for what?"

"For you to destroy Asmodeus. Or, imprison him, as it were. With him gone, no other demon will question my authority in Hell. I am now in control of every demon on this Earth and the next. Thank you. The others will now get in line behind me."

With a wave of his hand, the invisible bonds that kept her pinned to the wall disappeared. She dropped down to the floor, able to breathe freely again.

Belial sighed, "Now, I will ask this once: where is the ring?"

"I don't have it."

"I believe you, but you know where it is."

"Screw you."

"That's not a smart thing to say." He told her. "You'll get more out of this if you hand it over. I won't come after you. I won't hurt the ones you love. If you give it to me and stay out of my way, I will even leave your mother alone. I have no interest in killing her. She suffered enough at Ricky's hands. Just give me the ring and this is all over."

Dani shook her head. "I'll kill you first."

"Really? You think so? I am the Wicked One, girl. The first of Lucifer's creations. I am the King of Demons. You stand no chance of stopping me."

Dani felt the warmth flood her hand. It began to glow. "That right?"

Belial saw it, but didn't look concerned. He stepped back, holding out his arms. "Try your worst, lightbringer."

Dani gritted her teeth. "If you say so."

She threw out her hand and blasted him with the strongest light she could muster. The room exploded with a nimbus glow. Dani screamed and put her all behind it. The walls around her cracked and the windows shattered.

But, when she couldn't take it anymore and pulled back, the glow faded and Belial still stood there. Untouched. Even his clothes were unaffected.

He looked himself over. Then, with a flick his hand, he sent Dani crashing back into the wall, where she slumped down to the floor.

"I was made by the Lightbringer, girl. Unlike the other archdemons, I was forged from the power you have. You may have it now, but it will not work on me."

Dani stared up in horror at the creature. Her power didn't work. And if the power of the Devil himself couldn't kill him, she didn't know if anything could. She never met a monster that she couldn't kill. And she knew now, it was Dani, not Belial, who could easily be wiped out.

But he made no move to kill her. Instead, he wiped his hands as if fighting her made him unclean. "I'm not going to kill you, Dani. Not now, anyway. Instead, I'm going to leave you alive."

She choked, "Why?"

"Because I need you still. I need the Pentalpha. And you're going to lead me to it. Then, I will kill you. I'll even leave your mother alone; at least, until I need to use her. And you can live, knowing that I could take her from you when I feel like it. Until then, don't think this is over. It's far from over."

He turned to leave, the front door of the house shattering itself as he stepped through it. The demon left, walking down the stoop to the street and disappearing into the night. Painfully, Dani stumbled to her feet and ran to the broken. She held up her hand, summoning her lightbringing desperately, focusing on the archdemon as he disappeared.

But she didn't fire. There was no point. Her power didn't work on him.

The new leader of Hell was immune to the light. He was a darkness that couldn't be destroyed.

About the Author

Spencer Helsel was born in Culpeper, Virginia. He earned his Bachelor's Degree from Christopher Newport University and has spent the last decade as a middle school and high school teacher.

He currently lives with his wife Jessica and sons Adam and Sammy wherever the military sends them.

www.ingramcontent.com/pod-product-compliance
Lightning Source LLC
Chambersburg PA
CBHW051315250626
47155CB00007B/2326